Book 1

The Chant of

Cold Iron

by

Edward C.

Oliver

2

For Alexander,

You are I are constantly on the run and long may it remain so.

Dreams born from words, brother. And from these dreams a journey begins.

Also for

Chris Cornell

July 20, 1964 – May 17, 2017

Christopher John Boyle

Rest in Peace

Someone of whom I never knew personally but his music and especially his voice let me feel emotions and thoughts I never thought I was able to. Thank you and keep rocking out in the beyond, brother.

Acknowledgments

No book is ever written alone (anyone that tells you otherwise is a filthy liar) and ergo there is host of folks that will have to thank here. Firstly to my partner; Shannon who through long hours of me being far away in another realm entirely, still remained patient with me. Despite this lack of attention, she always welcomed me back with selfless love.

To Alex again and to Julian who patiently waited and watched the progress of this book, and serenaded me with some wonderful Gaelic inspired melodies . A shout out to RenflowerX for some truly beautiful map art. Also much praise must be sung for Fiverr and it's self funded independent artists of which the truly wonderful artwork makes me look oh-so-good. Many readers would be tricked into believing I am much better than what I am with your help.

Many, many thanks to all the members of Brisbane Writer's Group, but in particular to Peter, Cheryl and Lee whose invaluable input cannot be understated and to the Melbourne Writer's workshop crew. Praise be upon my reading groups- alpha, beta and gamma; you guys are my much needed testing audience. Though a special shout-out must be given for Joey, her insight is always second to none. Loki- the feline god of mischief and his little brother Rasmus of whom get some commendation for sitting on paw and tail and , despite not actually being capable of reading... Lastly but certainly not least; my mother and father for creating me and always believing in me. You guys are pretty decent.

When man meets an obstacle he can't destroy, he destroys himself.

-Ryszard Kapuscinski

Prelude

With all that was said and done

Nothing, nobody, no more and no one

The wounded Loner raised his gaze to the Far Above

And asked the simplest of All

'Why?'

Verse 11

Speakings of the Nameless Fallen Sculester and Pondly - 2722 arcs ATF (After The Fall)

They had arrived like an unheralded storm,
without warning on a day where the air had been
clear and calm, a day like many other such ones
before it, in the quiet inland village of
Letesah. Judeson could vividly recall every
taste, every smell and every sensation like it
was yesterday and that was what haunted him most
of all.

The town's farmers had been working the nearby
fields down from the plateau. They had been
sowing the earth beneath them and the harvest
looked to be plentiful the coming season. The
town blacksmith could be heard crafting metal
with his forging hammer, the echoing rings of
worked and piping hot steel sounding throughout
the vicinity. As always Judeson's own father had
been deep at work in his own endeavours, skinning
and cleaning the hides of elk for the upcoming
market. All those chores that intertwined the
close-knit community together in a well-
structured web that would all too soon begin to
unravel.

They would be engulfed in destructive turmoil;
consumed in an unforgiving tempest. The near-men
from the uncharted lands to the South, beyond the

Redland expanse would soon come and with them, a nightmare Judeson would never forget.

Just like a hundred times before, Judeson closed his eyes and recalled that day; the day, the Rakoni had come to his town and decimated his entire existence. He would never forget the nightmare. Never.

The boy fled as fast as his legs would carry him, nearly slipping several times and losing his balance on the grassy knoll, as he made his way down to the village of Letesah below. Terror gripped the young boy all over and his spine tingled, his heart pounded and cold sweat trickled down his brow, as he sprinted faster than he thought himself possible. At the bottom of the hill that had long since been called *Goat's Banquet* for obvious reasons, the young child did eventually fall, his elbows guarding his rapid descent onto his stomach. He scrambled onto his feet again, much the same way as the boy had seen a stag do when his father had shot it with an arrow, the similarity glaring.

The village's youngest member who would grow up to remember all this again and agai, nearly every moment he drifted to sleep.

Eventually he regained his feet and continued running after what seemed an entirety for himself, in his terror filled linear perspective. Judeson had hurried into the main avenue of the community of sturdy wooden and clay-work yurts and to his father's side where the older man stood facing the hill of which the town's goats favoured most of all. The stocky, broad shouldered man with a rapidly greying beard and serious eyes whispered to his intensely frightened son - words of which Judeson would remember for the rest of his days.

'Run and hide my son, I'll face these beasts.'
Judeson had stood frozen in place for a time
beside his robustly built father - Judisye.
Facing the incoming advance of heavily armoured
warriors. The Rakoni invaders were decked out in
plate maillee from head to toe, their armour
plain and well worn, their misshapen full helms
completed by a jutting spike on top of each one.
At their belts were; scalps, teeth and the
rotting loose fingers of their victims that
dangled unnervingly about. The hostiles charged
down the old mound in a rush resembling an
animalistic stampede. As they reached the edge of
the town they uttered challenging and brutal
howls and snarls.

Judisye once more urged his son Judeson to flee,
not with words this time but a gentle push. The
Letesah hunter and former front-line soldier in a
previous life, drew the gigantic bastard sword he
called Jude from its sheath on his back and stood
tall facing the dozen howling and heavily armed
invaders at the edge of Letesah. Judeson did give
in eventually to his father's insistent urging
and made for the safe cover of Judisye's store
front, with its hardy oak wood counter to conceal
him.

Six other villagers emerged from among the
scurrying rabble of now fleeing citizens nearby.
The six who would stand with the massive bastard
sword-wielding figure were not nearly as
appropriately armed as Judisye. Two possessed
cumbersome ploughs, the one woman among them held
up a meat cleaver that had recently been used,
red gore dangling from the blade's edge, two
elderly looking farmer types followed, one
completely bald, the other with a few loose
strands present. The bald worker wielded a broken
edged shovel his companion had a rack with leaves

still lodged in its hooks. The last remaining
member of the rag-tag group of fighters was the
blacksmith, a man of few words, a silent,
brooding type who many of Letesah's children
steered well clear. The blacksmith, still in his
dirty work apron and wearing an untrimmed beard
held a massive forging hammer in one hand.

There was little time for much in the way of
exchanges between the group; slight nods
sufficing before the Rakonian warriors charged
their position. The savage force and ferocity of
their initial attack made Judeson's blood run
cold. In mere moments three of the group of
Letesah villagers had fallen onto the hard road
below, in pieces of bloody mess and fluid,
twitching in death throes. One of the Rakon was
also felled, although the raider looked to have
only taken a minor wounding to the left shoulder
blade and staggered back to its feet rather
gingerly.

Judeson witnessed the woman who possessed; a head
of flaming crimson locks skewered and lifted from
her feet. One of the Rakoni had her with its odd
hooked blade run right through, the woman
screeched an unnatural howl of pain and Judeson
winced. The woman's cleaver lay buried half out
of the Rakon's shoulder guard, though it took
little notice as the creature violently threw the
woman's lifeless and blood smeared corpse from
its sword with violent gusto.

Meanwhile the blacksmith rammed his forging
hammer down upon one of the Rakon's helms with
deadly force. The metal helmet folded inwards
with a great clattering crash. Despite this the
enemy warrior only hesitated slightly in its
advance; before smashing his shield into the
blacksmith's torso, sending the man sprawling off
his feet. As he fell to the hard packed earth

Judeson witnessed thick crimson blood flow freely from his battered body. The Rakoni above him sank his blade deep into the man's unguarded throat. As the near-man did so a terrible snapping noise sounded forth. The blacksmith wriggled and squirmed violently around on the ground clutching haplessly at the blade for a few moments; as urine drenched the man's britches in his death throes.

The Rakoni murderer towering over the late-blacksmith did not however have time to react as the bastard sword of Jude swung by its namesake wielder. The blade was swung downward crushing the Rakoni's steel helm at the very edge of its crown and sliced deep into the crest of the near-man's head. In the weapon's wake wake it left naught but a hacked and bloody mess. The mortally wounded Rakoni warrior dropped to the ground in a heap. The creature leaked vitals from its head and twitching uncontrollably.

Judisye followed up his attack by narrowly ducking and weaving from another Rakoni who had charged in from behind. The near-man swinging a cumbersome double-handed battle axe in a hay-maker motion just shaving the air where Judisye's head had been half a moment ago. Judeson's father propped up on one knee in a half-crouch position and sliced his claymore across his aggressor's lower torso. Through sheer luck the amour plates had shifted aside exposing the soft, vulnerable flesh of the Rakoni's stomach. Thick crimson blood spurted out and splashed against Judisye's face. Judeson averted his eyes for a moment as the near-man raider's entrails spilled from his belly.

However Judeson could not avert his gaze for long. He was once again drawn back to the scene at hand. Only his father remained of the

resisting villagers and even he was slowly and
begrudgingly regaining his feet with sword in
hand. The six late villager's corpses lay
scattered about the road, broken and hacked apart
in varying degrees. Of the Rakon; only six
remained standing, those of which had formed a
circle around Judisye and scurried about. The
near-men shifted positions, their weapons readied
at their one remaining opponent. It was a sight
Judeson had seen before. The young boy remembered
seeing the great blonde lions of the Mornis
Hinterlands circle their prey of scurfy wild
goats in much the same manner. Witnessing this
sight on one of the many hunting trips he and his
father had embarked on together. Now Judeson
crouched chillingly horrified that his own father
was the prey being circled before the kill.

The Rakon were chanting in a low drawl something
unintelligible to Judeson, in between vicious
snarls. Judisye appeared helpless amid the
shifting ring of aggressors, yet Judeson could
not bring himself to look away. The child of the
trapped hunter made to call out to his father but
his voice was lost in his own terror. One of the
Rakoni closed in on Judisye from behind and
struck the man's back with its crooked timber
shield, sending him sprawling forward to the
opposing side of the Rakoni encirclement. In turn
those Rakoni pushed the hapless man back again
and a cycle of pushing and shoving ensured.

Judisye managed to regain his composure just
before a Rakoni swung its bulky metallic baton
toward his head, Judisye; by mere inches managed
to evade the attack by feigning ever so slightly
backward. The wild haymaker action the Rakon
favoured proved to be the creature's downfall.
Judisye counter-attacked quickly with the two
handed sword of Jude. Slicing the blade high in

the air toward the creature's throat. Sharp steel made stunning contact with the Rak's soft exposed flesh situated between full helm and the chest plate. The Rakon warrior's head arched unnaturally backwards and blood poured forth from the deep gash at its cut-throat. In mere moments the barbarian raider's head twisted backward with a sick-inducing snap, visceral showing. Only the white bones of the spinal cord remained; connecting the head to the body. The near-man swayed unnervingly for a moment like a leaf caught in the wind, before crumpling lifeless onto to the ground.

The remaining invaders encircling Judisye pierced an animistic howl at this. Judisye stood tall though his body was shaking uncontrollably now, either from exhaustion or fear or perhaps both. What occurred next was what forever haunted Judeson the most. All the Rakoni in that terrible circle stood frozen in time and Judeson himself felt distant, a world away at that very instant. Out of seemingly nowhere; a rapid dark blur of motion cut through the air and propelled directly into Judeson's father, throwing the man from his feet on impact. Embedded deep in Judisye's upper chest was what appeared to be a darkened cast iron arrow. No, Judeson had thought - *the arrow was of such a preposterous size, it was closer to a javelin.*

A Rakoni warrior appeared, this one much larger than the five who stood around the fallen form of Judisye. The gigantic near-man descended from the Goat's Banquet and strolled onto Letesah's main road which was cluttered with the dead and dying of both sides. Judeson could see the approaching warrior wore no helm. Instead the beast wore a huge blonde Plains Lion's head on it's own. The biggest Judeson had ever seen. The lion's skull was mostly intact, although the fur had long since blackened with mould and the eyes were but sunken hollows. Within the hulking warrior's right hand was a unfathomably long ivory-white bow, hissing, twisting increments cluttered the length of the weapon; dark vapour emerged from within the bow in spluttering puffs.

The five other heavily armoured near-men who cast the ring about Judisye shifted backwards to allow room for the formidable newcomer. Impossibly, Judisye made to rise from the ground but the Rakoni with the ivory-white bow strode over and assertively planted his foot on the man's chest taking up residence on top of him.

'Nekta Gozka.' The behemoth Rakoni grumbled in a long, deep resonating drawl, the words at the time were comprehensible for Judeson. Though much later in life he would learn their disrespectful meaning.

One of the five subordinates responded with a short burst of guttural phrases.

The giant Rakoni, in Judeson's horror leaned down and picked up his father, one handed and with relative ease like a child's play doll. Judisye awkwardly attempted to struggle against the beast's hold but his strength was all but depleted. The Rakoni wrinkled its nose in disgust at the middle-aged hunter and brutally yanked the cast iron arrow from Judisye's chest. In turn Judeson's father unleashed a chilling scream, just before all life left his body and no more struggle nor noise escaped again. The giant barbarian seemingly uninterested in Judisye's now limp and lifeless form threw the corpse to the hard packed earth.

From his hiding place Judeson went to shout out in agony. But he remembered himself and the predicament he was trapped in. Judeson swiftly covered his mouth with both palms. Despite this a whimper almost emerged, so he bit down hard on one of his fingers in an effort to silence his would be screams. Blood flowed down and trickled down onto his brown linen tunic. Nearby the giant savage that had executed his father motioned for its subordinates to advance into Letesah.

ACT I

All That Is Lost

First Stanza

Entry Four Hundred and sixteen

The more time spent among the Draul; the more
time I have come to the conclusion I have a great
deal more yet to learn. As soon as you believe
yourself up to date with their society. They then
go and surprise you yet again. They are a most
curious people indeed.

The Draul people's astute perspective on nature
and its workings differs drastically from
anything in the Confederated Tharldoms, the Cor-
Dazral Empire or even the Yunlands and Fartheilm.

This could be contributed to their delicate
relationship with the practices of Magik and our

seemingly dwindling supply of adepts in the said
Artform.

Journeys amongst the Draul - Part II by Sar Alverlin Ugusten Moor , 2001
ATF

Judeson awoke from his personal recurring nightmare with a started gasp. He proceeded to right himself from his hunched over position. He was at the root of an ancient fig tree. Sweat covered his brow and his body temperature ran feverish. He wiped a generous pool of hot moisture from his forehead. In his in his haunted memories Judeson was but the young lad; a cowering, whimpering boy. Now however Judeson bore an overwhelming resemblance to his late father, a square jawline, broad shoulders and a rugged wild appearance. He drew forth the two handed bastard sword from its sheath at his back. The sword of Jude itself was the pinnacle of Southrondor metal craftsmanship. The double forged steel blade had been in Judeson's family allegedly for untold generations. The sword of Jude was unfortunately the only real reminder that Judeson still possessed of his late father. Oddly and unequivocally the weapon managed to bring peace and clarity to Judeson. His heart's fierce movements pounding against his chest abruptly took on a more regular pattern as he gazed into the slightly notched flat face of the blade. The involuntary shaking he had from his dream eventually subsided.

Judeson had lived in the wilds of the world for arcs now. Most of his adult life had been spent in wooded vales, high mountains or desolate plains now. He had ventured man leagues after fleeing his shattered home of Letesah. Now Judeson had found his way into the forest of the mysterious Draul people. Rumours and legends flew the winds like loose leaves about the Draul. Though personally Judeson did not care for rumours.

Judeson placed Jude back in its scabbard and checked his provisions twice, slung his knapsack across his heavy set shoulders and set out deeper into the dense and gloomy woods ahead of him. The air all-around was moist and temperate; the shadows of the overgrowth cast themselves prominently about, obscuring the daystar somewhere overhead. The ground underneath Judeson provided an ever-increasing challenge as he traversed the thickly woven roots of ancient trees and the unsteady elevations and depressions beneath them.

The Draul he had hitherto met were a most curious people Judeson mused, as he slowly trekked through the copious foliage and tangled vines. Not since the day he had entered their territory had they specifically communicated in person with him. When they had it had been particularly brief and they appeared to have taken very little interest in him. Yet an intuitive sense lingered that they were watching him constantly.

A movement among the branches here or a scurry across dead leaves there was a fairly common instance in the last two days of Judeson's journey. He knew he was most certainly being scrutinized from the shadows but he knew not why. The two near-men Judeson had met on the borders of this land had addressed themselves as Draul *Watchers* and they had seemed adequately approachable enough, to a certain degree. However, only one of them had actually spoken to Judeson, the other seemed incapable or unwilling to. The two Draul had been dressed in dark green and olive full-body-length cloaks almost eerily blending in completely with their surroundings. Judeson remembered taking note of their peculiar dark-ashen and azure skin colour, their cerise coloured eyes and their thin wavy midnight black hair. The one that had discoursed with Judeson had spoken in a strange melodic accent that Judeson had difficulty following along with. The pair had seemed indifferent to Judeson's presence but at the same time he had discounted a lingering discernment they were quietly judging his person.

This was the only true contact Judeson had had with the mysterious peoples of the forest realm. Face to face that was. On one other occasion Judeson had been observed from afar by a duo of Watchers.

Judeson's sense of time and its duration had become flawed within these dense woods. The thick canopy overhead provided an unsettling obstacle to ascertain the correct flow of the daystar's path, although Judeson was not entirely sure if it was daylight at all at the present point. What Judeson did know was what the Draul Watchers had told him earlier; that there was a calling for work to be done by *'Outsiders'* (as they seemed to title anyone non- Draul in pedigree), work the likes of which Judeson had become well suited to. Hopefully it would get him closer to finding what he needed himself.

Slowly trekking through the uneven terrain of the forest, Judeson was quickly becoming overwhelmed by the journey. Every path seemed similar to the last and his sense of direction was losing out to the ancient woods. Still if Judeson held true to his senses and source directions the Draul welcoming party had given him he decided he would eventually end up closer to the Draul Settlement the Watchers had mentioned.

Judeson had taken in very little in the way of a recognisable civilisation, although it was clear there was an abundance of life in the forest demesne. Brown coloured hares darted about everywhere and birds frantically fluttered about the tops of the canopy. Wherever the Draul Settlement was exactly it had to be particularly well hidden.

A brief rustle of branches and the sound of leaves crunching under booted feet brought Judeson from his musings, the young man turning to the source of the disturbance, battle ready with Jude drawn from its resting place in strained instant. A single Draul, dressed in similarly shaded garb as the Watchers Judeson had met days ago, stood mere paces from him. The Draul stood much taller and leaner than the previous ones Judeson had met, roughly around the same height as himself but much lighter in frame. The new arrival, a ageless looking stranger was a similar skin colour to the others, a peculiar pale greyish-azure though he bore a head of long wavy silver hair, the likes of which Judeson had never seen before. The near-man had milky and pale-red eyes unnerving in a manner that Judeson could not entirely place as to why. The tone of the being's skin was what interested Judeson most as the Draul looked to have never been touched by the burning star of the day. This was entirely possible as the seemly near-darkness of the forest cast a constant shadowed shroud everywhere around the woods.

'Welcome Aurman, to Draul'estla-thielm.' The Draul announced in a melodic flowing accent. The Draul held out both his hands, palms facing upwards to the Far Above, arms outstretched before him.

The greeting was an unfamiliar particular for Judeson but he proceeded to respond with his own people's action in such acknowledging circumstances. Judeson commenced stretching his right arm to half-length, his palm facing out

toward the Draul ahead of him and his backhand
levelled with his eyebrows. The salute seemed
quite ridiculous in the current setting as its
origins symbolised the warding away of the
daystar's light. In this forest where the only
sources of light came from minuscule breaks in
the leafy canopy high over- head, the warding
away of burning light of day seemed pointless.
Still Judeson deemed the action respectful.
The Draul appeared to share the sentiment of
Judeson's action and continued his greeting.
'It is always good to see a new face in our lands
Aurman but I respectfully wish to inquire of your
business in our *theilm*' said the Draul who seemed
to be balanced on his toes, ready to move at any
given moment.
Judeson knew the Draul was not alone as flickers
of man-sized apparitions danced all around them
both.
'I am a Southron from beyond the Boundary
Mountains and my business concerns what your
border rangers told me of, work to be done, work
concerning an important youngling and possibly
the Rak scourge' replied Judeson, keeping a keen
eye on the movement of Draul all around the
outlying shrubs.
The Draul let out a brief chuckle, even as far as
inclining his head sideways with the effort
before responding.
'It has been quite some time since an Aurman from
the South visited our lands.' The Draul stated.
'I'm not familiar with this term. My name is
Judeson, son of Judisye, may it please you well'
responded Judeson with a slight hint of
annoyance. The near man's cryptic qualities were
growing tiresome quickly.
'Apologies, friend Judeson, I meant no offence to
you. Let me explain.' said the Draul who's ashen

face of blue and grey was lined with numerous
scars probably caused by battle. 'Aurman is what
Draul call your people. In fact Aurman is used by
most in the Lands in the Nerthiem.'
'Right...sorry, I was a wee hasty in my anger. Do
you have a name to go by?' Asked Judeson.
'I do, I am named Raijin and I am to escort you
to Tzsu'Teng friend Judeson.' The Draul paused
and raised two fingers upward into the air, more
than likely signalling his yet unseen
compatriots.
'Finally' Judeson said. Then remembering just how
blunt he was previously to the Draul. 'Uh..I mean
thank you.'
'Don't thank me just yet. The others don't trust
you, we will have to make camp for the night.'
The Draul Watcher stated carefree and loud enough
for the others to hear him.
Judeson sighed and began unpacking his equipment
and rolling out his swag to make camp.
The Draul gestured for him to get up. 'No, not
like that. Judeson. You see the Draul abandoned
sleeping under the stars, many many arcs ago.
There is a work camp not far from here.

*

Less than a league away the forest parted into a
clearing. Felled trees and stumps littered the
open expanse, as did at least a dozen log cabins
aligned in a perfect ordered row. Three long
makeshift warehouses took up a patch of raised
earth in the dead centre. Draul of all shapes and
sizes marched up and down, some with axes and
huge bulky saws in hand, others pulled along
small wagons filled to the brim with matured and
fresh wood logs alike. Well-to-do dressed Aurmen
stood off to one side with a loud Draul who
seemed to talk to them and not with them.
Judeson found himself taken back at the rapid

change in environment. The day-star could be seen clearly now. Although a thin layer of low lying mist persisted. Ever since he had crossed the Boundary into the Northern Realms this mist had settled over everything. The winds that sometimes passed through, parting the fog was chilling to the bone. Judeson was not sure which he disliked more.

'Where are we, Draul?' Judeson questioned.

'A lumber camp, more and more of them appear each week.' The stick figure Draul uttered almost too quiet to hear, looking off into a distance at something.

'And are we close to this city of yours?' Judeson inquired The bustling scene around him almost blocking out any speech so the young man was forced to step closer to his escort.

The tall Draul turned suddenly and looked puzzled at Judeson. It was clear the near-man had been a million leagues away inside his own mind.

'Yes we are friend. Coincidentally as close as you would have ever have gotten.'the Draul uttered, as a contingent of armed Draul approached, their leader's face painted a dead-pan brush of seriousness.

'Without me, of course' The Draul man continued, throwing Judeson a smile. 'Now please let me handle this.'

The head of the grim looking bunch approaching Judeson and his escort, hoisted up his blade belt. The stout, short Draul began speaking in a voice that was a hoarse scratching affair. His words, serious and short, matching his physical stature.

'Raijin, bringing in the dregs once more, don't you have hoodooo-shit to sprout somewhere in the woods?' The leader deduced, insulting Judeson as if he were not even there.

Raijin, the tall Draul that served as Judeson's escort ignored any hostilities offered by the other Draul.

'Excuse us Watch-leader we have important business to attend to in the Capital.' Raijin stated not bothering to meet the stout man's challenging gaze.

'Your papers if you would then, *Magi*.' The Watch-leader replied, if the man had used vitriol in his speech previously. This past statement though was drenched in acid. The Draul's tone was transparently hostile, uttered beneath clenched teeth and alluding to something so unforgivable as to be hangable for treason.

'We shall leave you with your engines and push onto progress Watch-leader' Raijin muttered and ushered Judeson forward, the two of them walking past the Draul Watchers who kept an ever steady gaze on them as they passed.

2nd Stanza

The Nertheilm or the Northern Realms as we in the South more commonly know it as,

is cold, misty, sodden continent. With seemingly endless rain , the place barely gets a hint of the day-star's light. How any of the Northmen and women function in this miserable place is beyond me. Somehow despite all this, their various civilastions and factions are thriving above and beyond anything the Hand of Kingdoms can produce in the modern times, more investigation into this issue pending review.

The Charm of the North - A Southron's account of the Northern realms

Shamil Dura of Kirilenko

'Eckard, I know you are up to something. There would be no other point to you coming back here. Please be careful, is all I ask. I will see you soon. Don't be an idiot, please just this once.'

Eckard heard the words induced to him from another mind. The thoughts were from someone who he knew very well, or at least he thought he did. He had, sometimes. He could not never sure, he had not seen her for many arcs and even when he had he was never sure. It was always an interesting experience receiving someone's thoughts, especially from *her*. Of course the manipulation of the Arcane Sea was just as intriguing. For magik had many a purpose and long distance communing was only but a single one.

'They're late!' The rotund and erratically pacing man known as Lucian Nonkar announced loud enough for anyone in the general proximity to hear and stirring Eckard from his thoughts.

Luciarn was endlessly parading up and down their humble camp-site but Eckard remained calm and indifferent to his plight. Eckard sat on a felled and rotting oak stump securing his pack to set out, that and acquiring his travel flask from his leather carrier bag, a task of equal importance.

'Since when are Draul late, what is going on?' Luciarn asked of no one in particular, this time with slightly less volume and gusto than his last statement.

'I'm sure the Far Above is about to fall at any given moment now Luciarn' Mocked Eckard as he unclasped the lid and readied the vessel to his lips.

The insistent and neurotic pacing of the keg bellied and hastily balding Luciarn ceased in a heartbeat as he turned to face his younger companion.

'This is serious, Eckard' Lucairn said, noticing the seated Eckard was now drinking from his flask earnestly.

'Really, at this hour of morning?' Continued Luciarn.

'I was not aware the hour of morning was cause to dictate all of a man's actions.' Eckard answered whilst placing his flask away and regaining his feet, to begin setting off.

'You always have an answer for everything don't you?' Luciarn snapped.

The younger man simply held up his right palm to silence any further protests from Luciarn as he had heard movement from the dense woods ahead. Feather light footsteps upon dead leaves and the slightest brush of cloth against the leafy foliage was enough for Eckard to take notice, for he had trained extensively in such sensitivities. Despite the overwhelming possibility that the approaching unseen apparitions were actually their Draul welcoming party, Eckard had learned long ago to not take chances on such assumptions.

The tall, dark haired and broad-shouldered Nerthanlander named Eckard dropped his pack close by his person, uncommitted his repeating cross-bow from its resting place on his travel pack and assembled a quarrel to the weapon. Taking cover behind his previous seating position Eckard motioned for Luciarn to follow suit nearby. The round bellied (now sharply unnerved) middle aged man did so in a somewhat exaggerated roll to safety, behind an outcropping of algae covered rocks. Eckard shook his head at Luciarn's antics and then proceeded to take aim with his well-worn crossbow in the vicinity as the yet unseen arrivals. Brushing a loose, dirty, makeshift beaded braid of onyx hair away from his peripheral vision Eckard attempted to make out any disturbances within the overgrown groves of birch, oak and protruding pines ahead of him.

Minimal shadows cast their positions on the ground, as the day entered its late stages. Eckard could just make out the slightest swift blur of movement among the thick foliage. Scattering images of passing faded emerald cloaks darted in rapid succession every which way, and Eckard knew they were being flanked. Probably an entirely cautionary measure by the Draul, although an Outsider like Eckard could not be entirely certain of such presumptions. Just as Eckard cast his eyes about the typical Draul flanking manoeuvre in the surrounding woods, a sudden flash of images overwhelmed his mind. His perspective shifted inwards to the recesses of his mind's eye, a brief glimpse of a Draul cloak bound and armed with a drawn readied re-curve bow and arrow, crouched over a moss covered rock. Through the eyes of the stranger Eckard saw himself crouched and ready with his own sturdy crossbow. The concept was a curious one to experience but Eckard was not a new arrival to the possibilities of Magik.

Returning to the normal vision of his own eyes, Eckard readied the safety latch and placed his crossbow down on the moss covered rocks beneath him and stood up to make his case known. Almost immediately apparitions in forest green mantles emerged from the encompassing woods around. Surrounded on all points by at least six armed Draul Watchers, Eckard proceeded with the traditional parley procedures that were typical of such occasions as he found himself in now. Placing both his hands upon the back of his head and intertwining his fingers together, the symbolic and practical gesture of dis-arming was widely accepted in many lands including the Draul Theilm. The Hunter directly ahead of Eckard withdrew its arrow from its cocked position on the near-man's bow and placed it back in the quiver at its side. Pulling back its hood the Draul revealed itself as a female, ashen faced with low set eyes, probably from one of the Eastern isles Eckard mused. Relatively plain looking by Draul standards, she did however hold a fierce fire in her stonewashed crimson eyes.

'What brings you here, aurman?' The determined-eyed Draul Watcher inquired in broken *Cestral*.

'The gathering about to take place tonight' Eckard replied, carefully eyeing each of the armed and hooded figures around him one by one. 'Well that and the resulting search party that is to be assembled from the said gathering.'

'And how did you acquire such knowledge?' The Draul asked.

'My name is Eckard Delmose Farth, nephew of Semus, Semus the Bold who I'm sure at least one of you have heard of. I have been informed by sources reliable to me of the nature of the ForeSeer sapling.'

'What do you know of the ForeSeer, Eckard o' Semus?' The Draul Watcher inquired whilst eyeing off the clearly obvious hiding place of Luciarn Nonkar.

'That he's missing' Eckard said bluntly, shrugging. He turned away to call to call to Luciarn.

'Lucairn get up they already know you are there'. Luciarn Nonkar, ever the mistrusting and suspicious type (being a merchant after all) gingerly came to his feet and strode to a position close beside Eckard. The Draul proceeded to eye him off just as they had his younger companion.

'And what of this... one?' The ever-distrustful Draul Watch Leader inquired, regarding the now dirt-ridden Luciarn.

'This one, is the South Farthielm representative for the gathering tonight' answered Luciarn mimicking Eckard's respectful disarming action.

'You must be Krikza's Shralett? Yes?' Eckard said looking directing into the fierce eyes of the unusually stocky Draul woman. "Hence the questions, the many, many questions"

The female Draul Watch Leader's expression soured somewhat and she merely grunted in response to Eckard's query. Instead of words, she turned back towards the outcropping of dense ancient woods and motioned for everyone else to follow suit. The other hooded Draul Huntsmen fell in, striding off with the woman and almost in unison, they unsteadied their arrows from their bow. Eckard proceeded to collect his belongings and weapons once more. As did Luciarn who paused for a moment as the two men began following their less than hospitable welcoming party into the woods.

'Eckard you are walking a fine line with this one' Luciarn uttered as the two Aurmen attempted to keep pace with the vigorously brisk march of their Draul hosts.

'The Draul value strength, merchant. Thus I gave it to them' Eckard retorted as he adjusted his backpack on his shoulders and strapped his crossbow back to its resting position within the outer netting of the pack.

Eckard and Luciarn witnessed the Draul contingent ahead draw up stationary positions just off in the shade of the first of the ancient wild oaks and birch trees. The Aurmen duo paused in their discussion and ceased moving forward at the all too familiar sight. The full framed female leader amongst the Draul held up dual blind man's cloths, one in each hand. Eckard and Luciarn looked between each other and both understood immediately what was to happen next.

*

Roaming aimlessly and blinded through deeply tangled undergrowth, curled abrasive vines and all, Judeson quickly lost track of how far exactly he had travelled with his Draul hosts, the journey itself was made harder by the terrain, the Southron ever stumbling about and losing his sense of direction. At one point Judeson mused, as they had crossed the shallows of a river he remembered almost losing his footing completely in the lapping and bitter chilled waters.

If not for the assistance of the Draul he had curiously acquitted earlier on he probably would have fallen into the river. His Draul guide indeed seemed to relish the chance to aide him and had even utilised a few choice curse words Judeson had taught him earlier, although almost too anxiously like he had been waiting for just the right moment. The river now seemed hours past and where Judeson was now exactly he could not completely fathom. The sounds of the lively gushing waters had long since passed.

A sudden draft of a cool but fierce breeze wafted up into Judeson's face as he carefully strode forward. They had reached a clearing surrounded by rocks or cliffs Judeson realised and quite possibly an expansive one at that, as his footsteps seemed to echo all around. Just as the

man from Letesah went to take another step
forward he was seized by the steady grip of his
Draul guider's somewhat bony hands.

'Far enough for now, friend Judeson' The Draul
Watcher said releasing the blind-siding binding
from around Judeson's eyes. "You'll need wings if
you wish to go further." The other Draul Hunters
around let out a hushed chuckle at this.

It took a few moments for Judeson's vision to
adjust to the brightness of the dying light
overhead. When he did the young man fully
realized the sights of the vast expanse around
him. Just mere paces ahead of him the lands
dropped down dramatically into a deep depression
completely covered by woodlands. All around the
edges of the valley was covered by the far-
reaching forest groves as well. Judeson could
instantly relate to the Draul's jest prior to his
blindfold being removed, the sheer cliff face the
party were situated on was a narrow span of
ancient worn rock outcroppings overhanging the
valley below. Peering down, Judeson could make
out little apart from the extremely distant and
dark emerald canopy of the treetops, nor exactly
where the ground was below it. The bordering
escarpment cliff face all around them portrayed
no clear indicating signs of a way down to the
valley below. Judeson somehow doubted the Draul
intended to take him down to the underground
forest beneath them.

The entire party of Draul backed away from the
cliff's edge and made their way to a narrow cave
mouth covered in overgrown weeds nearby. A small
but steady stream trickled into the hollow and it
was here the Draul paused to take up defensive
positions. It was the first time Judeson had
noticed there were five other Watchers apart from
the one he had spoken with. Judeson presumed his

acting guide was the leader as he made his way to the forefront of the pack facing the cave. The lean near-man closed his eyes and looked to be in deep concentration as Judeson followed him. Though what exactly he was concentrating on Judeson was uncertain of.

All at once the cave seemed to shift in its formation unnaturally by some unknown force. Not in the violent manner of an earth-shake as Judeson had witnessed before in the Southern Plains but in a way the young man could not begin to describe in any true sense. Rocks and tangled vines seemed to gradually scatter apart into minuscule particles as if they were just a mere dust cloud to begin with. The ground underneath parted ways and physically formed what could only be taken as a ditch, although far deeper into the earth than any Judeson had witnessed before. The stream flowed down into the bleak hollow as the cave that once stood in place seemingly disappeared entirely.

'Coming?' The head Draul Watcher said as he broke from his odd semi-conscious meditative state and advanced directly into the hollows path.

Glancing back the Draul motioned Judeson forwards with his hands, before stepping directly into the hole and falling dramatically out of sight. The other Draul to Judeson's amazement followed their compatriot into the impossible hollow.

Disappearing from view Judeson mused as to what exactly had happened just now. All of a sudden another party of Draul approached the scene from Judeson's behind. Much like his encounter of being blindfolded before his current predicament, the Draul group possessed two men with them, stumbling forward with their own cloths banded over their eyes. A stocky built female Draul pushed forward from the group and halted the blinded men, one being quite older and larger than the other. With the blinding cloths removed by the female Draul the younger and far taller man spoke:

'Hail fellow Draul prisoner' the young man with a head of thick midnight dark and haphazardly braided hair locks said. The man was absurdly tall, even greater in height than Judeson, who had always been considered quite tall by many he had met in the South. Planted firmly on the young person's thick dark bearded face was a mischievous grin as if he were up to something no good.

'Why have you not entered the Gartia, Aurman?' Inquired the female Draul whose eyes seemed to peer right through Judeson.

'By the Queen, what the hell is going on?" Judeson answered peering round the group before him and back at the hole in the Stone, *as the* Draul woman as so titled the hollow in the earth.

'The charming lass means the hole, hop in it, would you kindly?' Answered the bearded young man, almost bursting out laughing in the process. Judeson hesitated not fully understanding whether this strange circumstance he found himself in was a jest at his expense or something else entirely. Although where his own Draul guides had disappeared to when entering into the hole he did not comprehend either. Just about to advance towards the hollow. Judeson was bypassed by the rushing form of the young man he had previously been discoursing with. The man quickly vanished into the *'Gartia?'* in much the same way as the Draul had done earlier.

'Alright Aurman, you saw that fool do it, now get into the Gartia' demanded the female Draul Watcher behind him.

Judeson ran, defying his instincts telling him otherwise and jumped into the hole ahead. Instantly everything around him was swept up in an odd and eerily blur of motions. The feeling was not at all akin to falling to Judeson. In reality gusts of fierce winds swan about him as all movement downwards seemed to pause momentarily. Then all of a sudden his whole person was propelled vigorously downwards in impossible speed. Hurled about just like a used cleaning rag into the depths of the forbidding hollow Judeson began to feel sick to the stomach. Just as it became almost unbearable to experience any longer the chaotic process ceased.

His fall had not met the inevitable end at the ground that he expected. He was alive. Judeson came to his senses eventually, crouched over in what could be taken as a small pond inside an expansive dim lit cave. The cave walls themselves were almost comprehensively covered in thick vegetation, much the same way as the forest far above. The dark haired stranger from prior to the leap of faith appeared before Judeson and held out his hand to help him to his feet. Judeson obliged the courteous gesture and with assistance brought himself upright and out of the shallow waterhole in the centre of the gigantic cavern. Standing up once more and attempting to steady himself from his traumatic prior encounter, Judeson felt overwhelmingly ill again. His head swam with motion sickness and he turned away from the trench coat wearing stranger and began vomiting excessively and violently onto the cavern floor.

'Nothing quite like a good Gartia hurl' chuckled the scruffy bearded man with sky blue eyes standing off several paces from Judeson with his back turned.'I've had mine already. It gets easier on the stomach the more you do it'

Judeson felt horrible, he had eaten very little on the journey here and before long his stomach acids poured through his throat and nose, the beige bile burning as it passed. The young man continued speaking in a hushed tone as more of the Draul arrived within the cavern from the forest above. Judeson noticed they seemed almost completely undisturbed by the process unlike his person.

'Though in hindsight I probably should have chewed my stew a little bit more than I did' Said the stranger nearby as he spat onto the turf. Noticing Judeson had finally ceased throwing the contents of his stomach up, the man aided him back to his feet once again and offered him an unimpressive looking drinking flask.

'My name is Eckard. Here drink this.' Eckard continued in his odd deep-voiced gruff sounding accent.

Judeson gave the man a grateful half-smile and took the flask from him, downing some of its contents. The liquid was a bitter and intense mouth burning alcohol, although not an entirely unpleasant substance in the current circumstances.

'Judeson, son of Judisye of Letesah that was.' Judeson said in a painful croak, handing the simple metal flask back to Eckard.

Eckard took the flask and drank, wincing as he did so. Judeson noted the stranger did not seem to think much of the substance either. Eckard spoke again in answer:

'That's quite the mouthful of a greeting Judeson, though I'm not really sure where exactly Letes…."

'Letesah, its south of the Boundary Mountains and beyond the Edging Waters, roughly a hundred

leagues or more south by south east of here'
Judeson said cutting off Eckard from his failure
to pronounce Judeson's home town.

Eckard took on a clear appearance of intrigue and
wonderment at this statement. He made to speak
further just when; the two men were interrupted
by the generously built Draul Watcher who had
arrived last into the dim-lit cave.

'Hurry up you two women and move onward' ordered
the female Draul, pacing towards them.

'No reason to hassle yourself, Shralett with
these three Aurmen. I can escort them to
Tzsu'Teng if need be. After all it is adamant you
return to your crucial patrol duties. My own
Bardreli is to return to the surface shortly once
resupplied anyway. They can may-hap follow you.'
Interrupted the leader of Judeson's Draul Watcher
group, who stood in what could be taken as the
only viable passage out of the cavern chamber,
narrow as it was.

'I'm under direct orders of Krikza to take these
Aurmen to him, Caster' The Draul Watcher replied
sternly, stressing the last word in a bitter tone
most of all.

'As I myself am under direction from the rest of
the Lord-Protector's Council to escort them
directly to the Hall of Gatherings'the Draul *Mage*
replied with a coy but challenging smile to the
solid-set Watcher.

The Draul warrior uttered a rude grunt in reply
and turned around, motioning for her patrol to
band together in the cave's waterhole. The lean
built Draul Mage gestured Judeson and Eckard to
him, Luciarn followed suite after finishing his
own discharge of prior meals onto the cavern
floor. Following in the wake of the huddled and
crawling form of the Mage into the darkness of

the tunnel leading out of the cave, Judeson,
Eckard and Luciarn knew they had witnessed first
hand the social politics of the civilisation
ahead of them. The bleak, pitch black darkness of
the humid and smooth faced moist limestone tunnel
offered little comfort to the Aurmen and when
they finally passed through into the world beyond
they came into the hidden Draul city of
Tzsu'Teng.

3rd Stanza

The Draul have turned away from their old ways
and began down the path of what those in the Cor-
Dazral Collective like to title 'Modernity'.
Magik is nigh on extinct in practice with many of
the youth, its workings being shunned and
illspoken of now by both young and old.
Treelopping and harvesting of their incredible
woods has become a massive competent for their
industry and many customs that were in place are
being thrown to the Four Winds. This is not an
isolated case however. The rest of the Nertheilm
is on a very similar road. This particular
signature indicates 'progress', but what are the
implications do us or the Draul really know?

A retrospective study of Journeys amongst the Draul by Professor
*Danian Avlerin Selk, head of Extra-Race Studies at Tamisk University, ancestor
of the late Sar Alverlin Ugusten Moor , 2951 ATF*

Never before had such wonders been beheld by Judeson. All around him now were some truly astounding visuals, like he had stepped into an entirely extrinsic alien world.

The Far Above was still obstructed by the dense canopy overhead in this underground forest, much the same way as the woods above. Surrounding them were dazzling lights harmonious syncopation. In hindsight, Judeson wondered how it was that this underground valley was un-sighted from the woods above. The flaring luminescent lights of fierce cobalt blue seemed to flicker and play about in the air. In actual fact these flickering streams of light were trapped within thousands of see-through lamps scattered about in chaotic disorderliness. Pathways of intricately placed sand coloured tile stones served as roads. Crowds of Draul walked up and down them, interacting as they went by in a unfamiliar tongues and phrases.

Dozens of figures in similar garb to Judeson's host seemed to march about, whilst other apparitions in simple discreet tunics strode carelessly around. From the tree's branches; banners of words not known to Judeson hung, while in other sections of undergrowth more of the intriguing lamps were suspended. Just as Judeson was contemplating where exactly the Draul actually made their homes in this strange place, a lean figure emerged from a barrow at the base of one of the great oak trees. A carved wooden door was the portal that the stranger opened and closed as he went on his way. Curiousness became an insurmountable feeling for Judeson as he made his way further into the world of the Draul.

'Pretty fancy ain't it Southron?' Eckard

explained in his melodic up and down voice, a mischievous smile on his unwashed face.

It was definitely something to Judeson, although what that particular something was he could not pin point exactly. The pathway they walked on was lined by several smaller varieties of the elongated lamps with swirling blue lights within. It was staggering to think that without the lights the darkness would be absolute. The general populace of the eerie woods seemed unfazed about such issues and paid little attention to the group as they passed by what could be taken as busy market stalls and trading plazas; As if reading his mind Eckard answered Judeson's thoughts oput loud.

'The lamps don't go out if that's what you're thinking, been here a few times and it ain't going dark in a hurry. Magik energies you see, *Wisps* the Draul call them. The trees produce the Wisps they are kinda like gas clouds but well you can see, different.' Said Eckard.

'Wisps are spirits I heard, some of them vengeful if you do not do as they say.' Luciarn Nonkar answered pushing into Eckard and Judesons paths to make himself known to them.

'The Lights are not Wisps, friend, they are gifts from the Wisps, the power of light is given to the Draul for protecting their home from harm.' The Draul Mage ahead of them uttered over his shoulder, not bothering to turn around.

'Harm from what?' Judeson inquired as the group passed by a contingent of generously-armed Draul soldiers marching in the opposite direction.

'From any who attempt to harm this Thielm Judeson.' The Draul Watcher answered pulling up in his trek to motion the end of their journey abruptly. "We are here"

'Here being?' Asked Judeson who peered around, not noting anything remarkable in contrast to the rest of the forest they had been witness to.

'The Grand fucking Gathering Hall.' Eckard announced, moving his arms high and wide in a rather mocking fashion in front of him.

The Draul Mage ignored Eckard's over-dramatic announcement and strode a few paces to the base roots of a massive auburn-rose coloured tree. Reaching out a hand to place it upon the hardwood surface the Mage closed his eyes in concentration much the same way as he had done before at the hollow leading down to the underground realm. Judeson made note to peer around the area for any shifting changes in the ground, nothing happened. Not immediately anyway.

A tingling sensation spiralled up and down Judeson's skin making him flinch with the feeling, as if he; were being generously stroked by a sharp thorn all over. A series of chaotic chiming sounds made themselves upfront and prominent, seeming to originate from everywhere and nowhere in particular at the same time. Within moments the world around Judeson seemed to blur and become distant. The very ground seemed to shift and turn en mass everything was in rapid and fluid motion.

A brilliant flash of blinding light pronounced their re-entry into the corporeal world. Judeson for moments stood stunned in awe and struggling to readjust his vision. When he did he soon: he made out Eckard, Luciarn and their Draul Mage just ahead of them as if they had not moved, in actual fact the setting he found himself in was a drastic metamorphism. Instead of emerald greens and shadows of the expansive dark valley woodland, a marble floored hallway drew out all around for at least half a league.

The walls and roof of the gigantic open space chamber seemed to have been literally carved out of sheer rock. The misshapen hard stone-walls and ceiling added a differing contrast to the elegantly patterned marble tiles of the floor below. Several paces ahead lay an obsidian black stone disc, impossibly large in scale and populated by several different figures, all Draul. The members of the chamber situated at the odd table sat on misshapen, rustic chairs carved from oak and pine. Seven in number the Council quickly evaluated the arrival of Judeson and the others with intense stares. Judeson possessed the overbearing sense they were being judged even before they had spoken a word.

**

It was brighter than he anticipated. In fact he was slightly disappointed that the Lord-Protector's Council of the Draul peoples; was not more ominous and foreboding in appearance. Of course never being present in the chamber before Eckard had adopted certain fallacies to entertain his imagination of the place. Disappointment was a usual concept when one actually did enter such an elusive venue.

It was reasonable to discern for Eckard that his imagination was just far too high in its expectations. Of course the journey through to the chamber was what really mattered to him more. The experience excited him and incited his imagination to ponder further uses for such powers. The Green and Blue schooled Mage known simply as Raijin, the one that had brought them here to the Gathering Hall, Eckard had met before on a few occasions he had however never seen his potential at work

Of course Eckard knew the chamber was probably entered via prior employed *Wards and Enchantments* but the experience of *Pathing* at work was still an insightful one for him. After all one day soon he was going to employ it himself.

The young man rubbed his rough now intensely itchy beard and grimaced; trying in vain to remember the last time he had taken time to shave his face. Looking among the others Luciarn clearly looked nervous rubbing his sweatcoated palms together in unison. How that man could sweat so much was beyond Eckard, it was not even remotely warm in the Council Assembly Room. Raijin was closer to the onyx stone table and discussed something in hushed whispers with the others before respectfully bowing and wandering off to the far side of the hall. Looking over at the young sturdy set Southron named Judeson. Eckard noticed the Aurman looked overcome with amazement. Of course he had been of this way for some time now. His jaw was practically wide open and his eyes were abuzz with intrigue. It was to be expected however, Eckard imagined he, himself probably appeared of the same persuasion to the Draul when he had first come to Tzsu'Teng.

Raijin seemed to be no longer involved in the Gathering about to take place, he stood off in the distant confines on the opposite side of the room. All attention was to be drawn to the obsidian centre table. The Lord-Protector's Council itself was arrayed about in no particular order and it was fitting as Eckard well knew the balance of power among them was a shared one, even if certain figures believed their sphere of influence was more paramount then others. The focus of such thoughts had taken up residence on the far left hand side of the table and it was of course Krikza.

A heavy set Draul Elder male sat in an almost pompous pose eyeing off the Eckard and the two other men intently. The Lord-Protector bore a head of platinum blonde hair, (common amongst Draul of the Rosewood Isle) and was dressed in glimmering, recently polished Draul military attire complete with commemorative leaf shaped-medals and plate maille.

The remaining members of the Council had not decorated themselves so extravagantly, apart from; Malciero who wore his usual golden trimmed ceremonial temple robes. Despite their differences in certain matters and unresolved debates among them, Eckard knew that what was about to take place here was a cause every Council member had concern invested in.

'Good tidings Aurmen, you may approach the Council if you will' Announced Malceiro whose demeanour in public displays was almost always displayed theatrically.

'Welcome to you all, my Lords and Ladies. Good health and may *Falhaset* bless you all.' Luciarn Nonkar said to them as the three Aurmen approached the stone table. Eckard well knew Luciarn was not a religious man and hearing him utter the God's name seemed ironic, still it sounded relatively respectful in a tactful way that Eckard supposed Lords and Ladies would be interested in.

'We gladly accept such generous blessings merchant. Let it be known that the Wisps of Tzsu'Teng look kindly upon you as well.' Krikza said, seeming to puff up his chest in an unmistakably pompous manner.

What a load of shit. Eckard mused, finding himself grunting somewhat loudly after the Draul

Lord's spiel. Krikza gifting him a none too subtle glare of disgust. The rest of the Council seemed to ignore all of this and a female member whose name eluded Eckard continued on with the Gathering.

'Master Luciarn Nero Nonkar, Chief of the East Farthling Merchant Company what is it you wish to discuss with us.' The Draul in question, another Islander fair-haired and paler then her mainland kin, uttered officiously.

'I wish to present to you my Candidate for your Search Party in the Reclamation of your ForeSeer-to-be.' The merchant said gesturing towards Eckard's direction.

'And the other Aurman is what?' Krikza inquired forcing himself back into the discourse.

'My companion, he is to join me.' Eckard abruptly interjected much to the clear abhorrence of the surrounding Council Members. Judeson stared at the man astounded.

'You may only address the Council when spoken to Aurman.' Marciero stated matter-of-factly staring down his rather generously broad nose at Eckard.

'Apologies my Lord and Ladies, Eckard does not understand the laws of you Theilm in such matters. I wish to disclose that I did not anticipate his rude behaviour in your Great Hall.' Luciarn said, lowering his person into a bow and glaring back at Eckard to make his distaste known.

'You are well understood Merchant, however for the duration of this assembly only you are permitted to stay. Your Candidates shall be henceforth displaced from this Hall.' The unnamed Lord-Protector said and she turned towards the Draul Mage on the far side of the chamber.

'Shralett take these Aurman warriors back to

Tzsu'Teng and then onward to their temporary quarters.' She commanded.

'At once my Lady' Raijin answered, immediately trekking over to Judeson and Eckard's position.

Luciarn looked back at Eckard and nodded at the man, knowing his part in the Gathering had been fulfilled. The rotund Merchant pivoted back into the direction of the Draul Council and continued.

'Now on to business, shall we?' He said continuing his rehearsed speech.

Being led back to their original point of entry before Pathing into the assembly hall by the Draul Mage, Judeson and Eckard faced each other. The Southron looked to be noticeably perplexed by the whole encounter. This was understandable to Eckard.

'What in the high fucking Far Above just happened?' Asked Judeson as they found themselves back at their previous position before the Magik's induced entry, the Mage readied in deep concentration once more.

'That's the Draul Council for you. I got you the job anyway. You did want the work didn't you, why else had you come here?' Eckard said as the tingling buzz sensation that went with Magik induced tele-portation came back in a rush.

'Yes I did. I heard of the problem that arose and the involvement of the Rakon in it. But you lied to them I have never met you before now, let alone been your companion.' Judeson answered as the en-kindling goose bumps crawled across his skin and the sound of chaotic chimes echoed all around them.

'Yes well it was getting kind of dull. I thought we could use a drink.' Eckard shrugged indifferently.

Before Judeson could respond they were once again

swept up into the improbable darkness and seemingly vanished from the world.

*

They had spent hours wandering down dim lit forest pathways that all looked the same. Judeson began to doubt he, Eckard and the Draul Mage Raijin were heading in any particular direction. Judeson's sense of aim and location was henceforth thrown to the winds. The Draul and the strange boisterous Northman appeared to be in relative peace, in contrast to Judeson.

At least some people knew where they were going, Judeson thought.

The stick figure Mage leading them ever onward into the dark woodland realm abruptly stopped in his tracks and hummed for just a blink of a moment, the noise to Judeson's surprise seemed to carry all around echoing off the ancient surrounding trees.

'Here we are friends Judeson and Eckard. You're…
' said Raijin turning towards them and smiling a beaming grin. "Lodgings I believe you Aurmen call it."

'Thanks for your hospitality, friend Raijin.' Judeson replied to the Mage and saluted him in the Southron fashion.

'I believe there is something else we are forgetting friend Eckard' The Lean Draul Watcher stated looking directly at Eckard now.

'Oh fine here you go you smug bastard.' Eckard said back to the Draul with a grin of his own and passed across a leather bound, tombstone of a book from out of his small backpack that barely looked capable of accommodating such a large object.

'I'm not saying friend Raijin either, it sounds creepy' Eckard continued, still grinning.

'I believe parting ways, in Aurman tradition you state the period of the day yes? Well… night to you friends' replied Raijin as he began walking over back the way the group had come, holding up the large book in his hands as he did so.

'Right bed and booze I suppose.' Eckard said tapping on the side of a nearby sturdy hardwood tree.

In the moments after he did so a door seemingly out of nowhere at all opened outwards from the tree's base roots. A descending stair case was seen to be leading underground from the door's portal. At the bottom of the stairs sat a decently sized room with two simple beds and one of those curious candle lamps lit and hanging from the ceiling, the warmth of inside was alluring to Judeson at the current moment. Eckard motioned for Judeson to be the first inside of their temporary residence. Judeson obligated.

'I know it's not much but it's thoughtful never the less and look they left us a treat. *Kormai Firewater*' Eckard said as the men walked through the portal and into the quiet warmth of the small residence.

Judeson quickly noted the Northerners source of interest through all he had heard from the man in their brief time together. A simple long necked glass bottle filled with ochre liquid; and two rustic clay tankards rested on the room's solitary wooden bedside table between their two sleeping cots. Kormai Firewater was of course alcohol, Judeson instantly knew. Judeson made his way to the left hand side bed and removed his pack and unslung the sword of Jude from across his back. Living up to his reputation Eckard had already filled the two mugs with the tawny liquid before he threw down his own pack and stripped his weapons off and necked his first drink in one single mouthful.

'I do hope one of those is for me' called a quiet feminine voice from behind them.

On the edge of the door's portal at the topmost stair stood a female Draul, a rather pretty one at that, though she seemed to hold a deadly serious gaze as if she were born to it. Her long black hair which was embellished with magenta beads furled down loose about the shoulders; and despite her grave regard she bore a mischievous twinkle in her faded emerald green eyes, disconcertingly similar to Eckard in an odd way. Dressed in a Forest green Draul cloak she began down the stairs. The young woman was small in height yet quite rounded in figure, she was not fat nor was she startling thin like many of the other Draul, she stood out and not in any unpleasant way.

Walking past him she seemed to glide almost elegantly as if she were hutched up on tiptoes ready to start dancing. Without hesitation the young Draul of slight the greyish-blue hues, took the mug from Eckard's hands and drank down slightly, holding Eckard's quizzical stare on her. Although she did not nearly meet his height, her close stance to the man indicated a certain level of trust between the two.

'Always a pleasure our nighttime liaisons milady, unfortunately I'm not alone on this occasion. Pity really' Eckard said, pouring another mug of Firewater and handing it onto Judeson.

'Oh shut up Eckard, I'm not your Ladyship. I have however come to *liaison* as you put it, probably not in the manner you like to imagine either. Business strictly.' Replied the young woman as she planted herself onto the right-hand side bed, her words did not seem to be hateful however, more playful, like she were toying with him.

'That's a shame, I'm not too good at business usually, well not political shit annyway' Said Eckard now drinking out of the bottle at light fast rate whist refilling the others own mugs.

'Who's this?' Inquired the young woman looking at Judeson briefly before returning her gaze to Eckard. Judeson found the woman's stare unnerving in a way; she looked determined and mature beyond her clearly young age.

'His name is Judeson, he's from South of the Boundary, we met in the woods.' Replied Eckard before Judeson could answer.

'Excellent, I'm happy you found someone.' The Draul woman's crimson eyes seemed to linger on judeson for moment as if she were studying him.

'Krikza believes him to be a Kobold spy. Our favourite Lord-Protector is trying to use this to his advantage, propaganda and all that' The woman warned, accepting another drink of Firewater from Eckard.

'I am no Gnome spy' Judeson retorted in earnest, both Eckard and the pretty stranger looking at him curiously after he did so.

'You call them Gnomes? How very condescending of you. Nevertheless you two fools being here in Tzsu'Teng, at this time is not good. Not good at all.' The young lady replied, placing her mug, still half full on the counter top. She proceeded to tying up her her beaded locks to the back of her head.

'That's why we are both leaving, off to fetch the ForeSeer boy. Luciarn the fat bastard is sorting out the rest with the Council. We shall be out of Krikza's patch soon enough. No reason for us to stay, we have an important identity to rescue.'

Eckard shrugged, re-pouring Judeson's mug of bitter sweet tasting Firewater, Eckard made to refill the woman's but she refused handing him back the mug and standing up.

'Good. Because Krikza is spreading the word, as unfathomably stupid as it is; that the Kobold kidnapped the boy. Your friend being alleged to be in cohorts with them, as untrue as it is, will seem…well unseemly.'

'Of course Krikza is. What shall I call you tonight then? Ahma, Lotus, Betty? Asked Eckard.

'You know full well Eckard and Betty is not one of my aliases just you know. Kail will do tonight.' The young woman answered.

'Kail. You know the Raks are involved in the kidnapping don't you? Spreading dissent amongst the Draul and then the Kobold.'

'None of us know that for certain. You wish for some conspiracy theory to exist just as you always do Eckard.'

'The Rakoni are terrible beasts that have no mercy in their hearts' Judeson announced angrily, feeling an inner fire build within himself at mention of the Rakoni.

Kail now fully risen up from the bed, passed by Eckard after a momentary sustained stare. She once again seemed to delicately glide across the room to the doorway where she turned back to speak.

'I don't need to remind you of the importance of the child to the Draul.' 'Be careful, try not to get killed and all. I shall of course cover your exit, *as I always seem to do*' She whispered the last six words as she exited, shutting the door behind her.

Judeson felt yet more confusion build to a crescendo, this strange place and people were not easily read. Eckard did not seem inclined to answer any questions Judeson may have, as the Northman was now presently sculling the remaining contents of the bottle. Judeson made to speak but Eckard was first once again.

'Well big day ahead in the morrow, Judeson. Night night' blurted Eckard in a slur as he threw the glass bottle smashing it against the far wall and collapsing onto his bed face down.

Judeson sensed this was the extent of the heights his conversation was going to reach and settled down into bed himself.

*

Eckard woke up with a start uttering a gasping breath as he did so. His face felt numb from lying on one side for hours. The young man brushed his loose tangled braids away from his face and got up to stretch out his arms and legs. It was good to sleep in a proper bed every now and again; the hard earth was not a forgiving companion when traveling throughout the wilds for so long. Sometimes a little hint and slight sniff of civilisation was just enough to keep one sane. Eckard checked his belongings nearby, a force of habit entirely but one that was important to him. Back pack, crossbow, boots, sword no problems there, Eckard did however realise his problem. His head was pounding. Kormai Firewater, it was not the first time. Noticing the all-too serious Southron Judeson was not in his bed, nor was the man's gear. Eckard made his way out of the cabin, to the outside world.

The robust built Southron was close by, as Eckard has already sensed despite the throbbing head. Roughly ten paces from the threshold of their temporary quarters the man stood, back pack and sword on, looking ready to depart at the very first sign. Eckard smiled despite himself, he liked this one. He had a sort of certain… simplicity to him. Not thick like a township's fool but simple like a good helpful man, the likes of which Eckard was always informed he was not.

Judeson seemed to have a sense of honour about him, it also helped that he possessed a rather obvious deep fixed hatred of the Rakon. Perhaps Eckard had found another man who he could actually work with he thought.

'I'm ready to go out on this quest of ours I guess. Well that is to say I have been ready for some time now.' Judeson said as Eckard gingerly made his way over to him.

'Well yes of course you have but you my friend did not drink most of the bottle of Kormai fucking Firewater now did you? Besides we are not in a rush anyway. We are in fact waiting.' Eckard replied sitting down awkwardly at the base of the nearby oak tree.

'Waiting for what?' Judeson asked quizzically.

'Raijin. Ah there he is.' Eckard said stretching out both arms at full stretch and painfully realising he had to get back up on his feet. Raijin had arrived. The large book he had borrowed from Eckard still on him, the Draul carefully cradling it in his arms.

'What do you think?' Eckard asked the Draul as he finally regained his footing and pointed to the Book from the old bastard he had given the Draul.

'I believe it is time to go friend Eckard. However this work by Sar Wrendal makes for interesting reading I must say. Obviously you have been employing some of the writer's concepts I suppose.' Raijin said.

'I could tell you were coming before you arrived,

I followed a stream.' Eckard replied with a rye grin.

'Good you are learning, slowly which is to be expected but learning nevertheless.'

'Are we going or are we having a Council gathering of our own?' Judeson interjected flinching in his steps as if he could not contain himself any longer.

Both Eckard and Raijin laughed in unison at Judeson's impatience, although the man seemed to take it to heart. Glaring at them both. It seemed to Eckard the South must have been wasteland for humour. *The man was absolutely serious.* Nevertheless he was approving of Judeson more and more with every moment, he had steel in his veins. *That was a commodity they needed.*

*

They travelled back the way they had come, through the dark eerie forest that the Draul called their home. Both Eckard and Raijin spoke very little merely trekking through the woods silently, perfectly fine for Judeson. Passing through the Gartia upwards this time felt as straining on the body as it did in descent. Judeson wondered as to how the pathway had ever come about in the first place or indeed how it even even worked. Though Judeson also did not wish to divulge further into such matters of Magik, as he did not wholly trust it.

At the threshold of the entrance to Tzsu'Teng the trio were met by another Watcher Party, thankfully the large Draul woman from yesterday was not amoung them. Just like the journey to the edge of the valley the Draul requested the two men be blindfolded. Following Eckard's position on the matter, Judeson obliged again, although he still did not enjoy the feeling of being unarmed and wandering blind through unfamiliar country, though it was the laws of their realm and fully due respect. It seemed odd to Judeson that Eckard's stout friend had not returned with them but he did not bother Eckard with asking. In fact Judeson had long since decided against thinking too much on all the unknowns around him. Ignorance was indeed bliss.

Before the blind cloths could be applied completely over Judeson's eyes Raijin paused in the application. Several paces off from the group stood the slight figure of the mysterious Kail, she was relatively concealed behind a tightly drawn hood and in the shadows of the trees close by. Raijin motioned for the other Watchers to fall out and they did so. Kail did not approach; she only peered at them for mere moments before sliding away into the hidden confines of the forest. Judeson looked around at Eckard who let out a considerably brief bittersweet smile as she vacated the area. It was not the same as the troublemakers grimace planted firmly on his face at the Council Gathering, it was much sadder and reserved in nature. Eckard briefly looked up at the Far Above before motioning for Rajin to finish his blinding cloth, Judeson's turn was moments later.

The whole world enveloped back into darkness and uncoordinated stumbling followed with walking blind through the woods. It was not a welcome return for Judeson, but this time he did not bother to voice his opinion on the matter at hand.

Instead he preoccupied himself with the curious scene he had been witness to before. It was clear there was a history between Eckard and the enigmatic Kail, if that's even what her name was. Judeson remembered the exchange between his two new acquaintances well. The Southron supposed it was no use prying into such matters, even more so now as the situation did not really favour idle conversations; just another unanswered question from his time in this odd Realm.

Judeson realised the journey back as it always seemed to be a great deal easier back than it had been on the previous trek in. Of course not too many times Judeson could name himself being blindfolded whist travelling but it was beside the point now. He had slowly come to accept the disposition and sort to benefit himself from it. Judeson did not nearly fall as many times as the first excursion on the way to Tzsu'Teng nor did he slip into the gushing waters of the all too familiar river.

Indeed Judeson felt some sense of direction as their group passed the respectful waterway. From that critical point however the cooperative of Draul Watchers and blindfolded men did not travel as far as Judeson had on the way in. Indeed Judeson mused it must have only been one or two bells before Raijin called a halt to the trek and pulled away the cloths around Judeson and Eckard's collective eyes. Where they were now was anyone's guess.

Walking forwards mere paces after the blinding clothes were removed Judeson viewed the scene before him with askance glances. Beyond the dark confines of the woods the land stretched out wide and expansive before him. Scattered groves of immature pines and redwood spread about all directions from the group as they stood at the edge of the Draul Forest. Further down the steady depression strewn with trees lay a valley of rolling emerald grass and auburn dirt plains until the land once again layered back up into sparsely forested hills far off in the distance.

It was landscape the likes of which were to Judeson similar to that of his homeland. Although the North bore with it far greener meadows then his own and a morning chill of bitter cold and oscillating mists obscuring vision, those last points were a swift departure from the South's climate.

Breathing in the air of the open outlying lands was a simple pleasure Judeson had surely missed, within the eerie woodland realm of the Draul. Raijin and his group of Watchers drifted back towards their forest seemingly uninterested in traversing further beyond. Raijin paused momentarily to bow to both Judeson and Eckard before wandering back into the shadows of the great oaks behind. Eckard at Judeson's side let out a brief smile and waved at the retreating Draul emphatically before turning towards the lands ahead of them.

'Ah South Fartheilm here we come then' Said Eckard breathing in an emphatic inhale through his nose and letting out a brief subdued exhalation moments later. As if he was consuming a stockpile of air for the journey ahead. *Everything with this man, was over-the-top even breathing* – Judeson distinguished.

'What is Fartheilm? Is that the name of a Kingdom nearby? Your merchant, came from here, no?' Judeson asked, taking in the outlying landscape.

'Nah, the fat bastard is from the North Fartheilm, we are in the South Farth, quite different. Well sort of anyway' Eckard laughed before continuing, though Judeson could not see what the joke was.

'It's not a kingdom, nowhere in the Netheilm is anymore. It's the name for the lands all around here, from the edge of the Yunlands and the Cor-

Dazral Collective to the west and in the North Farth- as far north as the Testerment tablelands, of course bypassing the whole Draul Theilm and heading due straight east to the Reacher's Coast at the end of the Continent. Fartheilm is in plain words, well it's fucking big. No central leadership no Capital City to call its own. Just dozens and dozens of townships and settlements scattered about living the simple life. A bit poetic I guess. Well if you count out the corruption guild in-fighting and religious zealots in some parts.' The Northman continued.

'There is that word again, Theilm? I am unsure of this term' Judeson said.

Judeson felt should focus on acquiring little tid-bits of information. If he attempted to keep track of everything the beanpole Northman said, his head would explode.

Eckard motioned for Judeson to follow him as he began slowing trekking down the slight descent of the foothills on the frontier of the forest behind them. There appeared to be paths etched into the sides of the slopes, not by tools or man-made structure but simply the feet of those that had passed through this land before. Judeson supposed it must be a well-travelled venue if this current disposition of the ground was anything to go by. Mere moments had passed in their journey before Eckard continued in his explanation to the Southron who did not bother to face Judeson as he spoke, just walked onward at a brisk pace.

'Theilm is a Draul word, it more or less equates to realm. Far is an *Cestral* word of course. I don't think the country folk around here have too much in terms of imagination so they just plastered two words together from two languages.

Fair enough I suppose. I mean Aurmora isn't very original either.' Eckard said kicking a loose pebble down the slope the two were on, into the valley plains below.

'Aurmora?' Judeson asked, taking in the rest Eckard had stated.

'You sure don't know much about the Nertheilm do you?'

'Well where I came from Letesah wasn't really a very happening place. Small town is an understatement, it didn't really have many interactions with outlanders, the occasional game hunter or tracker every now and again but not much else, not even any contact from the Hand of Kingdoms.' Replied Judeson, remembering back on how simplistic his life was in the days long ago past.

'I can't say I have ever heard of Letesah or any of those things either, Jude, can I call you that? Shortened form of Judeson right?' asked Eckard

'Jude is the line of my Family and its sword on my back, Judeson will do please.'

'My most humble apologies, Judeson it is. Why did you leave your Letesah then?' said Eckard.

Judeson was not entirely sure if the man's first sentence sarcastically mocking him or not as Eckard faced away from him. Eckard's voice had portrayed very little emotion, there was a great deal Judeson was not sure about this man yet.

'It was destroyed, burnt to the ground and its people slaughtered.' Judeson said with a bitter taste in his mouth and his voice coated in venom.

Obviously clear to Eckard was Judeson's change in tone and character at this sweeping statement, was it that the Northern man halted in his tracks and turned to face Judeson, bearing a serious demeanour.

'I'm sorry to hear that' Eckard murmured meeting Judeson's eyes briefly and then looking away. "It was the Rakon wasn't it?'

'Yes.' Said Judeson as he too looked away and then trudged past the stationary Eckard further on the path down to the valley. Judeson however stopped in his own tracks as Eckard then called out to him from behind.

'My mother and father bot died at the battle of Wanderer's River.' Eckard paused for a second. 'They say battle now but there was no fight, the Rakoni slaughtered hundreds'

Judeson meet the man's troubled eyes and saw a look he had seen in his own eyes many times before. It was as if Judeson were gazing into a reflection of himself. That same hollow look of dismay he had seen on his own face, in a mirror on the surface of lake, he now faced on the face of another. Judeson could not believe he had met this man. It was uncanny that another had been so unfortunate to share such a similar fate as to his own and he would just randomly meet one day in the woods.

'Anyway I guess that's why you are here, to make a difference to turn that tide. Come on then, best we keep going. We have some ground to make to track down the ForeSeer child.' Eckard continued on down the well-travelled pathway speaking.

Judeson fell in behind keeping pace with the rapid movement of the tall Northman. A new and welcome exchange had been made on this road. Judeson had met another who knew what he had experienced; he had met a man who had taken up the sword much as he had done, to fight what was inevitably coming. For Judeson was convinced the

Rakon were to invade these Northen land much the same way as he had been witness to in the Southern Realms beyond the Boundary Mountains. Few he had met since arriving to this demesne had shared much with Judeson, though in Eckard he had found someone he believed he could trust. The man from Letesah that had grown to harbour a unfathomable and unshakable hatred for the Rakon, the fierce near-men creatures that had destroyed all he had held dear in his early days; had found another who could finally assist him in his ultimate aim.

4th Stanza

Magik is not inherently evil as so many in this court claim it to be. Magik is the metaphysical act of altering the world around us. Enacted by mere mortals who have studied the arcane practices, for Magik to be 'evil' or 'sinister' as several of you so claim it to be; it would need to have been created by someone or indeed something who is in turn malicious themselves or possessing an unstable and destructive mindset.

The Magik Arts did not create the Plague, Magik did not wage wars that saw the deaths of countless innocents. Magik is not to blame here. Just as every terrible thing that has come to pass; every war and every slaughter is almost always the actions of a select few that hurt the rest of us, who bring ruin upon us. If you so wish to cast blame let all here today; in this chamber know of your own Council's actions in all that has come this past arc.

Section of Sar Wrendal's Address to the Confederation Council

The Trial and Un-Knighting of Sar Wrendal Dastin Morke (Various Sources)

Nertharnlands Confederation, Aurmora, Reclaimers Isle

Confederation Council Chambers

on the eve of 2978 arcs ATF (After the Fall)

'As I must stress my Lords and Ladies, nothing of any sort has been occurring within Nero or Ortika.' Announced Luciarn.

'Nothing that you know about Merchant,' Krikza said, layering on his most malicious tongue in steadily heightening proportions.

'Easy, Lord Krikza the man obviously has no knowledge of such matters.' Another Draul Council member stated from across the stone table.

'Easy. Easy you say we Draul are to rest while malevolent forces all about us make their moves and muster their strength. Perhaps we are to sit calmly by whilst the ForeSeer-to-be is missing. Kidnapped and going to be bent against his will to serve a dark cause against our people and their Theilm.' Krikza replied, throwing on the dramatic pauses and punctuation to his pinnacle best. Hushed whispers by closely seated Council members broke out.

Luciarn did not trust this Lord Krikza. The others all had their faults, sure enough. Marciero tended to enjoy the sound of his own voice but the Councilor was dependable to follow on an agreement in the end. This of all things Luciarn respected the most. Although the Draul did not have any form of monetary system, the various caravans run by the Merchant Houses of the Fartheilm went to great lengths to trade resources with the forest dwellers. Krikza and his followers (which was a foundation quickly elevating) were entirely disagreeable to Luciarn. Lord-Protector Krikza did not seem to favour reason and often possessed an unshakable view of how he perceived the Draul should be in all matters, self-idealism in so many great proportions, was indeed a dangerous thing. Although Luciarn had prepared for the man's accusations and malingering, he needed himself to be at his best and indeed need patience to remain so. He had planned for Eckard to be out of this chamber from the beginning they had got here and indeed getting out of the theilm as quick they had had been a much added bonus. Eckard had proved more than capable of helping in that regard and now two allies were their boots on the ground now. With the Southron they had unexpectedly met in the woods (a welcome coincidence for certain), at least they had that much going for them against Krikza and his goons. Without help of Raijin, the Draul Mage and confident as an ally, Luciarn knew he and Eckard would have been subdued and accused of treason or some other such preposterous ridicule by Lord Krikza. Indeed without Raijin and Kail's hidden actions in the shadows. Kail of course was steadily subverting Krikza's own power cycles and moves. Luciarn estimated that he and Eckard probably would not have made it past the border, let alone the Council Hall without Kail and Raijin. It was not always this way though Lucairn could fondly recall; there was a time (what seemed countless arcs ago now) when the Draul and the Merchant Houses of Fartheilm worked as one, helping and assisting each other at every turn. Krikza's unforeseen and rapid rise to power within the Draul realm had ensured the gradual demise of such relations, as the Lord drew on more and more radical indoctrination into the fold. Luciarn knew even now, even with all they had done it was entirely possible that they were too late to stop Krikza now.

'Has anyone of you in this Council come to

consider the reality of the Kobold being behind the kidnapping of the ForeSeer.' Krikza piped up once again in his shrill voice, bringing Luciarn back to the now from his musings.

'If I may my Lord the Kobold are not behind the kidnapping it is more than plausible by our own reports that the Rakoni have involvement with some of the more…enterprising crinimal in the greater Fartheilm.' Said Luciarn hastily and with as much respect as he could possibly muster to the brash comments of Krikza.

'What evidence is this all based off of, merchant?' Krikza bellowed, narrowing his intense beaming gaze in Luciarn.

'I have given you all my documents in the last meeting we had, with all due respect. My lords and ladies you all know this.' Luciarn replied. *He was losing ground.*

A momentary break in proceedings followed as the Council elected to converse amoung themselves' in hushed murmurs again. Krikza followed suit and turned inwards to the discussion but not before gifting Luciarn a prolonged challenging stare. Well that was being generous Luciarn reckoned, *hateful* was probably more accurate.

Luciarn knew from previous encounters that these closed off whispering could very well continue on for any given amount of time and took up a seat on the fancily tiled marble floor, resting in preparation, for the next onslaught of political maneuvering. Though next time was probably going top be the last here.

**

Judeson gradually stirred awake from his slumber to subtle murmured sounds of sheared fur, the noise of which he had heard many times before from his father's own skinning and shaving of beast pelts. The young man soon discovered in this case, however, there was no animal being prepared for sale. Judeson rolled over from his sleeping position on a simple bed mat on the bare earth to find Eckard cutting off large swaths of his unruly braids of dark hair with a rather large hunting knife. Eckard grabbed a generous handful of hair in his left hand and sliced the curved edge blade across precariously close to the base of his chin. The beaded and braided locks falling to the ground nearby, Eckard with this done looked up and met Judeson's eyes.

'Just cleaning up. How was your nap?' asked the other man who now looked semi-presentable, even if his haphazard haircut looked extremely uneven upon his head.

'Fine, as good as it ever is sleeping on the ground.' Proclaimed Judeson who gingerly made his way to his feet and limbered up, the young Southron noting the Day-Star's approach on the distant horizon, mere moments from dawn the man well known.

Eckard nearby seemed to contemplate taking the broad-edged hunting knife to his thick full beard but thought better of it and inserted the tool back onto his belt. Judeson glanced over to the long-dead embers of the burnt out fire the two men had constructed for their camp site at this mound on the grassy plains they found themselves on. Blackened and charring remains of what was once Eckard's flask sat atop the ash of the fire pit. Judeson not saying a word looked quizzically at the man after seeing this and the Northman seemed to once again read his mind.

'No drinking whilst working, it's a rule of mine.' Eckard said standing up and collecting his belongings that lay scattered about the camp.

Judeson finished up a sequence of stretches, now
fully limber, made to move out. In that exact
moment Judeson heard a sharp piercing whistle
from behind him. The young man turned around just
in time as Eckard hurled a tightly wound straw
sack in his direction at chest height. Judeson's
sharp reflexes kicked in and received the sack in
a taut catch. Unwinding the bindings Judeson made
out a whole loaf of multi-grained bread in a
strange oblong shape and wax lid clay jar inside.
Once again Eckard had produced the items from his
rather small backpack, just as he had done so
with his book for Raijin. Judeson began to doubt
the dirty looking bag across the man's shoulders
was entirely what it seemed. Eckard held up
another item, this time a simple clay mug filled
with a strange dark, thick liquid. It was
steaming out of the top and Eckard held the
container out to Judeson.

'Kafra?' Inquired Eckard passing the simple mug
across to his travelling partner.

'I'm sorry? I have no idea of what this is'
Judeson replied, taking the cup gratefully
nevertheless.

Eckard clearly perplexed by Judeson's response,
yet another varying difference in understanding
between the two, Judeson mused. The Northlander,
however, did attempt to give Judeson an
explanation as they began to set off for the
day's journey.

'It's kind of well not really… I suppose you
could compare it to tea. You do know tea don't
you?' Eckard said as the two men started off down
a grassy knoll.

'Of course, there were fields of tea in the
southern lands, east across the great inland sea
from Letesah. Probably not there anymore.'

Judeson said, noting Eckard taking on that far away distant look so familiar to Judeson, the Southerner returned the topic to lighter matters. 'Staying on topic though, I do know what tea is, I have drunk it before, but this…this Kafra? Does not smell or look anything like the tea I have had from the Southrondor.'

'Well, that's because it isn't really anything like tea. It's far stronger for one, it wakes a man up quite well. Kafra is from beans, husked, roasted and dissolved into boiled water' Eckard replied, Judeson now remembering he had seen the Northman possessed an odd sideward bow when they had first met back in the Draul forest, where that strange weapon was now was beyond Judeson, as Eckard no longer seemed to possess it. Sensing the man was looking at him, Judeson decided to continue the conversation.

'Beans?' Judeson said holding up his cup of steaming black liquid to his lips.

'Beans' Eckard stated, giving the man his best; wicked smile.

Not another word was spoken between the two young men for hours as they journeyed further west across the dense high grass mounds and fields that were the primary terrain, albeit for the occasionally scattered shrub. The lands before them were absent of any sign of settlement and Judeson welcomed the setting, growing up in and feeling the most comfortable in a wilderness such as this one.

Sleeping in a proper bed back in the Draul city of Tzsu'Teng was more or less welcome exchange from the norm. Nevertheless, in Judeson's eyes nothing could never replace the feeling of open plains, clean air and wild tracks beneath one's feet, especially when the day-star descended at one's back.

In the present Judeson and Eckard came near to the hills that had appeared to be so very far away back at the edge of the Draul woodland realm. The two men's self -facilitated silences were respectfully broken when they came into the pine enclosed sanctum..

Judeson peered up at the scattered birch and pine trees, leaves of green and faded brown and down below witnessed small rodents scurry about the leaf-strewn floor as he and Eckard passed further into the woods. He soon noticed the marks and patterns of felled trees, the likes of which could only have been from men or near-men able to wield the tools necessary to have done so. Etched into the ground all around the small grove of trees were footprint patterns and signs of trees being carted away by the owners of said feet and animal hooves.

'Beyond the woods is Heatra, our hunt starts there.' Eckard announced, the man lifted a curious looking oblong shaped instrument from his seemingly bottomless backpack.

Judeson saw Eckard flip the strange object's copper-hued lid and a swathing mass of curling smoke pushed out as if it were viper uncurling itself, the smoky mass drifted off into the night. The object's lid slammed shut by Eckard who stood watching the pitch black. Judeson's hair hung up on its ends and he breathed heavy, deep in shock though he did not really understand how.

He glanced at Eckard who had fallen to his hands and knees and had his eyes firmly clenched shut aqnd head downcast. Judeson made to pull the man back up but just as soon he made to move, he was witnessing Eckard rise back up to his feet and open his eyes. In place of the sky blue Eckard's eyes was a curling mass of the deepest black. Twisting dark shadows in the man's eyes.. No whites or pupils at all left on his orb, the blackness was swirling about as if it were alive within. Judeson shook himself awake.

Judeson hastily and firmly grabbed the man with both his hands clasped on Eckard's broad shoulders. Face to face Judeson witnessed the dark shadows fade gradually away from Eckard's eyes as if they were never there in the first place. Eckard quickly broke out of whatever daze had possessed him and granted Judeson a single furrowed brow as he pushed off Judeson.

'And what was the purpose of fucking putting me in a hold?' Eckard inquired of Judeson, the Nertharnlander once again returning the mysterious trinket.

'I thought you were being possessed by some unseen evil.' Judeson said.

Eckard threw his head back in laughter and a rude snort resounded from his nose in answer to Judeson. The mischievous smile Eckard seemed so attuned to produce returned for a brief moment. Eckard regarded Judeson directly before turning and continuing on through the scattered forest hill. Judeson took his turn to look puzzled as he stood like a statue attempting to decipher this strange Northman's reaction. *What in the Queen?* Judeson's head spun, like he was intoxicated. Noticing his unlikely companion had ventured off into the grove of pine and birch, Judeson followed suite. He strode through the dispersed stalk trees, after a time Judeson caught sight of Eckard just paces ahead on the other side of the mound. Beyond, the land fell dramatically back down in the way of steep narrow cliffs and loose pebble-strewn tracks. Beneath this mass of sharp and dizzying falls lay a sprawling river and an emerald green valley.

Situated on the low-lying fertile banks of cyan blue-river was a rustic village of wooden log cabins with simple thatched roofs. More than a dozen such houses stretched out in the surrounding green river banks. Placed in the relative centre of the group of lodges was building clearly larger and more structured, even from the height Judeson and Eckard stood at that much was easy to read. The centrepiece structure possessed several chimneys at its rear side, which produced copious clouds of ash-grey smoke into the air above it. Judeson musing there must be many forge-fires burning within. The building's front section opened out onto an open span of varnished wooden decking complete with tables and chairs. High up above the settlement the people below appeared to Judeson as insects scurrying about. In particular, the centre building possessed an extensive foray of activity about it.

'Heatra?' Judeson Inquired in regards to the settlement below.

Eckard nodded his head in approval and began to make his way to the beginnings of the steep bluff beyond the forest they were currently in.

'Where the ForeSeer is?' Judeson said following him in the gradual descent.

'Perhaps' Eckard answered not looking back but gradually climbing down the first of the many elongated dramatic slopes to the valley below.

Both men made slow progress, favouring caution over a speedy descent as they looked for foothold crags in the narrow jutting cliff face. After a prolonged time of gradual downward rock climbing and sliding both men found the beginnings of a narrow winding track skirting the cliff face around, the makeshift road seemed to safely course down into the valley. Both Judeson and Eckard made note of the status of the track, however, the ground underneath were but loose shale rocks and they slowly trekked along, lowering their centre of gravity and holding their arms out for balance. It was not uncommon as they moved carefully about on the loosed surface to nearly slip and slide on the shale-rock. They both endeavoured to shift their weights according to the rough terrain and made note of every sharp turn in the tapered trail, Eckard and Judeson willed each other along, discussing their climb as they did.

'Now the time we get down this escarpment will almost be dark, just in time for some nice ale.' Eckard evidently stated in a series of heaving gasps, the man clearly tiring under the arduous journey they undertook.

'What happened to your rule of not drinking on a mission?' Judeson asked with a gasp similar to Eckard's own.

'Ah yes you see I had to burn the flask, did you taste that awful filth in it?' Eckard replied, skidding along slight on his left foot.

'It was awful, yes.'

'It was goat-shit. And to divulge into technicalities of the "no drinking" rule we are tracking our mission once in Heatra. Henceforth….'

Eckard let out a great gasp of air from his lungs as he ungracefully slide down a slick mossy slope. Judeson followed suit and stood with the man on a thankfully stable portion of mould-blackened rocks, just paces ahead was a rather nasty stretch of loose slate. Eckard to continued his dialogue, when both men stood together again.

'We will not technically be on mission. Besides, the tavern will be our first source of information' Eckard continued

'.....you believe they know where the ForeSeer and his kidnappers are?' Judeson said attempting to draw steady breathes between regaining his spent energy.

'He has passed through this way' Eckard vaguely replied and puffed out an intense waft of air before, cracking his neck and walking on to the next loose pebble pathway leading gradually downwards. Judeson quickly caught up and began to follow.

'Your rule is flawed by the way.' Judeson said as the two warriors slide and skidded haphazardly once more.

'The world is a harsh mistress, Judeson, Absolute Rules are always being twisted and turned which-way-to the abyss.' Eckard replied and they climb on climbing down.

*

The varnished glimmering wooden deck halls seemed quite extravagant for an establishment cluttered with empty drinking mugs on tables and unnumbered persons either engaged in drunken mayhem or deep in slumber. Yet somehow the variation between venue and patrons suited the place somewhat or so Eckard reckoned. Noting Judeson's face at such a scene, Eckard smiled.

It was not that the Southron was sour towards such dispositions it merely seemed to be the man had rarely experienced much of such matters before. From what Eckard had gradually learned of Judeson it would seem the man was better suited to the rugged wilderness the two had minutes ago arrived from A wild man at heart, that was perfectly fine by him.

Ignoring the hint of mild disgust painted on the face of Judeson at ordinary weekend Farthling social interactions, Eckard proceeded forward. At the oak counter top Eckard raised a single arm to hopefully get a hold of the establishment's barkeep. In the background the steady melody and simple rhythm of a six-string and a pennywhistle passed over them as they spoke.

'Two of your finest ales please' Eckard uttered leaning in, casually on the wooden bench to be heard.

'Coming up, my girl will bring them to you, traveler, take a seat' The generously proportioned publician replied in a gruff voice, turning to away from Eckard.

'Actually, make it a pitcher then,' Eckard said.

'A what?'

'Bring the largest fucking container that you have that can hold liquid, please.' Eckard said smiling at the rough looking individual, winking and passing a well-sized sack of coin up onto the oak bench.

The man, in turn, acknowledged Eckard well and nodded with more than a hint of approval present on his face as he looked inside the twine sack at its contents of Nertharnlander Shards. The likes of such were solid iron chips that had a rust-hue, not for neglect by any means, the colour was unique to the Nertheilm. Small etchings wrinkled the dirty iron chips to distinguish value.

Eckard and Judeson in this bastion of human amusement and debauchery found chairs at a relatively clean craved wooden table nearby. Taking up residence on a pine chair Judeson dropped his pack and sword and stretched out

making himself comfortable. Eckard followed up
one further, slipping off his rustic leather
boots, he leaned back in his chair placing both
his feet on the dirty table top of nut shells and
spilled ale. Judeson gave the man a questioning
look but Eckard shrugged it off, with no small
dose of smug satisfaction.

A few moments passed until a young and golden
haired girl emerged from behind the bar counter
carrying a generously sized timber keg. Eckard
glanced over and saw Judeson take note of the
young woman who placed the container on the
tabletop, she brushed away the debris and
Eckard's feet rather forcefully in the process.
Judeson smiled at the woman and she returned the
gesture with good humour. Eckard was not fazed
and gave the young lady a polite nod, asking him
to remove his feet would have been just as
effective.

After walking back to the counter top the young
waitress returned to the table and placed two
simple kiln-fire-bound ceramic mugs (*not the
biggest, Eckard noted*) beside Eckard and Judeson.

'Evening travellers.' Said the waitress as she
placed the cups on the table and proceeding to
fold her arms across her chest.

'Evening Miss, how are you?'Judeson replied
almost immediately in response.

'Rush hour at the moment, run off my feet you
see. Not long till it's all over for the night,
outlander.' The young woman replied, rearranging
her tightly bundled ponytail of sandy blonde
hair.

'I am called Judeson and this is Eckard. We bid
you fair tidings and good health, thank you for
this drink, kind miss' Judeson said.

The young barmaid appeared taken back by the

courteous nature of Judeson's dialogue and idol chat. It was several moments before she responded. In that time between; Eckard proceeded to fill the two mugs the young lady had prearranged for them and placed one right in front of Judeson and the other in close proximity to himself. When the young tavern employee did re-establish her wits she responded in a very different voice and demeanour.

'My name is Vestras and you are very kind, Judeson, it is a pleasure to meet you.'

'Likewise' Judeson answered standing up and saluting her in the Southron manner before retaking his seat just as quickly as he had risen.

Eckard observed the two intently whilst drinking deep from his ale. After several prolonged moments of silent looks passed between the almost statue forms of Judeson and Vestras, Eckard uttered a resonating croak from the back of his throat rather noisily and rudely to break up the awkward affair.

'I'm quite well by the way, not that it's important.' The Nertharnlander interjected wiping amber ale froth from his expertly shaved dark beard.

Both Judeson and Vestras the barmaid turned towards Eckard at his snide remark and raised quizzical stares at him. Eckard raised his mug in response and then set it back down and generously back in the wooden deck chair he was in. Vestras through force of habit topped up the man's drink anew. Judeson had hardly even touched his own ale.

'What brings travellers to our humble community of Heatra?'Vestras said standing over the table, all the while peering about as if she would make way to any other table at any other given moment. Although right now it seemed to be that the pretty young girl's attention was drawn to Eckard and Judeson's table, Eckard smiling to himself realizing that this was probably because of a very simple reason.

'We are searching for…..' Judeson made to state before Eckard interrupted him.

'We are just passing through. Do you know of any lodgings we could acquire?' Eckard motioned.

Vestras did not seem to notice any irregularities.

'Bursal our town steward and the man behind the bar can assist you with that, he owns a journey-house on the southern side of town' Vestras answered peering over her shoulder at the now vacant front counter where the mentioned Bursal had been present.

'Although I don't know why you would wish to stay even a moment in this Gods- forsaken place.' The barmaid whispered in a gentle murmur, leaning closer to the two men seated at the varnished timber table.

'Pray tell what has you so frightened?'Judeson softly spoke back to the woman.

'Bandits, people missing in the night, strange times,' Vestras answered keeping in a low cautious voice looking about her as if they were being watched.

'Can you tell us more about such things?' Eckard said perking up from his casual slouch in the seat, also in a low drawn whisper.

'I dare not speak here…..where unfriendly ears may listen' Vestras answered the two men and hastily took off from their table, to return to her usual rounds in the tavern.

'Something here clearly has her tongue walled

within her own mouth,' Judeson said once Vestras had departed them.

'You would be talking about her mouth wouldn't you, you old dog?' Eckard jested and raised his mug to Judeson as a salute.

'I'm sorry?' Judeson asked, engaging his best pretend quizzical look on his face. Eckard could instantly tell the other man's thinly veiled excuse for lying was of a poor standard and he knew that Judeson was probably quite a terrible liar in general.

'Anyway, something tells me we'll see the lovely Miss Vestras later on. Besides your good looks and charm Judeson, I believe she wishes to tell us something.' Eckard said, peering over into the direction of Vestras, who stood collecting used plates and mugs on the opposite end of the tavern's timber halls.

Judeson turned in his chair and looked in the identical location to Eckard and knew by the bitter-sweet sorrowful smile held on Vestras' face that the young woman hides something deep inside herself, a secret that she probably wished to disclose to anyone that would listen and perhaps indeed help.

***

A rattling unsteady knock on the hardwood surface of the door frame resounded throughout the small confines of the journey houses single room. Regaining his feet and putting aside his bastard sword and sharpening stone, Judeson strode over to the room's solitary door and made to open it. Eckard sat crouched over int he solitary timber deck chair near the door with his unusual crossbow in his lap. Eckard motioned to Judeson to wait. Using a straightened palm, quite clearly a universal sign for patience. Judeson nodded and

waited for Eckard, as the Northerner cocked a
quarrel onto the bow and rushed over to hide
behind one of the beds in the room. Eckard nodded
to Judeson from his concealed spot, Judeson
retrieved the sword of Jude and began to
unsheathe it. Judeson with his back against the
opposite wall from the window, sidled across the
varnished willow panels. He reached out and
grasped the solitary door in, Judeson turned the
handle, pushing the portal slowly and steadily to
come ajar on it's own. Slowly surely.

In rushed an obscure cloaked form unsteadily on
its feet stuck halfway in the doorway. Judeson
jumped into action unsheathing Jude and flanking
the cloaked figure, just as Eckard aimed his
crossbow right at the exposed target that stood
on the threshold of the journey-house. An
unmistakably feminine squeal of discomfort came
from behind the drawn hood of the mysterious
cloaked figure.

Judeson released his grip on his sword and
resheathed. and Eckard lowered his bow.
Withdrawing the tight wound dark russet hood the
enigmatic figure was revealed to none other than
that of Vestras. The service maid Eckard and
Judeson had met a few precious hours ago in the
dirty, populated tavern.

'By the Abyss beyond, you two could have murdered
me,' Vestras muttered in a series of gasps and
wheezes; she stood frozen in place and wild-eyed
in terror, her whole body shaking as if caught
nude in the snow.

'Forgive us. We were merely taking precautions.'
Judeson said taking the woman's cloak from her
and shutting the door she had come in from.
Eckard placed his loaded crossbow on the bed and
stood up once more, though his right hand did not

stray too far from his curved short sword at his hip belt. Eckard gave Judeson a raised eyebrow and coy smile and strode forward to greet the shaken bar maid, Still the man's hand did not leave his belt.

'So I take it you came to tell us something,'Eckard said, peering at the windows into the dark outside.

'Yes, I did I'll tell you everything. Someone in this town needs to.' Vestras answered.

Judeson helped the clearly traumatized blonde waitress to the nearby bed and seated her down and stood close by. Eckard took up a stance near the door and picked up his crossbow as if they were about to become besieged at any given moment. For several quiet instances, all three persons stood and sat in silence respectfully, Judeson over the shaking seated form of Vestras on the nearest bed and Eckard pacing about the cabin crossbow in his arms, until the hush was finally and gratefully broken by the sound of young Vestras' overexcited voice.

'Heatra is being held captive. We are all forced to harbour brigands against our will.' Vestras blurted out in rushed slur of words.

Eckard seemed to not be willing to be involved as the tall dark haired Nertharnlander continued to pace about. Judeson crouched down and proceeded to hold Vestras' hands in an attempt to calm the fair-haired woman.

'Wait, slow down, tell us everything but slowly, you are safe here with us,' Judeson said. Eckard halted slightly off from one of the windows and not bothering to turn around, grunted in response to Judeson's announcement to Vestras.

'Thank you Judeson you have been very kind to me. Not many still left in this village are like

you.' Vestras answered. Judeson gave her a smile
back and found he was slightly blushing despite
himself, heat rising in his cheeks. *Was she
complimenting me?* Judeson thought to himself.
Vestras gave him a sorrowful smile back and
Eckard turned around and saw the two, raised a
furrowed eyebrow and pivoted back to look out the
window.
'Bursal, our town steward…' Vestras continued
accenting the bar keep's name with some venom.
'…he's in league with the brigands, raiders of
whatever they are you see. He has been for a
while now. They gave him the en ar'gine. He lies
that he bought it off a Collective merchant but I
saw them, well I have seen them several times
now.'
'Who are 'they?' Judeson asked, squeezing
Vestras' fingers while he did so.
'I told you, killers, highwaymen, terrifying
people,' Vestra said.
'Can you describe them for us please Vestras?'
Judeson inquired.
'Big, all decked out in grimy armour and
formidable. Well, those were the ones that did
not speak.' Vestras said.
'They never spoke?' Judeson asked.
'One of them did. He looked and sounded like
proper gentlemen, well-dressed he was, well-
mannered but there was something about him.'
'And what was that exactly?'
'His eyes and his words. His eyes were cold and
empty looking, like a man that had lost
everything and did not care anymore.'
'And his words?'
'Well, it wasn't exactly the words he used it was
the way he said them. He threatened Bursal and

ordered him about but not like anything I had heard before. Not like a any old thug. He spoke like Bursal was nothin but a grain of sand beneath his feet, like he was born better' Vestras sniffed and breathed in. ' Well Steward Bursal did everything he told him to like was indebted to him. But I guess his friends helped a great deal in getting the speakin man what he wants, what with all the full metal dresses and growling and all.'

'So they did speak but they growled?' Judeson asked. Though he had a rising dread over what Vestras was saying. His blood was growing cold, he knew what 'they' were already.

'They growled and snorted all rude like, I remembered now.' Vestras said everything in a mad rush, she was clearly frightened of something. Her low droning accent becoming tangled with raw emotion.

'Raks' Eckard uttered in a faint whisper, finally turning away from the window frame and looking back at Vestras and Judeson. A sudden jutting chill ran up Judeson's spine with the mere mention of the Rakoni. *He knew it,* but hearing that particular; *word,* made it just that touch more real for him. He perched up and looking directly into Vestras' eyes.

'This is important Vestras you need to tell us if you have seen a Draul Youngling with them.'Judeson asked.

'A boy with hair, silver like the colour of glowing lights in the Far Above is that the Draul? He was always standing like a statue, a rock, not seen a child ever like him, did not move or laugh or anything' Vestras asked clearly frightened with even remembering the details.

'That's him.' Eckard said.

'How do you know?' Judeson interrupted the man and looked back at him.

'That's the ForeSeer.' Eckard answered in the deadpan delivery of a man explaining something to a child.

'He was right beside the smooth talking Aurman when I saw them, he looked petrified' Vestras said.

'Between the Raks, there was an Aurman?' Judeson asked looking back to Vestras.

'The one that talked yes, only one that I ever saw the face of, he was, well-bronzed him, kind of looked like a Dazral or a Corisi I think' Vestras answered, beginning to settle down gradually, as she slowed down her rapid speech and sharp movements that were so prevalent previously.

'Where are the bandits now do you know?' Eckard queried Vestras as he settled back into the crevasse of the cabin wall, and cradled his sideward- bow.

'They have a house, right here in Heatra. Well more like an estate really, it's quite… well huge really.' Vestras replied gently pushing Judeson's hands away and attempting to stand up she continued. "I can show you to it if you like?"

'No just give us directions, we will……uh.. Investigate on our own.' Eckard stated as he rose up and swung his crossbow over his shoulder whilst heading to the doorway out of the cabin.

'You be will safe here.' Judeson said reaching out and steadied Vestras as she got up.

Eckard opened the cabin's portal out into the dim light village and Judeson proceeded to follow after getting directions and a sorrowful smile from Vestras.

**

Pushing aside a loose overgrown scrub lodged deep in the gutter confines on the rooftop Eckard perched on, the Nertharnlander took aim with his crossbow in hand and peered downwards into the darkness of the village below. Shuffling through the narrow expanse that consisted of the space between the two timber lodge residences, (one of which was where Eckard currently squatted on the edge of), was Judeson. Eckard acknowledged the man as he came close to his position, nodding and gesturing for the Southron to head onward. Judeson signaled Eckard with a simple and clear hand raised in the air and preceded stealthily onward through the dry stock littered alleyway around him.

Eckard watched as Judeson passed through the threshold between the two buildings and into the sumptuous garden patches ahead, the likes of which were separated with several small wood picket fences.

Straight ahead as a crow would fly lay a slender rickety looking wooden bridge spanning the narrow expanse of the river bordering the village. Situated on the others side of the river was an affluent housing estate, bordered by high granite walls was the mansion proper, a brick enclosed affair with a simple wooden thatched roof like the rest of Heatra. Clearly, this had to the estate ground being utilised by the Raks and the Aurman that Vestras had spoken of, of this Eckard, was no doubt at all.

Eckard noticed two shadowy apparitions move onto the bridge, he whistled a distinctive three chirp tune that slightly imitated the Gimloc, a Night Bird. The signal had been one he and Judeson had agreed upon in their rush to their current hiding positions.

Peering down the end of his loaded crossbow, Eckard noted the arrival of the dark figures on the timber bridge ahead emerging into the vicinity of the nearest lamp light post. A scruffy ginger coloured hound stepped forward, a solid chain around its mangy neck being held back by a man-like figure dressed from head to toe in a dark cloak with its face concealed. Breaks in the black cloak's concealment on the apparition's torso and at the arm's sleeves revealed the ever-slight glimmer of well-worn plate maille in the flicking lamplight. The battered hound raised its nose into the air and took in the scents around it.

Eckard sweated on the next move, it was an easy shot he had in his sites on the armoured patrol guard and his dog but he realised he had no idea how many others of his ilk waited in the dark shadows beyond.

Judeson finally seemed to have taken in that the bridge was guarded and the Southron pitched off silently to the river bank where a generous crop of matured corn and wheat stalks grew. The man seemed to have taken in a relatively concealed spot for hiding as Eckard quickly lost sight of him, but not the presence of mind.

The mangy dog seemed to have picked up a scent as it attempted to edge its rather robustly sized master forward. Remembering his carrier on his back Eckard reached across and retrieved the Magik educed case and pulled out a small side of cured meat wrapped in a cloth sack. Retrieving the piece of preserved pig inside, (the last slice Eckard had for now) he proceeded to hurl the food into the darkness behind him. The sound roused the attention of both armoured guards and their hound on the bridge ahead and the animal took note of the item's scent instead of what it previously had; *quite possibly me or that hulking Southron* - Eckard mused. The hound pulled with greater zest than before and evidently, the master allowed the dog to lead the guards into night (and the other direction of Judeson and Eckard) to retrieve it's hurled prize.

The bridge was clear for now. Judeson came out from concealment and made his way across the rickety planks across the creek. Eckard climbed down from his perched position on the thatched roof on the seemingly abandoned residence. Once he had made it to the loose dirt road, Eckard with a crossbow in hand and curved sword at his belt raced forward as quiet as he could manage and met up with Judeson at the foot of the bridge. Peering about every which way Eckard could not discern whether any hidden eyes had seen them yet, though his other senses told him they had not. Judeson motioned the all clear paces ahead sprinted forward across the bridge with Eckard just moments behind him.

Into the shadow ridden hazy light of the bridge, Eckard soon lost sight of Judeson as he disappeared into the dark on the other side of the river. High over ahead in the Far Above very few stars sparkled and the moon was cast in a cloud. Black was absolute all around out of the light laid by fire. Reaching the other side of the bridge Eckard was pulled sturdily and sharply to his left side by two strong hands. Just managing to keep his feet Eckard glanced over and made out Judeson's blurred yet distinctive facial features in the obscuring dark.

Several paces down the pathway leading directly off the bridge they had run across stood another cloaked hulking apparition with an all to substantial mace in hand. The clearly armoured figure walked into the vicinity of the lamp pole lights and glanced about sharply and Eckard and Judeson huddled down onto opposite side of the thorn-ridden foliage of the nearby river bank. Though the flora provided very little cover, the gradual decline of the river's bank and the blackness of the night may suffice in concealment. Ahead the shadowy apparition turned its head to look about into the surrounding area around Eckard and Judeson.

Eckard hastily stretched over with both arms to steady Judeson as he made to pitch up and attempting to pull his sword from the scabbard on his back. Judeson without very little fuss calmed down and withdrew his hand from his blade, Eckard looked into the same direction of his companion and witnessed what had so enraged in the man. The mace-wielding figure ahead had pulled up its hood and revealed its face, the face of a Rakon.

The creature's face was bone-white as if all blood had been drained from it, and deep blue veins pulsating out of its face like tangling vines at the jungle floor. Scar stricken and covered with red pulsating welts, the Rakon glanced about the riverbanks shrubbery, with a solitary unsettling milky white eye that protruded outward likes a bug. The creature's other eye and where it should have been was replaced by an odd gleaming metallic eye patch, all the more fucking ugly, by Eckard's reckoning. Judeson looked directly into Eckard's eyes and queried silently as to why they had not attacked and Eckard, in turn, shook his head, the Northlander knew there had to be other Raks close by and running head on at the creature on the end of the bridge was not a great notion to consider right now.

A resoundingly shrill shout from some distance away screamed out. The words indecipherable to Eckard but he was certain they were those of another Rakon. The armour plated Rak guard on the bridge looked about in the direction of the sounds and answered in saying all too familiar to Eckard and indeed Judeson as well, as the other man seemed to pick up and take note of the Rak's words;

'Nekta Gozka'. The preceding words unknown and undistinguished to their Aurmen ears.

Judeson made to get up with one hand firmly around his bastard sword hilt ready to draw. Eckard pulled Judeson down to the ground and held him there as the other man gave up resisting in mere moments, wise of him despite his rage in not giving away their concealed position. The lone Rakon at the light post was soon joined by several more and in time at all there was five of the cloak shrouded and plate mailleed warriors standing, scanning the surrounding expanse of riverbank and pathways around them. Judeson looked questionably up at Eckard and the Northlander in response let go of him and crawled over across the ground as quiet as he could Aurmanly manage.

'We should get the fuck out of here.' Eckard voiced anxiously to Judeson in an exaggerated and excitable whisper.

Eckard made to move away in a staggered crouch from the gradually swelling ranks of Rakon ahead of them and peered back at Judeson to make sure the other man was coming with him. For a few precious moments, Judeson seemed to linger in his current position and Eckard feared the Southron was going to give into his more primal intuition on the choice subject at hand: the Raks.

Judeson did follow in Eckard's stead evidently. The the two were off; on all fours attempting to sneak along the dark sloppy mud bank of the Heatra River. Eckard nearly slipped into the murky waters as one heavy booted foot slide out across the mud towards the water's reach that was if not for a firm grip extended out from Judeson at his rear. The Rakon behind them seemed to sense their quiet movements and began towards their retreating positions ever so slightly.

'Zadma's mercy. We need a distraction.' Judeson hissed under his breath at the approaching company of Raks behind them began to speed up exponentially as a collected group.

Eckard opened up his seemingly bottomless Magik enabled backpack and produced the first item that came into his hand; a cylindrical loaf of solid looking brown bread. Judeson looked quizzically at Eckard, longing to understand what application a bread loaf would have for them. Eckard hurled the food item as far as he could manage from a crouched position and the heavy set bread tumbled into the previously calm waters of the Heatra River, ripples emulating out all around the point of impact. The Rakon warriors nearing Eckard and Judeson turned as one to observe the river's sharp awakening. Only mere paces from the shrubs where Eckard and Judeson were hunkered down, the Raks bolted away back down the river's banks towards the bridge, back towards the sight of the river's disturbance, moving as a close knit pack as they did. What a fucking luck-turned throw Eckard reasoned.

As quietly as one could manage in near darkness but with excitable haste Eckard and Judeson moved away from their hiding spot, the men quickly striding into the opposite direction of the pre-occupied Rakon. Their motives at first unsteady and disorderly but once both the men had found their legs they raced away from the scene at hand. Several moments of rushing into the imperturbable gloom head on ceased as Judeson pulled Eckard back and they both came to an abrupt halt at a narrow strand of the river bank.

The opposite shore from whence Heatra lay could be sighted not more the average two man' lengths away. With the solitary bridge spanning the river occupied by their armour-clad Rakons some way behind, the concept was a straight forward one to Eckard, and clearly, Judeson who had pulled him aside. They had to jump.

The contrasting river shore was but a mere blur in the shrouded darkness of night, and Eckard knew flinging himself across the gaping expanse was a sure fire way of arousing attention. If he fell in, the Raks back some generous distance now would surely realise Eckard and Judeson if they plummeted into the gushing waters. Eckard drew a deep prolonged breath, run at full pace and threw himself across, an absorbing dizzying feeling sweeping through him, out of place out of time, as he hurtled through the air across the gloomy river's length. The ground was restored to the North lander's feet as came across to the other side, the full force of Eckard's weight and momentum dragging him further than expected and he lost his footing, quickly falling forward in the process. Eckard recovered in time to roll onto one shoulder and distribute his weight safely, regaining his feet in a crouch after a short shuffle across the dirt strewn path around him. Judeson came through into Eckard's sight in a swirling blur, the big man's huge form jumping out of the darkness and rolling and skidding on the village track.

Amazingly Eckard and Judeson heard no clear sounds or signs of pursuit. The Rakon had not heard them nor had they moved from where they stood around examining the area around the rickety timber bridge, surprising as it was, Eckard meant to take absolute advantage of this scenario. He laid a hand on Judeson's broad shoulder checking if the other young man was alright. He was, as it seemed. Judeson had retaken his feet, up without incident. Eckard motioned for the Southron to follow him as he carefully paced forward into the village's fastness ahead. Broad hard timber walled and thatch roofed residences arrayed about them in orderly rowed fashion as the two men made stealthy back to their journey house past an old wind mill hovel. The Far Above seemed to open up without warning and heavy bitter cold rains fell freely as they ran.

5th Stanza

It was a new era, new times and new ideas. All around the world was changing, shifting from the Olden to a Brave Dawn of Innovative Beginnings and seeding creations laying the framework of the modern man. Of the numerous happenings in 2900 arcs After The Fall none were more curious then the climatic fruition of the Kobold/Aurman cooperative invention of Oyra-Tech or more specifically Technology powered by applied super-heating of a rare compound of Ore with the addition of specially enhanced water. This 'Oyra-Tech' as it was so aptly named marked and interconnected the occurrence of so many events to come......

Fragment Missing

Most inquisitive then was the Kobold for all their cooperation and insight into such matters of Oyra-Tech advancement, almost the entire group of Guilds save for a few Shamed Ones would practically leave the Nertheilm and disappear from all Collective and Confederation eyes in the arcs to follow. Indeed after the first day break of 2901 very few Kobold were ever seen since and their stories would leave the pages of all the

Northern Continent and become their own.

The Turn of the Century '2900'

Marten WordHand

City of Dazra, Cor-Dazra Collective, 2902 ATF

'But they did listen' Kail offered, cuttingly to the other two occupants of the modestly decorated room, whilst pouring them both a glass of Kormai Firewater.

'To a certain extent' Luciarn Nonkar replied in response casting his eyes down and appearing somewhat overcome in his silk padded wooden chair he seemed to sink right into.

'It's something at least, you will have to leave the rest to us it seems.' Kail stated as she neared over to Lucairn and offered him one of the elegantly shaped glass goblets in her hand, with a generous portion of Firewater present in it.

Luciarn kindly received his goblet and Raijin the ever-inquisitive Draul Mage in turn took up Kail's gift of Kormai Firewater. Kail took up residence close by on a seat facing the two forming a sort of semi-cycle in the process. Luciarn made to get up and Kail looking questionably at him in the process.

'Forgive me, I forgot Draul drinking customs for a moment, I'll get yours Kail.' Lucairn announced meaning to make his way over to the cabinet from whence Kail had poured his and Raijin's drinks.

'Do not trouble yourself I have had more than enough Firewater for my whole week thank you.' Kail hastily said as she motioned for Luciarn to retake his seat.

'With Eckard?' Raijin quickly asked in a coy smirk, slipping on his beverage as he did so.

'And the Southron' Kail hissed and granted the Mage a clearly unfavourable narrowing gaze. At least she hoped the Mage actually took notice of her disapproval. *He was definitively a stirrer, Raijin.*

Luciarn choose to wisely ignore the two and drank down hard on his Firewater, necking almost all the contents in the process. A sharp burning sensation as per the beverage's namesake rushed through Luciarn's throat and he coughed vividly in response to the occurrence. Raijin stood up and patted the merchant on the shoulder gently.

'Easy friend, the Kormai drink packs quite a hit.' Raijin said chuckling as he retook his seat.

'Back to the topic at hand' Kail said holding a narrow gaze once more on Raijin before swinging her head round to look at Luciarn. "It would seem Krikza had more influence than we thought by what you say."

'Even more so than last I was here.' Luciarn Nonkar answered choosing to look out away from his companions towards the balcony of the tree-top house were they presently resided in.

Even the cool night air outside lay enclosed about the tangled vines and tree tops of the Tzsu'Teng valley, an ever so slight beam of brilliant piercing light from the moon in the Far Above shone through a small gap in the foliage. The shining light met the surface at the dead centre of the outstretched balcony pad, which was a semi cycle disc of intertwined vines and branches. Curiously flattened out and sitting almost level centre to the Draul treehoue confines.

'If this is the case, Krikza will move soon. His desire for power will drive him onwards. Tzsu'Teng is no longer a safe place for ones of our kind.....' Raijin implied twirling a last remaining dribble of FireWater in his goblet transfixing his gaze across to Kail and raised a heavily graying eyebrow.

Luciarn looked away from the solitary light beam cascading down onto the balcony deck and rejoined the conversation.

'Krikza would not dare to take on the Lord-Protector's Council. Would he?' Luciarn said at first seeming sure of what he was stating but then questioning himself as he saw flashes of Krikza's aggressive and loud image in his own mind.

'The Draul prefer the surroundings of darkness and shadow I myself enjoy the occasional glimpse of the light, even if it is but the reflecting light of the moon.' Kail stated looking out at the light beam on the balcony and then back at Lucairn decidedly watching the man's peripheral vision. She continued, adopting on a more serious and grave tone: 'The rest of Council is weak and bankrupt; the arrogant bastard Krikza has arms, soldiers and resources.'

'How curious it is that you Draul refer to wealth and bankruptcy yet you have no currency to speak of.' Luciarn said, looking back out to the outer tangle-wood railed veranda of the tree house.

'We have wealth, merchant and a Draul is measured by it just as in your Aurman theilms. The difference however lays in the conceptual idea of riches. You speak of your currency as if it were a necessity, yet your coin offers no practical value, a Draul is rich when he possesses land, arms and physical resources like metal-ore or Rosewood or….Firewater. Products of of the world that is not what you are aurmen envision it to be.' Raijin rebutted, downing the rest of the rusty amber hued alcohol in his glass after looking at it quizzically.

'Where will you go if Krikza ceases authority over the Council?' Lucairn inquired not turning to look at either Kail or Raijin.

'When Krikza does, not if.Luciarn....when *he* takes power. When Krikza does we will have to leave…... quickly.' Kail announced, Luciarn turning in time to see the young Draul lady standing up and walking over to the far side of the room where their collective over layered cloths had been hung on simple tree branch coat racks. Kail's and Raijin's deep emerald forest cloaks hooked up side by side next to Luciarn's own dirty brown tattered overcoat complete with many holes taught by age among other things.

'And where do you suppose to go from here? Neither the Collective nor the Confederation is any place for two Draul Enchanters. The Yunlands are pitched in tribal war and the formerly mentioned nations' interference. Fartheilm….'

'Is good this time of arc I have heard.' Kail cut in. Raijin seemed to have found some humour in this and laughed half-heartedly out his nose in wiry sniffle and chuckle.

'Fartheilm is dangerous. Unrest is rife too and as you know the Raks have been sighted in numerous places.' Luciarn said.

'Where would you have us go, merchant?' Raijin queried standing up and making his way over to the coat rack Kail seemed to be finished with.

'You can come to Nero with me then.' Lucairn answered in an unrestrained sigh.

'Of course we shall, thank you.' Kail said, now with her cloak cast about her person and in the act of lowering her hood down over her furled dark locks.

'This was your original plan wasn't it?' Luciarn asked standing up somewhat embarrassed by being outwitted and gushing deep rosy blushes despite himself.

'Perhaps.' Raijin chuckled as he drew his cloak about himself.

'Did I ever have a choice?' Luciarn questioned while gripping his heavy patch worked overcoat in his hands.

'We shall hopefully meet Eckard and his charming companion on the way.' Kail announced, she was choosing; ignoring Luciarn's probing queries and making for the room's sole exit doorway to its spiraling timber staircase below them.

'On the way? It's in the opposite direction. How will they know where to meet us?' Luciarn asked.

'We have to walk a roundabout way. Eckard will know. Let us hope they succeed in finding the ForeSeer.' Kail said entering the room's threshold and Raijin following shortly after.

Lucairn stood not moving in inch, in the former residence of the young Kail. A generously sized, roughly round shaped room carved directly from an impressive behemoth of a tangle-wood tree. Casting his eyes about the tree's growth rings and the mark and nooks in the wooden surface Luciarn could not help but feel wonderment for such a place. Knowing he was probably being waited on Luciarn paced towards the open trap door double time. Beneath the trap door was a jutting dark wooden staircase leading downward and it in turn led outside.

'Here's hoping.' Luciarn whispered under his breath as he climbed on hand and knees; the first step down.

**

The cushioned hardwood doors rolled on their tracks to the side, parting ways from the closed position as if an egg hatching a new born. In stepped a broad shouldered Aurman wearing a simple woolen coat, his heavy military leather boots resounding on the polished timber deck floors. Trailing the man came two armoured and black cloaked figures their features obscured in the gloom of night and hoods pulled down low. The heavy set nature and the plate maille worn by that of the former two apparitions caused the floor boards to creak and grown under a greatly immense weight.

Bursal the Heatra town - Steward and tavern owner strode forth from behind his main service bench and came out to meet this new arrivals. He instantly dreaded what was to come too. The overweight bar-keep pushed back his greasy short cropped grey hair. An action he did out of habit when nervous, even though there was not much hair to push back now. It needed to be done.

'Sar Holloway I was not expecting you at this time of night.'Bursal stammered, gulping back deep down, trying to steady his voice. His anxiety getting the better of him it seemed.

'I'm not a Cavalier, sit the fucking abyss down, Bursal.' The Aurman said, the one that was at the spearhead of the trio before Bursal. The man - *Holloway* indicating to a seat nearby with a pointed index finger.

Bursal followed the athletically built man's forceful instructions and took a seat out from behind the closest table and sat down.

The other two cloaked figures to either wing of Holloway, stood close by.

Holloway, a handsome man perhaps once, but now various aged scars and deep burns mapping his face in dominance, stood almost on top of Bursal looking down at him from overhead.

'It would seem some of Heatra's residents do not honour the cooperative we have worked so hard to maintain.' Holloway said first not allowing

Bursal time to speak.

'Everyone understands their place my lord.'
Bursal stated anxiously, a cold, anxious sweat
bead forming on his brow that he brushed aside at
once.

'Oh yes? Well your serving wench, the pretty
little thing..'

'Vestras?' Bursal interjected gulping down in
more dramatic fashion.

'Whatever her void-damned is. Well that little
bird is chirping away right now in your journey-
house to the two outlanders.' Holloway announced
sliding both arms across the back of Bursal's
chair and bringing his solid frame down to crouch
intensely close to Bursal. Face to face less than
a hair's breath away from each other, Holloway
seemed to be smiling at him such as it was.

The smile that Bursal looked back at was much
more a grimace, with no good nature nor mirth
behind it, only a unspoken challenge.

'Are we not friends, Bursal?' Holloway asked of
Bursal, not pulling away inches from his face.

'We are my lord.' Bursal said, stuttering in a
disordered rush the words seeming to blend
together.

From nearby to either side of Holloway; harsh
eerily laughter seemed to come forth from beneath
the hood, the mere sound of which caused Bursal'
hairs at his neck stand on end and his throat to
dry up.

'I'm not a lord.' Holloway said releasing his
grip on the timber seat and moved back from
Bursal. 'Not any more...' The Middle aged
Corgisi-man seemed to whisper to no one in
particular as he turned his back from all three
others in the tavern.

Bursal gulped down hard and attempted to steady

his breathing the state of which was far gone
from normal patterns. In turn his heart thundered
in his chest without reprieve. The township
Steward made to get up which proved difficult
even on the best of occasions, now that his
courage had deserted him; his legs wobbled
uncontrollably like the waves of a sea underneath
a raging tempest.

'What is to be done….uhh boss Holloway?' Bursal
whimpered shaking all over in cold sweats.

'The waitress will be killed like the two
vagrants with her. Just as everyone else who has
come to meddle in this tiny little shithole.'
Holloway said in matter of fact tone, motioning
for his two accomplices to follow him out the
open doorway.

'And then you will take the Draul boy away?'
Bursal asked the words jumping out, he clearly
regretted voicing, as his hand raised to his
mouth, looking more like darting out of the
current scene at any given moment.

Holloway turned back in his tracks and stalked
over to stand side by side with Bursal breathing
on top of the man as if he were nothing. Bursal
clearly smelt the odour of smoked *saisr* leaf, in
Holloway's teeth, the yellowing to follow, that
was how close the formidable stood to *poor old
Bursal*.

'The boy will go to the Woldte where he belongs
and then…then we will return to finish this whole
business. Do not miss us too much and keep the
engine running.' Holloway said smirking at Bursal
through a barred grimace of yellow teeth.

Holloway paced back towards the doorway with his
two companions and departed the tavern premises
into the night beyond. As they passed out of the
building proper, Bursal clearly took in the

sounds of that vicious droning laughter he had
heard before this time more intensely vigorous
than before.

Bursal felt bitter cold chills run down his spine
all over again. *Poor, poor old Bursal.*

**

Judeson sprinted across the muddy pathway towards
the journey-house he and Eckard had taken up a
short-stay of residence in; only once slowing his
brisk strides to move around the cluttered wagon
and oak barrels in the journey-house's front
yard. Disregarding the steady sounds of enthused
rain fall on the earth, the scene all around
remained eclipsed in unsettling silence. Judeson
could tell something was wrong. It was too quiet,
in all was in moments just like this one that
something terrible was about to him to him.
Something, he sensed, he knew, he had stumbled
right into.

Nearing the journey-house's front door with
Eckard in toe close behind, Judeson called out
Vestras' name and he rushed into the threshold
reaching out for the worn unpainted handle....

...Judeson's hand never made contact on the door,
as it just that moment the wooden casing swung
open rapidly. Caught completely off guard Judeson
staggered back half a pace reaching for his giant
sword across his back. A haste filled rush of
teeth and fur jumped through the open doorway at
him in a brown-copper hued blur. Judeson was sent
sprawling into the rain saturated earth outside
the journey-house.

Large canines chomped viciously at his face,
dripping with moisture and smelling fouler than
anything he had experienced prior, Judeson
resisted. Pulling his face from harm's way and
shoving back hard with all his strength Judeson

threw his fur clad aggressor off, the creature
landing three paces off in the damp midnight mud.
The Southron regained his feet pushing himself up
from the blackened wet earth he now was now
decisively coated in.

The snarling, biting apparition that had rushed
Judeson, righted itself and the man saw it was
the feral dog they had saw before, on the bridge
with the two Raks, which *meant...Queen's Mercy no
- Judeson thought.*

The animal had been held secure by the leash of
the Raks on the bridge at the opposite end of
town. This however was leashed no longer and the
animal curled its nose back in a snarl, it eyes
ran wild with feverish hunger from pale milky
white irises. Judeson knew how this particular
act played out, this was not his first encounter
with rabid wild predators, after all.

The creature leaped high in the air directly at
Judeson's throat, it mouth open and teeth seeming
to extend out towards its intended target.

Bastard sword pulled from scabbard in less than a
heart beat Judeson had the blade leveled just as
a mass of scruffy wild fur came into direct
focus, mere inches from just underneath his nose.

The swords of Jude bit through flesh and organs,
sinking deep into the maltreated dog's frame. The
animal whimpered and yelped in pain as Judeson
pushed and twisted down sending the creature into
the rain drenched earth. The Southron curled his
fingers round his swords pummel and jutted his
weapon out twisting and weaving the blade out
through a shoulder and hacking a chunk of bloody
flesh away with it. The scruffy dog coated in its
own blood now in the black mud. The wild animal
threw its self about in several short lived
spasms, before falling silent in a sprawling of

outstretched paws. Judeson withdrew Jude from the carcass.

Judeson turned back to look for Eckard remembering his companion. The Nertharnlander sat crouched with his back against an upturned rickety looking wagon that previously had pottery in it. Scattered remnants of the pots laid in the dark earth close by. Eckard sat with crossbow in both hands and primed for release. Judeson made to walk over to the other man but halted as Eckard shouted something indescribable out to him.The exact words were caught up in the heavy rain and muffled in obscurity.,

'Qu, fff...ck ing moo..!'

Judeson was sure he heard although the words of which were hard to distinguish in the intense downpour from the Far Above. Before Judeson could answer with a reply he heard a rapid moving object whizz past his head, the item's trajectory cutting a swathing path through the air as it travelled. Judeson turned his head to witness an arrow buried in the mud just three paces to his left-hand side.

'Judeson, there's fucking sharpshooter! Get to Vestras!' Eckard shouted again, this time Judeson could make the man's voice it was dramatically clearer to his ears, despite the gushing rain not subsiding in the least and the Eckard not even looking at the man. The words had come from *inside his own head*. *No that was not possible* – Judeson reckoned. Reclaiming his real world perspective and senses; Judeson bolted for the journey-house not glancing back.

The simple timber framed door of their prior-arranged rental cabin came into view as Judeson sprinted for the temporary residence of Eckard and himself. Anxiety rushed over him in an eclipsing fold, he flew through all the possibilities that could be or happened in the journey house since their absence. Judeson panicked into an outright sprint, pushing aside the light timber framed door using his trained body to cast it out of his path like a loose branch on a dead tree.

The worst of Judeson's fears came into full view, not a feet-full of paces from him in the simple room's front entranceway slouched the sunken, defeated form of Vestras, still sweetly appealing in her appearance though now she had taken on a persona of horror for all to witness, clear as day printed on her freckled, pretty face. Behind Vestras', holding the young bartender was a Rakon wearing full plate maille, a horned helm encasing its head and bearing a forbidding hooked blade to her throat and a large hand at her back, holding her firmly down. Judeson tensed, drawing his bastard sword from his back and taking up a battle ready stance.

The Rakon combatant restraining Vestras back hunkered over the young woman with his wickedly curved short sword in one solitary chiselled away hand. The savage creature with a sharply shaved head and fierce white orbs for eyes slightly tilted its long head and seemed to smirk at Judeson, though the Southron could not be entirely sure as to its expression. The Rakon perched forward and a low rumble emerged from deep within the creature's thorax.

'Steady on Gozka'kel.'

'Let the lady go, you filth!' Judeson found himself snarling back at the near-man.

The Rakon indeed seemed to become incensed at this reply from Juedson and it pulled the battered form of Vestras closer in its hold even as the young woman tensed in its grip, looking helplessly at Judeson through full frightened eyes. Judeson tensed his grip on the hulking bastard sword of Jude pitched forward ever so slightly. The Rakon pulled slightly backwards in response and issued forth a curious misshapen chrome hued stone in its left hand, almost gesturing with it to Judeson.

'You fear the Qhrasa, Gozka'kel but I will deliver us.' The Rakon boomed at Judeson as it seemed to smile from ear to ravaged ear.

'Let the lady go Rak, now!' Judeson let roared at the scarred Rakon Warrior with as much gusto as he could put forth, tensing up his grip on the bastard sword of Jude, Judeson edged on tipped toes, ready to lunge forward.

'Very... brave Gozka...but the Qhasa...has spoken..' The broad shouldered and menacing form of the Rakonian warrior asserted once more gripping his hapless prisioner, the blond haired Vestras in steel hardened grip. Thursting forth the odd shaped little rock the Rak prolonged his hardened stared on his battle ready Southron adversary.

Judeson began forward with a careful half step, but that was as far as he got. The entire journey-house cabin was englufed into a brilliant luminescent explosion of washed out white. Judeson's ears rang with an overbearing buzz and he was thrown backwards as if he were nothing but a mere rag doll against it's impressive force. All around cinders and fragments of log were thrown assertively in prolonged chaos. Judeson felt himself tumbling ever outward from his original place and all of a sudden the bitter chilled air of the outside returned and Judeson knew he had been hurled from the cabin.

Feeling himself flung rapidly across the ground as he gradually came to a rest in the sloppy mud road, Judeson felt dazed and disorientated beyond clear comprehension. His vision was distorted and he could barely make out greyed and shadowed shapes of the world around him. His head rang as if being pounded against a forge stone a thousand times over. Judeson felt warm fluid seep from his eardrums and nose and down against the down his neck.

Pushing himself up with what little strength that still remained within Judeson, the Southron saw the extensively charred and burnt out remains of the previously sturdy set journey-house log cabin. Barely half of the structure stood intact and even that appeared to be lopsided in such a manner to be dangerously close to falling down into the mud.

Railings of tinder and uneven chucks of disseminated hardwood logs sat placed haphazardly about the vicinity of the late journey-house. Judeson fell into a frantic state of confusion swinging his peripherals back and forth about the place for signs of something...he could not place what, but something nevertheless.

The big Southron made to get up but his body ached all over and his head rang with a migraine the likes of pain-filled threshold he had never experienced before. Wincing with heavyladen puffs of frosted breath, Judeson dropped back down. Tensing with pain and attempting to piece together what had happened. His mind could not recall, and he found himself screaming out in a frustrated yelp of what remained of his vocals. He saw dirty blonde curls flash before his mind and he felt himself recalling his first hunt for a Red Loin in the Mornis Hinterlands so very long ago now.

A chain maille clad and grey-cloaked arm came
into Judeson's blurry ridden focus and a hand
reached onto his charred deer hide cloak. A
coarse black-bearded face somehow familiar came
into a semi-distorted view. A voice also being
more than vaguely reminiscent came to him also.
'Get up lad, no time for settling in now...'
And with that Judeson felt himself being steadied
onto his feet and his head rang more
exponentially as he gained height until all his
vision turned to black and he passed out
unconscious.

******

'Ah Void kissed shit' Eckard muttered to himself
as he pulled back as hastily as he could manage
as yet another broad tipped arrow whizzed past
his head into the mud at his feet. Around a half-
dozen sat buried deep into the wagon's frame he
had taken up as cover, as well as the unnumbered
arrows that had been lodged into the mud road
behind him. 'He must be getting low soon'
contemplated Eckard as yet arrow broad iron arrow
flew past his peripherals and into the misty
surroundings of the rain drenched village.
As if fate had decreed its decision measured
Eckard's own, the arrows stopped flying then and
there. The North-lander took a moment to close
his eyes and ease out a long drawing of breath,
sensing where the Rakon was by feeling the
trajectory angle of the near-man's arrows through
weaving together the lines. Eckard took a hasty
peek into the roundabout positioning of the Rak
who had been firing on him and saw the Near-man
scrabbling about on a clay tiled rooftop to
attempt to get away. The pounding bitter-cold
rain made vision blurred but Eckard pulled up his
already loaded crossbow from his lap and pitched

upwards onto the arrow riddled cart. Taking up aim on the Rakon who looked down at Eckard in curiosity for a prolonged moment.

Eckard loosed the quarrel and saw it sail in toward the Rak who seemed to stir awake in time, pitching sideward on the tile top roof and evaded the full force of Eckard's crossbow bolt. The Rakon bowman did not do enough however as the quarrel still made contact, pummelling into the near-man's leg. Eckard got up from his crouched position and commenced reloading his crossbow at his hip as the Rakon in the heavy rain ahead, evidently pitched from the rooftop onto the muddied hazel tint earth below.

Definitely the Rak made to rise as Eckard moved forward hastily cocking the bolt onto the crossbow once more, an action he had repeated far too many times to count. Eckard loosed a shot once more and the Rakon fell with a iron-head quarrel buried deep in his shoulder. However again the Rak attempted to make to his feet, though this time the creature was plagued with pain as it staggered between a crouch and a standing position upwards. Eckard withdrew his curved blade from the Rosewood scabbard at his belt, advancing further forward. The Rakon attempted to draw it's own blade forward. Eckard exhaled hard out and then closed.

Rain soaked iron cleaved heavily through flesh and armour as Eckard swung downwards onto the injured Rakon archer. The creature fell away in a bloodied heap, spluttering in the inevitable throws of death. Wiping his blade on his excessively wet, dark grey cloak; Eckard marched away from the Rak's fallen form and moved towards the journey-house where his newfound companion Judeson had hastily sprinted into previously.

The wooden-log framed journey-house ahead become prevalent with activity to Eckard's Mage-sight and felt something happening within...an explosive storm of blinding light and fire cut out Eckard's Magikal reach and forced him to stagger backwards from the blunt force of the fire-storm and its carnage ahead. Eckard pulled away just in time as loose debris and forceful gusting hot air passed by in almost every conceivable direction.

Once the smoke dissipated, Eckard noticed the shape of a fallen Aurman close by and suddenly realised it was probably Judeson. All doubt was removed when Eckard glimpsed the fallen man's sun tanned face. The rise and fall of his chest gave away presence of life still in him. From all directions Eckard made out black silhouetted shapes plunging through the thick sheets of rain cascading down towards him and the fallen Judeson. So they had passed through them.

Yahasa's mouldy sack! Eckard swore under his breath looking about to figure out an escape. The North-lander heaved Judeson with all his strength into a half crouch and attempted to right him. Eckard pulled the Southron along as best as he could possibly manage, he however quickly found himself exhausted by the effort and struggling to continue. Then Eckard remembered a technique he had learnt what seemed a lifetime ago.

The Day could not possibly get any worse. Eckard thought as he wove the threads of Grey Magik about himself and the his fallen companion.

***

Kicking loose chestnut brown mud from the roughened edges of his well worn travelling boots, the man some knew as Holloway looked up at the Far Above's reaches and the slowly dissipating rain within it. A grunt and shuffle of a nearby apparition brought Holloway's attention back down to the world around him. The rain drenched village of Heatra looked perfectly normal and sleepy as it always had; save for one completely noticeable earmark, the burnt out and incinerated remains of the late journey-house of Bursal the Inn-keeper.

'Gozka, the two Outlanders have passed on from here.' The Figure of Holloway's forced disturbance uttered. A grim cloaked and plate maille armoured from head to toe man-like apparition. Though Holloway knew it was no man he had ever met before.

'Yes, yes that is obvious; Mord'harja' Holloway replied being careful to speak the title-phase taught to him, as to avoid previous misgiving, for proper discourse with his associates. Holloway found himself soon looking about the various townsfolk cowering behind the close residences and businesses, afraid to come any further towards him and his armed companions, their expressions and movements clear to him all too well.

'We have to search the Gozka'kels, one of them has possible…talents, we must find them ...soon' The Mord'ha'ja seemed to whisper in a series of rasping noises.

Holloway always noted that this particular Rak always seemed to sound higher pitched in tone than the others. Although Holloway had never been able to talk with any of the other Raks, none had been willing to speak the Trader-tongue. Or they could and they did not wish to ever actually consult with him?

'Something tells me they haven't gone far.' Holloway answered the sole Rakon allowed or forced to speak with him.

*****

The incapacitated Southron was heavier than he
had an initially anticipated. Even with the
assistance of Magik, Judeson seemed as if a rock
that ships were possibly anchored to. At least in
Eckard's mind anyway. Glancing back the Northman
noted the pained expression on the other man's
face, written there in plain sight; anguish.
Eckard let out a heavy sigh and trudged through
the dense soaked woods around, attempted to
holster up Judeson's arm's onto his back once
more.

All of a sudden the whole process came undone. A
tense spasm of movement from Judeson's previously
dead weight disposition threw Eckard off his
senses and he dropped the other man in a heart
beat. A loud thud sounded off as the Southron
dropped on the forest bed of birch and oak roots
and leaves. Yet another sound too. One Eckard did
not anticpate; Judeson's voice.

'Ahhh...what the?'Judeson spluttered out in a
hoarse rasping breath whilst rubbing the back of
his skull.

Eckard turned cocked an eyebrow, this man was
sure was a surprisingly resilient.

***

'I don't understand why he killed himself though,
in the middle of the bleeding town. Did he want
everyone to see and hear then pass on word....'
Holloway repeated for the up-tenth time to the
Rakonian liaison officer or whatever the near-man
was to him. All the while he and the Rak briskly
marched through the sleepy valley town of Heatra
and its terrified populace.

'The Qhasa, Gozka he neared the Qhasa' The
Mord'harja said again as if this sentence alone

explained everything and that Holloway was simply just not listening.

Holloway turned away in frustration with the current line of discourse and began pacing out of the clearance of burned off embers and shrapnel littered carnage. They preceeded onto the outer limits of Heatra; the whole Rakon contingent moved about after Holloway began to pass. Holloway bothering a look back at them as the Raks did not seem to be intending leaving the clearly perplexed and intimated villagers hiding from them.

The generously shaped and hygienically ill-inclined form of the Bursal burst into the clearing, seeming to push other Heatra citizens out of his path. Though when he came close to Holloway, the Innkeeper made sure to steer himself as far away from the Rak warriors as plausible. Holloway slit his eyes to glare at Bursal's huffing girth.

'Apologise Bursal there has been an accident involving the two Outlanders and your own property. It's rumoured the girl you have working for you; Vestri or some such was killed in the resulting explosion.' Holloway announced matter-of-factually to the wheezing fat Innkeeper as stood next to him with his hands over his buckled knobby knees.

'Dead? Vestras....' Bursal was clearly shell shocked and his mouth gaped up and down like a fish out of it's watery home, no audible sounds to the Aurman-ear coming forth.

Holloway turned from the clearly bewildered innkeeper and peered back at the Rakon party that he had accompanied here, or was permitted to accompany (he sometimes mused). The Mord'ha'ja now had a compatriot beside him, a fellow

armoured Rakon, with similar concealing parted
coat. Holloway's breath caught at the new
warrior's position, a small dark cloaked figure
stood in front of the forbidding Rak, hood drawn
and child face downcast. The Rak stood over the
youngling with a chain-mailleed paw over his
shoulder, as if to make sure the children would
not run. As if he had a chance of such.

'Why in the Abyss is...?' Holloway made to
inquire of the new arrivals.

'We are leaving, the Gozka'kels have fled but
they are both still alive. We have drawn too much
attention to ourselves here.' The Mord'ha'ja cut
Holloway off, motioning towards the very young
cloaked figure; that looked like a mere slight
mouse (or insect maybe Holloway considered)
beside its keepers.

'The Runt goes now.'

'What? This was not part of our
agreement...Tiramene would have something to say
about this.' Holloway hastily objected stepping
into the path of the two Raks and the cloaked
child.

'Tiramene has issued the order, Gozka, now I
suggest you comply as our pact; as you so
proclaim it, only extends as far as you remain
compliment.' The Mord'ha'ja answered, extending a
hand towards the child near it an brushing its
grey skinned chin.

Holloway gasped, meaning to issues all his
thoughts and feelings on the matter to the
Mord'ha'ja but instead swallowed his tongue for
the time being. Curiously Holloway saw; the other
Rakon warrior had sliped its chain-link
gauntleted hand upon its weapon belt. Holloway
did not comprehend what to make of this, nor did
he believe he wished to. The Mord'ha'ja marched

past Holloway as did the other warrior and the Draul Sapling, the warrior pushing the boy forward with one hand, whilst it's other never strayed entirely from its sword.

'How did you get any orders? We have not received any messages from the Woldte recently?' Holloway questioned the Mord'ha'ja. Attempting to pry from them this odd circumstance.

The towering Rak warrior with the Draul Fore-Seer marched on seeming to effortlessly glide the child across the ground. The slightly smaller framed Mord'ha'ja turned back around to peer at Holloway, the Rak not as big as it's comrade but just as heavily armoured and quite possibly just as deadly. Holloway pulled his hands out from his sides in a gesture of non-threatening nature, though the Rakon seemed to be not bothered either way.

'You are receiving the blessing of the Shroud and the backing of Tiramene, Gozka. The likes of which are to fuel your vengeance an still you question us.' The Mord'ha'ja huffed with almost a scorning and downright hateful tone of voice.

Holloway straightened up to stand as tall as he could, pride was ever a shadow one must hold to give off the illusion of equal standing and power, ever more so in overwhelming situations such as this (of this Holloway knew well).

'My humblest apologies, as both men and as warriors we can get forget this misstep, Sar.' Holloway phrased in a tone only that of a former Nobleman and scholar could ever muster adequately so.

'I am not male, gozka, now come we have lingered too long.' The Mord'ha'ja replied pivoting back to her? original stride and marching on.

Holloway pulled himself out an unexpected daze

and rushed to keep up with his ever-surprising Rakon companions.

*****

Twilight fell upon the tangled ancient woods, as dusk moved on and the cycle of the day came to a close, the sun making way for the twin moons overhead. The chirping of eager nocturnal avian life came to the world around, and the scattering of tree branches could be heard as the beasts fed, fought and lived. The noise of many wild wolves' calls was heard from back and forth as packs met up and stalked the encroaching dark together. Two men were situated in the folding sanctuary of a grove of old cedars and birch, a fire place assembled in turn warming them nearby, as one watched the other rouse from a deep-set slumber.

Eckard pulled himself upright from his hitherto slouched position and seated on a mossy hollowed out stump close by him. Gently stroking a rough hand through his equally seasoned forest of a beard Eckard soon found upon a brown course leaf with which he throw out like an exile from rough bushy facial hair. Grunting out a half-hearted laugh at the thought of yet another leaf in his beard, and the remembrance of what a certain someone would have to say about the likes of such.

'Something shake the humour bone?' Judeson inquired looking up at the man from he lay on his bedroll on the leafstrewn ground close by.

Eckard offered the other man no reply and instead propped his body up and stretched out his aching back. Judeson all the while studied the Eckard from his from where he now rested both arms across raised knee in a relaxed sitting position.

Eckard raised a brow at the man and then offered him some of what remained of the bread roll from his pack.

'Any reason we don't have a fire, it's freezing out here, the earth is soaked through with this endless Northern mist you seem to have here.' Judeson spoke after the awkward pause between them.

'They are probably searching for us now after what happened in Heatra, it would seem our ambush has been upended, Southron and indeed now we are are the hunted.' Eckard answered the man while he placed his pack and weapons in front of his person, frowning at the lack of crossbow quarrels present, when did that happen?

Judeson let out a long heavy weighted sigh and passed pulled his deeply scarred palm against the back of his head, scratching an itch that probably was not there.

'What happened back there? I mean we were..I was trying to save Vestras....she was...' Judeson stuttered out, still clearly in shock and the hallowing look in his eyes made Eckard wince and avert his own vision away.

'The Raks are unpredictable Judeson, and they have weapons that we do not fully understand, their tactics are....' Eckard answered the Southron as he reached into his pack to retrieve something the Judeson would soon be looking for.

'I know all that I have fought them before, but that thing in it's hand, such devastation, it should of been impossible that I...wait where is Jude?' Judeson replied.

Eckard withdrew the heavyset and absurdly long bastard sword of Jude from the similarly impossible pack at his feet and handed it across to Judeson with both hand outstretched. The sheer cumbersome weight of the blade makde him strain himself to lift it. As Judeson took it stead, the Southron seemed to lift and then rise in strikingly dissimilar ease. Eckard's thoughts on the sword were confirmed in this moment and knew not how but somehow the weapon had proved to be Judeson's saviour back in Heatra.

'That blade, it's Invested, or *Embedded* as the others call it. Massively so, seriously refined *wards* on that one.' Eckard voiced his thoughts, not entirely sure he had meant to say them aloud but the words coming out all the same.

Judeson withdrew his inspection of the bastard sword immediately and placed the family heirloom down on his bedroll with concerned ease. Looking up at Eckard with a all-to-serious demeanour and his mood clearly darkening.

'What do you mean? Like the Black Art?' Judeson said gloomily, his eye narrowing to tense slits, symbolising his ponderous mood.

'Magik, weaving, shifting, flaring and turning, Jude as you so called it, probably aided you against whatever the Rak in the journey-house subjected you to.' Eckard answered sternly and abruptly as reasoned the matter was a closed debate. Why did this Southron scoff at the Arcane Sea? Eckard internally shook himself awake. Not everyone knew, very few.

The Southron in question spat onto the earth to the left-hand side of him in clear disgust and stood up in a forced rush, the previously mentioned corresponding events to happen upon him, undoubtedly catching up to him as nearly took a tumble over again, the man's own stubbornness seemingly preventing this. Mustering his strength at the last moment to hold firm on his own two feet, Judeson began make away from the campsite. Eckard steadied his back across his shoulders and making up with bow and blade onto his feet.

'Why does the mention of Magik piss you off so much?' Eckard asked, decidedly offending the Southron again by the character of face, though offending another was hardly much of a concern held by Eckard, so he held the Judeson's gaze.

'It's unnatural, like the Rakish curs and their....' Judeson spoke hastily his teeth barring as he spoke.

'The Raks don't use Magik and that that grenado that blew that house to the fucking Void was not Enchanted. There are elements in this World that we do not understand Judeson, neither you nor I. But I can tell you this as a Practitioner that I know for certain that the Rak's abilities and their devices are not of this world, they hold no place at all in the flow and ebb of the Arcane Sea.' Eckard said interrupting Judeson and cutting off his rant with his own.

'I knew you were a Conjurer of Black Art' Judeson answered, looking off into the night. 'But I did not want to believe it at first.'

'Why? Because you do not understand it, Magik is natural it is part of a whole, the Stone on which we live. Magik is just the altering of a course the shifting of a wind or the gentle sway of a blade of grass. Magikers merely help the spell be woven, all the resources for the Magik are already present around us...' Eckard stressed, clearly exacerbating Judeson's mood as the Southron clenched his palms into closed fists at his side.

'Enough.' Judeson breathed through barred teeth with the intensity of an Aurman possessed. "This is enough for one night, we have to recover our strength and search for this Young ling in the morning, if as you say the Raks are hunting us we best take sleep in picket-rounds. You can take first watch."

No more words for spoken between the two and Eckard was found taken back by the bulking Southerner's ire at being provoked. Before now Judeson had seemed tame of mood beside all issues Rakish. Eckard had clearly pressed upon a trigger that had hurt the other man, and that was indeed enough. Before now Eckard had wondered if the other man would ever wake and he had already been keeping watch, several uneventful bells had passed by in that time and those past moments had left Eckard already fatigued. Piled on this was the fact that his Magik had been put to the test in getting the Southron away from Heatra. Oddly to Eckard he did not feel like disrupting the already snoring Judeson and went back to where he had sat once before.

'What happened? I mean if you don't mind me asking.' Eckard inquired, passing a steaming cup of Kafra to Judeson who let out a heavy sigh knowing a normal fire had not heated the liquid inside the clay mug.

'There was a massacre, the Raks had arrived without warning and no one was ready. My father he was the only to stand...but then he was overwhelmed...he...' Judeson stumbled through recollecting a past that would never quite let him go.

'It's alright you don't have to tell me, I know what the Raks do.' Eckard answered.

'This...all of this I do for my father, to repay him some how..to make myself worthy of his courage that day...'

Eckard nodded in agreement and followed after the

brooding Judeson who had already sent off from their makeshift campsite.

The night had been a long one and Eckard had swore Judeson had slept for far too long but due to their earlier disagreement the Nertharnlander did not bother to wake his companion. The picket duty shift had dragged on without incident and when Judeson finally work in the very late hours of the night, Eckard had been relieved and he fallen asleep almost immediately. He would have stayed so too if it were not for Judeson who awoke him some time later with whispers of tracking after the Raks since they had not as yet discovered upon the two Aurman venturers. Thus they set off to search the pocket of woods just outside Heatra in the hopes of some signs of their hunt and also oddly enough their hunters.

Much of their trek consisted of Judeson scuffling about shrubs and the dense tangled forest floor looking for some tracks of possible Rakish incursion in the vicinity. Eckard threw out threads of Grey and Green Magiks hoping to pick up some trace of anything in particular. Finding only small rodents, insects and avian inhabitants in close proximity. Though Eckard knew Raks were in particular extremely hard to track with any Aspect-shade of Magik. Judeson however seemed to find something to follow, and of this Eckard was extremely thankful. It was only a handful of moments until Judeson led Eckard further into the forest-pocket to a dim light cave entrance heavily covered with tangled vegetarian. They made use of their blades and chopped though the feeder vines into the gloominess of the interior.

Sixth Stanza

Let slip forth; destiny's call

As the Lone Lion will utter a roar

A Red Wolf will say no more

A Thousand rise, A Thousand more will Fall

Without its Call, there would naught to be a New Shore

Arcs pass steady, arcs pass loose

The Long March is up upon the Noose

I had once seen a time without it all

But that time was never more

Fathomless Depths of the Demise

-Krakios the Grounded -Approximately 2022 ATF

note the Kobold poet's turn of phrase and prose is intentionally archaic

As to the symbolism that he alludes to, we have yet to diagnose as to

what this 'Krakios' intends nor if it mentioning real world features.

Afterword by Dawslen Maetinguldsali - Isle of Promqual 2948 arcs ATF

The Blinding light disseminated gradually as Eckard regained his peripherals. The hulking form of Judeson closed in close behind him into the mine head mouth. Just as Judeson made to speak with Eckard a sudden blur of shimmering motion in the gloomy darkness of the tunnel beyond caught the Northman's attention and he signalled for silence. Judeson obliged and made to reach for his behemoth bastard sword at his back. Eckard stilled the other man's hand and pulled him aside. Just in time as it turned out to be as large rapidly hurtling object squeezed past the two Aurmen and clattered in the mine head mouth beyond. Judeson pulled himself to one side of the cave tunnel and Eckard adjusted to the other corresponding side.

'What in the fucking Far Above was that?' Judeson stressed in between started breaths.

'A very old machine, quickly before it works out the reload.' Eckard responded bounding forward into the darkened gloom of the mine tunnel further ahead. Judeson fell in this time completely yielding his sword in its entirety, the blade clanging loudly in the enclosed throughway.

Eckard sprinted forward at a full pace not looking back to Judeson to make sure the Southron had kept pace with him. The machine ahead could be already being levelled at them both, it was a gamble going forward Eckard knew, they just as easily could have retreated back out, or be killed. Yet there was a hope the operator of the device ahead was struggling there was rumours, endless rumours of the Old Imperial's machine being greatly exaggerated or broken down through the many arcs that had passed. Or they were going to be killed.

A dimmed down torch light illuminated in a clearing ahead finally broke the awkward far-flung sinking feeling that had previously absorbed Eckard in his hasty sprint forward. A large Imperial machine stood ready, massive beyond comparison to anything else he had seen previously. A huge onyx bolt lay leveled in a huge narrow cylindrical metal holster. His Southron companion letting out a deeply held grasping draw in awe of the Ancient weapon.

'What in Queen Zadma's sweet mercy?.....' Judeson trailed off, pacing about the hulking monstrous creation, making sure to avoid the weapon's levelled trajectory path back down the tunnel he and Eckard had come from.

Eckard granted the other man a raised eyebrow in response and continued on past the machine and past its scores of heavily rusted cogs and gears, looking for evidence of any Raks being previously here.

'This, this thing..this...what is this?' Judeson

'Can you pick a trail in here?' Eckard inquired

of the Southron ignoring the other man's line of questioning towards the Old-Imperial ballista.

Judeson hesitantly forced himself away from the time swept killing machine and peered about the gloomy setting the two men were presently contained in. Eckard watched the other man slowly encroach a feathering touch with hazel hue gloves across the dust and mud caked floor of the cavern chamber. Judeson peering about oneway and then forcing his gaze another. What seemed like an eternity to Eckard; passed before the Southron stood up again and pointed down one of the many overwhelmingly dark drenched tunnels. Obviously indicating their desired path. Judeson passed for a moment however as Eckard began to follow the man's lead, Judeson briefly staring back at the ancient Imperial war machine.

'It kind of looks like…a sideward bow... giant one…but ...' Judeson began fixated on the hulking, rusting death trap.

'Yes?' Eckard responded immediately, a little irritated that the Southron would stop in the middle of their mission like this to ask a question about something from a meaningless and forgotten bygone era.

'How come there is no bow, no string or cord, no trigger? How did it possibly work?'

"That is a question that absorbed the whole Imperium, Judeson. Now can we go on?" Eckard answered, adjusting his belongings and hitching up his backpack, the process of which always made him just a touch more comfortable in clearly uncomfortable circumstances.

'Yes of course,' Judeson muttered, walking off in the pitch black abounds of the deeper mine tunnel.

*

Judeson found he was slipping and sliding uncontrollably his footing came loose and he pelted forward into the gloomy dark shadows ahead. From mere paces behind the scuffle of heavy boots could be heard and Judeson realised Eckard was close behind. The Nerthanlander almost pitched into Judeson if it was not for the other man's awareness to reach out with arms outstretched. A direct collision was abated but the two men were quickly distracted by the loud booming sound of stones and gears moving in unison. The squeal of ailing oiled cogs resounded throughout the darkened chamber cavern they were in.

Noting the direction of the arched entrance-way Eckard and himself had come in from Judeson saw much to his horror and awe the stone face shifting inwards closing about and the previous doorway hastily becoming absent. It was not long until the whole cavern they were in became swallowed in the absolution of pure darkness, blacker than any night he thought possible.

***

An overbearing thick blanket of darkness engulfed the room all around. Eckard strained his eyes attempting to make sense of his surroundings he and Judeson were enclosed in. A sudden flash of light shone through from above and the sound of a rust-ridden door swung open. Looking up into the overpowering light above Eckard briefly saw a figure move over the sunlit crevasse. A voice recognisable in the accent of a man from the Collective to Eckard called down into the decrepit confines Eckard and Judeson were held in; strong, clear and loud.

'Well, it appears your….nonsense is over now.' The voice announced.

"I believe we were just beginning to enjoy ourselves,' Eckard called back to the unknown entity.

'Ha…..still some fight left in you. I'm afraid you have lost, however. Before you….leave us, I have some questions.' The voice said.

'I'm afraid I will have to respectfully tell you to fuck off in regards to that, my noble Sar or Holloway son of some prick, Earl of an old burnt shithole, was it?' Eckard answered the voice while adjusting his eyes to the penetrating and harsh beaming light from above.

The figure that spoke down to Judeson and Eckard began to take form and Eckard saw him for what he was. Though still a harsh blurred vision, Eckard's eyes made sense of the voice's physical embodiment, a well-bronzed face clean shaven and wrinkled with age lines looked down at Eckard. The large brown eyes of the figure of Holloway stared intently down at Eckard until lifting up and the man himself pacing about the narrow grated opening in the roof above the cell. Holloway proceeded to light up an old brass smoking pipe he had in hand.

'My previous title matters little now. What were you two hoping to accomplish in harrying us as intently, as you have done." Holloway inquired puffing away on his now lit pipe and billowing out clouds of thick white smoke about him as he walked back and forth across the dungeon cell's murder hole.

'We had come to retrieve the Draul boy from your thrall,' Judeson said, standing up tall in the murder hole's shadow. "But then we found out a cowardly man was running a gang of Raks, enslaving a helpless village and we knew wrongs needed to be righted."

144

Holloway coughed briefly and loudly before taking his pipe from his lips and chuckling drily under his breath, finding something humourous in Judeson's discourse.

'Right wrongs? That's an excellent line haha. You know little of me and little of wrongs. Who sent you.. the Draul? They send Aurmen in their absence to retrieve their precious Magik child. Ha…you work for a people who care nothing for the plight of man and cower in their forest's shadow like selfish fools.' Holloway proclaimed in a loud booming voice, building in excited crescendo by the moment.

'And Raks do know? An alliance with savage creatures who know nothing but war, butchers of children ….' Judeson shouted in furious anger back up into the light above.

'The Rakon are not so different from us. You misguided idiots don't really understand what is going on.' Holloway piped up, cutting off Judeson and proceeded to dispose of his ashes from his pipe down the murder hole towards the two men below.

Eckard pulled Judeson back and attempted to silence him as he saw the man's look of ferocious rage present on his face. Surprisingly Judeson nodded and let Eckard speak ahead of him.

"Then educate us, Holloway, explain to us why the Raks are not so fucking different." Eckard voiced stepping forth into the light and peering upward at the stalking shadows above.

'.. you have burnt that bridge I'm afraid. The Draul boy will come of use and you two will perish in this hole, just as the previous meddlers have.' Holloway answered standing perfectly still now and peering at Eckard and Judeson through the iron bars of the murder hole.

'There were others?'Judeson inquired hastily glaring up into the solitary light source.

'Oh yes, quite a few, Draul soldiers, stupid and arrogant, some mercenaries, Aurman, little between their ears as well. But you two I must say have done quite well to make it this far, I stand impressed. The first to discover this place on purpose and track us here, the first ones to actually put up a fight, good work' Holloway said, laughing in refrained snigger. The sound of vicious more guttural fits of laughter carried down also and it was clear Holloway was companioned by an unknown number of Rakon warriors.

***

The Boy was right there. Judeson looked ahead and saw what must have been the ForeSeer he had heard all about. The child with a remarkable head of silver hair stood mere paces away. The young boy set upright to the side of one of the fearsome looking armoured warriors in the employ of Holloway. The ForeSeer's eyes were downcast and the boy trembled beneath his woollen cloak in the gentle breeze. Holloway caught Judeson's gaze on the ForeSeer boy and smirked at him in turn. The brief smile subsided as Holloway took on a serious demeanour once more and strode out from his company of warriors, much the same way as an alpha male from a pack of wolves.

'You had to complicate things didn't you two? You should have given up already and died in the hole. We will not spare you such mercy here." Holloway announced in a matter of fact manner in a quiet and calm voice.

'You will never give up Holloway, why should we?' Eckard said.

'Point taken if I were a more honourable man I

would respect that. But I'm afraid I can't offer such.' Holloway replied, drawing his rapier and his three Rakon charges following suite instantaneously after him, taking their respective weapons into their hands.

'Last chance,' Judeson offered; more as a formality that any real promise, holding up the bastard sword of Jude towards their would-be aggressors.

Not another word was spoken as the battle was joined. The Rakon warrior at the side of the ForeSeer had a bow drawn and he loosed a projectile at Eckard's head who seemed to just stand still not bothering to draw his sword or charge the attackers. The air around Eckard seemed to simmer.

Judeson had no time to see whether the Northlander had evaded the attack as he was soon set upon by one of the other Rakon bandits, swinging an axe wildly at him. Managing to clamor out of the way of the near man's initial bout Judeson righted himself into a battle-ready stance and closed upon the apparition with the axe. The Rakon reacted hastily and slammed his oversized weapon into Judeson's sword parry, both weapons meeting in a clattering voice of honed blade edges. The sheer weight of violence from the Rakon's attack forced Judeson backward and his footing soon slide, he quickly found his back hard pressed against the ancient bridge's stone frame behind him. The Rakon's face mere inches from Judeson's own now as the creature pushed forward with impossible strength, its warm heaving breath making Judeson winch.

Judeson drew himself back to an upright position once more, he released one hand from the hilt of Jude. He flattened the sword with the blade face

downwards against the Rakon's wild axe swing,
Judeson used his free hand to push against the
swords flat face. Mustering all his strength
Judeson propelled the Rakon's pressure and sent
the creature sprawling to the hard bridge floor.
The near man's dented iron helm went flying away
and the creature's head smashing on the stone
blocks in a sickening blow. Momentarily glancing
around at Eckard's assumed position, Judeson
found himself surprised to the see the man
righting himself to his feet from a half crouch,
the only damage sustained to his person, was a
small and thin gushing cut on his left brow. The
arrow that had been fired at Eckard seemed to
have disintegrated before him, splintered wood
fragments and the rusty arrowhead lay scattered
nearby at his feet. Holloway advanced, with
rapier onto the man.

Turning back around just in time, Judeson saw
another of the Rakon bandits rushing him, this
one with a morningstar in hand. Judeson pivoted
and threw his weight the opposite direction to
the Rakon's incoming charge. Shaving the air from
whence Judeson had been previously; the Rakon
attempted to redistribute his weight as to right
himself, in that moment however Judeson struck
across the creature's body with a downwards
slash, making contact. The sword of Jude slicing
through soft exposed tissue at the base of the
shoulder blade and down to the abdomen in between
the Rakon's flimsy copper coloured breastplate.
Thick, dark crimson oozing fluid spurted out from
the deep open wound across most of the Rakon's
body and onto the mossy ground around them,
Judeson thrust his long blade deep in the Rakon's
unprotected throat and swiveled his grip around
to work the blade through and out the other side,
blood coating Judeson's face as he did so. The

creature dropped to the floor, and Judeson reefed his sword violently from the dead Rak's corpse.

The bow-wielding Rakon bandit took aim once more with an arrow nocked this time at Judeson, the Southron stood frozen in place an absorbing chill running up his spine. The Rakon went to unleash on Judeson but his shoulder took a sharp blow as a curved hunting knife was lodged and perfectly buried deep within the Rakon's shoulder blade. The creature's arrow flies high and wide of its mark and the near-man, in turn, released his grip on the bow that fired it, the weapon falling to the bridge floor. Eckard had seemed to appear right next to him.

The Rakon made to snatch at his sword at its belt but Eckard had closed on him, Eckard's curved blade swiping at the creature's throat and making contact, a massive gash formed and spurting out thick red ooze. The Rakon went gradually limp and fell heavily backward. Judeson saw Eckard step toward the returning form of Holloway and he followed suite. Two massive tree trunks of arms closed about Judeson's torso from behind and pulled him into a stranglehold he quickly found himself trapped in. Unable to break free from the locked arms of the previously forgotten Rakon, Judeson involuntarily freed his grip on Jude, the sword falling away.

The air knocked from his lungs and his chest being crushed under the brutal force of the Rakon's hold around him, Judeson struggled relentlessly trying to free himself. The Rakon's breath discharged into Judeson ear and he squirmed away from the puffing hot air, tossing his head back to smash into the Rakon's own. The effort went unrewarded for Judeson as the move seemed to only serve to anger the Rakon as the creature strengthened his double-armed grip around his body, lifting him off his feet. Judeson lifted both feet parallel to his airborne self and pushed with his strength against the Rakon behind him. The action worked as the Rakon soon became unbalanced and began to fall backward, his grip however still held firmly about Judeson. Both Judeson and the Rakon fell tumbling from the stone bridge over the sharp edge into the river below as the Rakon ran out of the ground to stumble on.

**

The midday air reeked of the foul stench of the Void. Eckard had no time to take this in however as Holloway closed in on him.

Swords clashed together in a rattling barrage, steel striking against each other and the men behind the weapons shifting positions and closing once more, Holloway's rapier amazingly holding firm against the broader sided scimitar that Eckard wielded. Striking out in a clever pivoted slash Holloway bypassed Eckard's parry and sliced against the other man's backhand, it was enough and from sheer pain endured by such a cut, Eckard dropped his curved sword. Holloway countered up quickly with a coordinated thrust in toward Eckard's stomach. Eckard shifted backward much faster than Holloway's rush and narrowly missing the full length of the rapier's deadly point. Even then a slight brush of the absurdly sharp rapier against Eckard's exposed belly yielded an ever so slight wound upon him. Holloway slashed out his rapier towards Eckard once more as the Northlander ducked and weaved out of danger's path. Managing to get on the opposite side of Holloway's endless flurry of attacks and slashes, Eckard found the man unbalanced and unready for a hasty kicking to his unguarded back of the knee. Holloway fell down slight but just as quickly recovered and turned towards Eckard with his rapier out facing front and centre once more.

In between the unarmed Eckard and the advancing, rapier-wielding Holloway laid a cumbersome looking war-axe on the bridge's rocky uneven floor. Eckard hastily placed his front right front, toe just close enough to just touch the Rakon weapon and proceeded in righting it upwards to himself, a Magik thread cast out the axe flew up into Eckard's hands somewhat accurately though just an erring tinge to fast. In the very conjoining moment; Holloway cut downwards in a jutting slash the head of the axe fell away from the timber frame like butter on a hot knife, the cumbersome weapon similarly smoking hot at the cut end. The rapier in Holloway's hands impossibly undeterred by the action, *'it must be fucking drowned in the Void'* Eckard cussed to himself. Holloway grimaced at Eckard before again slashing downwards this time across the axe's main wooden body. Just like before the rapier cut clean through unopposed, Eckard acting quickly moving away from the rapier's reach and with the two splintered ends of the previous axe in each hand, twirling his wrists and hammering with pure blunt force into Holloway's temples at his skull.

Holloway staggered backward drunkenly, one hand clutching at the side of his head the other firmly holding on to his rapier at his hip. Eckard latched out at the man's out at the weapon holding wrist with burnt splintered timber axe-handle and forced Holloway's hand into the side of the stone bridge edge. The rapier, in turn, dropped to the ground in a defining crash, as Holloway's hand made contact with the jagged rock in the violent crash. Holloway recovered despite this and struck outwards with his other hand in a closed fist into Eckard's lower left rib cage, the blow sending Eckard backward in pain. Holloway followed up with his right punch, with his wounded left fist striking out. The action encumbered and slowed enough for Eckard to curl his arm around the Holloway's left respective arm in a fiercely determined coiled grip. Eckard holding on pulling Hollway in, using the other larger man's robust frame against him, struck quickly into the surprised Dazral dropping his knee into the former Nobleman's chest and striking with his upturned elbow into Holloway's face. Eckard aimed to shatter the man's nose. Stumbling heavily backward Holloway grasped at his belt hastily as Eckard advanced to charge him, holding a tiny clay ball Holloway squeezed and in mere moments was embodied in a vast billowing cloud of dirty white enveloped smoke. Eckard's attack met thin air and he clawed out, finding nothing. Eckard's lungs filled with the nasty toxic fumes of the smoke and coughed viciously in response. Pitching about in chaos Eckard evidently found his way out of the dissipating haze of obnoxious snowy smoulder in a desperate tumble and leap.

*

Spiralling down into the hitherto gentle calm of the settled river waters, Judeson felt the full force of the surface tension upon his back. The only relieving thought for the man was that the Rakon holding onto him was below and had taken the blow first. The sheer shock intended stinging pain across Judeson's body and he struggled to recover. Judeson's world had soon become that of swirling dim lit waters beneath the surface. The intense stranglehold the Rakon had on Judeson lightened as one of the creature's hands broke free entirely. The other Rak's arms stayed desperately clawing onto Judeson's torso as the Rak fell deeper into the depths.

Eddying bitter cold waters flushed past Judeson as he followed his captor down to the river floor. The densely weighted environment hastened his rapidly lightheaded daze which he found himself in. The grip the Rakon had forced upon Judeson before their fall into the gloomy Wanderers River had knocked the air almost completely from Judeson's lungs, and now is this underwater struggle Judeson found himself quickly drowning. In a desperate gamble Judeson stamped both feet down upon the Rak beneath him pushed upwards with all the strength he could muster. The Rakon finally let go entirely and Judeson surged from the river floor.

Just as Judeson thought himself free and heading towards the surface. A strong hand stayed one of his legs. The Rakon had recovered and its tenacious capacity to outmuscle the Southron had not died away at all slightly. Finding himself being drawn against his will back down to the near man's position, Judeson unsheathed his last remaining weapon on his belt, it was little more than a glorified pen-knife but it would have to do. Facing his death at the hands of a relentless Rak at the bottom of a deep river bed, armed only with a mere letter opener blade, Judeson felt nothing more than hopelessness. Hate had all about eroded from his mind, as water gushed into his throat and lungs forcibly, and it was with certainly that

His demise was eminent that he swam down firmly to meet the Rakon with pen-knife closing on the being's throat: The sharp pointed knife barely a finger's length long was driven by Judeson with

as much gusto as he could manage the pen-blade
rent into the Rakon's soft flesh between its head
and shoulders and tore through muscle and
cartilage alike. Judeson twisted and turned the
blade within the Rak's throat and thick dark red
blood billowing out into the gloomy cyan waters
around them, much like the way a cloud of smoke
would have emerged from a chimney. The Rakon
struggled and squirmed, the near man's sharp
edged nails digging deep and drawing blood from
Judeson's outstretched arms. The Rakon in moments
subsided and fell away from Judeson, lifeless as
the Southron released his grip on the buried
blade in its throat. Judeson felt all his
strength departing him in an increasing hazy
rush; he knew his fate would soon follow that of
his sinking victim before him. Just as he closed
his eyes to accept what would come, a sharp
twitch brushed against the back of Judeson's neck
and he felt unexpectedly more awake than ever.
All of sudden he a felt a rush build inside him
and threw his body upwards in a desperate bid to
reach the surface anew.

*

Eckard swept the gushing crimson blood flowing
free from his left brow with his palm, clutched
at his winded left side and looked into the
direction of the drunkenly staggering form of
Holloway. The running man was already to the far
side of the timber bridge that spanned the
Wanderer's River. Indeed it seemed to be that
Holloway despite being injured was still
remarkably fleet of foot as it were, and Eckard
being as wounded as he was now. It would prove to
be that there would be little to no chance of a
pursuit. Eckard remembered one of the Rakon
assailants had borne a bow and the weapon still
lay at the near man's fallen figure just mere

paces away. Both blood and the body's energy rapidly depleting from Eckard, the man hastily snatched up the composite built bow and nocked an arrow onto the weapon from out of the Rakonian's quiver. The figure of Holloway raced to the bridge's far end and snatched up a small, slender figure wrapped in robes. Eckard remembered the Fore-Seer Draul boy in a gut wretched horror. Holloway brought forth a fierce devilish looking hand-blade to the Sapling's throat after little more than a half struggle. Eckard spat onto the bridge's cobblestone ground a thick pool of phlegm and blood and let out a cry of frustration, the old man could sure hit some. Pulling back hard on the tightly threaded bowstring, Eckard took aim towards Holloway and the tightly bound up form of the Draul Foreseer and their staggered retreating mass, the likes of which was slowly evacuated the ancient stone bridge. Eckard breathed heavy, his heart pounded in his chest, his vision rapidly worsening at every moment. Holloway far ahead appeared to pause momentarily before raising his head to Eckard before; going on, to look back over at Eckard, his expression unreadable at such a distance. Eckard closed both eyes, he drew on all the conserves he had left, the man's mind turned to matters of Magik. He needed Magik now more than ever. The Northlander cast his concentration to the strenuous recesses of Magik provocation. All he had learned throughout the years he attempted to utilize now. He needed to. Yet it did not seem enough, his left rib cage burning now with warm fluid seeping out into his maille and cloak, Eckard realising Holloway must not have been empty handed, the full force only now being read as what it was. The adrenaline of the fight wearing thin, the true nature of the wounding becoming apparent now.

The shimmering shadows of Grey were weaved willingly around Eckard now, though his own head swam with fleeting energy and approaching screaming pain, his skin tingled uncontrollably as if he stood absently of cloth in a raging blizzard and he felt the overwhelming soaring sensitivity that accompanied; weaving. The raw feeling of opening access to the Arcane Sea was sheer thrilling and also just as dangerous. Then Eckard knew he was not alone in this Spell another presence had joined him. Pale red eyes seemed to stare back at him, even though he had closed his own.

Just as Eckard began to feel overcome with exhaustion, he opened his eyes he released the nocked arrow off the bow and fell to his knees in an unforced and rushed action. The whole act seemed strangely out of time for him. His head danced with intoxicating waves of nausea and it seemed to take an eternity but in reality, only it was several moments for his eyes to adjust to the light of day around him. Looking upwards and turning onto his side off into the direction of Holloway who had moments ago been retreating with the Draul Sapling in along the beaten track beyond the bridge, Eckard was surprised to witness the fallen, unmoving apparition of the mentioned individual, a single arrow lay buried deep within Holloway's upper chest or possibly his neck even. The Draul Foreseer standing over the Aurman, studying him maybe.

Eckard made to get up on feet and investigate Holloway's position. The mere effort to do so exposed his fragility for what it was. The young man's every conceivable joint ached with the attempt and he felt overcome with exhaustion, the pain was undermining his own willpower as he pushed himself upward, black edges distorting his vision as he found a handhold in the moss coated bridge walls. Eckard's mouth filled with blood and coughed up the thick liquid violently at his toes, as he struggled to his feet. Looking ahead to the rolling green hills where Holloway's body lay still and unmoving in the densely tangled grass mounds. Eckard felt a deep harrowing sense of regret for the killing of the Corisi man, it had been different; Eckard had never slew another Aurman before now, the Raks was a different story, and they attacked furious and unnerving they did not speak to him, not in a true sense of what could be taken as the discourse to him anyway. Holloway had. Eckard and Judeson had talked with the man. All of a sudden Eckard understood how much Holloway had longed for vengeance. How death was so absolute. He understood but did not agree with the other man's ideals.

**

Judeson strolled up awkwardly from the forested mud banks of the Wanderers River. It was evident that the young Southron was injured. The young Foreseer approached. A mere child, his slim framed form was embodied in a thick woollen coat, although he still appeared to shiver, whether this was from the River's cold was debatable Eckard knew. Judeson made his way over in a limp to Holloway's body, crouching down and placing one hand on the fallen man's head. Eckard peered at Judeson intently and in moments the other man looked back around at him. Sensing Eckard's unasked question Judeson looked over nodded extravagantly in response. Holloway was gone. The Draul ForeSeer boy made his way over to Eckard with Judeson only paces behind him. The young fair-haired child as he approached looked up at Eckard who swayed and breathed heavy on the windswept bridge that spanned onwards to the Hasperneara back the way Judeson and the boy had come. Eckard turned away from the Draul boy and beheld the other side of bridge's expanse. Dull grey stone shores and deep emerald groves of wild pines all around marked the borders of Fartheilm where their return journey would be.

'Tha..tha..nk…yo…' The Draul ForeSeer made to stutter, still intently shivering of fear.

'It's time to go home,' Judeson answered from behind him.

And with that said and done the boy and the two exhausted and wounded warriors prepared to gather themselves and then set off back the way they had come.

Interlude

Some in the Southrondor call it the Day-star, others the sun

In the vast reed wetlands and rolling, rugged hills of

The Yun it is so named by a people that title themselves in its light

That glaring, beaming, overwhelming brightness, gives life and burns it away

Much the same way as we mortals do to each other as if we are but replicating what

is above us all.

Writ of the Road

Author Unnamed

The gradually subsiding fury of the flaming bright embers gave way to a constant calming and warming glow. The fire was old now and would not last for more than an hour. A felled trunk of an ancient tree nearby provided adequate seating off the damp mossy grass for the young Draul Sapling and he was content. Glancing about to the sprawled form of a blanketed man, (the giant, black-bearded one) and over to his left to the lighter featured but unmistakably broader man, the Seer felt vaguely at ease. This was not saying much, he mused. The Raks had not been the most 'comforting' of custodians anyway. The one named 'Holloway', however, had been alright to him, he had been gentle and surprisingly kindhearted. The ForeSeer had always known there was always something else about Holloway though, something dark within the man, that ate at him. The Draul boy could sense such things in people, some called it a talent, to him it merely felt like second nature.

Peering around the makeshift campsite at the two men (his possible saviours maybe, right now it was difficult to tell). The Draul felt uncertain. He had only been brought into the world not long ago. Through the 'Ceremony' he had come to be. From there all the details dissolved into an indiscernible haze. The FarSeer ironically had no vision of what and where he was. Not just at this particular campsite but what everything around him was exactly. The dark-maned Aurman stirred, one arm rubbing at his nose as he sniffled, only to drop back down again into unconsciousness. Parting his eyes from the curious sight of this the ForeSeer caught the dusty brown one peering at him sideways. The Draul boy made to speak but as was usual at the current time, no words came out.

'Are you hungry youngling? Or did you need to relieve yourself?' The man said, casting his somber stare towards the boy keenly.

Feeling embarrassed from the attention granted by the Aurman the Draul ForeSeer looked away. He felt pins and needles lace up his spine. After several moments the Draul boy knew he was being rude in not delivering a reply to the light featured Aurman.

'n..No..No Gozka..' The Draul ForeSeer stuttered, the last word somehow piling into his sentence, the boy had no credible thought on how this became and berated himself from uttering it.

The Aurman made his way over to the Draul with a questioning look in his eyes. The FarSeer peering at the bear of a man.

'I am Judeson, you are safe. The Raks do not have you anymore.' Judeson said, never breaking eye contact.

The Draul boy found himself overcome by the stranger's (Judeson?) sight. It was all too much for the boy, how long had he been in this world, days, months? The Raks or Rakoni as Holloway had called them; had been frightening in a grim sense, yet the boy had felt safe. Everyone else around him had bowed, grovelled and averted their eyes. For Him? Or the Rakoni, he could not be certain. Holloway had been blunt, stating things and telling him it would be alright if he cooperated. There had been incidents between now and then, Aurman and Draul had attacked Holloway and the brooding Rakoni, the ForeSeer had witnessed a few of these moments. Holloway had attempted to shelter him from this. But the Boy had seen, men armed like his (current companions/captors) try to attack, all had ended abruptly and not well for them. Now, this Judeson character and the black-mane snoring away nearby had changed everything. For better or for worse, The youngling of this was not sure.

The broad shouldered and robust Southron averted his eyes from the Draul ForeSeer but not in embarrassment or discomfort like so many of the others. This particular man just looked devoid of ideas on what to say and went about poking the burnt out fowl carcass that was laid over the dying fire on makeshift spite erected from dry twigs. Grim and brooding company again it seemed. Yet these two were different than Holloway and the Raks somehow, exactly how they were of differing qualities; the Draul could not place. Sweeping long silver locks back across his face, the boy felt the grubbiness and oil seep through his fingernails, over the last few days it was getting progressively worse, he felt unclean all over, exactly how the Northman with that unruly beard on his face was coping, the Draul could not understand.

The thought of birds and insects nesting in the dense black forest on the man's face brought a laugh to the Draul boy and he found himself chuckling, such a simple gesture but one he had not had much chance to practice, in recent times. The ForeSeer did not realise how loud his laughing was. Judeson was now looking at him with a upturned brow as if there was something wrong. As if sensing the whole affair had been about him, the Northman had awakened from his slumber and sat up on his haunches. Sleep ridden eyes and a dreary look planted intently on his face. At the very edges of the Northman's forest-like-beard was a loose twig dangling as if it were a vine attached. The Draul ForeSeer lost whatever composure he had earlier developed and began laughing aloud anew, this time more excitedly than before.

Following the Draul ForeSeer's stare, the source of amusement become clear; Eckard looked ridiculous, well even more now. The black-mane raised an eyebrow in response and did very little else. Moments later even in the present hysterical laughter of the Draul-boy the Northman dropped his head and went back to his sleep. The Draul found himself wondering how casual of composure the Aurman seemed to be at the times. Not two days earlier Judeson and the black mane had seemed exhausted and heavily accosted to their wounds sustained in the violent upheaval at the Wanderer's River crossing.

Judeson had been bleeding the ForeSeer remembered the Southron seemed to wince at every move in the hours of their meeting. Now, however, he had seemed to have almost of recovered fully from what could now be taken as merely an inconvenient setback. The big, tall Northman had been poisoned, his veins had bulged and most of his blood had been taken. Felled by some unknown intoxicant, the black haired man had sweated and fallen into delirium at every given chance. Judeson whilst recovered from his own wounds tended to the man and attempted to do all he could. The Draul boy not noting what else he could possibly do to assist or whether he should exactly. And so he did what exactly any bystander would do and watched from afar.

Not a day passed and the black-mane's fever was broken and he, Judeson and the Foreseer were on their way. Judeson, in particular, seemed surprised how easily the Northman seemed to shrug off being poisoned. On their way back to the Draul'estla'theilm. Of this, the Draul was most unsure. Did he want to even go back? What exactly

did await him back there in the grim forest
obscured by shadows was what had his young mind
is a tussle with itself. In the all too brief
time present in the Draul homeland realm he had
experienced many, many things. Not all of them to
his liking.

The broad form of Judeson pulled himself up and
made his way over the slumbering Northerner who
had already awoken to greet the man. As if he
knew. The Draul Foreseer watched the two wearily
half caught between figuring out what exactly the
two Aurman were to him and whether he wished to
return his home again. Judeson slipped into a
woollen bedroll and drifted off with relative
ease laying on the damp sodden earth. The black-
mane took up residence on a rotten log close by
and whistled away a song that seemed to possess
no structure. The Foreseer looked across at the
Northerner who never met his gaze but looked over
into the distance ever intently.

'Take sleep youngling you will need it.' The
Aurman uttered as if it were fact absolute., his
eyes never turning from whatever ever he was so
intent on looking at.

The Draul ForeSeer considered the tall brooding
Northman's advice for he felt unbearably
exhausted yet as he lay down on the stranger's
bedroll swag where they had told him he could
sleep. The boy could not drift off his mind still
swam with all that had happened upon and around
him, for although his body longed for slumber he
felt unable to fall into unconsciousness. The
Draul boy sat pulled himself up and gazed across
at the black-mane. The man took no notice of the
Foreseer and instead had both his eyes closed his
face pulled tight into a concentrated appearance.
Magik energies swam about the North-man in an
intriguing dance of power. The Foreseer found

himself taken back by how strong the hue of the
man's aura.

As quickly as the Magik streamed around the air
about the man no sooner did it dissipate and
scatter to the winds. Waves of shrouded grim-blue
and twisting spirals of cascading luminescent
magenta parted ways and made off to the night
air, eventually dissipating entirely. The
Foreseer knew all too well from many, many
lessons granted him by his Draul instructors and
tutors that there many that could not see such
things he had seen. Magik and its patterns were
not subject to the viewpoint of those not fully
adapt- they had told him. Though exactly how
adept he was and how exactly anyone else viewed
the world was a mystery to the Draul boy. He knew
no other circumstance. Born into the world from
Magik he had no way of being without it, or what
it was possibly like. Though being without Magik
was a circumstance many already knew. In fact
from what Aroteph had been told; some of the
Draul factions longed to be in this case. Or so
the Foreseer had been told.

*

Eckard glance across at the Draul ForeSeer and
witnessed the young boy studying him intently the
Nertharnlander felt slightly uncomfortable with
the Draul's focused stare from behind those
penetrating deep crimson eyes. Remembering of all
the things the youngling was though Eckard
composed himself and made to speak, to lighten
the unwelcome situation.

'You have a name boy?' Eckard called to the
child, lowering his voice as the query dragged
on, remembering the slumbering form of Judeson
nearby.

The Draul ForeSeer shuffled uncomfortably about

and padded down his woollen coat at his sides, before finally answering his voice coming out as an awkward stammered murmur.

'Aroteph is the name they gave me.'

Eckard nodded his understanding and turning around to look upward at the Far Above. The Nertharnlander felt the Draul Sapling's eyes never stray from him, and let out a snide smile. A handful of moments passed and Eckard looked across to the sunken and slumbering form of the Draul.

***

Stirring awake anxiously in a startle. A loud apprehensive breath escaping his throat, his eyes straining to adjust to the obnoxious bright xanthic light hues of the day-time arcs, Aroteph found himself apprehensive and unsure of his surrounding. Two faces, one heavily embedded with a Stygian coated course beard, the other a tanned brown hue face with a heavily stubbled chin turned to meet him from above and a few paces distance off. Rubbing his eyes of sleep and adjusting his sight to make sense of the figures, the ForeSeer felt slightly more comfortable; his companions Judeson and Eckard were less imposing than the constant concealed faces of the Rakoni warriors that he had awoken to over the last couple of days.

The two men both tall, forbidding and broad shouldered, (though the Southron somewhat more so in the latter department) beckoned him to get up as they sorted their belongings and equipment. The Northman with the messily beaded black beard held out apple into Aroteph's direction, Eckard tilted his head in beckoning for the Draul to take the fruit. Aroteph accepted gratefully and watched the two men began a discussion about their current circumstances. The ForeSeer not really taking note of what they men talked about, happily munching away on his welcome breakfast until word of the Draul'estla'theilm was spoken.

'..and we take the Aroteph back to the Draul woodlands? If we can find the way back.' Judeson stated, the point almost lost on the ForeSeer who had joined mid-sentence, but now his interest was peaked with mention of his origin-lands.

'We will have to find Heatra which should not prove difficult. From there I remember the way back.' Eckard answered as he readjusted his wickedly hooked blade at his belt, stretched his neck from side to side and began to start forward.

'As do I now. However how are we going to find the town again, we trekked through that damned underground for near a day to get out here.' Judeson replied, motioning for Aroteph to fall in behind him as he too began forward in Eckard's wake.

 The Draul ForeSeer stalked directly behind the massive Southron in his shadow.

'The smoke from the Rak machine. Should be easy enough to see in a day's time if we follow due east.' Eckard said, looking at Aroteph and Judeson with hallowing sky-blue orbs of eyes. A determined look loomed on his face.

Judeson halted in his tracks abruptly and forced Aroteph to side-step away from crashing into the man's considerable bulk. The Draul boy looked up at Judeson' face and saw a sight which frightened him and made Aroteph avert his gaze from the stone cold gaze present on Judeson's face. The Draul remembered Holloway's face before it took the eternal sleep being much the same way many times.

'And the bastard inn-keeper will pay for his crimes' Judeson announced a steely tone in his voice.

Aroteph peered across to Eckard who now stood still looking back at Judeson. The black-mane Nertharnlander nodded in understand and pursed his lips in an elongated line beneath his haphazard beard. The rusty brown haired Southron seemed to find new purpose and began forward once more, walking past Eckard on the rugged hilly track, the Northman met Aroteph's eyes which lingered on him and again a nod. Feeling a cold chill run down his spine from the Mage's gaze the Draul walked past Eckard too who seemed inclined on waiting for everyone to pass him.

Minutes passed with no words spoken between the trio, just the sounds of the wild around them as they ventured ever east and the day-star in the Far Above passed over and evidently behind their line of sight. Aroteph followed in the bulky Southron Judeson's footsteps attempting to keep up with the man's frantic and unforgiving brisk pace. Ever since the mention of the returning to the town of Heatra had been uttered the Southron seemed a man obsessed with something. They must get there as soon as possible. Aroteph would like to think he too felt similar for his return to his homeland but of this, he was not even convincing himself.

A gentle cool breeze passed beside the group and Aroteph pulled his woollen coat close about him. Something seemed to whisper on the wind, like a voice, almost as if the airbrushing past was talking to them. From several paces behind, the sound of Eckard's up and down voice was heard.

'They are close.'

Aroteph chanced a look over his shoulder still keeping up in the frantic march imposed by Judeson. Eckard bore a half smile in clear satisfaction and winked at Aropeth as he looked. The ForeSeer was left confused as to what they curious Northman meant. A pace ahead Judeson had pulled up short in his determined trek. Across from the Southron, a ragged and malnourished Aurman bearing a long bent stick with a sharp pointed end strode out from behind a wayside of a mossy rock formation. The gangly balding apparition gestured with the makeshift weapon at Judeson and voiced in a shrill screech something inaudible to Aroteph.

The hulking form of Judeson stood firm in his path between the barely Aurman figure and the ForeSeer, shifting nervous eyes about the man fled back into the foliage as if a hare caught in a hunt. The Southron's big hands rested on the pommel of the massive claymore at his back. The sword not yet was drawn but his hand remained for a few moments until no sight of the haggard looking man was seen again. Eckard in his grey-tattered grey cloak paced forward pacing ahead of Aroteph and Judeson as if nothing had happened.

The ForeSeer was taken back, how could this man just keep going forward? Judeson close to Aroteph's side reached and brushed the young boy's shoulder gently pushing him forward onto the path of the grey-cloaked Northerner. Looking back Aroteph witnessed a gentle smile graced the features of the deep tanned lines of the face of Judeson. But this too like all things that made the ForeSeer comfortable disappeared all too soon. The Southron's features hardening like a dried shell resilient to the elements of the world. Judeson began forward and his long brisk stride leads him back into line with Eckard.

Aroteph rushed into a frantic sprint to keep up. Exhaustion seized him. Aroteph's breathing quickened even as he sat recuperating, with his back against a solid elm tree, his feet pushed out before him, boots off. The shrill cry of gulls far overhead was heard. The gentle breeze of the earlier hours of the day had subsided and a frosty cold takes hold with the settling fog clouds all around the surrounding hill country. From where the ForeSeer sat physically spent and mentally worn, the various pockets of woods lay scattered about, rolling emerald coloured hills separated the forests of the Fartheilm. A grim smog spiralling in billowing black and grey smoke into the air a few league distant off.

The crunch of boots sounded to the left side of the Foreseer, Aroteph turned and glimpsed the cloaked form of the Northerner; named Eckard. The Netharnlander regarded the Foreseer with a coarse cough and subsequent clearing of his apparent blocked up respiratory system, the mucus audible even to Aroteph.

'We shall make camp here young one, in order to recharge and steady ourselves,' Eckard stated, his deep resonating voice seeming to strike straight through Aroteph. The Northman paced over and placed a small bucket of water beside Aroteph, the Draul boy nodding gratefully.

The ForeSeer peered at the grey-cloaked man with the wild beard for a moment to try to understand the enigma. The Northman elected to give the Draul a gentle wink before pacing off back down the hill from whence he had come. Gathering up some liquid in twin cupped hands, the ForeSeer drank deeply not taking a pause in his consumption, a cough and splutter enacting to his undignified action. Wiping aside the droplets of

which scattered his face, Aroteph witnessed the
broad shape of Judeson sitting close by with legs
drawn up at sides. The man seemed relaxed with
his back turned towards the ForeSeer, the massive
claymore in its sheath resting nearby to the
Southron.

Judeson's legs stretched out before him, and the
Draul ForeSeer made to speak, only to find out
that he was unable to. What could he say to the
man? Why should he say anything at all? Aroteph
elected to remain in silence and just found
content to watch the man in curiosity. This
Aurman he trusted, he had not quite made up his
mind about the other one, the Mage yet. This
Southron this Judeson had something simple about
him, something comforting and with this thought
the ForeSeer rested his head against the base of
the old elm and drifted off to sleep.

**

Stirred awake by a gentle palm that roused him
from his slumber, Aroteph started up, mildly
surprised by the turn of the day around him. The
early morn light of the brilliant dawn sun bathed
him in gentle warming light. He had slept all
through the night. Though the thought made him
unsteady as he started to his feet, he realised
the exhaustion which had seized late on the
previous day must have indeed been significant.
He suddenly felt very foolish for attempting so
stubbornly to march so assertively onwards with
the two much larger and apparently much fitter
Aurmen. The cloaked form of one of them, Eckard
was nearby now, seemed as if a brutal reminder to
how out of physical standing Aroteph was with
against him.

The tall beanpole Northman had his grey mangled

hood drawn down tight and only his thick bearded chin could be seen downcast at the ForeSeer as he made his way to his feet, the gentle water droplets of the sun shower rain falling off it. Eckard grimaced and a rude snort erupted from the Aurman as brought an under-ripe and clearly hardened apple to his mouth, the crunch sounding off as if the ground had erupted. This performed act did not trouble Eckard one little bit and the Nertharnlander gestured Aroteph on towards yet another small cropping of elm trees. Circling round the immature foliage, Aroteph witnessed a weather-dulled cobblestone road, of much greater structure than the one the two Aurman and he had hitherto trekked across.

Just off a few dozen paces to the side of it crouched the imposing, broad form of Judeson, hunched over one of the travel burlaps the man had taken from the Rakoni in bitter cold waters of Wanderer's river. Aroteph shuddered at the memory of that place, not just from the remainder of the physical frostbite but of the cold-hearted battle that he had witnessed. The ForeSeer was not sure of such violence, he was repulsed by it sure enough, but at the same moment, he was curious about it, of how men could do such to each other. Hacking and stabbing, punching and kicking, biting, scratching, gauging, choking, breaking...

'Do you suffer in the cold, Aroteph?'

A loud gruff voice spoke, Aroteph looked up to observe Judeson standing close to him now, the man's hazel eyes looking gentle and warming. The ForeSeer must have given off the impression of illness of some sort for the Southron looked concerned now, the ForeSeer forced himself to shake his head in denial, though thinking on it, he did feel cold now. The sudden circumstantial

change was another topic Aroteph could not place
a hand on exactly. However, Judeson placed a
surprisingly warm hand on the boy's shoulder and
patted him, a broad smile eclipsing the
Southron's mouth. The Draul ForeSeer felt
comforted again. As if it there was never any
problem in the first place.

Few more words were uttered over the following
arcs as the two Aurman relentlessly pushed
forward, Aropeth begrudgingly following close in
their wake. Aroteph believed he was beginning to
keep pace with the frantic march of the two
Aurman warriors, either that or the duo had
commenced slowing down. The hazy distant smoke
had become drastically less, being that was. Now
the obnoxious smog seemed to be almost upon them,
as they rounded the crest of yet another untamed
hillock, if not for the shanty road, it was
quickly revealed to where the origins of such
smoke developed. A village that likes of which
was all too familiar to Arotep, the sprawl of
simple thatched roofs and one story wooden and
clay brickwork homes. The like of which stretched
out a thin slit of populated civilization; across
a narrow stretch of dirty brown river water could
be nothing other the Fartheilm town of; Heatra.

The two big Aurmen had already begun the descent
down the rocky hill to the town in the river
valley. Judeson and Eckard's long legs and
athletic characteristics taking themselves
several strides ahead as Aroteph ran to keep up.
Almost taking a tumble down, before composing
himself. Falling down the hill will not only be
an embarrassment but it could also prove quite
painful given all the loose shale rock littered
about the ground.

The Farthling town ahead had clearly altered
since he had been here and as the ForeSeer drew

closer to the settlement he saw how. Several buildings had had their roofs and walls smashed in, not enough to collapse the building but just enough to leave quite the harrowing impression on the structure. The dense murky smoke emerged from several such desecrated grounds, including the noble estate Aroteph had been held with Holloway and the Rakoni. No raging fire was unchecked however and most the flame tagged damage seemed to be on the decline, although the amount of such was staggering.

What seemed to be the collective population had gathered in the rough cut road-lines between the broken and shattered brick houses. Many faces that looked up at Aroteph as he and the two Aurmen approached were either old and wrinkled or so close to Aroteph's age he felt taken back. Wincing at the sight of frail elders cradling babies, and small children tugging on their tunic beside them. Judeson made to speak with several of the lost looking elders and he was gifted with hushed tones, voices nervous and withdrawn. The exact words, Aroteph could not make out. Aurmen had such unusual accents to the Draul Sapling he struggled to gauge the wordings when more than one of their kind spoke at once. Their drawing in and out of breaths and heavy tinged tone threw him off.

The tall black haired Nertharnlander paced past them all not making eye contact or discoursing with anyone, instead Aroteph saw him make his way over to the long-house at the dead centre of the Farthling town. Slighter larger than the estate grounds where he had been Aroteph had wondered as to what purpose the large buildings with the expansive varnished deck had. Judeson seemed to have finished with the Heatra townsfolk and broke off his engagement with them, seemed to nod and grant them one of his bright reassuring smiles. Aroteph followed without any gesturing and made his way with Judeson to the long-house where Eckard stood on the front deck, the man gently tearing a single piece of papyrus attached by a clipped off arrow-head to the building's front door.

'What is it?' Judeson inquired, attempting to look over at the paper sheet in Eckard's hands, while brushed at his brown mop of hair, clearly frustrated. "These people they won't say exactly what happened, just on and on about how they deserved what came to them, Zadma cursed nonsense."

'It's Yunsi, a Nertharn tongue, different from what you may know from the South,' Eckard answered his voice grim and quieter than his usual loud expressive self. Aroteph recalling the man sound similar on the night he had watched Eckard gaze up at the Far Above.

Aroteph like Judeson attempted to make sense of the papyrus written document as Eckard held it out, like Judeson, however, the words made no sense to him and he could not pierce its meaning at the longhouse and what it could possibly have to do with the changed Heatra. Eckard pulled the single pry sheet back to himself and looked it up and down. Whatever tongue this Yunnic was, Aroteph realised Eckard must know it or part there of as the man perused over the document and looked back at his companions. A darkened mood crossed his bushy haired face and spoke.

'It's a Kardesiu- 'a call to arms and gathering of resources',' Eckard answered Judeson looking at the man like he just fell from the Far Above. Aroteph held a similar feeling of puzzlement.

'The Preying Wolf clan of the Yunlands has made

claims on Heatra. The Raks were probably keeping them away before, now, now they saw their chance, war must have come again and the Collective and Confeds are on the move.'Eckard continued.

'What does this mean? The Raks held this town in their thrall and now raiders come and steal their resources, they left a note to tell them?' Judeson asked, hand out before him expressing his disbelief at what Eckard announced.

'Back to Void-Damned shit is what it is,' Eckard replied, throwing the note into the moist, trampled mud just outside the long-house.

'A war in the the Northern Realm then?' What does this mean? By your own words, the Farthielm was not a part of your other... nations...' Judeson started, but Eckard cutting him off.

'It's not, the Farthielm are free-towns, trading and bickering all by themselves without the self-righteous Reclaimers or the goat-taking Judicirum to dictate them. Neither were the Yunlanders, but that's all seemed to change over the arcs, another war and everyone is jumping in and taking sides to fight over the scraps.'

Judeson to Aroteph's surprise did not warrant the other man a reply and instead strode forward to stand at the door. Eventually, the broad Southron turned and looked back somewhere between Eckard and Aroteph who now felt uneasy about the whole exchange wishing that they had not returned to this bleak village. Wishing that this whole affair would end soon.

'I came to the North Lands to find allies, for in the Southrondor there is chaos, a great abundance of it. Anarchy and violence aplenty taint the countryside, men, and women are cut down like grass by the Raks. What little we have we guard closely and hide away when the need be given to.

But now....' Judeson started, his tone very grave matching Eckard.

'Now you discovered that the North is not all shiny and calm. That blood is paid in exchange for coin and dots of land.' Eckard interjected.

Judeson nodded passionately at this and Aroteph noted a great sadness painted in his handsome features. The Draul boy felt his heartstrings tighten and a cold chill ran down his spine making him shudder. Judeson seemed to notice this and looked more directly at the boy, an almost smile trying to form, but to no avail, his face remained devoid of emotion.

'At the very least the Raks have not overwhelmed you,' Judeson said.

'Not yet, the Confeds and Collective are pre-occupied with their own self-righteous bickering, the Yunlanders have seemed to have lost their identity and Raks are here just not a sizable force, but they have help, more like Holloway possibly. Or worse.' Eckard replied.

'How did you read this sign? And where have all the other folken of this town gone to? The Yunlanders you spoke of took them?' Judeson invited, gesturing to the muddy fallen Yunsi notice.

'They were conscripted into forced service of the Preying Wolf clan, a tribe aligned to the Collective. They took whatever resources they deemed fit for their effort. The Farthielm has long been a reaping ground for the larger nations to steal from." Eckard stated.

'Then why torch buildings and knock down walls? What is the point? Heatra offered no resistance the Raks had already taken that.'

'It was either by design of vengeance possibly against the Raks or simply out of malice'

'And where was their town Steward in all of this, the coward that sided with the Raks. That murdered, Ves....' Judeson paused and drew in a rasping breath between clenched teeth. 'Perhaps the Yunlanders stretched him em up?'

Aroteph felt distant in all this discussion of issues and places he had only vague knowledge of. He reckoned himself a ghost in this moment, being of incorporeal existence drifting about watching the affairs of mortals go about. Perhaps he was the wind, uncaring and fathoming little of all that lay about. These thoughts frightened him and he shook his head, were they his own? If not who's were they?Aroteph shook himself as if to merely shake off the undesirable thoughts that swam in his head, he felt himself slipping as if he hung helplessly on a proverbial edge.

The excessively audible screech of the great timber rolling doors being forcibly parted at the front of the long house brought Aroteph back to the world of the living and breathing. Judeson pushed through the now open threshold and on into the expansive recesses of the building proper. Eckard motioned for Aroteph to follow and started inwards of his own volition. The interior scene was a scattered mess heap, tables and chairs were thrown about haphazardly and the remnants of clay mugs took up residences in the spaces between. Aroteph tiptoed over the shattered pieces as he followed the trail of Eckard. This particular journey did not last very long and soon they were all standing still looking at the front serving bar area. Though its purpose was not one Aroteph could comprehend he did feel intrigued at the set-up of it all, large oak, clasp iron-fastened barrels containing something still inside. Why had the Yunlanders not taken these when all other food stores seemed to have been raised in some

form or another. Aurmans were alien to the
ForeSeer and he did not bother it another
thought, he had enough as it is.

A stocky and sweating mangle of a man came out
from the behind the varnished yet now grime-
ridden timber bar-front. The Aurman possessed
clear looks being perplexed by the new arrivals
in his vicinity. He held both fat palms out in a
sign of submission and gave an anxious looking
smile at them. Judeson closed on the man in a
blur of motion, both of the Southron's arms
closed about the thick woollen coat of the
barkeep. Pushing the generous form of Bursal into
the timber bench, Judeson stood over him
imposingly. Aroteph stepped back, frightened by
this sudden escalation of tension.

'Is this where you were whilst your 'people'
suffered? Hiding like a worm in fucking mud?'
Judeson hissed between barred teeth, his tanned
face a flash of determined malice. 'How could you
stand by and let Vestras be killed. An innocent.
How can you fucking live with yourself?'

Entailing the namesake insult imposed upon him
Bursal seemed to squirm anxiously in Judeson's
sturdy iron grip. The round shape of inn keeper
beneath the Southron warrior shrunk away as if by
sheer will of Judeson alone. Aroteph was
frightened all over again by how quickly Aurman
turned in emotions. Glancing back over his
shoulder the Draul witnessed Eckard moving from
the doorway, his eyes passing over Bursal and the
imposing Judeson. The big North-lander stalked
past them all towards the back room behind the
bar, relatively indifferent to the whole
unfolding scenario.

'Please...' Aroteph began, his voice a hoarse
broken whisper, escaping his lips before he had

time to formulate a proper argument for himself. Judeson turned around in a start his eyes grim orb of furious deliverance. The Southron's tanned, determined face began to soften at sight of what Aroteph realised must have been full of pain and fear.

'Let the pathetic wretch go,' Eckard spoke sternly, a hand resting on Judeson's shoulder, the Northman reappearing from seemingly nowhere.

The Southron proved unperturbed by Eckard's return and maintained eye contact with Aroteph, his prolonged stare shifting to a halfhearted smile on the Draul. Behind them, the sunken form of Bursal cowered into a dirty corner of the Inn, the big frame of the Farthling seeming to shiver uncontrollably. Like a pinned worm, Aroteph observed. A fittingly adequate description and one supplied previously by his friends nearby. Judeson extended out an open palm to Aroteph to take.

Aroteph quickly forgot the innkeeper and took up the Southron's offer. He felt comfortable again. Despite the awful devastation visited upon this small and sleepy community, Aroteph found himself at ease with his surroundings and in the custodianship of these two for-biddable men, he realised nothing could go wrong. At least the hope of which was something to hold onto. Pushing through the oak doors into the seething cauldron of wanton Aurman forced disaster, Aroteph, Judeson, and Eckard were encircled by the converging mass of Heatra survivors.

Ashen and close drawn faces gaped at them, unasked questions are written plain on their faces, like the mud and grime on their clothes. Somewhere at the back of the disorganised scores of solemn villagers, a babe cried out, an audible screech of desperate struggle, the sounds of which could possibly be a figurative sign of the surrounding scene. Aroteph shook at the encompassing forms of children and old female Aurmen. He wanted to do something, anything that could help somehow. Something. Aroteph closed his eyes and fell deep into concentration, just like he did when the two Aurmen he now had for companions fought for his release.

The cries of babes in arms gently shifted away like passing clouds. Murmuring unsteady tones seemed to cease and desist like they were never there at all. The broken down the world outside was no longer and a gradual calm was settling. Though it felt forced somehow.

If he assisted them in their time of need, he could surely do so for this despondent rabble. Aroteph found himself being tugged onwards, solid hands being his guide. The body heat and mumbling voices of nearby persons passed all around him once again. Realising he must have been pulled through the mass of Aurmanity. Another hand gripped his shoulder, not hard but firm, longer fingers than one around his hand. Eckard's deeply resonating voice sounding behind

'You need to stop ForeSeer.'

Judeson pulled up short in front of Aroteph and the Draul boy fell into his side, still tightly gripping his hand. Now with both his eyes open again, the boy saw the curious glances of the massed crowd of Heatra townsfolk, most of whom were curiously on their hands and knees all-of-a -sudden. A handful of the more elder in tooth lay sprawled on the ground, puffing out sighs of exhaustion. If fear was a dense paint on their expressions before, the layers of emotion had increased tenfold now. Nervous twitches and heavy bated breaths came out from the surrounding populace into the bitter cold winds of the valley town. Between the low lying mist that now spread throughout the village, the Aurmen elders and children pulled back from the trio of Aroteph, Judeson, and Eckard. Some even averting their eyes closing them altogether. Aroteph made out hushed prayers being spoken from some of the townsfolk.

'We have overstayed our....' Eckard began but choose purposely to cut himself short. The tall onyx-haired Nertharnlander instead stalking away from the crowd.

Beckoning Judeson and Aroteph to follow suit. Not with any real haste or panic, one may mind. Pure unfiltered calmness. A sentiment Aroteph found himself not sharing at this one tense moment. Everything seemed to have descended into something much worse than it already was. Not that such a metamorphosis of misery had only just occurred. As it was the current state of the broken down town was enough to speak volumes.

Judeson's strong hands gently pushed the ForeSeer ever onwards out of the town and towards a steep escarpment. Presenting yet another challenge on the road home. A testament to their how difficult Aroteph's life had become. The voice of Judeson behind him roused him from his thoughts.

'Hurry up young one we need to catch up with that spider legged Northman, he is not stopping for no one.'

With the hood down and cloaked wrapped tight about himself, the quickly disappearing form of Eckard some score of paces ahead only seemed to increase in speed toward the rocky natural wall ahead. Aroteph hastily threw both legs forward and yearned for the thought of any real rest from the world.

**

The cool night air set in as a steady mist
streaming through the Far Above, obscuring the
starlight. Aroteph pulled his thick woollen coat
tight about himself for the umpteenth time as if
the chill would abruptly dissipate if he
performed the action again. True to the form of
his luck lately nothing of the former mentioned
occurred. The night chill still fell about and
the ForeSeer was apt to shuddering and shaking
once more until the fire on damp wood was
started. Judeson crouched over the dug out fire
pit attempting to gauge a spark from the drenched
twigs and foliage.

The cloaked form of Eckard returned to the camp,
drawing his hood and looking between Aroteph and
the deeply focused Judeson; brilliant blue eyes
curiously evaluating the unfolding dynamic, a wry
half grin creeping across the black bearded face
as if a source of amusement was to be had in the
current scene.

'Step back Southron my aim is not the greatest,'
Eckard called out, his right hand extending
outward from his sides; finger tips stretched to
full length as if he were going to reach the fire
pit from whence he stood.

Judeson stood up not in any real haste and
granted a puzzling look to the Northlander. The
face of which Aroteph was sure he had now too.
Eckard nodding as if that alone was enough of an
answer. Judeson shrugged and walked away giving
the tall Northman his wish. A shimmer blur moved
about the firepit and a very brief and small
crackle and spark procured. Aropepth felt the air
around grow somewhat warmer somehow and then all
of a sudden the previously unlit pit was ablaze

with flames. Seemed a little over done however as flames licked up the edges and smaller fires started out around the campsite. Both Judeson and Eckard quick to stamp down on the rogue fires with heavy boots.

'Told you my aim is askew' Eckard chuckled out. Judeson shook his head and made his way back to the fire to get more fuel for it to burn, the big Southron motioning Aroteph forward, The ForeSeer very grateful for the exchange and the heat to stop the shudders that had overtaken him.

With the fire's life ignited the party sat in silence taking in each other's company, discourse minimal. But somehow Aroteph felt they were closer than ever before. Every now and again he would look up to the gentle warming smile of the tanned face of Judeson who sat shivering (although the fire was close) with his cloak pulled about him. At other moments Aroteph witnessed the lopsided smirk of the black born face of Eckard. The brilliant sky blue eyes giving nothing away, yet at the same time telling a thousand tales.

'You should be more careful with your *talents*, ForeSeer,' Eckard spoke, breaching the silence with a tightly closed sentence, the big Nertharnlander electing to not wait for a reply and bunking down on the earth nearby.

Aroteph tensed remembering the equally anxious moments back in the village of Heatra. When he felt separate from himself as if he were the very wind itself. He thought back to when all the people seemed so calm and collected, unlike their living quarters that had been visited by disastrous ruination. Yet that confounding and beautiful stillness had not been right. It felt off-putting. With Eckard's words spiralling

through his head in a hefty current, the Draul
ForeSeer felt shame and guilt flood in on the
tide within.

'Do not worry yourself youngling. Today is
another day.' Judeson voiced, a gentle smile
creasing his mouth. The big shouldered Southron
patted out the grassy earth beneath him and
settled down for the night like his taller,
hairier counterpart before him.
'Do not wear your troubles on your face boy,
otherwise the wind-banshees will come and
expression will be stuck like that awful mask for
all your arcs to come,' Judeson added as he layed
down.
The ForeSeer could not have felt safer now and he
had ever in his whole life, and he drifted off to
sleep near a steady fire and strong company.

***

Something felt wrong, every strand of detail out
of place, every moment flawed beyond repair.
Judeson had a grim feeling in his stomach and
could not shake it. Aroteph the small,
brilliantly sliver-hair Draul youth seemed out of
sorts and quieter than usual. A dozen paces ahead
Eckard strolled as if no worry in the world could
be had. The tall Northman whistled away a
chaotic, exuberant melody. But Judeson had that
feeling again. The one where he just knew,
somehow he knew something was about to go down.
Most usually it involved steel, fire, and mayhem
or perhaps all three.
Judeson peered across at the Draul lad who seemed
intent on dragging his feet in the soft wet
grass. Reaching a hand out to lightly tap the
shoulder of the boy. Judeson drew a deep breath.
'Your ah...talents?' Judeson began, quickening

his pace, to talk about such things as Magik were uncomfortable, to say the least for Judeson.

'Yes?' Aroteph spoke now scurrying after Judeson. 'I..ah...Do you sense...anything?' Judeson continued, gulping and regretting the words he had spoken to immediate effect.

The Draul ForeSeer pulled up in tracks and looked at Judeson intently. Puzzlement or intrigue perhaps? Whatever it was Judeson did not hold his gaze and averted his eyes from the lad. Half-ashamed by his questions now. It was strange and cruel in itself to think this boy held so much potential power. He looked barely past the age of crying at scrapping his knee from a fall.

'It doesn't work that way. I don't know exactly.' Aroteph stuttered. Down-casting his eyes and taking on a solemn look that made Judeson's heart feel like it would shatter into a thousand pieces.

'Don't worry young one, it was a foolish question to ask of you.' Judeson answered, making to turn back on their path into the Draul'estla'theilm.

'I see things, faces, places, names, times, those sorts of things. But it is most difficult to place the here and now. It is a real bother to make sense of what all of it means.' Aroteph blurted out in rapid succession.

Ahead, Eckard had stopped and about turned to face both Judeson and Aroteph. The dark hair enigma coming but six paces from them, to clear his throat in a clear pronouncement.

There is no reason to fret ForeSeer, you are being taken somewhere safe now,' Eckard said, the Northerner's gruff voice presented a reassuring and steady outlook on matters.

The Northman turned once more sweeping up the battered grey cloak of his and taking the long legged stride onwards, Eckard's over-the-top pace taking him far ahead once more and the Judeson and Aroteph breaking into a brisk march to keep up.

ACT II

In the Den of the Beast

...many theories allude to the origins of the incredibly strange mountainous fastness that is the commonly known as the 'Boundary'. Including a

bizarre left field theory of mythical Rock-Giants being the mountains themselves,

The creatures supposedly laid to settle in a hundred-thousand arc slumber.

A more popularly held belief that is the long dead Imperium and their self-titled

High-Born Masters created the Boundary Mountains, other scholars have vastly varying

alliterations but many of them frazzled and lacking in much of the way of solid detail.

One fact; solidly uncontested in all of this, is that the Boundary is most definitely not a natural occurrence and most probably a phenomenon caused by the mysterious works of Magik.

Curten Alder the Third

Stories of Mountains

1807 ATF

1st Stanza

The two continents stretch on and encompass; many, many peoples; Many languages, many thoughts, many ideals, all of which are differing and twisting threads. Knots of Aurman concerns, Kobold ambitions and Draul verses alike.

The tales one may tell of lands close and far away are a link in itself. For all the differences on the road an aurman can see is but lines in the sand. Sand on the beach of an everexpanding nature only held back by our own lessons that have yet to be learned.

Writ of the Road

Author Unnamed

There was no welcoming party. No signs of Raijin nor of the mysterious Kail to greet them. In fact, there was very little in the way of any Watcher let alone Draul anywhere at all for several leagues into the dense forest realm. Judeson knew something was not right now. He had never gotten this far last time. It was as if the Draul had completely changed their strict border policies altogether since last they had been here. No, something was definitely unsettling about this entire affair.

As if from a bad dream, the broad form of Krikza's sharlett appeared from between great oaks. The hood was drawn back and her hard features set grim, a look of determination clearly written on her face. Eckard nearby did not move and the lopsided smile that both confused and frustrated Judeson was taken up once again. The tall seemed to only find comedy in the dark look the Sharlett turned on him, hatred burning in her eyes.

Judeson's heart sunk back into the fathomless depths of a bleak existence. The Shralett and her fellow Draul Watchers formed a wall around the party of him, Eckard and the Draul youngling. An impassable presence intent on something he could not foretell. Tensing and peering about at the enveloping hunters with drawn bows, the Southron found himself sweating in the bitter cold. Fear was not really a feeling he harboured any longer, it was more of an expectation of chaos to be commenced that he employed, a calling to the carnage.

'The ForeSeer deliver him to us.' The robust female Watcher bellowed, without any discernible subjective emotion, an objective command at it's finest.

'No,' Eckard answered bluntly, a smile askew crooked smile crossing his face, his eyes alight with excitement. Judeson thought the Northman clearly mad.

'I hereby enact the official charter of The Draul'estla'theilm for an order of restraint against undesired Outlanders' The Sharlett continued as if Eckard's answer was worth no reply.

'From the new Seprithot Krikza the 1st of his name!'

'To the Abyss with the Tyrant!' A score of shouts rang out from the surrounding woods; everywhere and nowhere, in particular and all at once. Judeson glanced over and saw Eckard had not moved nor did he look at all fazed. Aroteph's face was painted thickly in fear.

The Shralett tensed, taken back and grim anger coating her face, she motioned her men forward and Judeson readied himself. Unseen Draul flanked around them, and the soft padder of feet concluded this case in point.

Surrounded outnumbered and in a fight, he was not

entirely certain of the cause. Judeson knew it
all too well. A sudden, unexpected and impossibly
loud hiss sounded out. It was if the very air
crackled around them. Tingles spiralling up
Judeson's spine and he made to turn to Aroteph
and Eckard. Who were no longer visible, a thick
billowing smoky haze obscuring everything around.
Shouts of frustration and clearly audible
trampling of the forest-realm foliage accompanied
the new hazy revelation. Shadowed movements of
activity and panic become the norm and chaos took
centre stage.

*

The hissing sound was incredible and awful all at
the same time. Aroteph founding solace in
covering his ears with hands in an effort to
block out the audible nightmare.
Eckard turned and winked at Aroteph, the boy had
no time to respond when the surrounding woods
become enveloped in a sudden and impossible fog,
the Northman lost in it. The unfathomable
provided a murky cover and seemed to unfurl from
nowhere and everywhere at the same time. The
blind fog clouds were as dense as oil and as dark
as a starless night. Screams and protesting yells
sounded out all around, the thunder of hoofs and
footprints on the soft foliage of the forest came
on exponentially and louder with panic. The Draul
ForeSeer was thrown into confusion and everything
that was before was suddenly and steadfastly
gone. Vanished, no more, Aroteph forced himself
forward into the gloom, a strong hand stayed his
progress and he heard the gentle flow of Judeon's
voice.
'Easy now lad, I believe this is our chance.'
Aroteph was confused and frightened, but the
staying hand of Judeson provided both a physical

guide and a calming presence for the ForeSeer. Being led onward and over the rain-drenched earth and tangled tree roots Aroteph's pounding heart forced its way up his throat. The Draul boy was awfully grateful he had the big Southron to assist him now, the thought of being alone in this moment unthinkable.

*

The Nerthanlander Mage stalked his way through the dense Magik induced fog clouds. Making sure of his path by checking his footing and surroundings as best he possibly can. Eckard cast threads of Magik outward and around, sensing the scurrying of panicked and confused Draul Watchers. Streams of arrows darted past misplacing their intended marks and falling around in a scattered haphazard nature with the marksmen unable to sight their targets properly. It was well known circumstantial fact that the Draul with their crimson piercing eyes could see far better in the darkness than any average Aurman could. But in this Magikaly enhanced fog-ridden chaos they were as disadvantaged as anyone else. Screams and shouts of frustration rang out in various Draul tongues. Heavy footfalls sounded all around and Eckard snicked through, with a clearly defined goal in mind. Keep track of the big all-too-serious Southron and the ForeSeer boy and make sure they made it out.

The Mage knew the Southron was an expert tracker by now. Eckard also knew Judeson would rely on his intuition and skills in these curious circumstances and not ride his luck. Of this, he did not have to worry himself. However, if they made it out of the fog Eckard also the Southron would be furious to learn the Mage had known what was to happen all along. That would have to wait.

Passing a dense foliage scrub and bypassing a small stream and intricate crisscross frame of ancient oak roots, Eckard made for what he felt was the way out of the fog. His Magik senses alerting him to a cropping of birch ahead a few paces away. Out from the flora came a blurred shadowy figure, armed and moving towards Eckard. The Nertharnlander threw off images, shapes, and sounds by Grey Magik, but the apparition had somehow stumbled closer to him with a poleaxe in hand.

Eckard shrunk past the apparition closing in on him and moved to the side of the Draul Watcher. Laboured breathing of the border guard was heard by Eckard and with the lightest of breathing, he flew past him and out of any clear line of sight. Beyond the cropping of scattered birch, the fog seemed to be clearing up and despite a rogue arrow whizzing by Eckard's head by at least ten paces, the Northerner could not sense any Draul Watchers nearby.

Making his way up a slight muddy incline into a forest ahead, Eckard noticed the fog reducing. Somewhere ahead a mere dozen of paces the murky gloom was clearing up. The audible screech of a blade being withdrawn from a scabbard sounded just behind Eckard. The Nerthlander turned sharply and shifted his weight to the side as a wickedly curved blade darted past him. Readying the Salmian rapier he had taken from Holloway and a hunting knife in a heartbeat, Eckard waited on the attacker's next approach for him.

Iron on iron rang out the rapier parried another carefully directed sweep by the hooked blade from the shadowy apparition. Fearing somehow a Watcher had tracked him down Eckard soon found himself face to face with his perceived adversary as he moved to the side in the dance of combat with the figure. A brilliantly coloured and chaotically patterned face mask obscured the attacker and a loose fitting woolen coat laid over glimpses of plate and chain maille for the rest of the figure.

Preparing another charge the masked adversary tilted forwards but Eckard moved first casting out a Magik projected illusion of himself at the figure on the full on charge, as the Mage shifted to the side and flicked his rapier across the confused attacker. The rapier bite through the painted mask's edges and met soft cheek flesh beneath, the masked aggressor attempted to pivot and adjust his stance to meet Eckard but the Northerner moved again, sticking the serrated hunting knife through the back of upper leg just shy of the lower buttocks, T=the masked attacker falling to the ground in agony and clear agitation.

At least a dozen footsteps sounded all about the vicinity and Eckard saw glimpses of other painted masks, all very different from the other ones around them. Now he was getting closer.

'Sar Eckard Delmose Farth' called out a familiar feminine voice in a fastidiously serious tone. Finally.

*

Judeson domineered through the impossible fog cover, with a one-handed but steady grip on the bastard clay-more of Jude, his other hand firmly pulled the Aroteph- the ForeSeer boy along. Figures clashed in the shadow-stricken gloom and the sounds of combat, steel clashing and parrying sounded all around. Frustrated shouts and beckoning calls in numberless tongues and accents were everything. Judeson made sure for up tenth time the Aroteph was right next to him in this terrible murk and pushed forward towards what he thought and hoped was a clearing.

Right into the path of at least a dozen armed combatants; arrayed about expertly in a defensive wedge formation, hooked blades at the ready and terrifically coloured masks obscuring their faces. They wore heavy woollen coats were almost collectively worn by them all and their stances were eerily similar in nature. If not for the incredibly differing face masks on their adjacent faces none of them could really be told apart.

Aroteph tugged at Judeson's side sleeve and the Southron glanced momentarily over at the Draul boy, seeing fear and anxiety plain as day on the boy's features. What he portrayed, Judeson felt inside now, tense and battle ready. The sword of Jude would be called into action once more...if not for a tall and familiar person making themselves' known through the crowd of colourful but fearsome masked men.

'Well met friend Judeson, but your blade is not needed now,' Raijin stated, gesturing for Judeson and Aroteph to follow him into the mysterious crowd of masked men.

2nd Stanza

….as well as the Isles of Kormai and RoseWood and rumours of a Draul colonoy in the Lanka jungles of the Southrondor. There is also a sizable population of Draul peoples in the distant Eastern Khasas.

On the Tribune Isles, Draul and Aurmen had existed alongside each other for generations. A booming fishing and manufacturing industry is growing and bright things can be seen coming on the horizon for them. Veroncea is a little difficult to learn much from due to their strict isolationist policy, but there were a number of escort ships with Draul sailors on them when we skirted their coast earlier this arc.

One of the stranger cases of Draul peoples is certainly that of Taurnton. A island just over two leagues from the bustling city harbour of Freeport. Isolating themselves in exclusion, much like Veroncea, these Draul cover themselves' head to toe in monk's garbs, constantly wear ornamental masks and worship the sea as if it were God. My study of Taurnton was limited to observation from the safe distance of a ship or from the very few that came to Freeport to trade. Further study will be needed of course in future volumes...

Journeys amongst the Draul - Part III by Sar Alverlin
Ugusten Moor, 2009 ATF

The masked enigmas stood off to all the sides around the arguing main group. Backed up against trees and hooked blades sheathed but idle hands staying on hilts. Every single one of the warriors was poised to jump into action at any moment. Ever vigilant - this lot were Judeson noted. Closer by Raijin - the lean Draul Watcher, the mysterious Kail, Aroteph, Luciarn, and Eckard all stood around in a loose circle in a dim lit clearing of the forest. Luciarn's mouth worked away, words and phrases of places and people Judeson had no prior knowledge of sounded off one by one like a call to arms.

Kail interjected every now and again reinforcing points the well-rounded merchant spoke or arguing against them. The woman that seemed to look like a Draul yet was clearly not from the vastly differing skin tone from Raijin's own; had a cold edge about her and when she argued her point was well taken beneath layers of certainty and a certain air of authority. Raijin stayed with his ever-quiet and singsong tone, only speaking between breaks from the previous two. Aroteph looked between all of the members, his curiosity-filled glance staying on Judeson and also Eckard the longest. As for the giant North man, he never said a word, with his hood drawn and seemingly his glance focused off somewhere into the trees.

Luciarn Nonkar once more argued about an island called 'Kormai' that Judeson was inevitably unfamiliar with. The subject of Luciarn's concerns laying in something to do with the supply of something the Southron did not know and tinkering of a religious cult of 'Reachers' in the local affairs. It all made very little sense and as Kail continued the topic at hand Judeson lost interest once more, wondering how long they would linger here. Until the words became familiar; the discussion started to click into place.

'...Aroteph will have to go with the, it is the only way and Kormai is far from safe Luciarn, supposedly neutrality does not apply to him.' Kail stated her opinion, her voice dripping in acid and direct to the point.

Judeson tensed, he found his palms sweating, despite the bitter cold chill of the morning air in the forest. What was all of this chitter chatter actually about. They briefly mentioned Arotep, and sending him somewhere. Gods he wished had been playing more attention to the conversation previously. Now was a good enough time as any to voice his concerns with all that was said.

'Where is the boy being taken? What for?' Judeson spoke up, his voice unbroken and precise, surprising even himself with his profound confidence.

The rest of the party seemed to all turn on him at once and bemused expressions crossed their faces. All except Eckard who sported that lopsided grin he so favoured.

'Judeson, not here' Eckard voiced, his tone soft and serious, arms still crossed and his expression remaining neutral.

'No, no, I need...we need to know what is happening. Why is Aroteph being taken away from his home? When was it our original mission to bring him back? The meeting at the great hall, was it all a charade? What was the point of it, if...' Judeson spoke, his voice giving out and felt himself trembling. Reaching out an grasping Aroteph's hand on his own. What had it all been for? Everything suddenly seemed relentlessly pointless. Aroteph going off with strangely masked warriors, Vestras, sweet unassuming Vestras dying.

'The Draul who are running the theilm are not to be trusted. Krikza has absolute control and is not to be trivialized. They have fallen so far there is no chance now. The ForeSeer had to be taken away, Judeson.' Raijin interjected. The tall drink of the water of a Draul moving towards the shaking Southron.

'This was the plan all along though, wasn't it?' Judeson huffed, clear annoyance on his face and tone.

'The North is not what it first seems, Southron. The charade that was played was always in progress, it is unfortunate that you were caught up in all this.' Kail retorted, her brilliant emerald eyes focusing on Judeson. Calming him somehow, ensuring him that every word she spoke was the uninhibited truth.

Judeson lets a maudlin demeanor take hold, he suddenly thought himself mawkishly sentimental towards the whole endeavour. As if the party around him save the ForeSeer child were all calm, collected and dedicated to the task at hand. His emotions getting the better of him, and he knew he was better than that. Nodding his understanding at Kail, she returned the action and the party set off once again.

They moved as silently as possible through the dense undergrowth, each member of the advancing party taking carefully constructed steps. Over ancient tree root systems, across steadily flowing cold streams they made their way forward. Judeson following in their wake, a sense of somber hallowing set upon him. Attempting to read the expressions or the scattered and rare speakings of the others to gauge if they felt any emotion similar to his own. Raijin seemed relaxed even somewhat relieved, yet that was how he always seemed to appear in the limited period of time Judeson had known him. The pretty young woman known as Kail was deadly serious and did not so much as make a noise. Eckard remained how he always seemed to be. And thus Judeson was left to keep following in silence and begrudged confusion.

The masked men ushered them forward and away through deep foliage and out into a narrow valley where the ground had fallen away over many arcs. Deep set willow tree roots sprouted from the earthen walls and some ducking and weaving were required to avoid entanglement. Out of the close set quarters of the old valley-trench, the party made theirs into a clearing of sorts where a puddle of stagnant water had fallen from the canopy. Standing on the edges of the rain water pond and facing towards the narrow trench in a defensive formation. The masked ones raised swords and shields.

'We are close now.' Raijin voiced looked ahead with his eyes closed in concentration. 'Just over the other side of these woods and beyond the river.'

'We are close to what?' Judeson inquired looking about the others for any betraying signs of something to tell him where they were headed.

'East-watch, Raijin's temple,' Eckard said in response moving with both his thumbs tucked into his weapon's belt, motioning the others to follow him.

"And what is Raijin doing? Why is he just standing there." Judeson asked, making a slow trot forward with Aroteph's hand still on his own.

'Making sure we make it there in one piece. Turning off all the wards and traps.' Kail explained following Eckard.

"Why would there be traps in the forest? Who would put all of those there? How is he turning them off with..just..standing..." Judeson began.

Lucairn walked by him and tapped him on the shoulder and signalled forward into the direction of Eckard and Kail.

'To safe guard the last Haven on the mainland of the free Draul realm. We did. And Magik, lad' Lucairn stated matter of factually, moving ahead to keep up with the others.

**

The bayside temple of East-watch was more of a fortified keep than a place of worship. Murder holes galore, high battlements and steep, winding stairs awaited them. Judeson found himself confused as to why Raijin insisted the place was really only for devout pilgrims and not really a manageable fortress. Or so the Draul Mage had insisted on the way to East-Watch.

'You think it is an ideal castle don't you Southron? That Krikza and his followers dare not touch anyone here?' Eckard asked. Walking ahead of Judeson to the base of the stairs.

'If there were anyone here to defend it, that would probably be a close truth.' Raijin answered before Judeson even had time to contemplate an answer of his own.

'Then why are we even here if we are not safe as you all so proclaim,' Judeson spoke back, making sure he was not forgotten this time round.

Nearby Kail laughed, more so a brief giggle than anything.

'The Southron raises good points, if he knew more it may even be an excellent one,' Kail stated.

'Then humour me, what is it I do not know.' Judeson voiced. Turning to look among the entirety of the group in anticipation.

The answer came from none of the adults of the company. Instead, Aroteph spoke up from where he stood with the majority of the mysteriously masked warriors.

'It is time for rest, for all of us. Judeson answers are the wind, it comes back around when needed. And all your questions are in the wind. But now, now we have to revise.' Aroteph said, his voice, serious assured and unlike anything, the boy had sounded like beforehand.

'The ForeSeer wakes in his homeland.'Eckard proclaimed, taking a swig from a bottle in his hand. Where did he even get that? Judeson thought.

Eckard gestured for the others to continue forward across the narrow vine-tangled, obsidian bridge that spanned across a slim Saltwater stream to the seaside keep of East-watch. One by one the company proceeded onward. Three masked warriors paced forwards followed by Raijin, Luciarn, Kail, Eckard and Aroteph. Judeson followed in the wake of the remaining masked ones. The impressive nature of the seemingly run-down keep ahead bringing awe and a welcome departure from increasingly confusing situations presented to him, that he saw little chance of abating him now.

**

Judeson awoke to the flickering daystar's light seeping in through the murder slits in the blackened stone walls. The East-Watch keep proved to trap in a chilly temperament, and Judeson found himself shivering, drawing the thin silk blanket about his person tighter. Footsetps sounded off nearby as someone approached his quarters. The heavy oak door creaked open and in came the dark complexion of the merchant Luciarn - whom Judeson had first met in Eckard's company.

'It is almost time for us to move out, Judeson,' Luciarn stated. As he handed down a clay cup of steaming kefra onto the benchtop near to Judeson's bed.

'Tell me Luciarn, was it a profitable trip for you to lose your Draul connections, see off a child from his home and make a renegade of yourself here?' Judeson asked as he propped himself up.

Luciarn huffed in heavy exasperation as he dropped himself onto solitary stool of the perfectly square room.

'All that has happened, has happened for a purpose Judeson. All of it concise, purposeful. Aroteph is safe now, and a tyrant's reign is damaged.' Luciarn stated, his mousy-brown eyes meeting Judeson's own and holding there.

Judeson felt a sudden chill run down his spine and he twitched in response. He felt a sense of light headed-sens overcome him. It was not the sleep, he had felt refreshed when he had awoken. In place of his irritation withy Luciarn as he walked through the door and all the others who did even bother to answer his questions; he now felt eased; far less stressed and free from all his worries.

Lucairn ahead of him looked determined and serious. The balding merchant's eyes focused solely and directly on Judeson. Never seeming to break away or even blink. But the whole strangeness of Luciarn's gaze did not perturb Judeson. Should it? What was happening? If the situation was wrong and out of place it did not feel so. All Judeson felt was relieved, soothed; like he was back asleep when in truth he was awake.

'It all makes very little sense to me...I...came here...' Judeson started, finding that his words did not flow all too freely when spoken.

'It is a difficult time for us all,' Luciarn replied.

The merchant looked out a thin murder hole slit, drawing closer to it as he did so. A faraway expression was present on him now. Judeson stood up from the bed and elected to look out an another of the tiny openings in the obsidian . walls. The forest realm below was wild and tangled. A healthy flow of glistening waters tumbled down the hill onto the shoreline. The woods broken up here by rough black and grayish sands and eventually the dark waters of the sea. Of what Judeson had seen of the northern lands, it was all much darker, much colder but beautiful nevertheless.

It was very much different from Judeson's own home - the Southrondor. But it some ways it was vastly similar. He had to return. Though he had imagined under differing circumstances, his return would have been more fruitful. He had to work with what he had - one of his father's favourite expressions.

'I have to return to my homeland soon. Though I came here for allies, something to help us. I will gladly accept whatever I can get as service for my own to you.' Judeson finally said.

'I apologize for dragging a man of purpose into our own chaotic tangle.' the voice of Eckard

called into the room, even as the beanpole
Northman stepped into view.

The tall Nertharnlander had his usual grey, messy
cloak about himself and his wild mop of dark
curls now untied altogether, the black untidy
beard almost seeming to merge into the hair of
his head.

Eckard motioned for Judeson to proceed forward.
Beyond the cobwebbed stone, of the portal way was
an open hallway devoid of any traces of dust. The
encasing walls of the chamber, however was coated
in dusty grime. This contrast led to an
intriguing image. In the cleaned down, centre was
a broad sweep of old oak workbenches, dim
candles, and pine stools. Luciarn took up a
position on one table with Raijin, as Kail sat
down at another across from them. Eckard gestured
for Judeson to sit; as the Northman left the
hallway.

'We should come clean with you, Southron' Kail
suddenly spoke, her little voice seemed to
resonate now, louder and more firm within the
confined obsidian walls.

'It would be nice' Judeson answered immediately,
attempting to not sound reverentially harsh in
his tone.

'We are all Mages if that much was not clear by
now, and we have been informed by Eckard you are
learning of Magik at a steady beginner's pace'
Lucairn interjected.

Judeson held back his apprehension of the
unfolding scenario and nodded. These people
seemed trustworthy, too honourable to be indebted
into the Black Arts and in turn be subservient to
the wicked ways of the Raks.

'We are members of an Order, a Pact if you will,

established long ago, many many arcs before now: That is determined to defend and uphold freedom against the Rakon and their Masters.' Raijin now said, in turn the chorus of speakers growing and all looking far more determined and serious than he had seen before.

'Eckard wants to induct you, wants you to become part of this Pact, that we will honour, Southron. But you must take care of what is to come.'

'And what is to come?'Judeson asked even when the voice of Eckard called out, impossibly loud and pronounced.

'Ready folks!'

'Hurry up knight we are starving' Kail said, laughing in a soft soothing voice, her hitherto serious demeanor passing momentarily.

Eckard returned as if waiting for the most dramatic entry. Knight? Is that what Kail had called him? Judeson thought. The Northman (Knight?) pushed in a trolley of various exotic looking fruits, loaves of whole grain and still warm bread and a delicious looking plate of dried red meats. Judeson could almost salivate at the sight and smell of it all.

'Stuff yourselves silly!' Eckard bellowed, raising both hands up.

3rd Stanza

The Draul have withdrawn more and more in recent times, due to the chaos of the Plague in the Southrondor and all the unfolding events from that. As far as we academics in the Confederation know, there are no colonies of the Draul in the South. The esthla-theilm is open to trade but with highly strict regulations for the Confederation, the Collective and the Fartheilm.

Most of our information concerning the Draul mostly comes from the exiled 'Oathbreakers' in the towns of the Fartheilm, the prairies of the Yunlands or the isle of Kormai. It would be highly beneficial for study purposes to be able to access the Eastern Khasas, but recent developments in the civil unrest on the eastern coast of the Nerthielm and the unprecedented extreme increase in storm patterns in the Omakis ocean east of the Tribune has made study of the East, very difficult to say the least.

A retrospective study of Journeys amongst the Draul
by Professor Danian Avlerin Selk, head of Extra-Race Studies

at Tamisk University, ancestor of the late Sar Alverlin
Ugusten Moor , 2951 ATF

The main foyer that had served as the makeshift
gathering hall of the group was now all but
devoid of everyone barring Eckard and Kail, the
latter had propped herself up on an old work
bench. Eckard guessed the foyer area had probably
once served as the main hall for religious types,
priests, and acolytes, scurrying about with all
the fear of their gods in tow. Kail had swept
away all the settling dust with Magik, the
interior relatively clean once more. Though most
of the historic scarring and natural
deterioration remained. Kail now sat opposite him
and made no conceivable move to speak or even
acknowledge him.

'I read part of his surface thoughts, he seems
genuine, honourable and a perfect companion. We
need folks like him if we are going to try to do
anything right.'Eckard broke the silence.

'Right? You speak of right but you use Magik to
read the man's thoughts?' Kail answered, giving
off one of her trademark questioning stares. The
ones she always seemed to hold so very well.

'Excuse me, missy, you just Magikly swept the
floor. How is not an abuse of power?' Eckard
probed, smiling mischievously back at the woman;
who now had her eyes narrowed at him.

'The floor is quite different than a living,
breathing Aurman you wish to recruit Eckard.'
Kail stated, crossing her arms.

By Yahasa she looked good when she did that. -
Eckard thought, *all these arcs and she still made
him feel like a silly boy sometimes*.

'And do you think your new-found ally will
rejoice to know someone has poked inside and
stolen thoughts from his very mind?' Kail

continued.

'I remember a time when some else poked inside of my own mind' Eckard answered before he could stop himself. His crooked smile faded as did his excitement from earlier, and he held the young woman's staring challenge.

'That was a long time ago, Eckard' Kail said, as serious as he now.

'And yet it still occurred.' Eckard's smile returned, as Kail started her own in answer.

'Now you mock me, ha ha. I remember apologizing and you forgiving me.' Kail expressed. 'And that was a very different time and place.'

It fucking was.

'All true, I can see Judeson doing the same when he understands just as it took me awhile to understand it all back then. The Southron has a future with us. I have seen it.' Eckard assured, standing up and stretching.

It was almost time to set out again, a pity, moments between them seemed so few and far apart.

'You read with the ForeSeer's perception, didn't you? I knew you would not be able to help your self Eckard.' Kail stated, narrowing her eyes once more.

'I could hardly not do so, the boy projects his *senses* all out in the open, you have felt it by now surely' Eckard said.

'Which poses the question I had worried about, how much did the Raks already get from the child before you took him back from them. If his sense were out, they may have read something from him, their unnatural affinity to the Void and all' Kail replied, folding her arms over and pondering her own question.

Always in the worst of moments, they were

together again.

Eckard wondered if there was ever going to be a dull moment in life.

**

Judeson waited outside, near the huge wooden panel gates of the citadel proper, the courtyard behind him, as deserted, dusty and ridden with cobwebs as the rest of forgotten fortress. The others joined soon after. Kail coming first, dressed in a deep emerald cloak near to the colour of her beautiful but deadly serious eyes. Raijin comes next, also cloaked but peering about with a slight smile as if there were not a worry in the world. Eckard and Lucairn came of the latter. Bearing packs on food and drink.

Raijin strolled up to Judeson and dropped his smile. Motioning for the Southron to follow him in tow back into the wild tangle of woods that was the Draul esthla'theilm.

'Come then if you must see it you must' Raijin stated, his quiet and calm voice suddenly filled with regret and a morose sadness.

'We will catch up afterward. And to the Southrondor you and I will go.' Eckard said his wry grin sported once more.

As the party departed each other's company, the different members going their separate ways back into the dark woodlands. Kail followed Eckard and though she did not speak - as if to just be absolutely certain the other's did not hear them - she asked him a much needed question.

Do you think he will be able to handle it?

Kail spoke into Eckard's mind with Magik-induced resonance.

I bloody hope so. Was all Eckard could manage as he kept trekking forward.

Though it was not much of anything at all, it was finally good to see Eckard did possess a certain level of realism still.

**

The trek took them almost a day away from the others, and Judeson found himself wondering if Raijin was leading him in any real direction at all. The dense woods all seemed to look so very similar after awhile. Each tree unremarkable from another, each gentle stream identical to the last. Yet through it, all Judeson did not bother in asking Raijin as to their path. He felt comfortable in the beanpole Draul's company and even though he had only known the strange near-man for a very short time he felt he could trust him utterly.

"We have arrived, friend," Raijin stated suddenly, pulling up in his long strides.

The current location did not appear any different from the last few dozen places the duo had visited. Just as if in answer to Judeson's as yet, not vocalized query, Raijin motioned with one raised arm to a slim hollow in an ancient oak tree.

'I'm sorry for what is to come' Raijin spoke solemnly this time, a pained expression crossing his ashen features.

Judeson nodded in understanding and went into hollow and the blackened abyss beyond.

***

As the night set in Eckard trounced his way across the leafstrewn path and its gradual upward turn. As the Nertharnlander neared the top of the slight elevation in the valley terrain he caught sight of her. The slight frame of the beautiful young woman stood still but on a casual lean. Her long midnight black hair swayed with the gentle

sequential movements of the wind about them.
Eckard like he always did, in the moments like
this, lost one of his self-proclaimed natural
abilities, his voice. The young lady Eckard knew
by so many names to so many others, but as Kail
most prominently did not utter any word either.
Instead she motioned for him to follow and she,
in turn, walked onward to the ancient beyond
description, towering fig tree ahead of them.

Both the giant Northerner and the slight framed,
the raven haired woman knew this place well and
on nearing the gigantic, many-limbed behemoth of
a fig took up positions on either side to climb
the natural beast. There were established
footholds ingrained into the tree that both
Eckard and Kail knew all too well, and their
climb was brief and unencumbered. On reaching a
vast sprawling ledge created by twisting branches
that had long ago fused together in growth, the
man and woman hoped off their climbing escapades
and sat down on the room sized collection of
branches, they overlooked far reaching sections
of the woodland below them.

After the natural sequence of huffing and puffing
that usually accompanied the aftermath of
physical endeavors such as climbing a hulking
ancient fig tree had come to a steady halt; the
two persons looked at each, only very briefly
before turning to observe the wilds below.

'So well done I suppose, although now Krikza is
claiming the rescue as his own, an imposter
standing in for the ForeSeer. At the very least
we have the real ForeSeer safe once more.' Kail
said first, flicking strands of her thick furled
dark locks back behind her shoulder.

'Only a half-victory then? A typical Delmose
trait that, doing everything only... half-right.'

Eckard answered, unleashing his most mischievous grin forth.

Kail slapped Eckard's broad shoulder with her backhand ever so slightly with a feather touch, more playful than anything else. Eckard leaned over the side of the branch's ledge where both their feet dangled off and pulled lightly at Kail's leg at the ankle to unsteady her balance. It seemed that the young dark haired woman was not entirely ready for such a counter attack and almost tumbled over the edge if not for Eckard flinging both arms out around her and pulling her towards him. For the briefest of moments; time slowed to a crawling halt as Kail's black curls brushed against Eckard's face, their sweet scent sending his head swimming. Her slight frame barreling into his and he felt her welcome warmth against his chest, her piercing green eyes cast up into his own and he quickly found himself lost in their gaze. As hastily as that brief moment came so too did it fade, as Kail quickly pushed herself away from Eckard and sat back, propping himself upright.

'You're an idiot.' Kail voiced brushing her hair back from her face and turning away from Eckard who sat unmoved.

'I'm sorry milady.' Eckard murmured under his breath.

'How many times do I have to tell you I'm not a noble Eckard,' Kail spoke out beneath clenched teeth, glaring at Eckard through silted eyes.

'I know, I know apologies.....Lisiarna' Eckard answered, rapidly turning away from her and looking out at the forest to hold back his laughter which would only incur more of Kail's certain incoming and retaliating storm of insults.

Moments passed in silence as Eckard bit his tongue down hard and looked off into the distance before turning around to scene he did not anticipate. Kail instead of bursting out at him sat with her hands in her lap and eyes cast down to them. She had returned to her original appearance, the masking faded, the Draul ears and skin tone went. The beautiful young woman released a small smile with her own face.

'You remembered.' The young woman said as Eckard looked dazed and confused at her as she raised her deep green eyes to him.

'Um…well…it's….'Eckard muttered, taken back and unable to form a competent sentence structure.

'It's nothing I know, but thank you.'
Kail/Lisiarna replied before standing in a half crouch and latching onto the thick trunk of the fig tree the two were on.

'Now what have you done to your face Eckard?' Lisiarna continued.

'I was not aware a beard was a depravity' Eckard replied, regaining his feet and following Kail's lead for the descending return climb down the ancient tree.

'It is the way you wear one.' Kail said whilst beginning her descent. "Come on we'll try and correct your mistakes. Oh and Eckard?"

'Yes?' Eckard said looking back at the dark haired woman holding on to the outcropped footholds around her.

'I'm well aware I'm wearing rather………. rather open attire at the present point in time. Could you try and refrain you sight upwards as I climb down?' Kail asked Eckard was more than certain she was speaking in regards to her currently half-exposed cleavage from the flimsy Watcher cloak, the equally liberal tunic dress beneath she sported. The cloak of which was pulled open as she climbed downwards to the forest floor.

'Oh but how shall I possibly see the footings?'Eckard answered, grinning furiously as he followed her down the tree.

'Try not to enjoy yourself too much up there.' Lisiarna called out.

'I can't promise that I'm afraid.'

'You never were very good at promises.'

'I can learn.'Eckard said.

***

'So another come to mock me then?' cried the voice from the bleak darkness beyond.

'Quite the opposite, I would speak with you.' Judeson said striding forward into the gloomy interior of the Draul dungeon.

The decrypt prison walls of hard packed earth leaked thick oozing moisture and the smell of humid rot ran rife through one's nose. Judeson clenched his teeth at the horrid atmosphere he found himself in. Behind a large metal barred cage, barely large enough to hold an upright Aurman, slouched the Voice's physical host. Barely more than a sack of wasted away skin and bones, a sickly shadow of a man squinted upwards at Judeson. The harsh croaking voice Judeson had heard before came from the nauseating shadow of the man's devastatingly parched and cracked lips. Judeson saluted the crumpled and chained figure.

'A Southron? By the sounds of ye you are. Who are you boy?' The yelping cry rang out around.

'I am Judeson, son of Judisye of Letesah that was.' Judeson answered.

The sickly prisoner yelped out a halfhearted and horrible sounding chuckle. Coughing madly in fits and wincing in clearly excruciating pain after

the man attempted to upright himself in his
decrypt iron bar cage. He failed in his efforts
and fell heavily upon his rear end. Slouching in
defeat the silhouetted figure uttered a single
groan of frustration. Judeson placed both hands
on the iron bar cage and tested the sturdiness of
the prison confines, finding them remarkably
strong and somehow impossibly cold as to burn, he
withdrew to stand close by. How was the metal so
low in temperature, like the frozen ice cap of a
mountain when the prison room around them stewed
in blistering heat? Judeson found himself
pondering.

'I was named Thorgal, once upon an arc when names
mattered still.' The sickly caged apparition said
looking up at Judeson.

'Your name still bears meaning, even if you have
been wronged in such manners as now. Were you of
the Southrondor? Of course, your accent gives
that away.' Judeson replied.

'Many arcs ago, yes. Before all the trouble I am
in now of course. I came from a place named
Sharstern.'

'I know of it, Seventy odd leagues southeast of
Letesah.'

'It was, just like Letesah was once as you say.'

'What happened?' Judeson inquired, although he
believed the answer he knew already.

'Raks happened. Hundreds of them, bringing
madness and death.' The wasted away prisoner
Thorgal answered.

Judeson tensed and shivered with disgust and
anger at the response by Thorgal.

'I know this too well...but how...are you here?'
Judeson eventually staggered out to the sick and
despair ridden prisoner.

'There was more us...survivors, we can through

the Old Passage north, very few of us survived
the journey, both the Silversands and the
Karchelch teaming with Raks and other... other
things, most of them sick and wounded by then,
bitten the whole way. Many did not survive the
crossing. When we had finally gotten to the edge
of these woods. The Watchers they....they...they'
Thorgal replied with a hollowing regret ridden
voice sounding out.

'What did they do? Thorgal you can tell me. The
Draul they do not know I am here.' Judeson
replied bending down on his knees to make sense
of Thorgal's spluttering and painful sounding
dialogue.

'In truth?' Thorgal asked.

'I swear on my Father's name'

'The Watchers they attacked us.'

Judeson raised both eye brows and took on a
wanton expression of disbelieving trying to make
sense of what his fellow Southron had uttered.
Yet Thorgal replied straight away after rasping
out a husky cough.

'Not at first you see, it took some time. The
wee-gnome man we were with, well he tried to
reason with them over something. And that's when
the arrows started flying.'

'But the Draul....they...'Judeson stammered, his
mind adrift with conflicting thoughts thrown
about in an inner maelstrom.

'They slaughtered us Judeson until it was just
me...stepping over the carcasses of my fallen
friends they had numerous arrows trained on me
and I knew it was Zadma-damned hopeless.'

'But they did not kill you. Why?' Judeson pried,
attempting to find one small spark of any sense
whatsoever in the morbid conversation he was in.
Thorgal in his dim lit and dank jail-cell of

drenched mud and rotting foliage croaked out a
painful sounding yelp and proceeded to spit onto
the enclosure's floor. Judeson lowered himself
and neared his person close to the prison cell in
an attempt to get closer to this very unfortunate
man. Thorgal's face lifted after a time and a
harrowing gaze of horror greeted Judeson, making
the man feel ice cold spears dance across his
neck.

'Why? Why-fucking-indeed? They did not kill me
because they said they wanted me to do
something.....' Thorgal answered in clear
unleased distaste.

'What Thorgal? What did they want?' Judeson
inquired, breath heavy as he gripped a sturdy
jail bar between him and Thorgal.

'At first, I resisted, of course, us Southrons
are not so easily pushed. But then they showed
me.......and I did as they wanted.' Thorgal
started sinking his head into his lap and
shivered, not from cold at least but something
else entirely.

'Please Thorgal? Zadma's mercy man, tell me.'
Judeson said, as the malnourished prisoner rocked
back forth in a tightened ball of arms and legs
on his hutches.

No answer came and Judeson backed off feeling the
meeting was proving fruitless, then just as he
turned, a loud breath started from behind. The
sickly figure of Thorgal began upwards and
balanced vicariously onto the ancient jail bars
of his cell. He commenced speaking between
exhausted and painful sounding breaths, the words
that flowed forth rocked Judeson to the core.

4th Stanza

There is no substitute for a sharp and reliable blade, keen learning mind and someone who can cook delicious food from raw product from the wild. Practical, reliable and flexible abilities, that is what is needed. No Laws, Rules, Judges, Coins or Requisitions can keep one warm, safe and healthy. This is the ultimate argument.

> – *Opening Statement of the Knight-Reclaimer Squire Handbook*

*First Ascribed 3 arcs after the Reclamation of the Nertharnlands

Eckard leaped down off the last ingrained footing over enthusiastically and tumbled across the soft grass mound to land in a sprawl at the bottom. Kail released an unrestrained crowing laughter close by and to Eckard's ears he swore a snort? Perhaps, perhaps he had heard it before even. Lying down his back and in no real sense of pain Eckard voiced a gruff clearing of his throat to draw attention to himself. Kail did come over. Holding two hands near her face and still giggling away the beautiful young half-breed Draul withdrew her arms to her side and made a disapproving face at Eckard.

'I know this game Eckard, I come over to help you up and you pull me down on top of you. Hmm?" Kail said, shaking her head of midnight black locks.

'Void-dammit! You worked that one out, huh?'

Eckard answered, sporting a rye smile as he regained his standing reluctantly.

Kail shook her head at Eckard and raised one thin dark eye brow at him. Eckard winked to which she slit her gaze in response.

'By the wisps and slutty Yahasa, what in the world did you do with your hair?' Kail inquired. "And here I was taking note of that ridiculous thing on your face. Your head looks like it was cut by a drunken gardener with blunt shearers."

'Hunting knife if you must know.' Eckard answered.

'Somehow that doesn't surprise me.' Kail said, holding her hands on her hips in crystal-clear disgust. 'Perhaps we should do something about this? Hmm?'

Eckard nodded knowing that resistance was futile and threw up his hands to accept his unconditional surrender.

**

Judeson felt himself shake, not with the cold winds drift past him in the dark woods, but from something far more personal far more primal; rage. Undiluted, pure rage. Curling his hands into fists, teeth clenching to the point of straining Judeson felt the unassailable shaking of his entire person come to. The last time he had felt like this had been the day after his father had died. The Southron had vowed for vengeance that day, even as at only a meager 14 arcs old he had decided what his prime purpose was. He had to c it by blade into stone. Now he felt the same refined anger build up etching into his mind like the stone's engraved marks.

Vengencence – that one cardinal basement of being that he had come to absorb. The essence of his existence. The meaning for his journey to the

North, yet now this just set ablaze a fire that had never died. The Draul were not to be trusted, Judeson realized now. The others he had met, he could not be certain. At least he doubted much more now. But why had they insisted he sees him. They could not have been part of it. He hoped so anyway.

**

Eckard squirmed and moved about making the act of cutting off his deeply tangled and wild crop of dirty hair that much more difficult. He was always difficult no matter the task though. Lisiarna tilted his head once more to get to the back properly, momentarily glancing at his intricately scarred back, from an altogether different time. Lisiarna woke herself from the well of her memories and had to fight against the worming and wiggling form of Eckard.
'Would you stop struggling, and not a peep about your little nuisance' Lisiarna joked.
'I have not said anything. And that's new...'Eckard answered. Tilting counter-productively to what Lisiarna needed.
"What's new?" Lisiarna inquired. Moving the big Nertharnlander's head back around again.
'Never been called little before,'Eckard stated.
'Oh you poor man, how will you ever recover from such an unprovoked attack?' Lisiarna teased, keeping a straight face despite the internal laughter within.
'The exact same way I always do push on against the odds.' Eckard said, snorting out his nose at the end and losing his constructed seriousness.
'Oh of course, how heroic of you.' Lisiarna burst out laughing.
Eckard turned on the ancient tree stump and raised his half-trimmed face up at her, his

crooked stare holding unnervingly long. A
lopsided smile crossed his face adding to the odd
yet somewhat handsome visage.

'Are you going to finish this or what? Witch-
woman?' The former knight uttered, a short-lived
chuckle becoming part of his act.

Lisiarna narrowed her eyes and tried to play the
serious reporting act as the situation demanded.

'For that son of Semus I will cut your hair down
so far you will actually fit in respectable
society and not look entirely like a vagabond
ever again.' Lisiarna announced mockingly, though
firmly with a touch of pride.

Eckard beamed furiously back at Lisiarna. And
shifting her Blue Magik back from herself so her
original appearance was cast, Lisianrna began
again with clippers in hand on the unreasonable
jungle that was on the young Northman's head and
face.

Much later as the day-star had begun to drift out
of its glory and it's light waned. The chill
breeze of twilight drafted in and the nightly
mist cast off of the forest floor obscuring the
flurry of insects underneath. The two realized
they were both dirt riddled and in need of a
bath. Before all light dissipated from the world
they indulged themselves in a swim by the stream
just ahead of the clearing.

The water was cool and serene. Worries drifted
away like the dirt from calloused hands and
pores. Though as Eckard well knew, the past could
not be avoided only contained sometimes. No man
or woman could run or in this case swim from
their' collective purpose. Despite this lingering
thought, Eckard found himself in this moment at
least to be free and genuinely happy.

'You still swim like a Drowning rat I see.'

Lisiaran called from out in the middle of the chilly fresh water creek.

Her. Lisiarna. That was both a lingering worry and happiness for him.

The glistening clear blue waters stirred and swirled as Eckard in his Draulning rat prose swam toward Lisiarna who smirked at him. He looked at her, the original her, with strawberry blonde curls and freckles, brilliant emerald green eyes and mouth that seemed too small.

Lisiarna smiled, and the world grew brighter for Eckard. He moved closed, eyes closing and lips parted as Lisiarna, in turn, seemed to do the same.

'Stop!'- Lisiarna's voiced inside his head screamed. The link between them as close as ever it had been.

'Stop Eckard, please' Lisiarna stating gasping and then proceeding to swim to shore.

Eckard follower her in turn and climbed back onto the shore where Lisiarna threw her cloak about herself.

Once again. The Pact was still the prime concern above all else.

***

The robust Southron stalked past Raijin in a rush, furious rage painted his face clear as day. The Draul Mage knew better than most to not pull up a man in a fit of ire as Judeson was currently. Instead, Raijin let him pass and followed him into the woods. Though by follow Raijin would mean to somehow catch up with the hasty and visibly fuming Southron to perhaps lead him in due course to their actual desired departure location. For in truth the Aurman had no idea where he was going in his fit of rage. Moving deeper and deeper into the wilds of the

Draul'esthla'theilm would not help him, but at the present moment time; he did not care.

Raijin eventually caught up with Judeson who had stopped after quite some time to perhaps reflect, or just simply to catch his breath from his forcibly emotive and hasty march. Whatever the reason for the halt to the raw emotional state, Judeson looked back at Raijin with visible tears streaming down his face, though his gaze remained steely.

'Why would? Why....' Judeson stammered.

'As a Greycloak we have seen such atrocities committed before and of this is what we have spoken we are fighting. For all that honourable, for all that is right in this world.' Raijin answered, not giving too much away but providing something of comfort for Judeson at least.

'Join us, Eckard will accompany you to the South where you can right the wrongs visited upon your people.' Raijin continued gesturing for Judeson to follow him in the right direction.

Judeson said nothing in reply; nodded and then followed.

*

As they made their way back on the green shore, Lisiarna glanced back at Eckard who now looked solemn, even disappointed. Biting her tongue, Lisiarna found herself torn both wanting to so desperately embrace Eckard but at the same time push him away. History was repeating itself all over again. Damn the man to the void, it was always so difficult. The Nertharnlander in question reached out a hand to Lisiarna.

Lisiarna pushed away, an avalanche of emotion flooding forth, Draulning her far beneath. She found herself unsteady on her own two feet, her breath lost in a moment. Absorbed by the roaring of tension compounded from a kiss that never was. Composing herself, she straightened up and faced the tall Nerthlander who had made his way to his feet once more.

'You must go now, Eckard we both know what we need to do,' Lisiarna muttered more to herself than him really.

Eckard nodded, silent and composed. Though his beard and hair had been cleaned up he stilled lingered in an unmistakable level of scruffiness. Perhaps it was the ill-fitting cloak he adorned or the armour that he refused to change. The tall Nertharnlander marched off toward Judeson and Raijin who had appeared with horses in tow.

'Eckard!' Lisiarna called, her well-constructed walls slipping slightly. Forcing herself to recompose once more, she thought she should say something, inspirational, something comforting but she realised the words eluded her. With a smile to mask her unease, she evidently stated. 'Don't die out there.'

Eckard turned around to fully face her once more, a rye smile that likes of which so irritated but amused her all at once.

'No promises, but I shall try my best.' Eckard said, the smile waning and a serious turn of voice taking hold despite his attempted gibe.

'Farewell...for now … Sar ruffian' Lisiarna called out, at least she thought she did, the words coming out in reality as the gentlest of whispers.

Eckard either did not hear or he did not bother to respond, the tall Nertharnlander marching away towards the mounts where Judeson now stood. Kail remembered the man never did bother to say farewell, another trait that struck through no matter what. And as night fully descended and the two aurmen rode off south, Lisiarna felt conflicted as to whether she would miss all that. Again.

*

The dramatic mountain fastness that was the Boundary stretched on for leagues upon leagues wide, though very narrow from north to south in spots. Its namesake sometimes ill benefiting of it, Judeson and Eckard had taken little over two and a half days to get to the end of it. Judeson questioned why anyone sometimes called the jutting rocks that pushed up from the dense dark earth 'mountains' at all. The word mountain dictated a certain authority about itself, an edge of realization that provoked wonder and astonishment. Mountains were supposed to be large or even majestic. The Boundary was more a collection of stunted rock formations.

The length may not have been long in duration but it was harsh and exhausting every-time it was attempted. Judeson toiled across the rugged terrain to rest on a sandy embankment nearby. His wet tunic and pack soaking up the sodium crusted soil. The crashing crescendo of waves from the dark sea brushed up against the ragged sides and tore away at the sand surface. The progressive struggle of between land and sea was a fitting background for the exhaustion Judeson felt. Salty foam tumbled over a stuttered cliff nearby, and somewhere further beyond that Judeson knew the shores of the Southrondor awaited them.

The intense rushing waters spiralled past. Taking loose turf and weeds from the banks around them. A darkened storm cloud somewhere overhead pillowed onward through the dying light of the Far Above, ominous looking clouds. The likes of which never seemed to truly disapparate within the range of the Boundary. Judeson sighted Eckard on an outcropping of loose shale and found the man looking skyward with a bittersweet smile curiously painted on his face. Perplexing all round that one. Judeson did not bother to pry and pushed onwards with the Northman on a close trail behind him.

Close to what Judeson believed was two hours by way of the day-star's movement: The two men drifted through the rocky crags of the wilderness around. Very few real words exchange, both of whom were welcoming the silent and solemn mood to reflect. Judeson personally taking in all the events that unfolded in the North. From Vestras being blown apart for seemingly, no justifiable reason to Thorgal's direct accusations of the Draul maliciousness visited upon his people.

By daybreak, they had crossed the escarpment of which Judeson swore had seemed much steeper on the way to the Nort, all the while Eckard smirking at him in his most tedium inducing-layered manner when he thought to mention it. Then had about an hour after that incident, they reached the pass that Judeson had come to be known as the 'Late-man Passage'.

'Jutid Hilabenz - or Stump-rock hill, in the common Cestral tongue' Eckard voiced loudly, his eyes scouting off to the south and the close shoreline wear the rocky jagged hills met the bright blue waters of the sea.

'What's that then?' Judeson inquired, not fully understanding where the Northman was going with his statement. This was a fairly apt metaphor to utilise for everything about the elusive Mage; ambiguous and frustratingly difficult to read for Judeson.

'It's what a Berussi sailor told me it was

called. They said it was the gap between the shore and the Boundary Mountains. Very few places that are easily accessible to enter or exit this void-damned range apparently.'

'Late-Man's Passage is what I know it as. What the folks on Shorne called it.'

'Hmph. Then it is not such a secret then? The Berussi felt they were the only ones that knew how to cross the Boundary. Varihale being too dangerous, other passes being too steep to the east and the never-ending tempest of the western waters making it near to impossible to cross via ship. But it seems many Southrons already knew there was a way. The man that you saw he said such, no?' Eckard stated.

Judeson finding himself taken back by how much the beanpole North-man spoke. No more than two words had been uttered by the other man in the two and a half days they had spent crossing the unforgiving jagged hills and deep ravines of the Boundary mountains. But now, it felt as if a great weight had been lifted and thoughts could be shared between the two again. In that, though the thoughts now were not entirely pleasant of disposition.

'Thorgal, he was of Sharstern; another distant memory now.' Judeson said.

Trying to sight how he exactly ascended up the Lateman's Passage the first time around. The scene of the ancient storm ravaged hills look only vaguely similar now. Perhaps his memory of the place was not as precisely taken as he thought; although his own tracking skills and recollection of physical places had always been considered second to none by many. Doubting himself was not needed now. Not when he still had much to do.

'Regardless this Thorgal; he and many others knew of this place and how to cross the Erasmus, it could be ascertained that the way through is well known.' Eckard continued, the Mage somehow tip-toeing around something, he seemed incapable or unwilling to talk frankly.

'You could say such,' Judeson answered him, his gaze lingering on the strutted growth of shrubs on the limestone edges of the nearby quarry.

'We should make camp before the next storm rolls in,' Eckard started moving down into the valley below them.

Judeson followed him, wondering if he would ever get to know an answer to any question he asked Eckard.

5th Stanza

Oh what folly we should have run

Void damned fools what have we done

Irony is a cheap one

Pleasure is a short lived one

What have we done?

With no more to say

The toil and regrets of time

Most assuredly; the blame was mine

Fathomless Depths of the Demise

-Krakios the Grounded -Approximately 2022 ATF

Dark and gloomy reverberating storm clouds hung low over the makeshift campsite of the two travellers. It had been two days of this horrid and unaccommodating climate and Judeson was sure he had had enough. The bitterly cold rain bucketed down in absolute unyielding torrents, turning the rocky hillsides to mud. Although Judeson had experienced the unrelenting character of the Boundary Range on the trip over into the Northern Realms prior and on this return journey he still did not feel welcome. The bleak Far Above high overhead seemed a distant murmur of a memory from the sun drenched South.

Judeson kept his mind busy, sleep not taking hold as easy as it had seemed to have for Eckard. The Northman was snoring peacefully in the back of the stretched out canvas on two poles at the edge of the rocky edifice their campsite was backed up against. Judeson peered over at the slumbering Mage momentarily. As if he knew he was being watched Eckard stirred awake and sat up, still in chain maille armour and sword at his side.

'You probably want some explanations to everything that has been happening lately, don't you Judeson?' Eckard said, his awareness seemed to be on full readiness as if he had never been asleep at all. This was probably not altogether untrue - Judeson felt.

How did he do that?

'Well that would be nice I suppose,' Judeson answered bluntly, ignoring his own pressing thoughts.

'We are all members of the same group, met at varying, points and have bonded since then,'

Eckard replied nonchalantly.

'Well, thanks for sharing in such lengthy detail,' Judeson said, no small manner of sarcasm caked onto his tone.

Eckard looked off into the star-laden night, despite the lingering but slowly departing tempest; of the Far Above away from Judeson, clearing his throat in a dramatic manner: He swung his gaze back to Judeson and continued.

'The Pact of the Grey Mantle is our name. Most of us are Mages and Enchanters but not all. We have existed for hundreds, if not thousands of arcs, working in the background. Behind governments, religions, wars, disasters, we have survived and helped others to do so too.' Eckard voiced, with no smile, no glitter of mischief behind his sky blue eyes. Was he, we he...actually being honest?

'And everything you have been doing fits into this Order? This secret group?' Judeson

'Pact. But...well mostly, the fun and booze is our own little twist on it all' Eckard winked.

'Once again, the conversation goes nowhere.' Judeson sighed and turned away to focus on the vastly important (or distracting) task of poking the muddy earth with a stick.

'Conversations are like journeys, we tip-toe around and go off on a tangent but we all get there or thereabouts in the end.' Eckard finally replied. The man had stood up with the pack in hand and sword by his side.

The two warriors trekked across the rough outcroppings of razor sharp shale rock and moved further down into a low-lying valley. Ahead a cave mouth opened up and sea spray was sighted on the far side. Judeson realized just how close they were to the familiar sights of Late-man's Passage they were.

Moving through the narrow cavern's passage and emerging onto an equally small rock edge; Judeson and Eckard sidled across the cliff face with the dark churning waters of the Erasmus sea beneath them. The Erasmus was the short yet treacherous waters that separated the Northern Realms from the Southrondor. And in the South was where Judeson would finally face what he should have done arcs before. His vengeance would be complete.

Eckard seemed to have somehow pushed ahead and interestingly he appeared to know his way or perhaps luckily found the right footfalls in the narrow passage to pass go. Judeson caught up to the taller man and looked out at the whipping and crashing waves of the Eramus, and just two short leagues beyond the Southrondor.

'We must signal the ferry-men for passage across.' Judeson shouted over the tremendously loud cacophony of waves splashing against the shores. 'Could you help with the fire.'

Eckard nodded in understanding and knelt to help Judeson build a fireplace with tinder, flint and loose branches from the Southron's pack he had collected. Eckard seemed quite intrigued by Judeson's announcement of a ferryman to give them passage, by the inquisitive look on his face. Though not once did the beanpole Northman inquire about the statement.

After several moments of structuring the fireplace and attempting to cover the pit from the harsh weather all around them the man gave up. Judeson thought it prudent to question why Eckard had not turned to his unnatural prowess at lighting up objects yet.

'Why don't you try your sorcery on this? Judeson said, wincing as he spoke the words, taken back by his gradually more liberal view of the Black Art.

'Magik' Eckard stressed, with iron eyes 'Does not simply conjure something from nothing Judeson. Shifting the balance of the world is not as simplistic as the campfire stories of snapping of fingers and the speaking of some goat-shit garbled words.'

Eckard stood up and swiped at the air close by. The wind seemed to shift and pass by not coming close to the fire pit anymore and the rain impossibly appeared to follow the wind on an unnatural angle away from them. Sea spray too seemed to have shifted its course as if it were told to.

'Besides Grey Magik is an another rung on altogether different ladder entirely.' Eckard grinned furiously, though the Northman seemed to be hiding something underneath, something that pained the man a great deal.

Judeson shifted back to commencing the flame with flint in hand even as Eckard seated down next to him in a none too graceful fashion. A spark lit and in a handful of moments, and with the changing winds, the fire roared to life. In the distance, a ship began to sail over toward the two men.

The ship or boat, Eckard had stressed in calling in as it approached their position on the rugged shoreline of the boundary. Was exactly as Judeson had vividly remembered from his previous journey across. The ship was a broken, leaky old mess of a contraption. Grime rode and tattered sails swung from twisted ancient mast frames. A salt bleached and barnacle crusted portside swung into the shoreline, narrowly avoiding jaggedly sharp rocks in the shallow waters. From the messy deck of the vessel, three figures scurried about hurling an anchor into the crashing waves below them and pulling back sails ropes to hold their position steady.

'Lo there Captain!' Judeson shouted through cupped palms at the ship's crew.

'Lo there son of Judisyeand friend of ours. Come abroad, if you would swim, docking ain't easy picking Imma 'fraid' Called back the Captain with a thick Berberussi accent.

'Very well, Eckard?' Judeson replied to the vessel's pilots and beckoned for Eckard to follow out in the maelstrom of violent dark waters.

'Interesting choice of transport,' Eckard stated no sign of his trademark grin presented, nor any indication of laughter at all in his eyes.

The two men stripped down out of their armour attaching it and their weapons onto their packs and slinging them above their head. They waded out in the bitterly cold foam of the seas between the North and South continents, the waters between coming up to waist height as they waddled in fiercely cold waters up to the swaying vessel ahead. Immediately a strong current took hold and they found themselves being about like debris in the swirling, churning waters. Judeson taking a serious note of just how many shallow rocks seemed to alarmingly encompass them. From the shabby excuse of the ship, tightly bungled ropes were cast out to them and Judeson held tight as he and Eckard were pulled aboard the vessel.

'Eckard this is Captain Gursniy' Judeson huffed between exhausted breaths. Motioning to one of the ship's crewmembers, a scruffy looking fellow with a greying bread and shaved and misshapen head.

'..and the pilot Jarkins' Judeson continued

motioning to a short and spidery individual with a burnt smock and tatty headband as his only attire.

'..and lastly but not least of all Risdan the deckhand." Judeson finished, shaking the hand of the last man, a dumpy man with a deep reddish maroon birthmark on his brown hued face.

'Greetings, and many thanks for granting us passage' Eckard uttered, touching his right brow with his index finger, as all good Nertharnlanders knew to be polite and appropriate on meeting others.

'Welcome to the Undefeated blokes, now let's cast off and be under way already' Captain Gurniy shouted over the crashing waves, his voice seemed so shrill for one so deep, like iron chippings somehow.

'Can we get a move on old ladies, this here wind is a fucking chiller' the pilot Jarkins yelled in answer, though he did not shiver at all.

Risdan the deckhand lumbered over to the port side keel and dislodged the anchor line and pulled up the lines cast out for Eckard and Judeson. Curiously the Captain and Jarkins had strode up to the second story where the helm was requisitioned though neither man-made an effort to steer or even touch the instruments at all. For once Risdan was done with his duties below he raced up to the where the rest of the ship's crew were and began working both the wheel and rudder. Impressively so and with much effort. Neither the captain nor the pilot intervened.

'We are working the lad up, great training on one's own it is.' Captain Gurniy called down to Judeson and Eckard, though the grizzled man's gaze layout at sea.

Judeson exchanged words with the men after that,

laughter ensued and they all began pacing across the vessel pointing and such. It would seem Judeson was intently interested in how it all operated. Eckard did not take the same viewpoint and made his way to the starboard side away from all the commotion and carry on. The voices of the captain, Jarkins and Judeson sounded out with no discernible words coming to Eckard as he lost himself in the view ahead of him.

The heaving and turbulent waves churned up against the near shore of the North and swayed back against the edges of the Southrondor. A huge maelstrom curled around the ferocious waters nearby and threw up white spray into the evening chilled air. A storm rolled over the Boundary behind them and began to drift out to the mouth of the channel and out to open ocean of the Omakis Divide. In the descending gloom, Eckard could still sight the shorelines of isles of Dirke and Shorne to the west and east respectively. From all accounts, the small rock islands had not been inhabited for many arcs. The sheer scarcity of life was staggering. Seemingly never-ending tempests proved a difficult habitat to endure.

Eckard turned away from the enduring struggle of the swaying ship against the tumultuous seas and glanced back at Judeson and his intriguing crew. He did not even seem to realize who or more specifically what they are. The Southron for all his talk of despising Magik seemed to be constantly surrounded by it. Though not entirely certain how or why these men still remained abroad; or even how the dilapidated vessel still sat tentatively above the waves, Eckard sensed the whole scenario stunk to the Far Above of something vaguely Magikal in origin.

'There are two seas in our existence, one a thing

of waves and water, the other Arcane, mysterious
in nature and the source of oh so much study and
contemplation by us fucking crazy Mages..' -
Eckard remembered the words vividly as if the
sour old man was right there with him. His old
teacher, the Pact of the Grey Mantle founder,
where was he now he wondered. Brought back to the
seas of the physical world, Eckard felt the ship
pitching to the right and almost just as fast the
vessel's course was redirected. At the helm, the
deckhand Risdan heaved at the wheel turning the
ship of course. They had come to close to the
rocky shores of Shorne isle and the crew fought
to right them.

'Lads there will be no spectators on board is a
hardy bitch of a tub!' The Captain shouted in a
hoarse outcry.

The burly captain motioned at Judeson and then
Eckard to take a hold of the bundled up rope that
would alter the sailing set ups. Gurniy held up a
halting palm to slow the men down from taking
action, clearly waiting for something. Jarkins
the pilot pointed off to the east across Shorne
as the both Eckard and Judeson reached up and
took up holds of the ropes.

'Over yonder eastwards, a squall comes to help us
turn this leaky wreck' Jarkins squealed his
shrill voice caught up in the harsh winds.

The Undefeated tossed and turned in the harsh
waters and the Captain seemed to stay his hand
for an eternity. At any moment it seemed they
would altogether capsize and been thrown into the
chaos of the dark depths below. Eckard remembered
just how poorly he swam and did not relish the
opportunity to be tested right now in this
turbulence.

'Now void-damn ya's!' The Captain bellowed even

as the squall pitched in throwing itself against the rickety Undefeated.

Eckard and Judeson pulled and the sails dropped down, the mast unfurling in its glory. For a heartbeat, Eckard stressed it would not be enough and they would all still make an early dry docking on Shorne's shore. But the Undefeated pitched back the other way as a wave pushed against them in tandem actions. They were redirected back toward the top of the Southrondor continent and safe for now.

'Not bad lads, not bad at all!' the Captain yelled above the chorus of crashing waves and hollering squall winds.

'Glad we could help, and not die.' Judeson muttered more to himself than anyone else, though Eckard heard him clearly enough from where he stood.

Both Jarkins and Risdan offered encouragement and gestured toward the shoreline of the Southrondor that lay staggeringly close now. Judeson turned and smiled at Eckard, relief was clearly written with a thick bold brush on his face. Eckard, however, could not push aside the interestingly precise thought that neither Jarkins nor Gurniy had offered any physical assistance.

*

Hours later and the day had all but run its course. Curiously the group had found an abandoned jetty and although several of its awnings and walkway planks had been missing, the general stability of the structure had proved sound enough to dock with. The Undefeated sat swaying on the tumbling rough waters of the Erazmus or the Egding Waters as the others had called it. Eckard watched the departing bulky figure of Risdan who had helped them lug their knapsacks, armour, and weapons and some additional food stuff the crew of the Undefeated had so generously granted them. Not that the other two would really need anything like that. Eckard chewed over that fact, granting Risdan a smile and nod as the rotund brown-skinned man.

Judeson nearby waved for the send off of the Undefeated and departed back into the gloom and hailing winds. The Southron turned to Eckard with a questioning gaze. 'What with the harrowing look then?' Judeson asked.

Eckard began up the steep sloping embankment, lugging up his knapsack and adjusting his new sheathed sword at his hip belt. He looked back at Judeson who began to follow him up from the shore. 'What do you mean?' Eckard answered.

'You spend a great deal of time avoiding anything that remotely resembles a question. You do it on purpose though don't you?' Judeson retorted, trekking past Eckard as if to impose himself.

'The crew of the Undefeated were well...interesting...is all' Eckard stated glancing about the terrain that had opened up to the two when they crested the steep embankment of the northern shore.

Though vaguely obscured by the nightfall, fields of high grass and numerous shallow rivers and ponds jutted out before them. Dispersed outcrops of small stunted trees and shrubs scatted the wild plains. In the near vicinity, a small mountain range propped up somewhere to the west while a series of rolling slopes continued on towards the east. Glancing back from where they arrived from, Eckard noted the stark contrast between the relative tranquility of the Southrondor. With its gentle swaying cool breeze and tumbling and clashing of storm clouds upon harsh seas within the Boundary and Erazmus sea respectively.

Eckard breathed in the slight chill night air and peered about the open landscape. 'Where about do we camp in this open expanse?' Eckard asked Judeson as he pulled out flint, tinder and a torch to be lit all from his pack.

Judeson who stood behind him attempting peer over his shoulder into the knapsack replied;' You answer my question first and I find us accommodating comfort.'

Eckard stood up with a lit torch and sighed over-enthusiastically. 'The captain and ship's pilot were both dead, while the deckhand manned the vessel by himself, possibly mute which would work in their favour apparently.'

Yahasa's balls, Judeson was proving to be more and more stubborn.

'Dead? What do you mean to say? As in ghosts?' Judeson inquired leading onward to a hilltop of scattered foliage and birch trees.

'Phantoms, spirits, wraiths what have you. For some reason, they offer a ferry service for us silly mortal souls. Something seems to be keeping them here, for whatever purpose.' Eckard answered, hoping that would suffice for Judeson, though from what Eckard had pieced together of the ever-increasing obstinacy of the Southron, most probably not.

Judeson huffed. 'Hunh' and then pointed toward the middle of the tiny birch forest. 'In here there is an abandoned food store, under a hatch some makeshift bedding and a little leg space, the barrels that were in there were moved to allow more room.' Judeson continued and pulled up a hatch from the ground. The wooden hatching leading to a small, dank underground room with three straw beds in there and not a lot of anything else.

'Not wise to sleep in the open with a fire I take it?' Eckard asked dropping down into the obscured room and dislodging his travel gear and weapons.

'There are a few Rak patrols that come through this way every now and again, best to be vigilant.' Judeson said, following Eckard and gearing down for rest.

Eckard pushed himself back onto the haphazardly stitched together straw bed and found some very slight comfort from it, Looking across the room at the bed opposite him he saw Judeson remained eye contact with him over the firelight that Eckard had stamped into the floor by the tip.

'Good night Eckard' Judeson said, reaching out to damper the flames with a wet cloth he had produced the solitary barrel nearby his bed.

'Good night' Eckard answered.

'Oh, Eckard one day I would like for you to answer some of my questions in a little more detail, please. Night.' Judeson said, the passive-aggressive tone clear and present.

Eckard kept his thoughts to himself as he had learned to do so well and just grunted in response. Drifting off to dreams, away from worry.

In the dawn's light of the new day the two men walked across a wild expanse of sparse woodlands, rolling grass hills low lying marshland. Judeson found important marks to remember his previous trek through here by. Eckard remained silent for most of the walk grunting and answering Judeson when he remarked on certain areas or the of the presence of bolting elks, deer, wild goats and all the various forms of winged life high over head in the stretching reaches of the Far Above.

The two men camped down at the end of a long day and indulged themselves with strips of the wild fowl caught the previous morning and salad of spinach leaves, dried chili, and oil of olives that Eckard had produced from his magikal bag. Judeson did not pry as to the property of the bag, that particular quest had proved almost entirely fruitless thus far. Eckard recounted how the night in the Southrondor did not seem nearly as mist-laden or in his words 'void-damned, balls shivering' cold.

The midday of the second day, they encountered a burn out hovel – a common enough sight for Judeson in these parts. Previous inhabitants or the bodies of such had long ago been taken away.

'Raks?' Eckard inquired.

'Most probably' Judeson answered. 'Though bandits have proved opportunistic in all this chaos.'

Eckard nodded and looked about the sight in earnest.

Judeson knew exactly where they were now, remembering seeing the smoke rise from this particular mud brickwork home and arriving at a scene devoid of life. Lessons of death and life were a cruel rhythm repeated so many times, many players forcing their influence on nature.

Judeson shook his head knowing such dark thoughts were distracting. He knew what he needed to do. Getting back to Letesah was just the first step needed.

Bringing himself back into the world around him Judeson began on his way and motioned for Eckard to follow in tow. The big Northman falling in step like a lithe shadow.

On the afternoon of the third day of their' journey across The Top- the name of the vast expanse of coastal regions that stretched the length of the Southrondor. They could not make out in the distance the wooded country of the Karchelch Tablelands where Judeon's former home of Letasah laid. However, for now, Judeson had a friend to visit and mounts to acquire. Zadma's mercy it would be a heck of a lot easier for him and Eckard to trek the wilderness with them.

'Names have a great meaning in the Southrondor, about where we are from and who we were born to.' Judeson announced, stirring at the flicking charcoals with a small twig.

The two men sat around a prepared camp fire while the wildfowl bird that Judeson had finally struck from the Far Above with Eckard's unbelievably powered sideward bow, cooked over the licking flames. Eckard tilted the roasting prong about the fire pit to tilt the bird around once more. The Northman had produced yet again more tools and interestingly a various assortment of collected of spices from his bag.

The bird had been an extremely arduous encounter, as Eckard's crossbow had been such an unruly weapon, to begin with. The repeating mechanism was hard to work and the bow had proved problematic at best. One quarrel had flown wide on the first attempt, and the second not much closer, Eckard had laughed and Judeson had preserved. The third bolt had struck true and the beanpole Northman had smiled and prepped the animal like an expert that had done so a thousand times before. Now the two men sat at a roaring fire and the roasting bird.

'That bag of yours is an endless well of surprises.' Judeson announced nodding at the fire and the improvised rotisserie.

'It's not endless, and it has just enough to get by in a pinch.' Eckard stated, winking at

Judeson.

Judeson held back his annoyance at the man's antics. And continued: 'As I was saying my name is from the proud line of Jude, a kindred that fought for the honour and the throne of Nesfahln, may the Queen guard them. My father Judisye was the bearer of Jude and his mother bore it before him. Connected in love and honour and by the weapon that guards Our House' Judeson storied along.

Eckard seemed to gaze over at the namesake Claymore which was currently resting against an angular slab of basalt. Judeson smiled proud of his lineage and his remembrance from what his father had taught him.

'As it does in the Nertharnlands also.'

'How so, do you have House-blades or symbols?'

'Not so much as yet, but we like to announce out steps from where we are from. Take my name for example'

Judeson beckoned for Eckard to continue, Intrigued both at the Eckard's story and that the man was speaking frankly for the offhand rare occasion.

'Eckard is my given name, the one I received on my birth, common enough in the Confederation, at least in my neck of the hills. Delmose is the name of my family or kindred as you called it. Taken after my father, though some choose their mother's family name, it's a matter of preference really. Finally, Farth is the town from where I was born, far to the north where the snow freezes your balls off and some half-wits call it the Onyx Summit, cause there is a big, dark, fucking cliff over there.' Eckard stated positioning the pot of rice over the flames now the wild bird had begun to cook through.

'Interesting. Good to know you Sar Eckard Delmose Farth' Judeson spoke.

Eckard laughed. 'I'm not a knight Judeson, the others do that mockingly.'

'But you were once?' Judeson inquired.

'Could have been.' Eckard bluntly stated in response.

'My grandmother was a Cavalier and then my father also, a knight in the court of Nesfalhn or so I am told. When the Hand of Kingdoms ruled the Southrondor and men and women were not butchered like animals and children were not taken as slaves.' Judeson

'Impressive.' Eckard stated.

Judeson narrowed his gaze at the Northman.

Eckard waved his hands in protest. 'No truly it is, my father was an erratic lunatic and my mother was too busy trying to keep me alive to be bothered to care about herself, or so I'm led to believe'

'You never knew them?' Judeson inquired, easing up.

'Nope. Moving on.' Eckard answered and began dissembled the cooked meat off the bird with the roasting prong and a small knife that had seemingly appeared from nowhere.

The two men stopped and devouring their simple meal, Judeson was impressed by how delicious it was. Eckard was obviously talented with food and cooking. The bird was perfect, the spices subtle but potent, the rice cooked with a hint of coconut wherever that had come from. Judeson found that he was enjoying food for the first time in what seemed many many arcs.

When the meal had concluded and camp had been broken the two men proceeded with their strides further into the Barrens. Scattered foliage and indiscriminately broken forests of immature aspen and elms could be seen going on for leagues. Judeson and Eckard bypassed a rather expansive low-lying bog and at the distant shore witnessed the burnt out remains of what was a homestead. Judeson personally had passed by this very way previously. So the trail they had set out was indeed a good one. On the journey northward and away from Letesah Judeson had scouted this ruin, though it had still been smoldering and though he had been in the relative distance south he had heard screams of anguish. Now the simple brickwork home there was no one that remained and the burning had left a hollow husk of its previous life. Eckard stood back kicking at cinders and ash. Judeson looked down at remnants of a child's necklace charm, the thread strand stretched and tore apart, dispersal of simple coloured beads laid next to it.

The necklace was just like those made by the children of Letesah, simple yet meaningful. Judeson felt himself once more returning to the grim thoughts of the past that returned so often.

'What's that?' Eckard called as the tall man scouted around the decimated ruins.

'Just another bad memory' Judeson answered, standing up and brushing his dirt ash ridden hands on his leather pants.

Eckard grunted and closed his eyes, considering something all to himself, before he nodded at Judeson. 'Raks?' Eckard asked.

'Could have been, hard to tell could have been bandits taking advantage.' Judeson said, remembering how he had witnessed this place first burning but had arrived too late to help whatever had befallen its victims.

'We do such stupid shit to each other sometimes' Eckard replied and walked off down south away from the residence.

Judeson lugged up his pack and trekked up to the man. 'Do you even know where we are going' Judeson inquired.

'Away from that bad memory and into another, lead on please' Eckard said, gesturing for Judeson to take the lead.

Judeson obliged and began on the trail, knowing the next night's rest would be more comforting, at least in the bare physical sense anyway.

*

'This looks comforting' Eckard stated.

Judeson led him up an old overgrown trail of a low hill to a quaint thatched roof cottage. The yard a shambles, and the fence that had enclosed the residence was in desperate need of attention. Judeson walked through the fence and past the knee high gate which had been dislodged from its hinges by rust. Eckard followed the big Southron and cast his attention to scanning the dead residents. The cottage seemed to be sturdy enough with all the walls and roof still intact. The glass windows had been long ago blown apart and loose shards lay near. A makeshift door of fence railings had been erected where once the home's door had been and Judeson strolled up to it.

Eckard looked around at the tangled weeds of the yard and noticed nothing untoward. Old habits proved too strong however and he opened up a stream of Magik and cast webs about, again nothing. No, a whisper at least outside, inside he sensed one life, but nothing of threat. The Mage closed his access to the arcane sea and raised a questioning glance to Judeson.

His companion took note and pushed aside the

barrier door gently and beckoned Eckard in, replacing the door as Eckard obliged. The room before them was dust ridden and looked to have not been lived in for several arcs at least, cob webs and buzzing flies littered the scene. The kitchen, in particular, was a great mess of broken and now mouldy clay vessels and discarded black iron pans.

Judeson walked further into the residence ignoring the vermin infestation and walked down the narrow hallway of warped wooden planks at the end of the house to a small abandoned room. The Southron knelt down and tapped on the tiles in a clearly rehearsed exchange. Eckard sensed the sole life underneath move into action. An answering conversation of gentle taps recited Judeson's own and the Southron repeated the verse again.

A trap door opened up at their feet and a slight framed woman of who was clearly malnourished emerged, crossbow readied and aimed at them. Judeson raised a steadying hand and the woman dropped her aim, a clearly relieved beaming smile crossed her features.

'Thank Zadma you are back.' The woman of wild brown hair stated, she dropped the crossbow and moved toward Judeson to embrace him.

Judeson picked up the woman in his arms and comforted her as she let out a sigh of relief. Eckard observed she had been shaking which seemed to subside as Judeson continued the embrace. This man certainly had a way with women – Eckard mused.

'Is your daughter still well?' Judeson inquired gently pushing the woman away.

'She's right behind me.' The woman answered, as a small girl bearing a similar visage to her own appeared.

Eckard knew why he had not sensed another life and found himself wondering once more if they would ever be done with the ghost of arcs past.

6th Stanza

Verse 27

In absent thought, pain subsides but is not
gone

Our mortal entrapment that holds as so, is
surely our undoing

and our remaking

For if our thoughts are only plagued with
death of innocence and

other such unquenchable morose

Surely we must hold to the afterword regard of Redemption's touch

Speakings of the Nameless Fallen Sculester and Pondly - 1722 arcs ATF (After The Fall)

'I just hope those two have not got themselves in too deep, we need them back here.' Raijin announced.

'Now who misses Eckard? Did he catch your eye?' Lisiarna teased, finding the act the more satisfying that Raijin had enacted on her previously.

'I would not dare to test your ire Kail' Raijin stated, a smile crossing his features.

'Ah, whatever then.' Lisiarna answered, raising her hand to knock on the wooden door they both stood at.

As if on perfect queue, the portal creaked open and the red, sweating face of Luciarn greeted them with a beaming smile.

'About time, you two quickly come in.' Luciarn stated, beckoning Raijin and Lisiarna inside.

The beanpole Draul waited for Lisiarna to pass before coming in and Luciarn swung the door to a close in their wake.

Luciarn fetched a ribbed glass decanter of Kormai firewater from a rosewood timber table and three

tumbler glasses. Lisiarna waved off the offer as
Rajin took a glass in hand and sat himself down
on one of the seat cushions. Lisiarna turned to
the window and peered outside at a chaotic scene
unfolding. From behind her Luciarn exchanged
pleasantries and tipped glasses together. A
carriage had overturned on the cobblestone road;
just two streets over down the steep hill from
them. The city-watch had turned out to control
and contain the tense exchange between
pedestrians and several other carriage escorts
that had taken it upon themselves to debate the
issue in the street. No blades had been drawn so
that was something at least.

'Well, most of our plans went to goat-shit.'
Luciarn uttered as he slumped into a plush
cushion.

'Krikza is an upstart, though his coup was
meticulously planned. We still have quite a few
options friend. Don't pull the rest of your hairs
from your head just yet.' Raijin replied, the
Draul's quiet voice barely heard over the rising
crescendo from outside.

'You two were more than possibly followed which
even if we have options, means someone does not
want access to them. Perhaps Krikza is wary since
we did spoil his plan of corrupting the Fore-Seer
boy.' Luciarn announced as he drained his fire
water and stood up to begin pacing.

Lisiarna turned toward the two men. 'Clever idea
merchant to cause a raucous and sidetrack our
would-be spies.' She said.

Lucairan nodded in reply, thoughtful still
looking aghast with worry.

'Krikza is too caught up in his pursuit of power
to worry about a band of runaway Magickers.
Besides the bastard is an insufferable clown and

would not have the finesse to organize recon on us. Perhaps his Shralett as more insight. Or maybe the Collective is far more involved than we realize.' Lisiarna continued.

'Though far more worryingly we did sense a Channellor stalking around somewhere. A creature such as that could sway many to do more than following us.' Raijin declared, refilling his tumbler with more fire water.

Surely they are not this far north, if that is so...' Luciarn started.

Lisiarna cut him off. 'Raijin is prone to describing worst case scenarios.' She stated narrowing her eyes at the beanpole Draul. 'The Channellor is most probably in the Woldte, either this Tiramene we have heard so much about or another. That would be the most likely situation, merchant.'

Luciarn nodded in acknowledge, seeming to calm down slightly.

'You are probably right.' Luciarn stated.

'Even if the Channellor or the Yun blind us all, more than one of those creatures are directly involved. It is still disconcerting to think Krikza has quite clearly made a pact with them. Now given we already know that certain members of the Collective are in cohorts with Channellors. We are fast running into a heck of a lot of growing enemies.' Lisiarna stated.

'As always you are a shining light, Kail.' Raijin stated turning to Lisiarna.

'Oh quiet you' Lisiarna replied.

'Well, the question remains what is our next course of action.' Luciarn said.

Lisiarna looked out the window once more and saw the dispersing crowd that Luciarn had somehow orchestrated. In the background, three figure fully cloaked stalked the peripheries. As the various retinues of onlookers, arguing carriage operators and city guards fanned out the three apparitions began forward up the hill to where Luciarn's estate was.

'I believe leaving Nero and away from prying eyes is in due course.' Lisiarna stated.

'And where pray-tell are we to trot off to?' Luciarn queried.

'Somewhere we can think.' Lisiarna stated, walking to the back exit, a simple affair of a timber door. Raijin made to join her and Luciarn followed in the Draul's wake.

'What are we plotting again?' Luciarn inquired.

'You will need to ready your most reliable assailant's friend Luciarn, we plan to strike them in retaliation. And we plan to strike them where it will hurt the most.' Raijin answered the man as they advanced down the rain sodden stairwell and out into the alley where a horse drawn carriage awaited them.

'Oh Gods' Luciarn sighed.

'Yep and Eckard and Judeson will provide the backup.' Lisiarna said.

Lucairn waved to the hooded carriage driver who returned the gesture and beckoned them aboard. Lisiarna went in first with assistance from Raijin who raised her small form onto the raised steps up into the concealed booth. The beanpole Draul followed her in and Lucairn back them up. Once inside the dim lit carriage booth. Luciarn sighed more prominently again. Lisiarna sensed the man's hesitation.

'We are left with very little choice merchant, we need to fight them where we can.' Lisiarna voiced as she pondered what identity she would enact once they were closer to their objective.

'Anywhere but there.' Luciarn voiced in frustration.

'Believe me, I would like nothing more than to never see that place ever again. But these Void-damned pricks need to be stopped before this invasion of theirs begins. And the Woldte is where this particular battle must be fought.' Lisiarna announced, memories flooding back to her, none of them particularly pleasant.

Luciarn nodded this time in reply and knocked on the front door for the carriage to take off.

**

'Ruth, we can't stay long there is more to be done.' Judeson said as the woman made top lay her callused hands on him again.

'Chasing the trails of war leads to nothing but heartache young man, stay here and be safe. Help us and we will help you also.' The older woman known as Ruth replied as she rested a staying palm on Judeson's chest.

Even with her deeply scarred hands, her touch was surprisingly gentle, Judeson realised. Her smooth, gentle voice was calming in direct contrast to the actual state of madness of the voice's speaker. This circumstance of an unstable mind seemed all too prominent now as it had been the previous visitation he had made on the farmhouse.

'Come back with us, we can take you to a safe place, the Karchelch it has many brave men and women. The Free-Fighters, we are strong and united and hold against any Rak threat.' Judeson stated, though his words even to him were weak and devoid of truth.

Ruth shook her head. 'No sweet Judeson my place is here at my home with my daughter.'

'Ruth please...' Judeson began but was cut short

as the older woman reached for his pants,
clutching at the belt.

Ruth let out a long unrestrained sigh and moved
closer still to Judeson. Her cracked lips parted
and she tilted her head inward to Judeson's own.
He was met with an aggressive but not altogether
unsuspected kiss. Ruth's withered hands reached
downwards across Judeson's tunic and she pulled
his leather belt.

Judeson pushed Ruth away and held her at arm's
length, a continued look of rapturous hunger in
her eyes. There was indeed madness within her. By
a stretch of the imagination was she ugly or
undesirable, a little old for him perhaps but he
would have welcomed the woman's attention none
the less had Judeson not felt a vertiginous sense
that her actions were not well thought-out. She
seemed to act on impulse and something had to be
broken within her mind. Pity was overwhelming any
desire Judeson could possibly have for this
woman.

'Please Ruth stop.' Judeson stated looked at her
as she struggled.

Ruth stopped and said: 'I'm sorry Judeson, let's
get your dinner sorted'.

For twenty minutes Judeson helped the woman
assemble their food, in excruciating silence.

*

Onita was not living; of that much, she was
absolutely certain was true. Nearly every other
facet of whatever her existence was exactly, she
had no grounded understanding of to be sure. How
very fitting it was that she could not even feel
the ground beneath her feet. In fact, she could
not feel much of anything at all. How she still
remained here was beyond her. What Onita did know
was that she was not living anymore; and that she

loved her mother. Her mother who had long ago lost most perception of what it was to be living too. Onita was not so upset by this though she was not sure if she could feel emotions anymore either, though the predisposition remained that her mother loved her and that was enough for Onita.

Onita was instructed to prepare a bath for the tall and dark-haired stranger just as Judeson had taken earlier. Though just as the preparation on the bath tub had gone for Judeson Onita had merely shown this next man where and how all the applicant materials were for bathing. This man seemed vastly different than the brooding Judeson (who her mother liked so very much). This Northman had something about him, something she could not entirely place but something.

The tall man in question had already stripped down, weapons pushed to the side of the room, chain maille off and shirt removed. The tall man raised one of his brows at Onita as if to ask a question but no words came forth or so Onita thought to make conversation.

'Do you require assistance Northman?' Onita questioned the stranger.

'You can call me Eckard and your name is?' Eckard inquired right back at Onita.

'Onita' Onita replied.

'You are a ghost, a soul-snared apparition you know that right?' Eckard said bluntly.

Onita was stung and took a step back. After awhile she composed herself and nodded back at Eckard. She knew what she was, it was just unsettling that someone else could see that too. Judeson did not take notice and her mother could not quite get past what happened before Onita's death, understandable at least Onita thought it should be.

'Why are you still here, I'm sorry but the realm of the living is no place for wandering souls.' Eckard said.

'What about ones that help hold together the living before they pass.' Onita replied.

'You know since crossing the Boundary you are not the first spirit I have happened across, the Arcane Sea's leavings lingers here very fucking strongly.' The Northman stated. 'Ah sorry girl, I'm a bit rough, forgive my tone.' He said, though his apology did not sound right to Onita.

'I don't mind Eckard of the North. I'm not really here after all, well at as a girl anyway.' Onita stated, smiling at Eckard, it did not bother her about this man and his roughness.

'Well yes, of course. But I don't wanna be corrupting the dearly departed as well as the living.' Eckard said and winked. The man went about removing his clothes and hopped into the warm waters of the prepared tin bath tub.'And since you are not really a little girl anymore I cannot possibly be indecent to you.' He continued.

Onita laughed. At least she felt herself laugh. Could not be sure. When the man turned around in the tub, Onita spotted a large scarring mark right down his back across his lower spine, an old injury but an extremely noticeable to be sure.

'That much along your back, Eckard, does it hurt?' Onita said, though even as a member of the dearly-departed she knew there were some things mortals may not enjoy discussing.'Never mind, I'm sorry.'

'Accidents and sharp things, Was hilarious, had to be there.' Eckard replied a mischievous twinkle to his eyes and rye grin sported on his face.

'You are a very funny man.' Onita said even as she found herself chuckling.

Eckard brushed himself with a sponge and moved about the bathtub as for all intensive purposes he did not practically fit with his huge height.

'You know what Onita, I don't get that quite enough.' Eckard said.

*

Judeson and Eckard sat across from each at the silky old oak table as Onita sat down at one end her mother Ruth at the other. Situated in the middle of the table there was a large ceramic bowl of steaming noodles and another with deep red coloured soup. To the side of these main dishes as an assortment of green leaves and hand picked herbs. Eckard nodded and smiled, it was not much and on first tasting it, it was a little bland but the thought and effort were well and truly noted. These two remaining family members, even if one was passed were quite capable. It was a feast compared to what he and Judeson who manage in the wilds.

'Excellent, thank you very much Ruth and little Onita.' Eckard spoke first, with a mouthful of noodles: The man winking at Onita who pretended to be interested in the food.

'You and your mother are welcome to come along with us.' Judeson said.

Ruth sighed and dropped her head into her hands. 'This again, Judeson please no more.'

'Mother maybe these men have a point' Onita spoke up in defence of Judeson.

'Sweetie please.' Ruth stated. Onita smiled back at her mother.

Eckard though better than to interject oneself in the tenuous situation and leave his input open to the vitriol that would probably come from the deranged mother and her long passed daughter. Judeson shifted in his seat and dropped his fork to the table.

'A story than to tide us over.' Judeson began. 'Long ago the wise woman of my village gave us a tale of a hoppit and plains loin that pursued it.' Judeson cleared his throat and commenced this tale with a brief look at the table. 'Many arcs ago there was...'

'What's a hoppit?' Eckard questioned, spooning more noodles into his bowl.

'I'll tell you a story, it is a mother and daughter that were set upon by savages.' Ruth interrupted.

'No Ruth..' Judeson said in dead seriousness. Ruth took no hindrance of Judeson's steely tone and continued on unabated.

'My husband and I were set upon in the yard by a group of scraggly looking bandits, aurmen if you could call them that. In their wake; a score of Rakoni, head to toe in black metal armour followed. It was cruel and cold. They killed him, my husband, stone dead with blows from clubs, one after the other. And the Raks watched on, burned our crops and livelihood and slaughtered the cattle for meat. The Raks watched. My older daughter Rubie was taken as was I. Vicious without a hint of fucking restraint. And then the Raks, the animals took my boy Tyrell away, telling the bandits not to touch a hair on his head, though he was already damaged on the inside now. The bandits left amused with themselves they were.' Ruth stated, tears welling in her eyes.

'This will not help. Ruth.' Judeson spat, his

tone if steely before was now fully armed to the
teeth in the hard cold to the touch iron. The man
had impressively imposing speaking voice when he
wanted to, Eckard reckoned.

Ruth broke into tears and Onita moved to her
side. Counseling her however she could, only
Eckard and Onita herself knowing her touch would
be impossible to pass upon her mother.

'Please Ruth. Let's not make ourselves upset.'
Judeson said as he stood and looked across the
table at Ruth who nodded and wiped at her tears
that were freeflowing from her face. Judeson sat
back and continued his story.

Judeson continued as if Ruth had never spoken
though he was visibly shaken. 'The hoppit lived
in a burrow close by to where the loin roamed and
hunted. Though the greenest and most luscious
grass where the loin hunted. The loin knew this
of course as he this was why he was there. He was
a predator and one of convenience. The hoppit
each day tried to get to the green grass and each
the loin would try to bring him down.'

Eckard looked across to Ruth who was now calming
down though she had hardly touched her food which
was not a good sign. Onita hovered nearby her now
and seemed to comfort the emotional woman.

'What in the Far Above is a hoppit though?'
Eckard said, grinning at Onita who chuckled and
Ruth looked across to her daughter. Ruth seemed
to forget herself and even smiled as her daughter
laughed.

Judeson nodded across at Eckard, knowing what the
man was doing. 'It's an animal with four legs,
though it bounds on two. It is fur-ridden and
ears like a rabbit you have in the North, though
far stiffer.'

Eckard smiled once more and Onita and Ruth

followed suit.

'Please continue Judeson.' Ruth knowledge Judeson had not finished his story.

Judeson nodded and obliged the request saying

'The hoppit was putting his life at risk each time. He knew he was in danger although each time he did narrowly escape, so that was important. Evidently, the plains loin gave up, his quarry was too fast and too cunning so he left for easier prey.'

'And thus the hoppit escaped back to its humble abode and the loins chased other game.' Judeson finished, leaning back in his chair with a smile. Ruth nearby returned to looking grim and began to cry again.

'I'm petrified of their return, and what they will do to us when they do. You have no idea of the fear I have' Ruth stammered, her top lip quivering, her arms shaking and her eyes welling up as before. The subject had shifted back.

'I'm afraid of heights, always have been. Letesah sits on a plateau of course and I was shit-scared to go too far to the edge. Other kids would taunt me and pretend to almost fall whenever we walked out to the borders. My father took me up Mount Ayrdio once, tried not shut my eyes as he practically carted me up the summit.' Judeson answered, stuttering as he always did when he mentioned his father. His story seemed to ease the nerves of their host however as she sat back down.

'I have an allergy to horse hair, stay away from the things at every chance that I get, terrible Yunlander I am. Lucky I am only a dirty half-blood.' Eckard added, joining in. 'And don't get me started on swimming'

'Those are all silly fears. The Raks are

dangerous and deadly.' Ruth screeched.

Onita turned on her mother. 'Mother listen all fears are as prominent as each other. We must learn to face our fears. And we must learn to survive. Judeson's tale is important that's why he said it. He spoke of finding safety.'

'I'm not leaving my home and neither are you, young lady!' Ruth screamed, standing up and her eyes welling up. She shoved her bowl to the side and it crashed off the table into a thousand smaller pieces.

Judeson rushed forward and embraced Ruth who seemed to fold into his arms. The woman tossed and turned in opposition to him. Her screeches and soft moaning turned animistic in tone but Judeson still held her. Evidently, she went silent and was obvious she had exhausted herself into the unconscious. Judeson picked her up like a rag doll and took her to her bedroom. Onita looked back at Eckard.

'Your mother thinks you are still alive doesn't she.' Eckard said.

'You wishes I were, I don't think she has accepted me leaving. But Judeson does not realize either does he.' Onita replied.

'Not many do Onita, it would be difficult to tell if one did not use Magik.' Eckard replied.

'Or if they touch me' Onita said.

'They cannot, the physical realm and beyond the past, the Arcane Sea never get to meet. Unless Magik is cast and their presence can be snared into being here. But never the body, once dead there is no return.' Eckard instated.

'You two should leave, my mother is like me, caught between the living and dead, in a different way sure but only I can understand how she feels, out of place.' Onita said and Eckard nodded knowing there time here was done.

*

'We could have handled that better' Judeson announced as he and Eckard made their way in a brisk march across a muddy field to an old rundown barn.

'There is little we could have done, they will look after each other' Eckard replied, his breath shallow in the evening chill and shivered, though he was not entirely sure that was just simply the frosty air.

'We are warriors, not healers. That much is certain.' Judeson said.

'Was that ever in doubt?'

Judeson shrugged in an answer and doubled his pace forward to the thatched roofed barn.

'I left mounts here, two from my last passing through. Ruth and Onita kept them healthy so we can get back to the Free-Fighters.'

'Oh great.' Eckard stated dryly, kicking at the muck at his feet. These free-fighters must be involved with the man's stubborn plans for vengeance somehow it would seem.

Judeson pried open one of the side doors to the stables and motioned to the Northman the horses of which stirred from slumber, saddlebags hung nearby on a post.

'Anything but fucking horses.' Eckard decreed.

Judeson laughed enthusiastically and began to prepare one of the mounts.

'It will get there faster. I take it you know how to prep a horse for riding. ' Judeson answered.

'Unfortunately yes.' Eckard replied.

7th Stanza

*The Hand of Kingdoms was ripped apart in frenzied
fervor, the plague and the civil wars left thousands dead
and tens of thousands in diaspora. The sudden influx of
refugees caused a strain on the Nertheilm nations. We*

are still reeling from this to the modern day. The strangest aspect of it all is that events of the 'Breaking of the Hand' are still not all clear to any of us.

– Reflections on the Southrondor-that-was

– Girgio Maskren Moor, Professor of History at Seljuk University

– 2989 arcs ATF

'You and her, you are lovers?' Judeson pried, the words stinging Eckard as he awkwardly pivoted back in his saddle to look at the Southron.

Eckard granted his companion a lingering look of disapproval to allude to how to unwelcome the inquiry actually was.

'Lovers?' Eckard queried, pulling down on straps and reining in just to the left of Judeson his horse stamping down in the dusty earth for being pulled up so abruptly.

Judeson looked across to Eckard who burst out in sudden laughter. Not a slight chuckle either, the man howled with laughter, the sound erupting from his throat and the sound belting out across the open expanse of the Karchelch.

Before Judeson could interject with any form of speech. Eckard stopped just momentarily and peered over at Judeson and then once more began urging his horse forward once more along the dirty old cattle track.

'Hmmpp..' Judeson replied, letting out a snort of disapproval and bedazzlement.

'Bah! Enough said about all that, there are far more pressing matters ahead, my friend.' Eckard said just ahead.

'Fair enough' Judeson replied under his breath. It was quite clear the subject was closed.

Eckard reigned in his steed further forward along the dusty trail. Judeson motioned for the Northman to follow him around a hollow on the ground ahead and more westward than they had been going, for Judeson had once more picked up the trail they should be on.

'You know in the Nertheilm we have a tale similar to the one you told back at the ranch' Eckard began as they skirted wide around a small dried out creek bed.

'Oh?' Judeson replied, not forgetting the man had changed the subject conveniently.

'Though in ours we replace your giant cat and big bouncing rabbit-thing with an ice wolf and hare darting away for his life from the former.' Eckard stated.

'BSo it is still essentially the same tale? That of a relentless predator but an adaptable prey, how a cycle can shift.' Judeson answered.

Eckard looked ahead where woodland began to take shape from the barren plain lands. Ahead of the scattered forests, lay a small lake, Judeson knew to be Mellow's pond and past that the plateau of Letesah. Home, finally.

'No not entirely, in the tale of the wolf and the hare, he wolf took its prey in the end, though the hare offered tough resistance all the way through.' Eckard continued after a brief silence.

'Then the point had shifted entirely, what was a tale of hope and progress is in the North a grim yarn of failure.' Judeson said.

'No, not failure, there is much progress in that story.' Eckard replied.

'How so? The predator kills its prey and gets what it wanted. This is nothing new, aggression has taken so much and answers are far and few between its stubborn charge.'

'If you choose to look at it from a very shallow point of view, yes, that is exactly how it could be viewed. But there a few changes in our telling of this that you may be interested in.'

'Which is?'

'The hare does indeed retreat and is safe for a time from the clutches of the wolf. Though whereas your tale ends with that one particular, our version continues with the prey returning to eat in the wolf's domain.' Eckard stated.

'Then it could be taken that you tale illustrates the lack of restraint on the Hare's part. That it was safe but it chooses to return. The predator failing once did not repeat their error again when gifted afresh with opportunity.'

'Well, there is that. But more importantly is the rest of the story. You see the hare returns to the wolf's territory because it knows full well that its life is at risk just as your hoppit tale. Though in our reiteration the hare makes its return because it knows the grass tastes the best from where the wolf makes its lair, and despite the risk continues feeding on that particular patch of turf because it desires the best for its self and the wolf pounces on its prey's unwillingness to give up.' Eckard stated.

'Then you ending is left with the impression of greed on the prey's part, that it could have escaped the predator given the chance but choose not to.'Judeson said.

Eckard nodded though he then smiled. 'Then I would ask you Judeson why is it you return to the den of the beast?'

Eckard's smiled dropped and he stared directly at Judeson now. The Southron felt a cold chill motion up his spine and he shivered though the night was not particularly cold.

'Because we are not animals and it is not grass we seek.' Judeson replied and brought his horse to a canter with Eckard following in his wake.

The two men pushed their horses into a canter as they neared the edge of the lake and the rising plateau ahead of them. Judeson gestured at the land mass and the township with billowing smog clouds overhead.

'Letesah, well at least it was once.' Judeson said.

'From the fire into the inferno.' Eckard stated and they continued on.

The eastbound fierce winds that like of which his father had named the Raging Gale drafted past pushing the various low tree and shrubbery pockets of the hills in its wake. Judeson took in the warm breeze and the windswept wilderness around him. Feeling somewhat nostalgic about the whole return to the Karchelch Barrens, the Southron reigned in his mount and slowed down, across the rugged Auburn dirt path. Judeson leaned to his left and spat off onto the loose shale rock outcropping nearby. Glancing back at Eckard who doused himself with water from his right hand, seeming to flick his hand from above his head and a tide falling about his head.

'Won't that rust your armour?' Judeson asked with a rye grin forming on his bronzed face, the satisfaction of watching the Eckard squirm in comfort ability was not worth hiding.

'This place is too Void-Damned warm.....' Eckard stated wiping the excess moisture from his face and hair with both hands.

'The Karchelch can be I suppose..but it's quite cool at night. You should travel further South beyond the River Furrow. Then you will know what warm truly feels like.'

'I pray to any God that will listen that I never have to then.'

Judeson shrugged more to himself than Eckard really, just the inherent action of which kept him alive, the conversation with his distinctly closed companion not so. The humour with the bean bole North man was interesting sometimes but that

was always followed by the grim and thoughtful
silence that accompanied their travels together.
Or so far Judeson could gauge of their time
together anyway.

Less than a league ahead the plains rolled out
onto a generous swath of upraised hill country
and atop that a lengthy expanse of scattered
woodland. The two men cantered their mounts up
the hill, Judeson pushing ahead knowing they were
very very close now.

Both men dismounted and tied up their horses in
the shade of an alcove of stunted pines. Judeson
whistled a short melodic line out into the
falling darkness of the forest ahead and from the
pines and cedar emerged a collection of harrowed
faces and malnourished bodies.

They certainly did not appear to be much worth.
The rag-tag company had very few articles of
armour even clothes seemed scarce on their
malnourished bodies. Weapons were few and far
between for the supposed 'Fighters' Judeson had
claimed them to be. Eckard worried as to what the
man thought these helpless denizens could offer.
Men and women with hallowed looking expressions.
Scarce few had anything that could remotely be
called armour. Thus these were the supposed
'Free-Fighters' Judeson had spoken of.

One of the scruffy looking Southrons rushed
forwards out of the pack, a woman with hair the
colour of flame, her clothes a mere thin cloth
coated in dirt. The young woman jumped at Judeson
and gathered him into an embrace, latching on
with an intensely tight interlocked grip. Judeson
looking alarmed at first now sported a grin from
ear to ear and Eckard needed no words to
understand.

'Thank the Queen you are back!' The red head

squealed with unassailable delight.

Judeson did not grant an answer and pulled her into an equally tight embrace and hugged her for what seemed a lifetime. Eckard found himself looking through the crowd of some equally halcyon faces, some still seemed stuck in downtrodden and not even the arrival of a wayward son could break them out of such; most peculiar still were the set of figures at the back of the welcoming party. There was no grins or delighted looks present on their face, just dark expressions of determination.

A big and brawny Southron man made his way towards the forefront and stood in close proximity to Judeson and Jehasli.

'Good to have you back Judeson son of Judisye, the hero of the Fall of Letesah.' The robust man boomed out.

The crowd around seemed to hold him in high regard as they took on his every word.

Judeson let Jehasli pull away from his embrace, although the young woman stood close by his side as he turned to the large man with tan skin.

'Cousin Yormeth it is equally good to see you once more.' Judeson stated dryly.

The lack of sincerity in Judeson's tone sounded a little too burdened with doubt for Eckard's liking. Glancing across at this Yormeth, Eckard saw no derision from the man directed at Judeson and Eckard perceived maybe he had hastily jumped to conclusions. Though Yormeth exuded a clear strain of prideful permissiveness with his arms crossed he strode through the mass of aurmanity who downcast their eyes on the man's passing. If Yormeth was in charge here, it may not entirely be from a respectful position Eckard speculated. From the very back of the crowd around himself,

Judeson and Jehasli; Eckard witnessed another curious insight. Around a score of Southrons stood several paces off from any of the others, the distance was clearly imposed but one group or the other. A short, angular faced man at the front of the separate score met Eckard's gaze and turned away just as fast.

'Come you and your ah...' Yormeth began turning to face Eckard dropping his arms by his side.

'Eckard' Eckard stated, tilting his head in respect.

Yormeth offered no greeting in return and turned back to Judeson.

'You and Eckard will join us for dinner and then after we would hear if you are ready. For our plans are almost complete now.' Yormeth continued and about turned. The rest of the Southron Free-Fighters turned with him and all as one they advanced further into the woodland.

As Eckard followed the group into the forest he saw that more and more of the shadowed figures were either too old or too young for any real fighting. Humped over old men and women waddled after Yormeth carrying babes, young boys and girls skipped at their heels. Of the mass of Aurmanity spotted here and there was a mere handful out of dozens of able bodies, carrying armaments. That particular minority of those that were armed did not have much in the category of the aforementioned. There was a rusty sword with no scabbard here and an old pick axe there. Eckard noted, somewhat sourly how illequipped these so-called Free-Fighters actually were.

From just behind Eckard, Jehasli moved in close whispering in Judeson's ear as they walked side by side. Eckard allowed a brief stream of Magik to be pushed out from oneself, focusing on their speech. Eckard picked up their words and increased the audible level to play back to him.

'Mind your steps, best you and Eckard remain wary of Yormeth and his vipers.' Jehasli's words rang out inside Eckard's mind on the Mana-stream. Eckard felt a strange pulse mark across his Magik flow, but it was not too small and insignificant to take much note. Possibly still feeling the effects of the Boundary and it's odd openness to the Arcane Sea.

Judeson did not answer Jeshali and just nodded. He held out his hand the redheaded woman took it in her ownself.

8th Stanza

Just as you would not wash cloth in dirty water

You would not sharpen blade on dulled stone,

You would not harvest wheat within the chill of Noctra

How can you possibly trust a person who never takes their mask away from their face?

The Issue with the Rakoni

Sandil Maseada Malik addressing the Confederation Reclaimer Council on the Rakoni's incursions into the Nertheilm

The Prodigal son has returned- Thought Yormeth. He spat on the dusty earth beneath his feet.

Water droplets began to fall from gloomy grey cloud cover overheard. Dust quickly turned to mud.

Looking up into the Far Above, dark clouds rolled on in the evening air and the clap of fear of thunder could be heard. Turning his attention to more earthly matters, Yormeth observed all his soldiers, the rabble of immigrants and miscreants and the new arrivals had all camped down together.

Void Damn the man. His cousin had returned and all the others seemed to shrug aside his words and concerns. Already that conniving bitch, Jehasli clung to Judeson like a leech. Yormeth had committed the hard yards. He had rallied the Free-Fighters and acquired all the necessary equipment and for all intensive purpose; trained all the warriors of note, here. Now, however that big, brawny dumb bastard, his void-damned cousin had strode in with some odd looking Northern wretch. Well, Yormeth would be thrown to the

Deep-Dark of the Void before Judeson wrestled his command out of his hands.

Still, Yormeth best keep face, at least for the others to continue in respecting him. Granted respect should be accommodated to him anyway, for all he had down for the little close knit community.

The new arrivals and Jehasli's other whores; the two were insufferable and far too scrawny women, had all seated themselves down with Judeson and his mung-eyed Northern friend. Jehasli had made her place very close indeed to Judeson. One of her whores made eyes at the Northman. Yormeth shook his head and gestured for his loyal men to follow the set order of camping down for the evening.

A fire was ordered to be made by Yormeth as to celebrate the arrival of the new guest and a returned Free-Fighter, much to the intolerable protests of Judeson and Jehasli. Yormeth chooses to ignore their insolence and knew there would be ample time for the chastisement of those two.

Mulled wine was made and shavings of pork and pans of Kirilenko goat curry placed beside the fireplace as the heat came into full bloom and flames latched at the cast iron casings. Greens consisting of broad beans and leftover broccoli stalks were prepared by the non-combative personal of the camp. Curiously Yormeth observed the lanky, midnight-haired Northman take up a knife from seemingly nowhere at all and assist with the food's preparation. No matter the odd man could have his eccentricities even if he jumped into a woman's work without any sign of hesitation. These Northlings were a downright fucking strange lot.

Yormeth gestured Marko and Duminee in closer, his

two most trusted grunts. Big, strong and not much
in the way of individual thought process. The
kind of dependable enforcement and physicality
needed to properly assert authority over a
hopeless mass of aurmanity that desperately
needed direction. With dinner on the ready
Yormeth directed Marko and Duminee to keep both
eyes and ears on the newcomers and make sure they
remained 'settled'.

'So cousin, welcome home once more.' Yormeth
announced, forcing a smile onto his face,
bellowing out his tone and opening up his body,
raising his shoulders and puffing out his chest
to physically impose the ultimate sense of
comparability in the elevated position he
commanded. This installment of pride was
important it made the others respect their own
standing.

Judeson gazed up at Yormeth, the differing
orientation of their height, a perfect
representation of the difference in power.
Yormeth thought.

'Family reunited is always a joyous moment.'
Judeson beamed at Yormeth. Who did not know if
the man was alluding to a passive aggressive
approach or not?

Yormeth like always seen his opportunit anyway
and proverbialy pounced like the predator he was.

'I fear moments of joy, Judeson, are all too
short lived in our current circumstances. With
the Void-Damnmed Rak goat-takers infesting our
lands like the vermin they are.' Yormeth answered
back, keeping his own smile held within.

The group settled down and bunked down for the
night around the erected campfire.

Judeson and Jehasli fell in together and sat in
such close proximity to make Yormeth do a double

take. The Abyss take them they possessed no
decency. In each other's arms once more, just
like before his oafish cousin had left them.
Yormeth wondered if the man had gained anything
more meaningful than the unnerving giant that sat
across from him. This Eckard in question looked
bored of all things, the hairy bastard was just
looking at the fire and not meeting anyone's
eyes.

'How goes all the preparation Yormeth?' Judeson
started up. Stroking the redhead bitch Jehasli's
hair away from her face.

Yormeth paused for dramatic emphasis.

'It goes increasingly well, the thick-headed Raks
don't know we have such numbers and such
organization.' Yormeth stated, proudly.

Judeson and Jehasli shared a glance. Those two
were plotting something even now. The giant
Northman still did not look up.

'You are confident then that we can retake the
village.' Judeson inquired after a momentary
break.

'Of course, we have a plan' Yormeth replied.

Jehasli started up from leaning against Judeson.

'The gate's mechanism takes a long time for it to
open and close. Which is a clear disadvantage for
them. One if we time it right we could easily
exploit.'

Yormeth looked over with a questioning gaze and
narrowed his eyes at the woman. She always had to
get her two coins into everything.

'So their gate then, but how do we get to it?
Across the plain we are vulnerable and they will
have ranged lookouts and probably more. We have
no siege equipment still by the looks of things
so what is our advantage?' Judeson asked.

Yormeth's stomach reeled and turned with seething anger. - This bleeding, Void-damned prick thinks he can just come back and question his command.

'Cousin? What is our advantage?' Judeson voiced again.

Our - The word stung Yormeth like an arrow in his shoulder. How dare this peasant prick try to make out like he was one of them, one of the brave Free-Fighters, noble, honourable and fierce. Yormeth concealed his inner thoughts.

'We need no siege weapons, we have acquired some of that Gnome-ore. We are going to cause a big void-kissed blast and smoke those bastards out, they will open the gate to send reinforcements and we will have a concealed raiding party in place to charge right through their fucking gate they use to hold our homes.' Yormeth said.

Yormeth hinted at the plan perfectly. He had given enough of a summary to his half-wit cousin to leave the man content. At the same time, he concealed enough so that the plan would work brilliantly. After all, he had come up with it. Slight input from Jehasli aside it would work.

'You are using Oyra then? Do you know what you are doing?' The big Northman said finally looking up at the fire, with his unnerving sky-blue eyes.

Yormeth contemplated his next course of action to subdue these peasants.

'Friends, come on. Enough dull and sober questions, come let us drink and plot our next moves in joy.' Yormeth waved at Marko on the edges of the flicking firelight. 'Marko, my brother, come bring some wine and let us enjoy this night as allies'.

*

The nights in the Southrondor were just as muggy

and humid as their daytime counterparts. Though the sun had set the humidity seemed to linger on like an unwelcome guest. In such stark contrast to the northern realms mists, one could see quite well in the encompassing darkness (as well as an Aurman could in the dark anyway). The sweltering conditions provided a metaphorical background to the flaring tempers present on this night. And despite all this, a fire had been lit.

Very few of the rag-tag company remained present at the flaring fireplace that served as both a beacon to the leaders of the Free-Fighters to come in and as a symbol of endurance; in that the Rakon had not taken everything from them just yet. - At least that was what Yormeth had voiced quite zealously to Judeson and Eckard.

Of that handful of Fighters that remained with the trio of Yormeth, Judeson and Eckard only two were remotely conscious. Though it would some merely just did not want to contribute anything to the discourse.

Of that they could not be blamed- Eckard mused.

'We must strike hard and with great haste.' Yormeth pronounced.

'And what advantage would we be pressing upon Yormeth?' Judeson inquired.

'You have returned, unlike that coward Irsthule who sulked away because I won command.'

Judeson started up. 'Irsthule is not here? He had twenty good men and women, that means we have fewer numbers than before.' He said shaking his head in disdain.

'May the Abyss swallow him, they deserted us as they believe our cause impossible.' Yormeth replied. 'They doubt we can deliver, but Letesah will be returned to us, it is certain now.'

Judeson threw Eckard of disapproval a look and

the tall Northman nodded in unspoken understanding.

'All Raks are the same and must die for what their kin have done.' Yormeth spoke up, breaking the silence that had settled into the camp. If anything the man always craved attention it seemed.

'Did you ever stop and think what they actually are?' Eckard retorted.

'It matters little to what Raks are' Judeson huffed.

'Why? Knowing your enemy well is a great step in the right direction of defeating them.' Eckard answered, thinking his own response logical.

'A philosopher it would seem you are Eckard. Killing your enemy so we may live in due course enough for me. Besides if you must know; some scholars in the South have pondered that the Raks were unnatural creations of the Deep-below, evilly twisted creations of Daemon kind.' Yormeth stated, poking at the blazing fire-pit.

'That speaks of reanimated warriors, that's horse-shit' Eckard stated, matter-of-factly.

'More or less. Undead I believe a man in Tahnbael called them.'

'You truly believe the Morba-Rakon are brought back from the dead to fight you. As in Necromancy?' Eckard said, standing up and brushing off the dirt, leaves, and twigs from his person.

'Ah, the 'forbidden sorcery' - my father called that.' Judeson piped up, ceasing his incessant stirring of the campfire pot.

'And what do you Northman believe then?' Yormeth asked, narrowing his eyes at Eckard in a challenge.

'Well, I cannot speak for the entire Nertheilm. But Necromancy is not Magik. It is not even possible. In theory, a skillful caster may be able to attempt, soul-snaring which in itself is quite a task and more times than not a massive gamble. But bringing a dead body back? Impossible.'

'Magik is not possible' Yormeth blurted pushing out his chest in emphasises and standing up to face Eckard from a higher angle.

'Still not convinced huh?' Eckard said, lowering his gaze at the self-proclaimed renegade leader.

'What then is soul-snaring and why is Necromancy impossible?' Judeson said, standing between the two men closing off an avenue for aggression.

'Soul-snaring is an incredibly intricate and precise technique of attempting to touch the other-side…death and releasing a body-less soul from across the Arcane Sea. Trying to make contact with a soul that has passed from existence. It is rumoured to in many texts and some hints of progress have been alluded to. But realistically it is all very up in the clouds of the Far-Above to be perfectly honest. Soul-snaring may or may not be possible it is difficult to really tell outright.' Eckard stated.

'And Necromancy?' Yormeth asked.

'Well, the short answer – dead limbs.' Eckard answered.

'Your right that is a short answer and one that does not answer anything.'

'On the contrary, it answers it perfectly.'

'How so?'

'When one dies their limbs will seize up like dead wood and fail to work as they did in life. There have been tales of folk's hands encased on their blade's pommel so tight the weapon could not be extracted after a battle.'

'And this explains your dark Magiks failing to work?' Yormeth searched, smiling in a challenge and in unmistakable arrogance.

'Even if one could somehow theoretically bring back someone from the dead - which as I stated is called soul-snaring is not an absolute resounding truth at all: The limbs are dead and unusable for the body. If you had an undead vassal at your command which applying to your reasoning Yormeth would be a Rakon ravager. That warrior would not have use of their limbs and could not fight. A pretty fucking, void-damned useless skill to possess.' Eckard said.

'And what's more, the Rakon is not any of that anyway. So this little argument that you are so inclined on pursuing is not reasonable nor is it of any worth, gentlemen, ladies.' Eckard finished (and finished for Yormeth) walking off from the camp fire and into the woods where it would be best to stay tonight.

Behind him, he knew Judeson laid a steadying hand upon Yormeth and was counseling him to not push the issue any longer.

Eckard walked deeper into the woods or what passed for woodland on the Southrondor. The trees were so scattered apart and ground so very dry beneath feet, almost nothing like the esla'theilm's damp and misty confines or the dense cluster of ancient oaks in the Confederation lands. Pulled up from his thoughts, he gathered his knapsack and other belongings from the concealed hollow where he had kept them safe.

**

'Judeson the man is clearly keeping something

from you, not to mention unpredictable. A
dangerous combination. Zadma Bless us.' Jehasli
stated, the woman, incensed. Her eyes marred with
passion.

Judeson felt there was something off if the way
she uttered the lady's name though he did not
think to question it.

'Eckard is an odd character I'll grant you that.'
Judeson replied, trying to lighten the mood
within the makeshift tent he now shared with
Jehasli.

'This is no joke, Judeson.' Jehasli said,
crossing her arms.

Judeson nodded. 'I realize this. Look Eckard has
done nothing but selfless acts since I have met
him some weeks ago. The man is unpredictable but
he is just and kind. I would be so daring to even
call him a friend. Though he is still quite
annoying.' Judeson admitted.

Even as he said it, Judeson felt himself
reminisce about the events of the past few weeks.
About how Eckard had thrown himself in danger's
way again and again and followed Judeson further
down a path of yet more hazard. Jehali's face
seemed to soften from her dark, brooding she had
previously born. The flame-haired woman's arms
unfolded also.

'Perhaps you are right, Judeson. I'm sorry I was
being just as judgemental as Yormeth for a moment
there. Any friend of yours can also be one of
mine too.' Jehasli said.

'No one can be as judgemental as Yormeth. No one'
Judeson replied with a smile.

Jehasli happily laughed in answer.

'That is altogether the most truthful verse ever
uttered from anyone, Judeson.' Jehasli replied
between fits of laughter.

Judeson smiled and then gave into laughing, it was good to see Jehasli again, even better when she was in such high spirits. He reached out a hand to her and she took him in, closer to her. Pulling him so their faces met and his arms curled around her waist and Jehasli's around his neck.

'Just like old times.' Jehasli said, a beaming smile on her face. By the Queen's mercy she was beautiful - Judeson though.

He never replied, not with words at least and instead and kissed Jehasli deeply.

*

'I've always wondered what it was like to meet a wizard.' The slim dark-skinned woman stated as she crawled into the tent pushing aside the canvas entrance.

Eckard made a note of her body language and she tried to slip closer toward him. He shifted back to look at her sternly.

'What are you doing?' Eckard asked though he sensed by the slightest inkling he had a fair idea.

'Getting to know you better, wizard.' The woman replied, seeming to purr in the process. Her eyes were hungry and she still positioned herself on all fours as if she were a beast ready to pounce.

'Wizard, an olden term used by Cor-Dazrals and it would seem Southrons.' Eckard said putting a hand up against his beard and somewhat covering his mouth. 'Nowadays we are usually referred to as Mages or Arcanists.'

The onyx haired woman was now less than a pace from Eckard. Her face close to his and she reached out a slight hand brushing the back of his palm.

'Words are cheap. What I require are insight,

knowledge, and learning.' The woman winked. 'Which sometimes words don't quite fill'

Eckard drew back further, now cornered against the canvas tent wall.

'I'm not sure I can help you, lady' Eckard said.

The woman licked her lips and replied; 'Well apparently you Mages can satisfy a woman in ways unheard of in normal circles.' The woman whispered, drawing out the word 'Mages' in a feline purr.

'What I do has almost nothing to do with that sort of pleasure.' Eckard replied, raising an eyebrow but holding eye contact with the woman. The woman shrugged.

'Come on handsome, beneath the twin moons we could teach each other and dispense with words, though much I am sure later we shall talk for hours in each other's arms.' The woman finally said, with heavily lidded eyes and her full lips parted.

Eckard knew something was up, he was not handsome, at least not conventionally so. Most sane women did not swoon at a crooked eye and lopsided smile, nor did many sighs on his lanky self-passing them. He was not interested in whatever scheme was being played on him. Eckard needed to make contact with the Kobold, if this night was any indication of how the Free-Fighters operated, then he feared they would have no chance of success in a pitched battle with the Rakoni. Between an arrogant, self-absorbed molehill tyrant for a leader and the strange accosting of him by this shield-maiden in the middle of the night, he had to scout out what other avenues he had.

'Kiss me' The woman said, she was attractive, this much was ascertainable Eckard reasoned, but she was too forward and Eckard never trusted when a woman offered sex so readily. Sex could be utilised as a weapon, and whatever conquest was on this woman's mind, Eckard was not going to provide the assist.

She moved forward, tilting her head and making ready in advance with the kiss she forcefully requested. He spotted a small making just at the base of her collarbone, quite invisible if one did not take considered and concerted effort to notice it, Eckard had witnessed the small thrice slashed markings before. Eckard gathered the smallest flow of Magik about him and he formed a shadow-weave within himself drawing from the Arcane Sea, the ebb and flow of mana passed against him his skin prickled against its otherworldly chill. The world in his vision became a mess of shadows and blurring threads. He gifted the woman an illusion of what she wanted to see and she kissed a shadow of himself even as he moved past her, collecting his bag and Holloway's embedded rapier and proceeded out of the tent.

When he had first started to use the Sea his illusions were obvious and far too distinctly flawed to be taken as real. Now his Magikal mastery was of astounding verisimilitude. Even to himself, he was taken back by how well he could allude and influence other's viewpoints. Glancing at the silhouetted form of the woman in the tent as she collapsed and Eckard too dropped his enchantment on her.

For she would have kissed an illusion of him and there would have been very little feeling after the initial shock of smooching on with thin air and not another. But the woman would never have had time to unravel the mystery for her lungs had been emptied of all immediate air intake through her fully parted lips. Eckard had left on his shadow-weaving work this detail as to give the woman a goodnight's sleep and hopefully in the morning she would be confused enough to not remember too much. In dropping the spell Eckard had allowed the normal flow of the air to return to normal so the woman was not left with excessive brain damage and she would evidently wake with no problems.

Well, I did take her breath away - Eckard though smiling to himself, all the best jokes came when no one else was void-damned around, though he was quite certain many would not find his work even remotely humorous, each to their own.

*

Feelings Judeson had thought long ago forgotten or unattainably flooded back to him. As he cradled the naked and remarkedly beautiful Jehasli in his arms, both of them sweat ridden and gasping for breath from their latest tryst. There had been two or maybe three previously Judeson was not sure now. The moments between each love making session had been sweetly brief and only a few words had converted between them, mostly about Letesah before the Raks, or of some of his adventures in the North, he was not sure what he had said nor of what Jehasli had asked. Judeson absorbed in hunger for her. He wanted more of her. Her smell, her body, her very essence was irresistible.

Judeson and Jehasli parted after a time and they each spoke through heavy breath.

'I'm glad you came back.' Jehasli said.

'As am I' Judeson replied and passed into unconsciousness as exhaustion took hold.

*

Judeson awoke, to an empty tent. Jehasli had

gathered up her bright coloured clothes and left some time ago. He did not begrudge her any ill will, she probably had something to do on this morn, her loyal shield maidens probably needed guidance or some such. Judeson collected his own clothes and dressed. Hefting up the bastard-sword of his family's name that lay at the far end of the tent he moved out into the woods beyond.

Passing by several other Free-Fighter tents, some acknowledged Judeson in a friendly wave or greeting some other ignored his passing, the latter parties probably being Yormeth's cronies, easily swayed by passive-aggressive utterances. Judeson knew his blood-cousin was trouble, he always had the man was truly insufferable sometimes but they all leaned toward the same cause. Freeing their homeland and for Judeson that was all that mattered.

Judeson came upon where Eckard had agreed upon staying. However, Eckard was gone, the Northman's knapsack and endless (and seemingly magikal) inventory with him. The tent the man had supposedly been in was empty. Judeson shook his head and puzzled as to what could possibly have happened.

Some places down the rugged hill a Free Fighter motioned for Judeson as others appeared. They were armed with short hardwood branches and a many of them were stretching or swinging the sticks about, a training exercise then. - Judeson reckoned.

*

Mere moments later, outside the Free-Fighter encampment, Eckard found the others Yormeth had previously made a mockery of. They looked malnourished sure enough, their pitiful slap dash of hemp tent sheets over malformed sticks made for a pathetic excuse of the organisation. In some regards Yormeth was right. In many others the intolerable man was wrong.

As Eckard approached a watch at the camp's edge hailed him over while another, gangly man held a drawn bow on him.

'Lo there, stranger, tell me with earnest if you are just passing through or if you are here of a hostile nature.' The unarmed watch said. He was a boy-barely even a man, with a short tuft of pale hairs on his lip.

'That's a very old fashioned fucking speech you have there, watchman.' Eckard voiced, a small smile on his face as he threw back his cloak and showed his weapons to the watch, with his hands far from the hilt of the blade.

'Yes well I was just trying it out is all, doesn't hurt to practice what we read, there is wisdom in the written word, friend.' The youth stated.

The older watchman lowered his bow only so slightly and peered at Eckard with his wide orbs of brown becoming more clear as firelight flared up at the camp edge. Another figure this one somewhat vaguely feminine in curvature had arrived and brought a torch with her.

'What do you want, Northman?' The older watch inquired. Clearly, this group was not under the thumb of a tyrannical madman but they were however still subject to the mistrust shared by so many of the downtrodden.

'Just passing through here, Southron. Does your camp have a leader?' Eckard answered, nodding at the youth who seemed to shy away as his elders talked.

The woman with the flaring torch answered for the watch.

'Irsthule he is in the center. Tell us, are you with Yormeth?' The woman asked.

'Shake the Stone and send it to the Void. By Yahasa's balls, no.' Eckard answered, with a smile.

The woman grunted and motioned Eckard to the centre of the camp. He passed the two watchmen, the youth smiling back at him and the older man giving no such pleasantries. *Trust is a fine thread we dance upon daily*. Eckard thought.

What Eckard witnessed from the other score or so of the camp's occupants was another beast entirely from Yormeth's followers. Happiness. The figures were helping each and conversing like old friends. They worked together in unison preparing what meager supplies they could for an evening meal, placing pans upon fires and bring sauces and blanching pots to simmer. And they decided what on sentries by communicating with one another. Some of them playing a game with haphazardly cut resemblances of thin wooden cards.

In the absolute centre of the chaotically arranged circle of makeshift tents, sat a tall Southron, dark of skin and with a freshly shaven head. The man sat cross-legged with a broad axe across his lap.

'I'm not with Yormeth, that's probably your first question and the prime reason your guards seem on edge.' Eckard stated.

The Southron the others had named Irsthule turned his head up and met Eckard's eyes.

'You came from that Void-damned taker's camp.' Irsthule answered, obviously alluding to the infamously charming Yormeth.

'My comrade, Judeson is there keeping an eye on things, I am sure nothing rash will happen.'

Eckard replied, winking at the man. Not an outwardly antagonising wink, at least by his warped reasoning.

To the balding man's credit; Irsthule laughed half-heartedly. He seemed somewhat pleased Eckard had a sense of humour. Perhaps he is relieved I am not like that stick-in-the-arse Yormeth - Eckard reasoned.

'Judeson is a good man, of that much I can believe from you Outlander.' Irsthule stated moving to sit down on a burnt off stump end.

'Well that is a starting point, I suppose.' Eckard replied, granting the man a smile, Irsthule grunted in response. Eckard began to wonder if any Southron had any slight semblance of a sense of humour.

'I knew Judeson since we were both younglings, hunting in the tall grass of the Mornis Hinterlands. His father Judisye was a remarkable man also. If Judeson and you have journeyed and fought together then that is indeed enough, however, I 'av to ask why he is not here with you?' Irsthule inquired, raising one of his bushy eye brows at Eckard.

'We fought with each other a couple of times over the last week too' Eckard replied, something had to give in this man, laughter was a good medicine for tough times after all.

Irthule's eyebrows elevated even higher as if they would leave his face utterly. Another grunt followed.

Eckard cleared his throat, though he was screaming inside from Irthule's misunderstandings of his own wit.

'It would seem Judeson is tied up at Yormeth's camp, with....err' Eckard began, though realizing he was quite possibly without proper execution probably crafting a joke again.

'Uh...' Irsthule stated.

This time it was Eckard's turn to raise a searching regard and equally raised eyebrows.

'Jehasli' Irsthule stated.

'Jehasli' Eckard nodded in agreement with the man.

'Those two were inseparable from a very young age.' Irsthule said.

'I hope they were not doing what I am only guessing they did last night.' Eckard replied, another joke, he really had to get down to business eventually.

Irsthule unexpectedly laughed. It was different not a subtle thing either, the man let out a raucous disjointed chorus of primal howls. It was awful and equally laughter- inducing all at the same time. Eckard joined the man, though not quite as dedicated to the cause as Irsthule.

After a few minutes of what was apparently laughter from the Irsthule, the man wiped away moist and glistening eyes, to speak again.

'You really cannot be with Yormeth then.' Irsthule stated matter of factly.

'Oh. Why do you say that?' Eckard questioned, finally this hard nut was indeed cracked.

'Cause you ain't no fucking prune.' Irsthule said, smiling.

'No void-damned way, not with that idiot's half-arsed plan.' Eckard answered.

Irsthule lifted up a kettle that had been suspended over the fire nearby and motioned for Eckard to take a mug from the table adjacent to him. Irthule poured a steaming brew that smelt of mulberries and cinnamon into Eckard's mug and motioned for him to sit down on a cutaway stump

that served as a stool. Irsthule sat on similar.
'Tell me of the jackarses plan' Irsthule started
again.

'It involved or or Kobold-ore I think you
Southrons call it, a possible distraction and
charging stupidly head-forth at the front gate.
Apparently, it takes awhile to close or some
such.' Eckard replied, the exact details were
cards kept close to Yormeth's chest though it was
possible the plan was not much more than what he
himself at said.

'Of course, probably a trap more like. Did he
state where he got the Kobold-ore? Irsthule
queried.

'He did not say.' Eckard replied.

'The Raks have been baiting for a clean fight for
weeks, they don't send out patrols anymore. Just
keep locked up in Letesah. Ever since they put up
their big walls, they don't worry about Yormeth's
raiders. Almost like an invitation to come at
me.'

'No disrespect to you of course, apparently you
were meant to be returning to reinforce Yormeth.'
Eckard answered.

'Zadma's Salvation, fat fucking chance of that
happening.'Irsthule frowned.

'Then what is the plan with you men and women?'
Eckard said sipping his tea.

'We are heading north, to safety and to fight the
Raks, tried this void-damned game for arcs now.
There ain't no saving the Southrondor, below
Garble's Run' Irsthule motioned behind him into
the gloom, Eckard reasoning the lands south of
Letesah must bear the stated name. 'There   are
thousands of Raks just below the Run, whole
encampments, tent cities, some more advanced
outposts, huge watch towers of that odd white

materia they use.' Irsthule stated.

'So you are looking for allies in the North? If you fight the Raks in the Nertheilm you will be eventually able to retake the Southrondor. ' Eckard replied.

'You move fast, a million leagues an hour you do, Eckard.' Irthsule answered. 'But yes more or less in simple terms.' Irsthule agreed.

'Well that I can help with, I am a member of the Pact that is against the Raks and more importantly their masters; the Channellors. If you can make it to the Nertheilm I can arrange a meeting, in a few weeks, there will be a major offensive. The details will flow. Unfortunately, most routes North are either blocked or very treacherous.'

'Well then, all good news finally not to worry Eckard, we already have a way north. No problems, well no more than normal in this risky business of war.'

'Really?'

'The Kobold has a secret that has been keeping, but with the right connections and the right amount of desperation. Of which we have fucking buckets, an agreement was reached.'

'Prestan' Eckard stated, the name coming to him instantly, what Irsthule said made sense, though Eckard previously imagined the Kobold had given up any hope.

'How did you know?'

'She was once part of her Pact, old habits die hard it seems'

'She?'

Eckard laughed and Irsthule this time could only look on puzzled.

'Of course, Prestan is not really her name.'

Eckard voiced, smiling at the transparently puzzled Irsthule. 'Kobold really enjoy the fact that we aurmen cannot distinguish their sex so they switch up their names for us, well their Shamed One titles at least.'

Irsthule shook his head.

'I must admit I know even less than I thought I did about those scaly bastards.' Irsthule said. 'Now I look like a bit of fool really.'

Eckard did not reply but nodded his head in agreement.

Irsthule poured more tea and the night grew long.

9th Stanza

-Witness 'Shira' – A Southron of Dosin origin, aged 38 arcs is called to the Stand by the Honourable Judge Markus Krist-

Witness - "The Rakoni view us *(presumably all of Aurmenkind, though the witness may also be referring to all non-Rakoni)* as the ultimate enemies, heathens of Most Unholy Union. They are born and raised to hate us, to fight us and to eventually conqueror us."

Honourable Judge Markus Krist – "Order, Recordists Hold Proceedings"

15 Minute break in proceedings enacted by the Honourable Judge Markus Krist *(Witness became unstable, took several moments to settle down by Attendants of the Court)*

Honourable Judge Markus Krist – "Witness to Continue"

Witness- "Whatever conflicts we have with each other, whatever distrust we have with the Draul and the Kobold, is really nothing.

Not when the Morba-Rakoni unite, for they will and they will come for the North just as they took the Southrondor. We were distracted, fooled by our own concerns, the real enemy exists across the Boundary and they are getting stronger each passing day...."

Honourable Judge Markus Krist – "Order, Court is Terminated"

(Attendants had to restrain the Witness at this point and take her to confinement for her own safety)

Manuscript of Salmian High Court – 2801 arcs ATF

Yormeth's new recruits were mediocre. Their
techniques, both individual and in battle ready
formation was deeply flawed, to say the least.
More than half the men and women present on the
training ground could not even hold a stance to

anticipate or even strike out an attack. Almost none of them wielded a weapon properly, that was if they even had a weapon on them. Most only had their cutaway tree branch. The supposed training ground, which was really just a clear space of land in the Karchelch forest was not ideal either. Judeson's anger was rife to boil over. This was void-damned ridiculous.

For what they unequivocally lacked in skill and technique the very much green-leaf recruits made up for in passion. They shouted, howled and swung their mock weapons about as if they were fighting for their very lives, backs up against the wall and nowhere to retreat to. Judeson was mildly impressed, though the last stand would do no one any good if the Rakoni slaughtered them all before Letesah was retaken. Certainly not at all beneficial if Judeson had any hope of getting his vengeance.

*

Prestan sat on a tuft of soft patchy grass against a granite boulder and waited. The tall stranger approached at a casual pace, a male aurman for sure but his heavily bearded face. Odd creatures those, hair grew everywhere. Of course, hair, in general, was an oddity for a Kobold, as they never grow such. Prestan looked down at the grass beneath her and smiled, the Great Mother's hair some called it within another Guild not her own, grass and hair were not similar but both had a tendency to sway in the wind.

As the broad shouldered man neared Prestan, she saw he was armed. A short, thin sword sheathed at his side, dark grey cloak torn and tattered but more than probably bearing more weapons underneath. A small burlap sack was held on his shoulders and swung as he walked as if weightless. The beanpole apparition threw back his hood and beamed a grin from long aurman ear to ear.

Prestan kept herself weary and regarded the aurman with a nod, it took her a few moments but she recognized that face.

'It's you again, what are the chances?' The tall aurman spoke.

'Prestan is the Shamed One name we took' Prestan replied.

The aurman laughed raised both hands away from his sides to show he had no weapons in hand.

'Shamed is hardly what you are now is it?' The aurman stated.

'What do you want, aurman?' Prestan inquired.

'Eckard is my name you never did ask the first time. How is your brother?' The tall man answered.

'Well. You are the knight that uses the Grey Art?' The Kobold replied, straight to the point and placing another question on the already preexisting one, a Silvershard clear attempt at avoidance.

'Yeah, that one' Eckard laughed, halfheartedly, though Prestan sensed a touch of discomfort from the tall man.

'Wrendal's nephew?'

Eckard laughed and began forward.

'You and I both know he isn't my uncle, nor was he ever much of one anyway.' Eckard stated holding Prestan's gaze.

'Indeed Eckard, but you also know we're not part of any of it. Not one bit, anymore.' Prestan said.

'And I don't expect you to be.'

'Then what pray-tell have you come all this way

for then?'

The tall Northman paced around the huge boulder against Prestans back and did a full circle until he stood face to face with Prestan once more. She knew what he was looking at in the distance and did not both to question him.

'Help, Krikza has taken the Draul into his sweaty little palms and is possibly looking to expand into Rosewood and Kormai. The resistance is not at all well organised and disparate, to say the least. The Yunlands is on the brink of civil war again and the Confeds and those snobby bastards in the Collective will probably make a scene soon enough.' Eckard declared.

'Then why are you not in the North with the rest of them cleaning up the mess?' Prestan answered.

Eckard laughed once again.

'The Southrondor has fallen to the Rakoni hasn't it?' The man said, offering no answers.

'More or less.' Prestan replied.

'And the Rockwall does nothing.'

'The Hand of Kingdoms broke itself apart and we survive as we always have done.' Prestan stated, trying to gauge the man beside her.

'Like when you ran from the North'

'Trying to bait us, Eckard?'

'Just gauging your reaction to the long staggering list of concerns that exist.' Eckard expressed throwing his hands up in emphasis.

'Come your questions are more for the Assembly than they are for us' Prestan stated, beckoning for the aurmen to follow her as she skirted the boulder, and made for the foothills of the Rockwall.

'Why did you leave the Pact?' Eckard asked as they began up the loose shale slopes.

Prestan let out a long exasperated sigh, shrugged and finally spoke. 'Because we had to.'

'That's it?' Eckard queried, one of the man's eyebrows raised, his wandering eye seeming to focus over Prestan's shoulder.

'There was no choice really Northman, our people are not in for the long fight. They needed all the help they could get and we choose survival over anything else.'

'How long do you think your survival will last?' Prestan was stung with the man's snappy retorts and sighed again.

'We won't, even now the Ashen-faces gather to the South of the Lake.' Prestan stated although she wished she had bit her tongue right off instead.

'The Channellors are uniting them' Eckard answered.

Prestan continued despite herself.'Slowly but sure enough, their numbers are great and their war machines and Oyra, a Heck of a lot of the stuff' Prestan continued as she pried loose a concealed metal box from a cropping of marked rocks. Eckard looked at her with a questioning regard.

Prestan did not answer the man and opened the box to take out the long elongated aluminium tool within. The aging Kobold released the long string at the base of the tool and the resulting flare bursting from it shot high into the midday of the Far Above. A series of concussive bursts flared into the air high above them and a dulled orange spray of Oyra dust scattered about clinging to the gusting winds as it fell.

An answering flare skirted the Far Above a league off at the base of the Rockwall Range. Prestan turned and acknowledged Eckard once more.

'Don't make us live to regret this Greycloak, or

we will be thrown into the Deep-Dark this time
for sure.' Prestan huffed.

Eckard replied with an over rapacious glint in
his eyes and beaming smile.

'Trust is a thin thread we all dance upon daily.'

'Wrendal's student through and through, how is
the old one eared bastard?'

'Haven't seen him for arcs' Eckard replied.

'Well, all we can say is better be a God-damned
reason you have to try to rouse the Rockwall from
its slumber.' Prestan voiced, mirroring her own
fears at continued inaction.

Eckard nodded solemnly, the smile fading like a
leaf upon the raging winds around them.

Prestan immediately felt a pang of regret.

*

'Yormeth this is void-damned fucking ridiculous!'
Judeson announced to the whole vicinity in a
booming voice, echoing off the hills and away.

Judeson brushed aside the attentions of one of
Yormeth's lackeys who deliberately left a
shoulder in as he passed by. Yormeth sat cross-
legged in front of a number of other of his
subordinates who cast Judeson cold glances in
unison.

'What is it, dear cousin?' Yormeth replied,
feigning a calm and controlled demeanour. Though
Judeson could swear he heard the man's teeth
barring together from where he stood.

Judeson gestured behind him and all around. 'This
all of this, whatever you think is happening
here?'

'We are taking Letesah.' Yormeth answered.

Judeson saw all an array of hostile, grimacing
faces in front of him from Yormeth and his

drones.

Judeson brushed aside his doubts.

'They will be slaughtered, cousin.' Judeson said between barred teeth of his own. 'The moment they attempt an assault.'

Yormeth's Free-Fighters laughed and hurled insults at Judeson.

'Coward!' They droned. 'Yellow belly bastard' Others delivered up.

Yormeth held up a staying hand and the abuse halted.

'Judeson, listen to me and listen to me well now so you don't fucking miss it.' Yormeth began saying.

Judeson listened, despite knowing what was about to happen already.

'While you were running off to the void-damned North, we were training and hatching a plan to take our homeland.' Yormeth said.

Judeson held his tongue.

'We held off the Rakoni patrols they sent our way losing many, Zadma blesses their soul, no less without you. We fought and toiled. Again I stress; without you and in two days time. The Kobold Ore will be ready and we will bring the Rak Palisade down. And murder the fucking cunts that took our home. With or without you.' Yormeth declared with no small amount of vitriol.

Judeson walked off knowing his situation was untenable in their' clouded over eyes. They would never listen to him. Not now. Judeson walked all the way back into the Karchelch woods and held his tongue even as a constant tirade of insults rang his way.

*

'I could not sway him, mistress. He used his

Black Art on me.' The shield maiden whispered in Jehasli's ear.

Jehasli stiffened and nearly dropped the bundle of clothes and clay that contained the saline in her hands. Jehasli managed to find a grip on the item though and she thanked the Queen of the Far Above for it.

It was only salt water after all. Jehasli need not worry herself. But the news her shield maiden had delivered threw a proverbial spanner in the works. This simple task they were assigned was becoming increasingly more difficult. The Pact was not supposed to be here.

Jehasli glanced over at shield maiden. The beautiful young woman looked miserable.

'It's alright, you did as well as you could. The rest will be up to us.' Jehasli whispered back in a hushed tone to avoid the attention of the other Free-Fighters who worked away at their tasks.

The tasks that had been designated via Yormeth and his lackeys were all to do with the assault in two periods of sleep time. Mainly the Oyra bomb; the hulking gigantic form of the hard packed boulder just before them, encased by compacted rocks the precious and volatile mineral inside would be their explosive battering ram, or at least Yormeth believed so. Jehasli knew otherwise.

The shield maiden who sometimes called herself Odetta seemed adequately relieved and went back to her preparations. Jehasli joined her moments later but not before remembering with and increased the supply of dread that their mission involved betraying Judeson.

*

The elaborately decorated hallway was just one of many that led to the inner domicile of the Kobold

Guilds. The Rockwall range was home to the Kobold. And in an existential syndicated harmony, be it a decidedly delicate one the Kobold was very much a part of their home. The Rockwall was maintained and existed, even thrived because of the Kobold. Local flora had been preserved and was waited on by Kobold gardeners. The intricate pattern work of cobblestones laid out before them in went off in dissecting paths. Eckard did not lose his perspective on the primal beauty and followed in earnest; the leading figure of Prestan.

The Kobold known as Prestan led at a hectic pace. It was quite obvious her anxiety was peaking to great heights. Even on the first entrance at the cave-mouth, they had to work their way down to reach the main fortified gate. At that particular foreboding entrance, they had been drilled on procedure and due respect for the Kobold culture and environment.

Large solid oak doors slammed shut. Down cramped hallways littered with potted shrubs; Prestan led Eckard who was never met with hostile glances but was never even looked at all. Scurrying figures of reptilian kobold hid and ran from them, downcast angular faces looked at Prestan as if she were a warning for them to heed, never at Eckard of course. He reasoned it was a trained reaction that if aurmen were ever to make their ways into these polished marble floors, that the kobold must at times avoid them, instructions that were currently devouring as holy words.

It was ridiculous really. Though he had vague recollections of the history between aurmen and kobold and the deterioration of said dealings, Eckard did not think this childish behaviour was warranted. He briefly glimpsed a nursery where the yet to be hatched eggs of kobold young nestled on beds of scattered straw, the door was thrown shut on his advance.

Down yet another corridor and Eckard witnessed kobold workers collecting up tools; spanners, pliers and hammers together as they rushed back into a workshop. Two kobolds slightly more muscular of build than most hauled a wagon into the cluttered workspace and slammed the large double steel doors behind them.

Only one portal remained before them. Huge solid hoop pine doors lay open, iron rings with half moons handles to each adjacent side, matching the iron bound casing that encompassed the door's frames.

*

A day had passed and Eckard had not made a return. Yormeth's Free-fighter's were moving to attack the following morning from now and Judeson was without an ally albeit Jehasli, who was proving void-damned difficult to track down.

How had he done something wrong? Was their love making all for naught? Had it even meant anything other than a fleeting moment of passion?

Judeson shook his head, women were incredibly difficult to comprehend sometimes.

Yormeth and his two hulking brutes of bodyguards approached vacant stares on those two, deadly serious eyes started back at the man from Yormeth. A man with an agenda possessed eyes like that Judeson reckoned.

'How can you trust him, Judeson?' Yormeth inquired, his voice masking no delusions to his ire as he stood up to face Judeson. They were on a mound just off from the main camp which was being readied for war. Yormeth stood a mere hand span higher than Judeson on a patch of elevation.

'Because he will do the right thing' Judeson

answered in a hasty rush. Turning away from Yormeth and his brutes to stalk back into the woods to think.

Yormeth grunted and nothing more, not answering challenge this time around. Judeson never turned from his viewing of the day's opening light as he continued due east further into the Karchelch wilderness. Zadma's blessing he was starting to feel choked here, his thoughts muddled. There was little point arguing anymore. The Free-fighters had already decided it seemed and there was no going back now. When all the words were spoken, when all the signs were seen there were only actions left to be fulfilled. He would return for the attack, he had to.

For now, for now, however, he needed space, Jehasli he thought must be as willing to wait as he was.

*

Height could be construed to be a position of power. Though the kobold was naturally less in stature than either draul or aurmen, they made up for it in many constructs of architecture. Where Eckard found that now was no exemption to this over-riding rule the squat reptilians seemed to adopt.

Standing at almost two metres tall Eckard was quite used to looking down at others. Towering over people was second nature. Letting them believe he was nothing more than a clumsy stick figure was a well-trained person.

The Kobold before Eckard were raised high above on a parapet stand, a fortress within the domicile. The kobold sat on the edges of the upraised battlements spires as if peering down at a besieging party on their form biddable high ground. The stained double glass windows high

over head shone down on the stonework the Circle
of Guilds perched themselves on.

In the middle of the castle within the room sat a
kobold who must have been the eldest of them all.
And perhaps even more arcs than all of them
combined. The kobold had a single furrowed brow
and onyx skin similar to the shade of Eckard's
hair. Admittedly Eckard brushed the short crop of
hair he still possessed on his head. Inwardly he
thanked Lisiarna once again for the trim, even if
he would never tell her so. The dark toned kobold
spoke, using Eckard from lingering internal
dialogue.

'We need your help.' Eckard declared, skipping
straight to the poin, a lesson that was still
lost on so many.

'We have been privy to witness our help with
those of your kind.' The dark toned kobold
replied, not illusions as for how this meeting
was to progress.

Same as always - Eckard reasoned.

'What is about to happens.' Eckard retorted,
meeting the snake eyes of all the kobold one by
one. 'Involves us all, all the races, all the
factions. What we will face is our own
absolution. And we must fight to preserve us
all.'

Eckard finally rested eyes on Prestan who
proceeded to look down, she was ashamed, a
reasonable reaction, but not at all helpful.

'The Guilds will not play host to your lies,
Magicker.' The elderly onyx coloured Kobold
stated, with no small degree of hostility in her
voice.

'I am not lying. Swear on the dawn.' Eckard
replied. Void-dammit would no one reason, was the
world really just going to fall apart like this?

He thought.

'We helped aurmans long ago and all they made of our assistance was destruction, your people fight each in petty, power grabbing struggles, there is no honour. There is no love of family and the Great Stone from your race. Aurmans abandoned reason long ago, they live and die by the sword. We kobold left behind your reckless abandon aurman. Your Pact is broken and we will not help you again.' The kobold centre stage announced, his word final and absolute.

'Then ask of you no I beg that you intervene, we need your assistance in what is to come. We were foolish, we were void-damned fucking stupid is what we were, but there is still time. The Pact is not broken, as long as the Arcane Sea endures, and we have thought, we can fight oppression in all its forms, Eckard said as he sunk to his knees on the ice cold stone tablet he had hitherto stood on.

The Circle of Guilds all looked down at him, disapproving scowls on their creased and chiseled faces one and all. The kobold leadership was ancient as far as Eckard knew, which he admittedly knew and understood very little of these people. Let alone their leaders.

'We the Voice of the Kobold have spoke, leave now Mage. Go in peace while you still live on the Great Stone. In the After the Deep Dark will swallow you whole for your sins.' The onyx kobold stated.

Eckard dropped his shadow weaving. Before the Kobold Cicle's eyes, he dissipated into a cloud of scattering dust.

*

'This is your fault, we will not stand for this.' Malus - the Voice of the Circle, the only kobold able to speak for some reason or another of the Circle proclaimed he stared her down; hitting the point home as blunt as a hammer at Prestan.

'You must make amends for allowing the aurman to deceive you. You must find him and stop him with whatever means possible. Until this time you are Shamed and not welcome in our home' Malus enforced, all the Circle had raised hands in unison, fingers pointed right at Prestan.

Prestan nodded in agreement and retreated before the Guild leaders steady scouring gazes.

She turned back, remembering herself and what she needed most.

'May Shame is absolute Voice of the Circle, but please if I am to track down this aurman please grant me use of the Felnarti?' Prestan requested as she thumped her tail on the ground anxiously. Her birth-makers had hated her habit of doing so.

The Circle shuffled about and evidently, Malus spoke for them.

'Go you have use of the Retrievers.' Malus stated.

Prestan scurried out of the Circle's quarters as the huge double doors parted for her exit. She broke into a full on sprint, not fully trusting the ancient ones would turn around and string her up for her insubordinate.

Inward she was relishing in the fact that her and Eckard's gambit had worked as planned. Outwardly she was anguished and distraught for shaming her people, again.

**

On a sparsely forested hill on Garble's Run, less than a league from the kobold homeland of Rockwall, Eckard sat waiting for his escort. Prestan walked up behind him, several another kobold in tow. The others were armed with blades and crossbows, concealed beneath their nondescript tunics.

Eckard pivoted around, remaining still seated. Resting on his laurels, with hands overs knees. His head still spinning from his long range shadow being woven so far. He felt a build-up of dry build and mucus in his throat and mouth. Some of his bread hairs had caught alight when he opened access to the Arcane Sea. The side effects nearly almost always fluctuated sporadically. No pinpointing.

Prestan stood with arms folded a mere two paces from Eckard now.

'He would not have appreciated the theatrics back there.' Prestan stated. 'The Circle is pissed, we are truly *Shamed* now.'

'You were not before?' Eckard replied. He knew who Prestan spoke of in her first sentence but he shrugged it off, not worth discussing at this time.

'We were on a probation of sorts, Mage. It matters little now. The other Retrievers are free now too, we are searching for you, to bring you to justice' Prestan proclaimed, gesturing toward the kobold who nodded their long snouts in appreciation back at her.

'You are not with the old man are you?' I know he is not here, but you are not doing this with his approval or that of the Pact.' Prestan said.

Eckard brushed off any burnt tendrils of hair from his face and rubbed his awake with his callused palms.

'We are the Pact, whether he is with us or not. Someone has to do something. Why not fucking us?' Eckard replied grinning, though he was pleased. Only exhausted, in more ways than one. However, a smile did not cost a great deal.

Prestan shifted nervously. The kobold met Eckard's searching regard.

'The Rakoni are mustering, in great numbers. They have constructed various shantytowns, cities really, to the south of the Remiourdan Sea. Their various nations vie for control, there are contests, duels, and raids from each faction onto the other.' Prestan began. 'Behind the scenes, something is happening, our scouts believe they are uniting, weeding out dissidents, someone is pushing for absolute control.'

'They are preparing for war. The Channellors are pushing for it.' Eckard bluntly reinforced.

Prestan titled her sharply angular head.

'How do you know, Mage?' Prestan inquired.

'The Raks are their slaves, they are being manipulated to commit their atrocities.' Eckard stated.

'Regardless the Circle will not intervene. If the Rakoni does unite for a war against whoever for whatever, the Kobold guilds will not intervene.'

'It affects fucking void-damned all of us.' Eckard hissed between barred teeth.

'You do not have to sway me, Mage. We here because we know the stakes, now come we have to be away from where the Circle has eyes. They will not fight the Rakoni but they will fight us with every snarl to stop us. Stubborn moss covered bastards. We will meet at a spot even they do not know about' Prestan replied. She and her Retrievers beckoned Eckard along.

Eckard stubbled onto his feet with great effort still aching from the effects of over exerting himself earlier. The Arcane Sea was never an easy one to navigate. Yahasa's crusty Gooch he was fucking spent. Eckard reasoned. But he would keep keeping going, they all had to keep going.

Ranks upon ranks of heavily armed soldiers passed by, their strides purposeful and directed. Their purpose matched their march which was due course onto war most holy. This was the Word of the Qhasa, the one, and only true God. Form unknowable, unsaleable by mortals. But by God's loving touch alone they were made complete. Wellstocked wagons rolled on the past, over makeshift floating bridges. Bypassing the flowing waters of the River Furrow. Camp followers, tradesmen and soldier's partners brought up the rear, the march had begun and the heretics would soon know their will and resolve, for the Word of the Shroud could not be denied.

From out of the advancing mass, her most loyal servants departed their ranks and came upon her position at upraised banks of the river's edge. The handful of Void Callers walked up to her position and proceeded stand at attention. There were adorned with their formal white cloth, luminescent white with gold trim on the coat tails. These were the marked colours of the Most Holy. It was picturesque and Channellor-Mistress Khrislo would almost appraise her subordinates, if it was not her duty to keep them in line, with an iron fist.

'May God smile upon you all' Khrislo uttered, with an approving smile.

'May the Light encompass you also, Madam-Channellor.' One of the Void Callers answered, their highest-ranking member was the only one allowed to speak to a Channellor in public of course. As is written within the Holy Doctrine. Their leader was a balding man with bushy grey brows and extensively wrinkled face much like a prune. The man's demeanour matched his personality, he a conniving power-hungry worm. Though Khrislo could not place the man's name; she knew through well-trusted sources the vermin coveted her position among the Pure Order. She would be mindful to keep an eye on this one. Sure enough, he would grovel and kiss her feet now but it was highly probable that in the near future he would stab her in the back at an opportune moment.

Khrislo motioned for the Void-callers to follow her into her command tent. Casting aside the thick hide tent flaps, Khrislo walked into the decorated confines of the interior, incense burned and the oyra-fuelled lamps over head cast a gentle warm light. As she sat down on the cushioned stool behind her workbench, she invited her subordinate Void-callers to seat themselves down on the many coloured cushions that adorned the tent's carpeted floor. Being a Channellor had its perks. For example comfort was only one such earthly pleasure that helped ensure success.

Khrislo adjusted her paper work into a nice neat and ordered pile. The broad printed sheets had various manifests of Rakoni military and trade activities. The modern printing press was powered by Oyra and sanctioned by the church was a literal godsend. It had cut out all the hustle and bustle of fidgety old scribes and their bore some scroll and cursive style writing. Khrislo thanked the Qhasa each and every day for the printing press. It had made her life tenfold simpler.

'Madam Channellor, not to be too presumptuous, but are we going to the front? Are we finally to teach the Holy Word to the heathens in the North?' The prune faced Void caller inquired, breaking Khrislo's chain of thought.

Khrislo proceeded to stare down the horrid little man. She wanted him to squirm and fully respect her authority. After it was she and not him who was chosen by God to be a Channellor. After almost a minute of silence and the man visually taken by, he was sweating and in some discomfort now, good Khrislo thought.

'Void-Callers, your holy mission will be in the north. You are to join Master-Channellor Tiramene at the Woldte.' Khrislo finally answered.

Each of the Void-Callers nodded eagerly and all but old prune face looked appreciative of the importance of their mission. Khrislo assumed the man still felt the sting of the chastising from her.

'We have contacted Tiramene and informed him that you five will be joining him soon.' Khrislo continued, she dipped her hand into her top drawer and retrieved her copy of the Last Orders, the most revered of all the Sacred Commands.

The dusty pieces were of the old scroll style and the text was archaic. Khrislo had been meaning to get a copy of it on the more modern print press. Though that was proving to be difficult as some other Channellors and Rakoni Task Master stalled her progress with their pointless debates on the Commands. Right on cue, an errand boy stood at the tent entrance one of Khrislo's Elite Rakoni Guards escorting the timid young man in.

'A message from Tiramene, ma'am.' The Guard proclaimed in his native tongue. He was a loyal servant and Khrislo trusted the soldier completely

'Thank you, Ruus.' Khrislo replied.

Khrislo choosing to use the soldier's name instead of his rank of Captain, a subtle nod to understanding those in lesser castes, the Void-Callers in the audience may or may not pick up her lessons, it was beside the point, she as their teacher she had a duty to uphold.

The errand boy began forward toward Khrislo's desk. Before reaching his destination he prematurely dropped to the cushioned tent floor in a fit. On his back like a turtle turned over and unable to raise itself of its own accord. The boy flailed his long limbs about and his eyes rolled back in his head.

Some of the Void-Callers sort to render the young boy assistance but Khrislo raised a staying hand.

'Don't touch him. Patience, students, patience.' Khrislo stated with a touch of authority in her voice.

The Void Callers backed off and the young errand boy eventually and inevitably got up to face Khrislo, the lad's face was drawn tight and solemn.

'Madam Channellor, you are sending more apprentices? Would there be any Zealots or Sentinels coming with them by-chance?' The boy stated in a sobering tone, far more mature than was possible for his arcs. The boy's mouth was moving as was conventional but someone else was doing the speaking.

'Master Channellor Tiramene, how goes the front line? Making good progress in the heathen North I take it? The troops you have requested are on their way in due course. This is still much to be done here on the Plains.' Khrislo answered the boy and one that was Channelling through with the energies of the Shroud.

'I am afraid Tiramene is absent on other business ma'am, I one of the Chosen Heroes, I have been sent to oversee operations and spread the Holy

Word here. All the fun, ya know' The boy spoke
again, the speaker behind this was very casual
about it all, frustratingly so for Khrislo's
tastes.

Khrislo was taken back. *Why was she not informed
of this? One of those blasted new Cultists had
supervision of the front in the North? Was this a
trick, a ploy by one of the new Factions? She
would have to look into all this after her Void
Callers had left her.*

'Very well Hero, that is all for now.' Khrislo
proclaiming, she was keeping face and not showing
an ounce of surprise to the outside world. The
Void Callers did not need to know her mind after
all. Nor so was the case for the Cultist either –
Khrislo rationalized.

The boy collapsed once more. This time the fit
lasting only moments until the lad lay still,
dead, the blood draining from his features,
leaving him ghostly pale.

Some of the Void-Callers whispered shocked gasps.

'Hush.' Khrislo beckoned her Void Callers, the
five servants uttered their horror but Khrislo
continued 'Students, students, the boy served his
purpose willingly. He will be fondly remembered
and his soul will be welcomed lovingly by the
Qhasa'

The Void Callers nodded and praised God with
downcast eyes and joined their respective palms
together.

'Let us pray for his soul, and for your mission
my children.' Khrislo stated, joining her
students on the velvet cushioned floor.

Khrislo closed her eyes and heard the Void-
Callers begin a chant, one of the newer verses.
As God's many deeds and names were uttered,
Khrislo wondered to herself if the foolish

messenger boy actually had any chance of ever
being embraced by the Qhasa. Although Khrislo saw
herself as devout, she doubted one so lowly
really mattered in God's eyes. It was a
circumstance she never feared her self, her faith
was absolute and her mission was far too
important.

*

Staring off into the blood-red wash of the
crimson smears coating the Far Above in the
waning afternoon hours, Judeson contemplated the
natural beauty of the Southrondor and how much he
had missed it. The brushing of foliage behind him
brought Judeson's attention round to take note of
Eckard coming over to his position on the
overhang. So he returned after all. The tall,
lean Northman sat down beside him in on mound
outside the forest grove where the other free-
fighters still dwelt. The beanpole Northman held
clay cup of steaming mulled wine in one hand and
loaf of dull grey brown bread in the other. A
light easterly wind picked up a puff of Auburn
dirt on its way past and the small dust-devil
reflected delicately but all too briefly
brilliant flare as it departed from Judeon's
vision.

'Why are you doing this Judeson?' Eckard asked
finally breaking the silence between them as he
turned to Judeson.

'Why are you following if you don't believe in
the course? Why did you come back?' Judeson
rebutted, not meeting Eckard's eyes.

'Why does anyone do anything?'

Judeson did not warrant a reply, not believing it
really needed one, the Southron turned briefly
and nodded at Eckard. That was enough. Both men
once again shifted to look out over the tranquil

dying light of day. Judeson saw flocks of faraway
birds take to the evening air and spun out. The
'constant wheel of life' Judeson's father had
titled all the small idiosyncrasies of life, all
those tiny yet beautiful moments. Judeson knew
that there was only a handful of arcs left before
they must act, and his mind turned to darker
matters.

'You went to meet the Kobold?' Judeson inquired,
turning his head to look at the Northman.

'I did' Eckard replied.

'And?'

Eckard shook his head and stared off into the
departing daystar's light.

'That well huh?' Judeson retorted. 'Seems you
have as much luck as we do'

'They are offering assistance' Eckard countered.
'Just not here, not now.'

'Not much use really' Judeson laughed.

'Fucking aye'. Eckard muttered, handing over a
bread loaf half and what little remained of the
wine cup he had had.

'Yormeth is going to lead an attack on the
morrow.' Judeson stated, taking the cup and
gulping down its content. The bread he placed
into his lap and continued staring off into the
daystar's gradual setting path.

'I take it this is the decision your cousin is
committing to?' Eckard inquired.

'I have to join him, Eckard. I will fight along
side, my brothers and sisters. I must.' Judeson
said.

'And the strategy is the same?' Eckard replied.

'It's void-damned stupid, I know.' Judeson

'Then why follow through on a plan that you
yourself know will not succeed. Your cousin is a

fucking single-minded bully, Judeson. He will lead your people into a slaughter.'

'I know! I know what he is Eckard, but he is family, and family sticks together! I have to go help or save him probably I cannot do anything.' Judeson howled, his voice quite clearly laced with agony, his eyes were ablaze with raw emotion as he turned his head to face Eckard.

'You have to do what you have to do.' Eckard answered, it was such a simple sentence and cliché one at that but Judeson thought it helped. He nodded in approval.

'I don't expect to risk your life for me.' Judeson said plainly.

Eckard looked serious for all of two seconds. Then that smirk he so favoured come out blazing. The lopsided nature of his mouth added a certain level of comedy and his crooked eyes darted about.

'I ain't got nothing better to do.' Eckard said, then looking thoughtful he stated: 'Have you got any water? No offence but that void-damned wine was fucking awful.'

Judeson answered with a grin and passed off his water skin.

The two men sat in silence for a time. The daystar now departing like a recent memory, the creeping fogginess of night taking hold. Judeson felt no intimidate need to break the quiet, it was not awkward at all. It felt... right. Few things recently had felt right for Judeson and that was enough for him now.

Eckard did not offer anything in answer. The Northman sat down next to Judeson on the rugged hilltop and just looked out as the daystar departed away.

'All I feel is hate, sometimes it leaves me and I

feel something else, but then I go back to how much I need to avenge my father.' Judeson said breaking the silence, the darkness was absolute now and precious few stars were out just yet. The Twins were still rising somewhere off on the unseen horizon.

Eckard stood up, brushing his trench coat off of foliage and rust coloured dirt. The darned man was still wearing his chain-maille coat underneath. Judeson thought the Northman was going to leave, but Eckard stood still facing straight ahead, peering down into the darkened plain and country below. The Twins glistened off the oil slick surface of the polluted pond below, various odd machine parts and ramshackle work huts constructed by the Rakoni were scattered just on the outer limits of Letesah. The only home Judeson had ever really known, and the one ripped violently from his life.

'When I was a soldier, there was a saying among the men and women.' Eckard stated, seemingly beginning something but not inclined to rush through it.

Judeson straightened himself up.

'When you were a soldier?' Judeson inquired.

'Yeah' Eckard replied. 'Arcs ago, the other soldiers always said you had to fight for something, they were doing their utmost best to comfort me, I was shitting myself. They told me you needed something substantial otherwise you would die the instant you entered the fray. There had to be a driving force to combat, there had to be a reason to run head-forth into violence. There had to be a reason to end another's life.'

'Vengeance' Judeson answered, a foul taste forming in his mouth, the nightmares on the preferential edge of his thoughts lurking closer.

'No not that, it is not simply enough to hate, you will only get so far. What I speak of is love, Judeson. Love is the only true force ever worth fighting for.' Eckard replied, facing Judeson now. His gaze was beyond confident and focused.

Judeson frowned.

'I am going to get revenge for the filth that ended my father's life.' Judeson said with an acid laced tongue.

'That's because you loved him, Judeson. Hate is not the driving force, it is a fleeting emotion devolved from the love you had for your father.' Eckard stated plainly.

'Enough!' Judeson roared, his fists clenched, he found himself experiencing hot and cold flashes. He was seething. But it was not at Eckard. It was at the Raks, it was always at them.

'One of the soldiers, my commander actually spoke of something just as important as fighting for love and not hatred that I never forgot.' Eckard imposed, the man was certainly persistent.

Judeson shook his head in disgust. This man did not ever rationalise when enough was enough. Always pushing. He took a deep breath and realised no good would come from losing himself in resentment. Judeson knew Eckard made good points, even if they were quite abrupt and illtimed.

'Fuck it all. What did you officer say?' Judeson replied, he almost lost in but restrained himself.

Eckard rubbed at his black beard that in parts strangely on closer inspection, looked slightly scorched by a fire's touch.

'The Knight-Commander spoke of cold iron.' Eckard said.

Judeson was struck by a moment of clarity. His father had spoken of such, long ago.

'I have heard of this cold iron. The mentality of some to suppress and withstand emotional turmoil at will..' Judeson replied.

'It is a state of calm and emotive expression all at the same time.' Eckard answered.

'But it arrives from being damaged.' Judeson answered bitterly.

Eckard nodded, grim face was drawn tight and then the man suddenly burst into an obnoxious grin. Judeson smiled back at him despite himself. He broke away from the moment at hand, cold iron or not they still had a task to be done.

'We should really get back to camp soon' Judeson said. 'Come.' Judeson continued, beginning to walk off back across the overhang and down the slope into the woods behind.

Eckard broke away tentatively from his faraway look and followed.

'Of course' He said.

'You speak of fighting for love. But the Rakoni and their masters you speak of..'Judeson proclaimed. Getting interrupted by Eckard who interjected:

'Channellors.'

'Yes, write them. Well what in the deep Abyss are they fighting for?' Judeson questioned.

'The most dangerous and addictive love of them all' Eckard replied, Judeson turned around to face the man who had stopped in his tracks. A hefty wind blew past the two men scattering leaves in pronounced gusto, as if for dramatic effect.

'The love of control' Eckard said.

Cold shiver laced up Judeson's spine. He swore

he could feel the conflicted tension from the solemn expression Eckard held.

'Their love is that of a God they have constructed to substantiate control. They wish to crush, coagulate and control all that supposedly stands in their path. The Rakoni are the tools of the Channellors, though I not know how this is so. Their God, at least the concept of it, is a self-fulfilling idea that is a source of absolute blind devoted love. That is the most dangerous love, Judeson. It lifts one up and brings them to ruin all in the same stroke.' Eckard said.

Judeson was taken back.

'That sounds like a very serious fight, Eckard. One I honestly do not wholly understand.' Judeson replied.

'Neither do I, not yet. But it is the only real fight worth being involved in' Eckard stated.

'How do you know their God is not real?'

'There is no God, not a single one, Judeson.'

'Zadma is.'

'Perhaps, hard to say.'

'Mysteries of life.'

'Fucking aye. Did you make up with that fiery little red-head?'

'Mysteries of Life'. Judeson countered. He hoped to Zadma he would one day figure out at least one of these mysteries.

*

Yormeth had the camp cleared up and organised. The Free-Fighters were arrayed into loose ranks of half dozen. Whatever improvised weapons such as hatchets, pitchforks, sharpened sticks and some blades were in hand of the Letesah exiles. Many of the Free-Fighters only had leather though some had some possessed bent cast iron breast plates and a few sported old black iron pots they had shaped to form helms.

Yormeth and his half a dozen cronies had breastplates, spears and swords equipped and were all mounted on horses. The Chargers were huge though looked slightly under fed. It was still quite a noticeable disparity in how much Yormeth's favoured and those unfortunate reminders that would have to face the Rakoni with farming tools.

Leading lambs to the slaughter- Eckard noted, looking around at all the desperate and starved expressions.

Two more horses, these particular ones more stoutly built and a measure shorter than the war chargers Yormeth and his men were on, came up from the confines of the forested hill. Being towed by the horses was rickety old carting wagon, probably used in past for hay bails or perhaps mining materials. Mounted on the old fourwheeled cart was a hulky looking boulder of black obsidian. Nestled in crags dug by hand tool into the boulder were dull flickering segments of the sedimentary material Eckard knew as Oyra.

The bomb the Free-Fighters had constructed was huge, against the crags were clay vials nestled within, that Eckard dreaded to know what was inside. It was well-stocked knowledge within the Nertheilm, particularly the Confederation just how oyra worked now.

The aurman nations of the north had been studying and using as an energy source; the blackish-brown sediment rocks for generations now. It reacted to water with a sort of flaring and opposing heat and against salt water it reacted violently, exploding with a force that could not be matched. This particular device that Eckard now looked at, if those vials on the sides were filled to the brim with salt water would be incredibly destructive. Eckard had witnessed first-hand before just how oyra could be utilised as an explosive charge.

Yahasa's bare arse, this was overkill – Eckard swore internally.

The oyra incendiary device would not only take out the gatehouse as Yormeth had planned. Eckard looked over at the walled tableland of Letesah in the near distance. It was plausible that the crude device would take out half the town if not more.

'What is Zadma's name is that?' Judeson inquired.

'This is our salvation, a battering ram like no other and hammer on which to crush the Rak savage and save our town!' Yormeth proclaimed his voice ringing out to the assembled mass of militia.

'This is fucking void-damned madness.' Eckard stated loudly. Several Free-Fighters taking notice. Yormeth's already beady eyes narrowed on Eckard in a direct challenge.

'Enough, if your ugly pet Northman is not going to assist in our just revenge he pisses off!' Yormeth announced in a course screech, his gaze now solely resting on Judeson.

Judeson barred his teeth back his cousin, Eckard could hear an aggravated hiss from Judeson.

Yormeth took no notice and ordered the advance. The battle would be joined.

Several low, booming blasts from a horn nearby sounded off and a score of Free-Fighters began forward with crudely made bows. Down the broken up and muddy slope was a body of water Eckard had heard several of the Southrons labels as Mellow's Pond. Round its edges were several work camps of small tents and deep walled edifices cut into the earth as if they were mining something. Figures scattered from the chaotically scattered camps and ran toward the walls of Letesah. The gate groaned a protesting creak and the iron balls began lifting up to part ways for its workers to return occupied the town.

In an opposing action; just as hasty, several heavily armed apparitions came running out of the gatehouse. Rakoni soldiers formed up. The Southron Free-Fighters open fire down the hill at the Rakoni. The Southron archers had no real practiced order and just loosed their arrows of varying designs, which they retrieved from the loose earth beside them. The aim by the archers was as disordered as their firing rate and though they possessed the higher ground only a handful of arrows found their marks.

The Rakoni in opposition held rank. In the front row, several soldiers held shield as long as them. They were slick looking wooden shields the arrows flung at them by the Free-Fighters seemed to indent only the surface and become stuck in the timber frames. Some Raks pulled the arrows from the wood and passed them to the bowmen behind. Some of the Raks held those intricately long bows, with gears and whistling spokes. Their arrows launched high and smashed down into the assembled Southrons causing chaos, though the foliage and trees provided cover for most.

Other Rakoni held huge two-handed cross bows, mounted up against soldiers and bearing only a tiny little bolt and bow at the front. These weapons made whistling noises and steam escaped the sides, billowing out. Some of these bolts launched uphill and some found their marks in Southrons unready for the barrage. One of the Free-Fighters fell nearby Eckard. The man grasping at his bloody mess that was his neck, with a bolt lodged halfway through.

Yormeth signaled his cavalry to take the wagon forward, his two strong men, Marko and Dumiee stayed by his side. The other mounted warriors brought their chargers and clamped large metal hooks with steel chains running from them onto the wagon. The four cavalrymen whipped their reigns into a frenzy and their horse broke into a full-fledged gallop. The stout, carrying horses in the front sensing the frenzy of their larger cousin also swung into top gear and the wagon was off at full pelt down the hill. To the gatehouse, to their' their goal.

'It has begun, my Free-Fighters. Vengeance is ours! We will be free again!' Yormeth shouted over the chaos.

About halfway across the plain land between the raised table land of Letesah and the forest where Eckard was, in the proximity of the surrender work camps, a plan went awry, and salt water mixed with oyra. The improvised incendiary device never made it to the gatehouse. The thing lit up like a flaring candle in the utter pitchblack darkness. The horrible screech of the horses crying out in twisted pain could be heard even from where Eckard and Judeson were. The harrowing screams of the unfortunate aurmen that were torn apart in aggravated howling flames. An intense flash of sudden blinding light flared up and then was gone a moment later. Dust, dirt, the remains of horses and carts and human mess flew up into the air.

The explosion cut off the line of sight for both the Rakoni and the aurman. The barrage of projectiles from both sides halted for the time being. Nearly everyone fell silent in shock. Judeson started toward Yormeth who was struggling

to steady his horse of which was twisting and
turning back in forth. Marko and Duminee looked
to be in the midst of a similar conundrum.
Judeson took no mind of Yormeth's bodyguards
around him, he dragged the disorientated cousin
of his from the saddle and pulled him down.
Pinning Yormeth to the rough ground with both
hands and a knee.

'Then it would appear, gentlemen, we need a
distraction' Jehasli called from the far flank,
ignoring Judeson and Yormeth scuffle and breaking
the tense silence that had crept into the
melancholic group.

'And what would that be?' inquired Judeson,
calling back to her.

However even before he had time to ask anything
further, Jehasli had sprinted forward and moved
at an astonishing pace, in her wake her two
shield maidens followed in a sprint. Though the
awe was not really particularly inspired in
Eckard who just realised his suspicions of the
lithe young woman were fulfilled. She would have
to have some flavour of Green to have moved that
fast, across rocky ground too. Turning was
clearly at work, both on her and her shield
maidens, impressive.

Judeson made to get after Jehasli, relinquishing
his hold on Yormeth, Eckard stayed his friend and
Yormeth suddenly got up from the earth, though
his purposes were entirely different.

'She is deserting us. Quickly one of you; open
fire!' Yormeth screeched, motioning for one of
his bowmen to notch arrows and shoot at the
rapidly retreating woman, though now they had
been lost in the billowing clouds of debris and
Auburn dirt.

'Don't you void-damn dare!' Bellowed Judeson as

he advanced on Yormeth. The man seemed to fold inward and shrunk before Judeson in face of his rage.

Eckard stayed Judeson once more this time stepping between the two Southron men.

'She is running the other direction of your town, drawing the Raks out you fucking mugs.' Eckard stated, gesturing with an upraised arm toward where Jehasli and other two had made great strides across the rolling Auburn and green hills to the west, now clear of the explosion's dust cloud.

In the woman's wake, a score of so of Rakon Ravagers raced after them, trailing in hard blackened and boiled leathers, axes and curved blades in hand. The three warriors seemed to disappear over a hill in the near distance.

Eckard felt a connection. The Arcane Sea Turned and Shifted before him and an unexpected ebb flew against him in a somewhat subdued wave. A familiar yet unexpected voice was in his head, a thousand words and images at once. Pictures from someone else's experiences, Jehasli's. She was doing quite well, albeit ill-defined and chaotic projecting from her distance yet for one to try to pierce Eckard's well maintained circles of Grey perception. Eckard instead allowed her to project her thoughts to him.

He won't understand - came through in a buzzridden whine, quite awful *writing*. The amateur practitioner was straining to project so perhaps not as talented as first thought. Her voice a serious of huffs, clearly physically spent already. Eckard weaved back, forcing the connection and flow to become stronger, he could see Jehasli worried and distraught, a decision of utmost importance had destroyed her both inside and out. Of course, Eckard did not allow the woman to see any of his reveries. No, she was not strong enough to see him.

Judeson would definitely not understand. Clearly, that was why she attempted to tell Eckard. Looking down at the Southron Eckard knew the brashly emotional nature of the man would not take the decision of Jehasli to act as bait for them would not abide. However, some things were better left unexplained when faced with the deep running emotions of love. Eckard did not claim to know a great deal in life but that particular subject was one he felt he had some experience in, especially so the running away and avoiding sections.

'You will need to move now, we have a slim advantage that is better used than not so.' Judeson said, remembering the conversation they had around the campfire two nights past.

'Judeson is right, quickly go now!' Yormeth proclaimed while his men were filing out of the shrub and onto the road ahead. Judeson's cousin pulled himself back onto his charger, throwing Judeson a hateful grimace as he got back up into the saddle.

The Free-fighters rushed forward across the flood plain between the forested hills and the escarpment fastness of the Letesah town limits. The score of free-fighters with their various assortments of weapons and/or farming tools hurried onto the slapdash high road. Weapons raised and bellowing voices rang out. Yormeth and his mounted bodyguards pulled ahead of the scurrying group. Not the kind of surprise attack Eckard would have suggested. But their efforts were notable, at least for zeal. Eckard despised what he had to do next.

The tall Nertharnlander held back Judeson's considerable bulk with one outstretched arm. Not meaning to grab at him but the notion was enough to persuade the hot-blooded and hormone fuelled fury that was the fair Southron. Judeson shot Eckard a questioning glance.

'What are you doing? We will need to catch up with the assault if we are to assist them?' Judeson proclaimed, his voice privy to his emotion riddled state.

'They will fail' Eckard answered.

'Most probably, they are not at all remotely trained or disciplined for that matter. But that is our home and we must fight for it.' Judeson stated in white-hot-rage.

'It is a trap and it always was.' Eckard gestured down the slope to Letesah. 'Leaving the gates ajar, sending out half the garrison for one girl, no watch on duty, no fortification for a siege that they know is coming. Ask yourself "why in the Far Above would the Raks do that?" They know about the Free-Fighters they always have and they luring you all into a trap. It's too all too perfect isn't it?'

Judeson felt a sinking sensation of demise and morose settle into his stomach. For despite all his rage he held onto, sometimes even he knew this whole entire plan of retaking Letesah was a foolish one. As if the epiphany of such had grown a hand and reached out to slap his face he reeled back. Eckard just looked at him intently, waiting for his response.

'I have to at least avenge my father's death, of that, I cannot be swayed, right now is the only time I will ever get.' Judeson stated, knowing full well how stubbornly foolhardy he would sound to the Northman.

Eckard simply nodded.

An image from Jehasli passed to him, a secret entrance into Letesah, possibly the same one Prestan had made a note of.

'We are not charging in head forth to the front gate like those fucking fools' Eckard said.

'It's possible with all the commotion we can make it across the plain unseen. In and out and then we find Jehasli.' Judeson challenged Eckard.

'Fine.' Eckard replied.

Eckard pulled into a sprint, using the conflagration of dust cloud as cover, Judeson followed close behind. The two men made for an alternative entrance in Letesah.

10th Stanza

A flavourless dish left out for all to swallow

Revenge is a flare, a bright spark, a dangerous promise

So few see the shortsightedness present

So few recall the taste before

For all the favours are brought to stew

And seasoned relentlessly until discontent is the only taste-

That we can possibly remember

Both Eyes closed and Blade held high

I stride forward with no other thoughts

Colm - The Only Survivor of the Ash Path

At the edge of the escarpment, another of the work camps went up like a candle and the Free Fighter charge was stunted. What could be taken to be another oyra-device exploded into a bright inferno of dust, flying stone, wood chips and free-fighter bodies. In the chaotic disruption, Yormeth was nearly thrown from his charger. Marko was not so lucky, tumbling off horseback. The big man fell with a sickening thud onto the road head first. Yormeth had no time to look back and he and Duminee bolted for the open gatehouse.

From the bulwark of the palisade walls to either side Rakoni bowmen with their odd crossbows loosed into the Free-Fighters who fell in droves: The Free-Fighter charge was funneled into the gatehouse by Duminee and Yormeth. The Southrons packed in like jam in a bottle managed to over the Rakoni gate guards through sheer force of numbers. The tight knit entrance was overrun and the Free-Fighters charged head forth into Letesah. Duminee and Yormeth rode through after the group.

This was all too easy. -Yormeth rationalised.

The gate behind them slammed closed. The forged iron bars battered into the earth. Steam and

hissing from escaped from the top of the
gatehouse,the embedded bars were joined by a hard
white stone slab that sides into place in front
of the bars with a groaning rumble.
Ranks of Rakoni soldiers lined up behind the
disorientated Free-Fighter band, ahead of them on
the narrow street up into Letesah proper, a
procession of Rakoni stood steadfast, weapons
ready on hand.
'Fucking goat-takers!' Yormeth screamed in
deference.
Those goat-takers had outwitted all of them and
now they were trapped.

*

The scattered remnants a timber plank ladder
dotted the cavern floor. Perhaps once-a-time the
ladder was held together by tightly strung rope.
The coils of such lay garbled about, bite marks
from rats unmistakably present. Shining the
candle lantern across rock face where the rope
ladder had once hung pointed out clear enough
what it had formerly been. However, now the
ladder was of no use to the men that wished to
scale a forbidding and sheer rock face in the
absolute gloom of the disused tunnel.
Back down the tunnel, the two men had waded
through kneedeep refuse and disjointed remains of
old constructions. The original settlers had
various wood-carvings and animal skeletons but
those had been beneath the metal shavings and
alabaster stone off cuts of more recent Rakoni
endeavours. Cities on cities, a life built onto
of life. The victors of history made a point of
using what they had conquered and remaking up on
top of it all over again.
Judeson and Eckard left their lanterns at the
refuse clutters cave bottom and proceeded to

climb up the steep rock incline. Attempting to
find foot-falls where they could and stabbing out
ones with hand-picks where they could not. The
desolate darkness offering no assistance though
Eckard attempted to project mage-light though it
did very little. By casting onto the fading
lanterns below. When a dim light pulse sparked
around them, the darkness soon engulfed it with
rapturous hunger. Countering their weight and
pointing out changes in the cliff as each other
respectively saw it. Spotting each other proved
difficult at times, and Eckard reached out with
tangling webs of Magik in an attempt to find safe
passage. After a long anxious and arduous hour,
however, they came up a break with the cliff and
what was possibly the cave mouth Prestan had
spoken of.

Judeson was the first to pull his person up into
the narrow rabbit-hole opening and Eckard
followed shortly after. The Nertharnlander threw
out his Magik senses and warding spells in all
directions to make sure there was no one nearby.
There was not, in the very near vicinity but at
least a score or more perhaps less than a league
away. There was however multiple tunnels
stretching out in the mountain-plateau, just as
Jehasli had also mentioned.

A subdued flaring firelight could be seen ahead
in the darkness of the tunnel seemed to expand
out. A timber door was pushed aside by Judeson
and the two men came from the absolute blackness
of the refuse tunnel and into a dimly light room
full of white stone masonry.

A particularly large hacked apart agglomeration
of the alabaster stone was covered with metal
parts, oddly elongated iron spikes and stretched
wires. Rakoni had well and truly made this place
their home. Huge timber barrels reinforced by

iron clasps skirted the walls and Eckard rationalized the fine dark powder of the crushed Oyra ore was the contents of the barrels. Judeson strode about looking confounded and Eckard could emphasise with him. Though where the former man's sheer confusion may lay, Eckard's was frustration. The Raks and their masters always seemed to be one step ahead of them.

'What is all this?' Judeson spat, the man's tone unmistakably venomous.

'They call it progress.' Eckard replied, shaking his head.

'Arcs ago this had been a grain store and the old granary keeper, who as younglings had named gaffer Anders whittled wooden horses for us if we helped him.' Judeson stated his voice and expression a hundred million leagues away.

'That's what happens now Judeson they build over the top.' Eckard stated coldly.

'Is everything a cynical joke to you?' Judeson asked, listening out for the potential slap of any feet outside but there was no trace of such. Eckard too seemed just as concerned with their arrival being discovered as he placed an ear to the timber doorframe. Slowly the Northman turned and in quiet, composed whisper answered Judeson.

'None of this at all a joke, and that's what makes it all the more concerning.' Eckard stated as he stood back from the door and drew out his enormous repeating crossbow.

Judeson unsheathed his family's long sword from his back and took up a battle ready stance just ahead of Eckard at the doorway. But the footsteps subsided and disappeared back down the opposite end of the hallway outside. Eckard dropped his bow back down and shrugged.

'Come on' Judeson uttered and quietly pushed back

the simple latch on timber portal. Slowly Judeson
eased the door open.

Out in the hallway, there was no one else. The
pattern of booted feet dissipated entirely.
Judeson scouted around and saw nothing but a
dusty, poorly lit and cluttered hallway. More
clasped barrels and timber crates littered the
path ahead. Stalking forward Judeson motioned for
the all clear as Eckard came out from the room
behind him.

At the end of the hallway, the building opened
out onto a narrow balcony. A Rakoni stood at a
watch. Back turned to Eckard and Judeson, unaware
of their presence.

Judeson drew a knife from his leather belt and
advanced on the figure. Eckard stood, unmoving
behind him. Judeson looked back the man puzzled.
The tall Nertharnlander scowled in absolutely
clear disgust back at him. Judeson elected to
ignore the man's bizarre behavior he instead
started forward. Drawing a hand up against the
Rak's mouth to muffle any sound that may escape
the doomed soldier. Judeson rammed his blade into
the Rak's side, puncturing the soft flesh between
the grooves of hardboiled leather and steel
plate. Hopefully puncturing the kidney in the
process.

The Rak struggled in his grip and attempted to
bite into his glove at its mouth. Judeson twisted
and turned the knife splitting apart the wretched
creature's insides. As the near-man slowly lost
the struggle, muffled screams trapped in Judeson
loves, Judeson slowly withdrew his blade, wet
slick blood free-flowing out, and let the limp
form of the Rak slowly to the floor without the
much raucous sound.

Eckard come up alongside Judeson, barely making

even a sound as he did so. The Northman continued to frown and looked down at the Rakon.

'What?' Judeson inquired from the man in a hushed whisper.

'It is not right to murder someone like that. There is no honour in it, no real fight from your opponent.' Eckard stated quietly.

Judeson was incensed.

'What? What are you blabbering about? This thing...was a monster. They have murdered and enslaved my people and yours.' Judeson protested trying to keep his cool and voice down.

Eckard shrugged. At a certain point this man was sometimes insufferable, this was unquestionably one of those times.

Eckard then sighed and whispered back:

'I follow a different code.'

The Northman strode forward in soundless footsteps.

Not turning around Eckard said in a quiet voice:

'It's a rather young monster there too more likely a lookout while the soldiers are out playing.'

Judeson glanced down at the Rakoni the near-man did not possess a metal faceplate mask. Instead, Judeson was looking at the exposed face of milky pale skin young Rakoni man, slightly feminine looking, soft lips, small jawline, perhaps young woman. Judeson shuddered, this...this.. thing did look at all imposing. It bore alien characteristics, sure enough, those elongated lumps and bumps all the Raks seemed to have. But no menacing stare no wicked sharp teeth. It almost looked aurman or maybe draul.

No. Judeson thought. These things butchered and burned your people. They are not people. Not really.

Judeson rushed forward as stealthily as he could manage. Casting aside his internal monologue. He did not distractions. Not now. Not here. Eckard was perched at the end of a slim timber catwalk the structure was propped up on the refined white sediment material the Raks used.

Eckard had his crossbow angled and sighted downward, crouched ready. As Judeson drew up beside the other man in stooping down and lowering his head under the timber casing of the catwalk to evade any prying eyes.

'There seems to be quite the commotion down there.' Eckard stated.

'The Free-Fighters or what's left of them must have got in, maybe they…perhaps Yormeth...you don't think?' Judeson purposed, he kept losing his train of thought, he had believed the others would have been all rounded up by now or butchered at the gates.

Judeson spotted another Rakoni down the hill on a small man-made redoubt. This particular Rak was short and wearing only a tight leather jerkin, a helm and a small blade at its hip. Withdrawing his pig sticker from his belt once again he sneaked forward. Eckard stayed his hand this time, a firm grip on his shoulder.

'Stop murdering void-damned look outs' Eckard growled softly.

The Northman closed his eyes in concentration. Judeson swore he heard waves crashing in the far off distance. As in implausible as that would be this far inland, Mellow's Pond had become stagnation since the operation and would never have any flow again most probably.

Down the hill, the Rak look out scampered off. The near-man must have heard or seen something.

'Ok let's move.' Eckard said, from behind Judeson. The man had reopened his eyes.

Judeson nodded. He did not question Eckard nor pry into what he had done.

Just add it to the list of void-damned nonsense- Judeson silently transposed.

Judeson and Eckard scurried down the pine timber platform and out onto a hard packed earthen street.

Eckard never made a sound even as his heavy boots hit the rough gravel street. The man seemed to glide as if he were a cloud and Judeson rushed to keep up with him.

'You know this is my town.' Judeson whispered to Eckard's back.

The Northman turned, still not making a sound.

'Of course, lead away Sar.' Eckard replied softly, an amused grin on his face.

He was infuriating, inconsistent in every single way and kind of insane. But he was growing on me. - Judeson realised.

Judeson sidled up against the mud brick wall of hovel nearby. He saw the open main road leading down the hill, a collection of fallen bodies adorned the through-fare. Far too many Free- Fighters and far too few Raks for his liking. The street ran crimson with the fluids of the felled. Judeson heard some activity up ahead and pulled his head back. Just in time as it turned out. A score of Raks rushed past in a flurry of feet and rustling leathers clanging steel.

'Doesn't look very promising for your beloved cousin.' Eckard said Rak's brisk march ahead left them.

'I am not leaving till I avenge my father's murder... and all the others.' Judeson started

choking on his words. How many had died this day?
He would fix that. He would fix all of it. He
rushed over the street and into the cover of a
stockpile of the white Rakish stone.
Eckard behind him simply grunted and followed.

*

It was not supposed to end up like this.
What the actual fuck. Zadma has mercy.
Yormeth was not really a praying man. He feared
and loved the Goddess just as every good man
should. Love for God was unconditional. They
created you after all. The least you could do was
love them back. Yormeth, however, found himself
questioning the Goddess's mercy right now and
here.
They had been led into an elaborate trap. The
slaughter was undefinable. The Free-Fighters had
been cut down like wheat in the time of Harvest.
Even now their corpses lined the street outside.
Brave and loyal Duminee had died saving them. His
limp and lifeless body now riddled with crossbow
bolts. Duminee had desperately yanked the timber
planks holding the door closed away. He had given
his life doing so.
He would not die in vain. - Yormeth reasoned.
From beside Yormeth the young girl who had
propped herself against the pine door to keep it
closed with him spoke.
'They stopped, boss, they stopped they did' the
girl who was barely that, a helm too big for her
adolescent head, a spear too blunt to hurt
anyone, let alone of those demons outside.
What had he done, he was far too headstrong, too
reckless. He had led these poor fools to a
massacre.
Yormeth beckoned the big block-headed man ahead

of him awho was a blond haired Grantumban with a
vacant stare in his eyes, to take up residence on
the doorframe just in case. Yormeth motioned for
the child soldier to follow him, the girl
scurried after him as if he would lead her to
salvation. She too had the same bereaved
expression on her face. Emotionally drained,
aurmanly absent.

'Look, boss, we found a little Rak youngun' A
Free-Fighter stated as Yormeth neared the man.

The Free-Fighter had an ugly albino creature in
his clutches. The hideous creature whimpered and
sneered in the man's grasp. Yormeth relieved his
subordinate of the creature and picked it up by
the colour of the maroon tunic its tunic.

'What in the Void are you?' Yormeth hissed
between barred teeth at the abomination.

'Gozka'kel!' The ugly child spat back.

Yormeth cuffed it across the face and dragged
across the work room floor by the collar.

The Free-fighters had retreated into a what was
once the old lumber mill of Letesah. The gigantic
circular saw Yormeth's pa had once operated had
been removed, only iron barred timber crates
remained anywhere. There was no lumber in sight.
No pine or cedar, nor iron bark or red gum. The
whole place was covered in plain old dust and not
that of sawdust or timber chips. Why ever the
Raks had left this pathetic little child alone in
this hollow dead place, Yormeth did not know.

But now they had a bargaining chip. The Raks may
be demons with the blade and bow but surely they
would not hesitate if one of their children were
in danger.

Yormeth began to piece together a plan. He would
get the Free-fighters out of this yet.

'Brave men and women, come with me.' Yormeth

called to the others, only a mere four now. The
blockhead of a child with an adult's helm and
two afro-sporting Dalhese twins followed in his
wake as he dragged the Rak child to the double
doors of the front entrance into Yormeth's
father's lumber mill.

On the return to the day-star's light, Yormeth
and the Free-Fighters were greeted by a score of
trained crossbows on their position. From up on
timber catwalk staircase creating the sharp
escarpment opposite the mill, a squat Rak with a
one shouldered cape of white and navy blue strode
down. Behind the caped Rak, another near-man
stalked behind, this one staggering tall and
hulking in its dark steel plate maille. The
taller Rak sported a Loin's decapitated head over
its own.

'I have a child of yours, throw down your arms
and let us pass' Yormeth stated, as commanding as
he could. A sudden wave of exhaustion battered
him a thousand ton brick. He shook aside his own
tiredness. He would get them out of this yet.

The Rakoni said something completely
incomprehensible to Yormeth. It was all in that
guttural gibberish the Raks spoke. The child
answered with one croak laden word.

'Speak Cestral, you filth' Yormeth spat in anger.

'I was reassuring the child that he would be
saved from the heretics.' The caped Rakoni said
in heavily cacophonous and accented Cestral. The
near-man and its bulky companion now only a
handful of paces from Yormeth and the four other
Free-Fighters.

Yormeth had heard enough. This was getting
nowhere.

'Void damn you fucking wretches! Then come meet
me face to face, leader to leader. This

Taskmaster of yours if he ain't got the balls to talk to me, least he could do is fight me, man, to monster in a fucking duel.' Yormeth hissed between clenched teeth.

The caped Rak with high-pitched voice nodded in agreement.

'Very well gozka-kel, finally you show honour.' The Rakoni replied.

'You will let my people go when I do.' Yormeth stated.

Both the caped Rakoni and the heavily armoured killer nodded.

'Very well' The caped one said.

Yormeth threw aside the squealing Rak he had held up and drawn his broad sword. The gigantic lion headed killer drew a twisted monstrosity of a blade from its sheath at its back.

*

Judeson led Eckard to a timber, thatched roofed long house. The doors were barred and the windows also. Hushed whispers drifted out from the inside. Judeson marched toward the main doorway as a man possessed.

This fool has a void-damned death wish. - Eckard thought.

Judeson raised his huge bastard sword and smashed apart the boarded up planks on the front doorway.

Judeson rushed in, Eckard followed and saw a sight that had left the big Southron stuck in his stance and speechless.

There were no Rakoni soldiers in the wide polished timber hallway. Not weapon on one of them. Though to be fair most these pale near-man looked far too elderly or adversely too young.

Eckard threw an arm out across Judeson. Just as a precaution.

'No, these fucking creatures....they don't get to whimper. They don't deserve mercy...they.'
Judeson said the man seemed to drift off into the unintelligible.

'There are no warriors here, just workers and students, doing their jobs, carrying the load forced upon them and trying to get by. You would slaughter all of them then?'

'No of course not.' Judeson sighed. 'I will not do onto them as what their kind have already done.' The Southron sheathed his blade back onto his back.

'Their kind, Judeson you would slaughter these people as defenceless animals. Your vengeance can't be completed by visiting upon your so-called sworn enemies the very same atrocities that you so strive to halt.'

'We have to do something, we can't just let them go after all this, after...'Judeson began as one of the scarcely clothed near-men or women perhaps backed away. Further away still in the gloom of the barn, a Rakoni babe cried out.

'And what shall we do?' Eckard inquired, gesturing around the dim lit barn.

'Who's to say these ones don't come back armed and slaughter more.' Judeson snapped in answer.

'They are civilians Judeson, they neither hold weapons nor the skills to wield such, they just want to survive.'

'I never thought the Rakon could be so..'

'Aurman?' Eckard interjected before Judeson could finish.

A scream of utter primal rage sounded off in the distance

*

Judeson froze a dual tone visage of horror and

sudden surprise, stung by Eckard's omission and
Yormeth's angry filled yelp. The big, broad
shouldered Southron faced the ruined longhouse
doors and let out an exasperated sigh. Several
Raks fell to their feet nearby and began what
could be taken as a prayer. The all-too familiar
words of gozka could be heard again. Judeson
swore he heard the Rakish term key in their
chants once more too.

He bolted for the doorway and beyond. Judeson not
bothering to look back, he somehow knew Eckard
would follow.

*

Yormeth attempted to angrily swing at the lion-
headed Rakon but the near-man shifted his weight
and pulled away from the Southron's reach.
Cursing himself the Dosintali realized with no
small quarter of horror that he had over-extended
himself. Yormeth's defense was exposed and
footing was all-mightily messed right up. The
Rak's weapon's arm came round and the wicked
blade sliced across; directed for Yormeth's neck.
The Southron managed to just pull his head under
the blow as it came by, cool air passing across
the top of his head. More luck than any real
skill in surviving the first attack, Yormeth
could not counter in time and the Rak's other
hand bearing his knife came from below and
pierced right into his side.

Hot fluid poured from the stinging wound and the
Southron found himself losing strength; his
thoughts becoming a broken daze. Black spots
began to cloud his vision and Yormeth swung once
more, trying to hit anything of the Rak who held
on with a fierce grip on the lodged knife inside
Yormeth. His swing was weak, Yormeth was drained
from blood loss and the huge near-man warrior who

was inexplicably fast and side stepped away from Yormeth's desperate, hopeless gamble. Yormeth messed himself and between his blood loss and luke-warm flow of urine he slipped down falling into his own filth.

Void-dammit! Yormeth shouted at himself even as the Rakon's sword bearing arm swung down and the blade came closer and closer to his head. The world seemed to fold in on itself and time was dragged to a crawl. The impending blow taking an eternity to make contact and the pain of Yormeth's stab wound only seeming to intensify every moment. Though the Southron realized this limbo of suspended time was an illusion of his own mind. He closed his eyes and embraced what he could not run from. Void-dam..and there was no more.

11th Stanza

My eyes were open

Though I was blinded by the Sea

The Truth of all

Was subject to flee

Right there in front of me

Ode to the Lost

Darus Orio -' the Wilderman' – 1872 arcs ATF

Freeport, Tribune Isles

From where Eckard and Judeson stood at the end of
the town hall veranda they witnessed the short
fight ensure and then conclude. They both
witnessed Yormeth fall with all the subtlety of a
landslide into a lake. The Southron died before
he hit the ground in twisted, unnatural spasms.
The snarling Rakon standing over him raised his
challenging gaze levelled at Judeson. Yormeth's
countryman roared in an answering call and
charged headlong forward, practically throwing
his considerable bulk self from the balcony.
Eckard pulled to the side and let the two
heavyweights battle it out with themselves. There
were other obstacles to be overcome.

Yormeth's companions were surrounded on all
sides, with stealth emphatically out the window,
the headstrong Judeson making sure of that.
Eckard would not have much use of shadow-weavings
to distract or confuse, not yet anyway. With a
score of Rakish crossbows to call on, the
remaining Free-Fighters had no possible means of
escape. One of them looked to be barely only a
child, shook like a leaf and sobbed audibly even
of the sounds of Judeson and the Rakoni meeting
steel.

A Rakoni bearing a golden half-cap on its
soldiers motioned for the crossbow wielding

compatriots to instead of fielding the remaining Free-Fighters in a cluster of pointed barbs. To stock, their weapons, draw blades and take in prisoners. The Raks followed orders like single-minded zealots. The Procession of Raks filed away with the Free-Fighter hostages in tow, very little resistance was offered by the desperate Southrons, though Eckard knew he could not begrudge them in their defeat.

'The Free-Fighters died in agony with no chance, God was always against them.' The cape sporting Rakoni said, in heavily accented Cestral. Though The guttural nature of the bear-man's voice did sound quite feminine to Eckard.

Eckard realized the cape wearing one must be their Mord'ha'ja – their liaison, interpreter and solitary speaker. The procession crossbowmen had now gone. From behind them appeared a far greater threat. One spoken of in hushed tones by deeply traumatised survivors, or some cases causalities that had been reached a little soul-snaring.

Two maroon cloaked apparitions that were previously strode forward toward Eckard. The Nertharnlander knew and dreaded what came next. For though he had never actually faced one; Eckard had heard many a tale from other members of the Pact about White-Mark Zealots or Dread Helms as some called them, for obvious reasons.

The cloaks were thrown away and metal encased arms and spindly steel legs came out. Thin pig-sticker blades in hand, that is to say- not so much in hand , the knives were part of their hands, built in. Long elongated and wicked looking blades right across the back of their metal palms. The Dread Helms made a rapid approach for Eckard. Blackened steel spiked headgear fully covered their faces leaving no

clear discernible features present. Beneath the
solid blackened metal plating; the sounds of cogs
and gears whistled, screeching disconcertingly,
dark choking steam spewing out of their
mechanical parts. The duo fanned out, flanking
Eckard.

'You will surrender now or face recompense for
your sins, infidel' The Mord'ha'ja declared
coldly.

Eckard knew it would be foolish to face two well-
trained opponents on the even ground. He threw a
smile which he hoped would disarm, or perhaps
antagonise enough to provide cover. He feigned an
attack, stepping forward with Holloway's rapier
in hand. Holding an aggressive stance the Dread
Helms began to attempt a blind-siding flanking
attack from both sides. Eckard cast a thin shadow
weave of his form in front, perceiving a
tentative hold on a flow from the Arcane Sea and
pirouetted and turned down a side alley in a mad
rush. If they had to fight he was going to draw
them away from Judeson's vendetta first and
foremost, even the numbers out.

Can't be fucking cheating now Raks. - Eckard
mused, his slap-dash route down a muddy alleyway.

For a moment it seemed the two assailants had not
followed his lead. Eckard felt he had left his
friend to face four opponents and the whole
burning bridge metaphor from earlier suddenly
seemed an unequivocally chilling conclusion. But
the twin Dread Helms came into view striding up
in an arrogant challenging strut, as if this were
no battle at all, but merely a practice round.

*Well fuck this, I'm not conceding to a fair
fight.* Eckard thought.

Even as he gathering the flowing ember of a weave
around him. Waves of fiery scarlet and off yellow

swam past him and he pushed those away. This town stuck of the Void, seethed in it. His head pounded from vile, gut-wrenching onslaught

Eckard hurled himself backward. He cast a shadow weave, an invisible web strung out behind him and literally threw his body against it. Not certain whether his ploy would actually work or not. He was violently thrown across the open courtyard behind him. Perhaps an old pig or goat holding pen, the fence long since knocked down. Eckard found himself at least fifteen paces from his foes, they looked about and eventually steadied glances on him with unnaturally glassy eyes.

Well, it had worked momentarily at least. - Eckard thought trying to be calm his pounding chest.

The beanpole Nertharnlander felt his back brush up against a mud brick wall. He was almost on top of or if he had of weaved his shadow a little more violently.

Maybe even thrown me inside the wall, now that would not have been fun. Eckard realized.

Eckard rounded the building until he found an opening in the form of an open face window. He climbed up and into the residence. The home was obviously abandoned. A broken table and chair set of varnished hooping pine lay scattered in a corner of the dining room.

The front door was brutally thrown inward off its hinges. Eckard pivoted to the side as the rusted bulk sailed past him into the back rooms and the two Dread Helms entered.

The twin steel-encased Raks fanned out in a flanking manoeuvre once more, around Eckard.

He backed himself into their trap. They would relish the chance for a close combat melee. He would die if he did so. Eckard would not oblige them.

Of the thousands of hours of mental training with the unrelenting Wrendal, the arcs of varying advice or criticisms from equally diverse sources, one tidbit of information came to mind for Eckard. It was the voice of the late monk - Marek.

You have an unorthodox technique both with the sword and with the way you weave the ebb and flow. Embrace that Eckard. You have a unique way about you use it to its utmost extent. - Eckard swore he could hear the ancient and wiry Kobold utter in that scratchy voice that he had had, all those arcs ago.

Eckard did not know why he had heard the deceased Kobold's voice right now, on the perceived advent of his possible demise. He was thankful, it gave a reinvigorated sense of optimism.

The Rakoni Dread Helms closed in like an opportunistic pack of ravenous wolves. Eckard remembered himself, back from reminiscing and on to the job at hand. He wove the ebb and flow from the Arcane Sea he had previously opened. Then Eckard did something he had not done for arcs. He turned his way on the Sea just as a Green-aspect Mage would have done. Not quite as capable as Raijin. Nowhere near as coolly disciplined. But Eckard persevered all the same.

The way changed. Eckard's vision of deep swirling shadows was altered to a diverse spectrum of many shades and tones. He saw the varying timber grains he could smell moisture inside and the damp outside. It had begun to rain and he could feel water drops impact and touch the house they were in and the ground around them. The Raks had thrust out their blade-hands in a dual enacted strike. As if they were the same soldier. Eckard could see inside their mechanical armour, tubes of varying size took black oil and minuscule pieces of shining or over their oddly spindly bodies.

I will be dead soon. Eckard felt as if he could feel his own death. In a way, he swore he could.

Eckard threw all the shadow weaves he had constructed outward from himself. He turned the moisture inside the timber frame of the house as hot as he could, bringing molecules to boil, come with a price, he felt himself sweat and become feverish in response. Eckard weaved and turned on the oyra, urging the mineral to become unstable.

All of this was in a matter of seconds. Three breathes...The Rakoni were now inch from him with weapons near to piercing him. Eckard threw himself forward, holding out Holloway's rapier before him.

The entire hut caved in after him.

Eckard did not encounter the luck he had in hitherto had had. His shadow weave casting threw him against the pine wall and burst out of it a violent shattering of wood chip debris. Some of which smashed against the rapier, his face and against his sides. He did not have time to realise this pain as he met the ground in a tumble of limbs, Holloway's blade flying from his hands. Eckard finally after a series of rolls, smashed into a timber and stone retaining wall, left shoulder first. It was possibly dislocated, worst case scenario it was broken.

Righting himself back onto his feet, Eckard felt the hot flush of blood free flowing from his ears. His nose was dripping with crimson liquid also. With the back of his hand, he brushed aside his own blood. Clutching at his shoulder, the bone still felt intact, with the last little flow of the Arcane Sea he could feel no bones had been broken at all. Fortunately. Eckard with his right hand popped back in his opposing shoulder.

Eckard winced in agony as he twisted his arm back in, a sickening pop going along with the unnatural motion. He held onto the flow from the Arcane Sea, his nerves calming somewhat and the pain subsiding. He looked up with teary peripherals at the decimated remnants of the hovel he had previously been in. Movement from the debris as the Dread Helms had begun to rise from the ruins.

A thousand faces and a thousand places flashed across Eckard's vision. He was somewhere else, or perhaps many other locales with people he did not know or did not immediately recognise. And then that was all gone. If it was ever there. Eckard shook himself. He was mere paces from the smoldering hovel ruins. To his right was the rapier. Eckard picked it up, marched over to the struggling rise of one of the Dread Helms. The creature had one arm and its legs still pinned down in the wreckage. The abomination had a free hand its head free. Eckard thrust the rapier toward the Dread Helms neck, the creature blocking his initial strike. Eckard pulled away, feigned a counter and then tilted his thrust into a brief swing. The blade met flesh between the metal plates and dark maroon hue blood flowed forth.

From behind Eckard the other Dread Helm has wrestled its way out of the wreckage. The sounds of timber chunks and loose earth being thrown off announced the arrival of the mechanical killer. The Rakoni creation charged Eckard and offered a flurry of precise blows and jabs. Eckard shifted back blocking as many of the creature's furious attacks as he could. Some of the blade arms

sliced across his chain maille vest and cut
through the cloth of Eckard's trench coat. The
thing seemed tired as with a furious it just
sliced the air between it and Eckard's own face.
Eckard countered and dropped his weight into a
downward slice, cutting across the Rakoni soldier
leg, steel parts and soft flesh parted in the
blade's wake. The femur joint split and the
Rakoni creation fell to one side. Eckard struck
fast the rapier skimming across the torso. Fresh
and blood against magiklly embedded metal. Blood
and bile seeping out like a fountain. Despite
being opened up the Dread Helm countered fending
off Eckard's killing strike on the return.
Holloway's rapier snapped against the other
blade.

*Not quite as well embedded as I first thought
that or it is used up*. Eckard rationalised.

Eckard waited for the unstable Rakoni to
overbalance. The creature struck out a blade-hand
toward him and he pivoted away from the
creature's reduced reach. With the remaining
broken end of the rapier, he threw his full force
and some flow from the Arcane Sea into a forward
thrust. The Rakoni twitched in an involuntary
spasm as the shattered shard of a blade went
straight its eye socket. Eckard lets go of the
shattered rapier and left it in the dying Rak as
it fell back into the debris pile.

He would need another sword.

*

Judeson met the Rak's almighty strike with steel.
The bastard sword of Jude was hammered against
the Loin-headed Rak's immense tulwar in a
sequence of brazen sparks. Judeson lowered his
centre of gravity, shifting away in a half
crouch, keeping his guard up as the Rakon came in

for another frontal attack.

Judeson caught his opponent's tulwar on the dead centre of his word. The sheer momentum of the Rak's downward swing sent Judeson skidding backward. He was barely able to stabilise himself in the all-consuming mud, Judeson's heavy booted feet sinking into the muddy earth. He tilted himself to the side, bypassing another blow thrown by his Rakoni opponent. Judeson was afforded a welcome break and pulled himself up from the mud. The Rak had run into a similar problem to himself, becoming bogged down and skidding past Judeson. Unfortunately for Judeson the hulking near-man somehow managed to keep his feet.

Judeson's respite would be short-lived he knew, so he moved as fast as the unsteady terrain permitted him. The rain from the Far Above had turned from patches of light drizzle when he and the Rak had first begun their dual to a fullblown heavy torrent. Clear visibility was obscured. Judeson pulled away to the cover of a nearby hovel, the thatched roof provided some cover from the increasingly heavy downpour.

The huge, imposing form of the Rakoni warrior came into view, literal buckets of water coming down sideways now. Other apparitions emerged in the gloom. The crossbow wielding Raks that had taken his people prisoner had returned. It was either that or as Judeson dreaded there were, even more, Rakonis in Letesah.

Judeson's dual adversary held off the other Raks, urging them behind him. As was common in the Southrondor the torrential rain subsided drastically; One moment a storm, the next a clear day. The daystar returned and the hulking Rak came at Judeson a new. Swiping, slicing, thrusting, the giant Rak was incredibly and unexpectedly agile. Judeson fended off a sequence of jarring attacks. He was exhausted and the Rakoni was relentless.

No, he would not give up he would have his vengeance these fucking creatures would pay for all they had done.

Judeson counter attacked, forcing the near-man back with a series of well-timed blows.

The Rakoni stood back, staggering his charge at Judeson.

What was the bastard doing? - Judeson thought.

The Rakoni tugged back the huge plains loin head from his own, to reveal a deeply scarred and unnervingly ghost-pale face. A small smile escaped from the Rak's thin slit of a mouth. Judeson had dreamt of this savage a thousand times over, his father's murderer. The Rak that wore a lion's head and yet…. The creature before him now was not him. It was not his father's murderer. He was sure of it this Rak was different, younger maybe, taller perhaps. It was so very hard to tell as to why Judeson doubted himself now. The nightmare was unclear, hazy. It was not him.

The shorter Rakoni with the cape from earlier had reappeared, the creature striding up to the giant Rak half collapsed and dying on the ground and resting a hand on the brute's shoulder even as the creature heaved and huffed in agony, vitak fluids spilling out.

'Well met, infidels. But now you must face your fate. We of God's chosen children will always prevail.' The cape-wearing Rak stated.

Quarrels and arrows bolted out at the ranged Rakoni troops and cloaked figures ran in from all sides. Judeson saw the look of shocked awe

painted on the faces of the cape-wearer and the
giant. That was enough, he pelted forward, sword
in hand for some form of vengeance that much he
had to have.

Where was HE?

'Shove your self-righteousness up your arse!' The
all too familiar voice of Eckard called out. The
bean-pole Nertharnlander striding in
nonchalantly.,. like a casual audition for an
amateur stage show.

*

Eckard threw himself against the side of tin
walled garden shed. Just in time as it turned
out. He had darted out of the path of a quarrel's
flight. The bolt lodged into the soft, rain
drenched earth, barely a few hand lengths from
Eckard's left boot. He threw out a strand of Grey
weaving from himself and found the presence of
two Rakoni snipers holed up behind an over turned
wagon-cart. Eckard took a deep breath, a foul
taste of his own blood and sick in his mouth. He
reached further into the Arcane Sea, his mind
attuned to the ebb and flow now, that stinging
cold taking hold, goose pumps laced up and down
his whole body. His head pounded.

Wrendel had called it - drowning. Eckard thought.
If one took much out of the Arcane Sea and forced
their way in, not closing the gate behind them,
endlessly casting without pause. They were
overcome. Magik was not without its consequences.
It absorbed life and altered it. It also had
nasty habit of extinguishing life if abused with
reckless abandon.

Eckard had been warned by Wrendel before, he had
been warned by Lisiarna and by Raijin about what
the Arcane Sea could do if a mage waere not
careful and wary of all their steps. But he had

to, this time he had no choice, he was outnumbered and outplayed. Just how far could he skirt the Sea without falling into its depths? Forcing aside the overbearing pounding in his head Eckard started forward. He threw out a shadow woven phantom of himself, some three man-lengths to his side, several quarrels falling upon his false position. Rushing ahead he took out his repeater bow from his bag and that other place where he kept his belongings. The crossbow already armed, he cocked the release guard and squeezed the trigger, weaving a thread of Grey with the shot. Three bolts flew out in quick succession. Magikly enhanced the quarrels passed through Rakoni armour like knives through warm butter.

The Rakoni soldier fell to the muddy earth in involuntary death throes. One made to rise, but Eckard snuffed out the near-man's chances with a knife buried in its arm pit. Struggling with the hunting blade stabbed deep, the Rakoni did not have to die wondering, as Eckard slammed the solid iron encased timber shoulder guard on his crossbow downward. The Rakoni half-helm crumpled beneath Eckard's urging.

Down with one hostile exchange, Eckard broke into a sprint, he could hear another in the very near distance. The clash of steel and iron, the whiz and whirl of projectiles through the still air and of course the unwelcome but inevitable smell of blood and bile. If Judeson were alone...

But he was not, Irthule had returned. The big Southron's score of patched together warriors held the ground against half as many Raks. From behind the Retrievers and Prestan had formed a flanking formation from out of the thatched roof hovels. An aurmen fell and a Rak followed shortly thereafter and then hostilities were abruptly discontinued. For the gold cape, Rakoni had become aware of their intangible position.

'Well met, infidels. But now you must face your fate. We of God's chosen children will always prevail.' The cape-wearing Rak announced as if they had the upper hand.

Eckard smirked to himself. He walked forward into the fray.

'Shove your self-righteousness up your arse!' Eckard called out.

The Rakoni leader glared daggers back at Eckard.

Prestan's voice rang out calling for a ceasefire. Hands still lay on blades and triggers, itching for a fight on both ends.

A sudden chilling realization swept over Eckard, as he witnessed the hulking form of Judeson stride forward, Claymore out before him, his face a mask of indefatigable red-hot rage. A huge giant of a Rakoni was facing up to the vengeful Southron with an equally preposterous blade on hand. Both the Rakoni and the Aurman forces had parted to let the two into a face off. The enemies formed a sort of guard of honour. Though there was clearly no love lost between the Raks and aurmen, spiteful dialogue in varying dialects went back and forth.

Eckard knew the Rakoni would not be so foolhardy to directly engage the aurmen Free-fighters as their flank was exposed to the kobold behind them. The Raks would be jammed into a pincer by the two flanking enemy forces.

But Judeson was throwing his life into the hands of the front line, against an opponent that reeked of the foul all-consuming scent of the Void. Eckard peered closer with his weaver's sight of Grey magik webs. The Rakoni giant

possessed the soft off milky white flesh of his
species, but to Eckard's dawning apprehension,
also had machine cog and gears very similar to
the two admonitions Eckard had fought not minutes
ago.

It was then that Eckard felt the Arcane Sea flow
out from another source other than his own.

*

Judeson experienced a second wind. His rage was
abruptly thrown to the four winds and a sort of
out of body sensation replaced it, as if he were
merely watching himself swing his sword and not
actually doing so himself. He thought he was done
for just moments ago and now, now he was not sure
exactly what he was doing.

This was not right.

Judeson's father had instructed him on no less
than fifty separate occasions about rage and the
battle fatigue that inevitably followed it. He
felt warm, not like unlike being next to a fire
or strangely enough have a spark of one deep down
inside himself.

It could not be.

Judeson saw an opening in the Rak's defense even
as he feigned and jabbed at his opponent. The
Rakoni had left a between blade and body. But
Judeson knew a sleight of form when he saw one.
The Rak was baiting him. Judeson pulled away and
threw a backhanded swing the opposite way the Rak
meant to lead him.

This was impossible.

Judeson's attack met the Rakoni just below the
under arm region. It should have been the
blackened plate maille pieces. But contrary to
the point of a rational warrior's thought
process. The sword of Jude met resistance with a
steely crunch. Judeson felt the blade sink in,

flesh must have been met, as the dark crimson blood all Raks seemed to process flowed out. But so too did a shiny oily fluid. A hiss of hot steam came out with the oil and the reeked of putrid sulfur.

The Rakoni before Judeson had been pushed back by the blow from Judeson's family Claymore and a swift and hard boot in turn. The blade which had come free from cleaving into the near man was now married on its surface with mess and slick oil. As the giant Rak staggered back Judeson realised that; he too had been struck by the Rak in a counter attack earlier. Judeson's coat had been ripped to shreds around his torso and his breastplate had taken some violence onto it. Somehow it was only slightly dented inward.

Judeson felt fresh like he had only just begun the fight. The hulking Rak was his polar opposite. The creature staggered and lurched on its feet. Hisses and twisting of gears sounded off from somewhere inside whatever the Rak was wearing.

How was this happening? What was happening?

The gold cape Rakoni drew Judeson away from his immediate adversary, the feminine sounding Rak, violently shook in convulsions. When the creature came back to stand still from whatever inflicted it, the Rak smiled, confidently. The white gleam of teeth could be seen even through the Rak's full face mask. The soldiers of its kin stirred behind and the aurmen and kobold tightened their grips on their collective weapons.

The Rak who had seemingly suffered a stroke, albeit for a moment. The creature then righted themselves; laughed and applauded in such a raucous manner everyone looked up perplexed. Judeson looked over to Eckard who grinned like a man possessed. But behind the big Nertharnlander's eyes was a deadly seriousness and in plain sight a knowing look of rage.

'Finally, the Pact rears its ugly head.' The Rak said, this time in a completely alien tone than what it had sounded like hitherto the 'spasm ' it had suffered.

'Why don't you show yourself, Channellor?' Eckard laughed out loudly, though his voice was edged with deadly seriousness.

The gold cape Rak laughed and offered quick exchange that it was. A low pitched chuckle, brief as a gentle breeze.

'All in good time, patience is the key to long life, Mage' The Rakoni soldier stated.

'Preaching does not work on me, you can shaft that up your arse.' Eckard grinned.

'Crass as always, enduring like mud.' The Rakoni said in another's voice.

Judeson restlessly awoke from his initial shock and awe and strode forward.

'Enough of this goat-shit' Judeson fired back to the stagnant parties. He found his second wind stirring his emotions once more. With the new-found resolve and strength, Judeson began forward to finish the job.

The hulking Rakoni monster of metal and gears stood unevenly in Judeson's path once more, the abomination joining in a chorus of laughter with its gold cape wearing master.

The Kobold and Free Fighters readied as the Raks too anticipated a recommencement to hostilities.

'We are Chosen Heroes of the Almighty, children of the Shroud and let God be witness to your damnation!' The cape sporting Rak enthusiastically proclaimed. The near-man then

fell to the ground in another chillingly
unnatural sequence of fits.

Judeson ignored whatever sorcery was occurring
here and began to swing at the Rakoni giant anew,
although now the creature was hissing out clouds
of tar black smog and shaking as if it too were
struck by some unworldly possession.

The Rakoni closed and their blades met. Judeson
shifting and jabbing at the hideous creature,
testing the waters. From all around, bolts passed
by and met flesh, both Rakoni and Judeson's
apparent allies. Eckard had taken the gold cape
Rak's broad sided scimitar and was covering
Judeson. Perhaps the man was not entirely insane,
he knew better than to interrupt Judeson from the
justice he deserved. Amazing in between a
sequence of clashing blades, Judeson saw Eckard
hold his ground and at least a dozen Rak crossbow
bolts lay at his feet none of which had come
close.

Judeson did not feel right, his lungs burned, his
head felt like a great weight. Something was
speaking to him. A voice, familiar but so distant
as to not be discernible.

Judeson - The voice said his name.

This was not happening, not now.

'Down everyone fucking down!' Eckard shouted the
Northman was somehow, impossibly by Judeson's
side, One of the man's spindly arms resting on
Judeson's armoured shoulder.

'Come on! Void-damn you!' Eckard screamed near to
Judeson's ear.

Judeson made to protest or merely shrug off
Eckard's loose grip. Completely unexpected than
was Judeson in that moment he and the Northman
flew backward like a heavy storm wind. The two
men crashed in a heap against a thatched wall of

a yurt.

On all sides, Raks emptied their wicked looking crossbows into the scattered positions of kobold and the few remaining Free-Fighters. If the latter soldiers had of been still fighting back many of them would have probably fallen. As it turned out, however, the kobold rushed away in all directions, in full retreat, pulling and tugging the Aurmen with them as they vacated the battle. Several of the Rak's bolts made contact on the fleeing Free-Fighters and their saviours cutting them down like wheat at harvest.

What were they doing? The little fools were going to be all shot in the back running away and all Judeson's compatriots would be taken with them.

Just as Judeson made to ask Eckard nestled up behind him, an impossibly bright luminescence and harrowing noise blanketed outward in a terribly ominous explosion. The violent denotation was exactly where the giant Rak and it's gold cape master had been moment ago.

The earth seemed to rock and the wailing boom rocked Judeson's ears until they felt like they burst from his already heavy head.

Many Rak's were caught up in the wailing wall of flame and cascading dust and lost it. The Kobold and Aurmen retreated behind Eckard Judeson and back up the main thoroughfare of Letesah.

'Come on you heavy bastard get up.' Eckard proposed from behind Judeson.

Judeson hauled himself back to his feet with great effort. The tall Northman made his way to his feet just as gingerly.

'It was one their grenades again' Judeson motioned, though it was not entirely an assured statement on his part.

'It was oyra, but something else too.' Eckard

replied.

'Come on you two crazies, we are making a break while we can.' a high- pitched voiced kobold offered as it bolted past in full flight.

Eckard broke into a run and Judeson followed him.

Several frantic moments passed Judeson ran as fast as his legs would take him up the muddy hill.

A ring of armed kobold and a score of aurmen waited ahead of them. Crossbows and blades in hand, the formation of soldiers allowed Eckard and Judeson into their ranks. Judeson spotted the familiar grim face of Irsthule. He granted the man an acknowledging nod to which the Tahnise man rekindled in turn.

'Think of your family, keep that thought in your mind.' Eckard stated, brushing past Judeson and making his way over the to the kobold who had briefly spoken to him and Eckard before.

'Prestan we have to get out of here, I hope you have our escape covered.' Eckard said to the lizard like creature.

The reptilian curled its short tail upward and nodded.

With most of the Free-Fighters and kobold down the tunnel, it was just Judeson, Eckard, and this Prestan remaining. Though where that tunnel led to Judeson knew not. For somewhere off in the distance, he could hear the blasting of Rakoni horns and the slow and steady odious drumming of the aforementioned near-men's drums.

Not yet, no. There was still much to be done. Had that giant been the one? No, then where was the goat-taker? - All of his carefully dreamt plans of justice and vengeance had gone astray Judeson realised.

'Wait, I need a moment' Judeson managed to croak

out, though his mind was a myriad of broken and confused thoughts. He knew, for certain he needs to stay albeit for one more fleeting moment.

'Go on, we'll catch up.' Eckard stated. A certain tinge of finality was in Eckard's voice that ceased any arguments from Prestan who nodded in exchange and began down the tunnel mouth, pausing at the entrance.

*

The rolling dirt hills on the outer southern reaches of Letesah became quickly engulfed in the cascading dust clouds as a Rakoni army marched on the besieged village. The shattered debris Eckard stood on seemed like a grim reminder as to what very little his friend was so intent on protecting. There was barely a purpose, a minuscule purpose at most as to why Judeson refused to retreat from the ruined settlement. That purpose was of course not at all practical. Although Eckard knew his Southron compatriot would not go easy on this issue.

'It's lost we have little hope of protecting your home. We should flee while we still can.' Eckard made into words what already harboured in his thoughts.

'We can't just run now, as soon as we flee the Raks win..they void-damned win...again. The whole cycle starts again and that tunnel leading out of here, the whole point of this mess, they profit on our failure and blood once again.' Judeson stated, anger now taking hold. After all this, it just ends the same anyway.

'Then choose the other option, the meaningful one. The Pact's founding members saw that blood cannot be quenched with blood. That the fight of vengeance and the war of right and wrong would never be won with back and forth blood-letting

and rage-filled slaughter.' Eckard stated,
burrowing the Rakoni axe in the bamboo framework
around one of the standing alabaster bulkheads.

'Speak plainly for Zadma's fucking sake.' Judeson
growled.

'Defence, the Rule by which I stand it is one of
purpose and promise.' Eckard began first; the
tall Mage began pacing around Judeson and
continued on. 'Revenge is hopeless, like drowning
a lake with buckets of water after it already
flooded your home. Don't you see Yahasa's
nutsack, man all of this...these acts you have
done against the Raks are for naught. You strike
down their soldiers and more come to fight for
their name. I'm sorry about your father I truly
am. But his death would not suddenly be avenged
and honoured by killing the Rak that did so to
him nor any other Rak.'

'What then should we do, if you have the answers
to this shit what then?' Judeson asked.

'I don't have the answers Judeson not by any
stretch of the imagination, metaphors aside. I
offer a better option at least one not wholly my
own. I offer a choice to you one in which you can
run head forth into that horde of Raks over the
hill or one in which you don't fucking die. You
fight another day and protect those you love'
Eckard stated.

'I cannot die I have more to do. If I cannot have
my own personal redemption I will have to fight
for those that have and will be wrong by those
who seek to impose their rule by the edge of a
blade. ' Judeson answered

'Then join us, the Pact of the Grey Mantle join
us and see how we will defend ourselves from the
tyranny at the end that blade. But this is the
most important thing to remember about that

blade.' Eckard replied.

'Go on'

'The blade is not the enemy nor is its wielder, the real enemy, the true enemy stands behind them, concealed and not directly involved. For behind the Rakoni, behind the Collective and behind every bandit there was a plan most fucking devious that drove those cretins those scum to perform the horrendous acts that you so desperately cry out against.'

'You speak of your enemy, your Pact's enemy, are they not the Rakon?.'

'The Rakon are not so different, just another race, be it an unusual one to us. But a Race still. They have families like us. And live the struggle of life.'

'Then you can continue on the path of reckless revenge and sail on the chaotic sea that only leads to torment and nothing else in particular. Or you can fight for something far more meaningful.'

'Fight a war for defense'

'The Channellors are the enemy? ' Judeson inquired.

'Everyone's true enemy, Judeson, the Channellors are the driving force they always have been for thousands of arcs now they have driven this progression this jump into the supposed modern era. The Hand of Kingdoms was not simply torn apart by civil war and plague, those acts were created and imposed by the Channellors. And in the Nerthielm, the division the void-damned stubborn unrest all products of careful; meticulous planning by the Channellors for they fed on aurmen's weakness for jealousy and foolhardy vengeance. The Channellor reaped return from the Kobold's unwillingness to enter the fray and finally, the Channellors preyed upon the Draul's desires to be all-consuming influence once more.'

'So what do we do now then? If we don't stand and fight what then?'

'Well, then we are left with one option.'

'Voice your thoughts'

'We burn it, we burn down the town, leaving no place for them to retake.'

'Madness. You dare speak such Void-damned goat-shi...'

'Judeson please there is no other way out of this.' Eckard proclaimed, gesturing around to the decimated village 'You know this. Either Letesah burns or we die here for nothing, all for fucking void-damned nothing. Your father fought to protect much more than just this plot of land."

Judeson lashed out in an uncontrolled furious rage, his fist closing on Eckard who this time did seemingly nothing to avoid the confrontation. The Northman's head tilted back from the impact and Eckard fell to his knees clutching his nose. What of the all his magik? Blows never seemed to land on the man such as this. Judeson thought in a state of confusion.

Still clutching his nose from which blood flowed freely now, Eckard stood back up and looked Judeson directly in the eyes.

'I'm sorry Judeson, I truly am, but you know what needs to be done.' Eckard mumbled between his hands and broken nose 'Now that is out of your system, let's get on with it then'

Judeson shook his head at his own foolishness, a blow not physical like his visited upon the Northman but one nevertheless more sustaining and detrimental. Letesah was gone and it had been for some arcs now. What was the point of holding onto a time long past? Like being on the edge of a cliff with no way back up. Better to free fall down and hope the landing was better than sustaining hopes of climbing to an impossible future.

Eckard turned around and followed the squeaky voiced kobold down the tunnel.

Judeson's attentions were drawn away by another demotion down the hill. Blazing red-fire hot flames licked up into the air. Black-smoke accompanying it hand in hand. Buildings all around were alight and the inferno engulfed Judeson's hometown of Letesah was absolute.

As he walked Judeson realised Eckard had wanted him to strike him as if the physical contact would be the argument solving point, the metaphorical shift that was so needed. The big Southron collecting his thoughts, Realized Eckard had been right all along of this whole wretched affair, of every coming back to Letasah, of ever besieging the Raks and most importantly and prominently of vengeance. That cold subduing force that so called to Judeson. Shaking his head at himself Judeson realized Eckard had stood by him throughout everything that had happened since they had passed over the Boundary. Friendship and brotherhood were a tense outing but one on which the road held firm when truth came to the forefront. Of this Judeson knew there were no cracks to fall down.

The two men made to leave, back up the hill, within the tunnel again and away from painful memories.

Bridge
A Stacked Deck

The card game of High March is predominantly a game of chance.

This is not to say there is no skill involved whatsoever, the skill in High March comes into effect in a very different manner.

Luck can be ridden, but the art of bluffing, boasting and general diversionary tactics cannot be understated in High March.

There is usually three to six players. Each player has a deck (the standard being forty-eight but some older rules dictate up to sixty four) of randomly shuffled cards. Each player may draw, hold, trade and barter from their' own deck or another player's one, with prior permission of course. Each player must draw and stay on three cards by the end of the game, or else they forfeit completely. Once each player has drawn a card they can choose to reveal, play on or raise or hedge their bets within the game itself. Cards can be traded between players if they see an opportunity. But therein lies the cloak and dagger tactics. Nothing is certain in High March and much of it is purely luck, though also purely ruthlessness at the same time. Luck can be ridden and a hand be more than meets the eye if one is clever enough...

Nicola Sueshi Kajvik– *Extract from the Guide of Parlor and Pub Games*

Nicola Tesrik Reldurn

Dusk District- city of Maseada, 2804 ATF

Lisiarna frowned back at her new face. She shook her head at her newly assumed body. The image in the mirror, the assumed appearance she had taken on did not look quite right. New was not an entirely accurate juxtaposition for her physical appearance. She had taken on a similar visual identity before. But this time she was intent on outdoing herself. Of pushing the boundary to what she could accomplish. In doing so she hoped for one single crucial important component to come into effect. Lisiarna wished to look as distracting as aurmanly possible.

The blonde hair was bright, thick and wavy, her eyes now much bigger than what she normally possessed. And her face was rounder, fuller and her cheeks rosier. All due process for what she intended. Lisiarna, however, did not feel comfortable and one major complication that was the ironic drawback of form-shifting was that the shifter was must be comfortable to continue the form. The loose fitting sundress she currently wore was not helping the situation. Otherwise, all manner of factors came in. If the form was not considered comfortable by the Form-Shifter wearing it, it was not a form one could pull off.

Lisiarna turned as a light rattle-a-tat-tat was gently knocked on the door behind her.

'Yes?' She answered the knock.

The door was lightly pushed open in response and the nimble frame of Raijin slid in. The Draul looked her up and down with his piercing crimson eyes. Not in the way Lisiarna reckoned others may, but almost as a physician examining a patient for the first time. Raijin seeming to closely profile her new adopted form.

'It's much better... endowed, than your last.' Raijin said, seating himself down in the worn out armchair to the side of Lisiarna and her full-length Silvern glass mirror.

Lisiarna re-examined her form in the mirror. Sure enough, Raijin may be right in some aspects. She had increased her breast size, men would be sidetracked by that alone, her hips were narrower through, though her legs were much longer than before. The legs she supposed were the primary the source of discomfort for her.

'Do you think it will work?' Lisiarna inquired at the Raijin who looked back up at her as she spoke, the man seems to lose himself in contemplation.

'It is difficult for me to say, ma'am. By all accounts, I believe the men of the Collective find this particular form you have taken to be pleasing. Your trunk and branches would be aesthetically pleasing, I'm sure of it' Raijin answered.

Lisiarna threw the man a smile. She knew the Draul attentions did not lay with women, and being a Green-Aspect Mage or Turner as they were more commonly known as it Mage circles. Indeed for Raijin emotion and feeling were not the most forthcoming for him. That particular school of Magikal learning required an unnerving amount of detachment, even Lisiaran who reckoned herself strong of will could probably not do what he did.

'Well, it is something at least.' Lisiarna said, sliding about the room on bare-feet, trying to conceptualise her balance with this new form.

The longer limbs were proving difficult to manage but a shift always churned up some sort of problem.

Raijin moved to the table looking down at a map of the Nerthielm which lay on the polished red glum table top, propped down with intricately craved placeholders. Lisiarna knew the Draul mage was concentrating on the marked spots of interest.

'I can never get past your Draul analogies sometimes, my trunk...'Lisiarna said, trying to lighten the mood. She knew Raijin was about to go off on a tangent.

'You have pretended to be Draul before. I thought you would be used to our expressions.' Raijin answered looking up to meet Lisiarna's gaze. Though he dropped his head a moment later. 'It

won't be straightforward you know, any of this.'
'Nothing in life easily attainable is ever
worthwhile.' Lisiarna said, running her fingers
through her long blonde hair. She did not really
like, too much going on to be sure. But honesty
was something she was genuinely skilled at
hiding. Much practice in earnest went a long way.
'Too true.' Raijin agreed.
The lithe Draul sat himself down near the table,
moving in long strides as he did so.
'Are we ready?' Raijin said, the Draul proceeded
to pour himself a drink from the glass brandy
decanter into a brass mug, he offered another
pour to Lisiarna but she declined with a wave of
the hand.
'Still, need the outfit to complete the
character' Lisiarna replied. 'And I know a
certain group of people who craft excellent silk
weaves that would do the trick.'
'Ah yes' Raijin acknowledged, he picked up one of
the pastries from the basket on the table.
Lisiarna rarely saw the Draul Mage eat anything
and following convention the silver haired Draul
offered the sweet cake over to her. Lisiarna
accepted earnestly. With all the elaborate 'prim
and proper' showcase to come in a handful of
days, Lisiarna was not going to pass up the
chance to eat like a normal aurman or at least
what she hoped most ate like.
Of what was going to come, Tteir plan that the
Pact or at least the active members of such had
been preparing for. The plan was simple and
should be effective. But as Lisiarna knew all too
well, even the greatest of plans unravelled at
the seams like loose thread at the best of times.
As it happened the recent times were very much
less than ideal.

Lisiarna devoured the pastry in three bites, the sweetness of the jam and the crusty flakes of puff pastry, a perfect combination for her unsteady hunger. Raijin raised an eyebrow at her antics and Lisiarna gifted the Draul smile in return.

'I have to cherish the memory of food and what may be construed into eating in an unladylike manner. After all, Nobles are above all that.' Lisiarna stated, grabbing at the pastries zealously once more.

'Who am I to judge what you do with your bodies?' Raijin replied, pouring himself another drink.

Lisiarna smiled again.

'Good, cause I am stuffing my face before I have to pretend to be all elegant.'

Raijin grinned back broadly.

'Present company would not be fooled into such ploys.' Raijin said.

The room's solitary door swung open and Lucairn huffed into the room; in a sequence of deep breaths and a startled expression painted on his face.

Luciarn shifted his glance between Raijin and Lisiarna at an erratic pace, like his head were on a spring. Seeming to remember himself the merchant slowed down and exhaled slower.

'I...err..apologies, I should have knocked. If you were indecent Kail, I ah..sorry. I mean to say..'Luciarn hammered out at ludicrously near incomprehensible rate.

'I would not be indecent, Luciarn. I would be have been naked if I had been. In which case you would have been most rude.' Lisiarna laughed in good humour.

Luciarn looked confused.

'I doubt Luciarn would be much interested in the female naked form. Come to think of that why would I be in here with naked you?' Raijin retorted, grinning like a mad man.

Lucairn shook himself, he still appeared bewildered but he ignored Lisiarna and Raijin's teasing.

Luciarn narrowing his eyes and grasping at the brandy bottle managed to pour our a more coherent sentence eventually.

'Tormenting me aside. I arrived as quick as I could to tell you, two insufferable devils, that a welcoming party of the Vigilant Hawk is here.'

Lisiarna breathed a sigh of relief.

Now they were making progress.

'Excellent, now kindly vacate, I need to shift, again' Lisiarna said, gesturing for Raijin and Luciarn to depart the room. A thought struck her, in regards to tormenting Luciarn.

'Unless of course you wish to actually see me naked, but by the Far Above; what would your husband say?' Lisiarna nailed a final coffin into the anguish of Luciarn.

The rotund merchant sighed, defeated and left the room. He would not take the incessant mocking to heart Lisiarna knew. Raijin filed out with a grin still painted on his ashen face, the stick figure Draul following Luciarn with both he and the merchant's drinks in hand.

Lisiarna threw off the loose one piece dress and strode forward to where her Yunsi leathers lay sprawled out on the room's bed. Remembering, fixating on that form, that size, that weight and the movements of her Yunsi character. The lithe, long limbed and nimble hunter that ran with the wilds, that knew bareback horse riding better than anything. Lisiarna shifted into Ahma. It had been years, but Ahma was never one to be forgotten.

Lisiarna's limbs shifted and morphed, her head changed, her hair grew darker and her face formed anew. The blond, tall noblewoman she posed as just moments previously departed the world. Ahma, the Yunsi scout, and master horsewoman stepped in once more.

Picking up the riding leathers and Yunsi wolf fur coat, Lisiarna fell into the familiar challenge strut that was very much a part of Ahma's psyche. The way someone moved was crucially important. A Form-Shifter such as Lisiarna knew that for her characters to be completely convincing they must all have their own walk, their own head tilt-their approach. Ahma was very different from Lisiarna's real self, the character of Ahma was arrogantly self-assured somewhat aggressively masculine and very protective of those she considered family. The last point was at odds with the previous two as Ahma approached a level of motherly care.

Though that was well hidden behind all the flexing and strutting, every conceivable person in existence was one of the contrasts and double negatives. Everyone had their complications. For a Form-Shifter to be truly successful, first they must look the part, but more importantly, they must act the part as if they were born to it. - Lisiarna remembered her journal entry she kept on her at all times. The words she never forgot on the dust of time, the words were her and she was theirs. Her training she would never abandon.

Lisiarna pushed her way out into the hallway with Raijin and Luciarn. Both the Aurman and Draul waiting for her patiently.

'This form looks more practical.' Raijin stated,

with a hint of amusement or perhaps it was agreement - Lisiarna mused, the Kormai native was exceptionally difficult to read sometimes.

Lisiarna led both men down the hallway and begun toward the single spiral staircase at the end of the hallway. The intricate floret patterns of the latticework followed Lisiarna down as she descended to greet the company of thorns at the bottom.

'Ahma' A course smoke laden voice called from out of the company of Yunsi frontiersmen and women.

Lisiarna knew the voice well.

'Afriti' Lisiarna answered in greeting.

'I thought my wild rose had forsaken the Yunlands forever' Afriti said in the native Yunsi tongue.

Lisiarna rolled her eyes in the most exacerbated theatrical manner she could muster.

'That's enough of that shit. Cestral if you don't mind, for the others and onto business.' Lisiarna replied in Cestral, no nonsense.

Afriti shrugged indifferently, outwardly, though Lisiarna knew the Yunlander would be a least slightly taken back.

'The stick bug Draul and the tub of lard?' Afriti questioned, this time in Cestral, the hard-nosed Yunsi woman gesturing in the direction of Luciarn and Raijin at the foot of the staircase.

'I am named Raijin' Raijin answered.

'Good for you' Afriti growled.

'He is a Magicker..'Lisiarna enforced, knowing that one always must be assertive around Afriti, otherwise one would never get a word in.

'And?' Afriti huffed, unamused.

'..and he is a leader among the Oath-breaker Draul. He will bring with him a company of the most highly skilled and trustworthy rangers you will ever bear witness to.' Lisiarna retorted.

Raijin gave Lisiarna a welcome acknowledging nod. The rag tag mustering of several dozen Yunlanders behind Afriti began whispering. The Yunlanders in the journey house threshold and outside in the courtyard strained ears and craned necks to listen in.

Afriti called for calm and quiet, her subordinates soon folding to the woman's wishes.

'We of the Vigilant Hawk are not ready nor are we willing to fight in your war.' Afriti said, no allusions in her tone as to how adverse her tribe felt about what was happening around them.

Lisiarna sighed. Not masking her frustration either. She let in out slowly and as loudly as she could.

'It's not simply our war.' Lisiarna stated.

Afriti narrowed her gaze, Lisiarna stared right back at the scowling hard as a stone faced the woman.

'I like your pretty face, my flower but your little Pact always stirs up trouble. We are perfectly content and at peace here' Afriti said.

Even incensed with prideful anger, Afriri still attempted to flirt with Lisiarna when she posed as Ahma.

'Make no mistake, Afriti. The Channellors; their Rakoni lackeys and all the other fools in their ploy will not leave your people be. Their eyes will be cast your way when they are finished with the other nations of the Nertheilm.' Lisiarna offered.

'As I said, your war my flower. We have no interest in it, nor should we.' Afriti declared her other subordinates in the Vigilant Hawk clan nodding their collective approval.

Lisiarna knew what Afriti was doing it was an old game. It was a game that required patience and stubborn dedication. What Afriti did not realize however was that Lisiarna's hand was well stocked and the game that Afriti was attempting to play was one Lisiarna now knew how to master.

'Your people would merely act as a distraction, a diversion tactic at best. More smoke than fire. We; ourselves will be assaulting the Rakoni stronghold of the Woldte.' Lisiarna said keeping the details masked in secrecy. Though it was very little risk to divulge parts of the plan to Afriti and the Vigilant Hawk clan, that slight hint of uncertainty presented too much of a risk for the Pact.

No, it was better we keep the plan as safe and secure as need be. The Channellors had eyes and ears nearly everywhere nowadays. Trust was a fine thread after all...

'You and who's void-dammed army?' Afriti responded, stirring Lisiarna from her inner musings.

'Raijin, the stick bug you spoke of is a prominent leader among the Oath Breaker ranks of the Draul of Kormai, the Yunlands and everywhere else in the North. The Pact itself has a few cards yet to play and Luciarn…' Lisiarna stated matter-of-factly.

'The fat goose egg one?' Afriti smirked between barred teeth.

Lisiarna turned back to see a stonefaced Luciarn, the merchant was clearly made of harder stuff to crack than Afriti gave him credit for. That and Lucairan was simply hearing more of the same old rhetoric. The big merchant nodded at Lisiarna's regard and she turned back to Afriti.

And here comes the first card...

'Luciarn has a vast store-yard of grains, yambal fruit, dried and smoked meats and various tubers. All safe and secure held by dozens of well-trained caretakers and guard escorts. The Yunsi of the Vigilant Hawk is suffering a famine, the likes of which has been one of the worst in many arcs. It would seem, the 'fat one' as you so ungracefully put has in his possession a fair few things that would be extremely useful for you and your people.' Lisiarna lets a small smile linger, keeping her eyes sharply on Afriti and reading the woman's challenging leer drop and subside into something far more open and emotional.

The murmurs from the other Clan members of the Vigilant Hawk began anew, Afriti called for calm, though it took much longer to settle her outriders and warriors.

'You need food we need your troops. I think you can read between those lines well enough.' Luciarn offered, no vitriol in his tone, no grimace present. It sounded like the man was reading to lecture hall of young budding students.

'Even now, contingents of the Free Draul or Oath Breakers are gathering at the edge of the Emerald Corridor. The Woldte will be our target. Just so as it is the pinnacle of the threat to our freedom, of all our freedoms, Draul or aurmen.' Raijin said, striding with his absurdly long legs forward to stand side by side with Lisiarna, his well-spoken tone carrying right out to the fringes of the Clansmen and women.

The second drops. Lisiarna mused.

'Will that be it? The food sounds...enticing...' Afriti struggled with the wording about the food, it was clear she was in a predicament with resources. 'A few outcast Draul to assault the impregnable nightmare that is the Woldte? A fortress built by the Old Ones that never fell, a couple of Draul?' Afriti was caving, Lisiarna reasoned.

'Eckard has struck a deal with the Kobold of the Southrondor and the Aurmen Resistance from there. Next week he will be back with more fresh troops.' Lisiarna said Afriti looked intrigued now.

Finally for the third card to play.

'Eight arcs ago, a sizable fortune came into our possession. With this we will raise an army of sellswords and the Woldte will be breached. We do not need a full besieging force from your people, Afriti. We, as we said, need a flanking ploy. The Collective and the Preying Wolf are lapdogs to the Rakoni tyrants, the follow their whim and they sniff at their laps. What we need from you my flower...'

Lisiarna paused, mainly for dramatic effect but also to centre herself and to rationalise her move, her final gambit; the one action which may prove pivotal in the events to come.

Afriti smiled, nodded and beckoned for Lisiarna to continue.

The deck wins a bittersweet victory.

'What we need, Afriti is you courageous and diligent men and women to reinforce our element of surprise. We are desperate. We need our stealth, it is all we have but with your help, once your people are supplied of course. With your help, we will prevail; the unbreakable Woldte will be breached, by us. The Rakoni will be sent packing; scurrying in the fear they so subscribe to inflict on us. And your people will remain free and most importantly safe to live and love another day.'

Lisiarna said, the words, the same ones she had practiced for in front of the mirror as she shifted back and forth between her chosen forms. She shook with anxious uncertainty, for her ploy was desperate and ill-advised, it was the most unsafe plays in a game of cards one was uncertain they could be triumphant.

The Clan-folk of the Vigilant Hawk fell deathly silent, Afriti included amongst their numbers. There had been an unspoken revelation in the wake of Lisiarna's speech, a resolute, collaborative acknowledgment of understanding.

At last a bit of luck.

'My flower, we will ride for you and we will place our souls in the line of fire for you.' Afritit declared her people behind her roaring in unreserved appreciation.

'No, not just for me. It is for everyone. For the Pact and for the freedom of all. We will not be controlled!' Lisiarna shouted, with vigour.

The crowd of Yunsi cheered and howled with glee.

End game. Lisiarna acknowledged in her mind's eye, though not without a hint of deception on her part. White lies but still deception.

The Yunsi fell into ranks and called for their horses from their stewards who waited nearby. Afriti urged her people onward, although she herself remained behind as the other leather clad warriors moved out. In actual fact, she had moved closer to Lisiarna and now stood a mere hand's length from her.

'One more thing my flower.' Afriti whispered, barely audible for even Lisiarna to hear.

Lisiarna followed the woman's lead and leaned in to orchestrate a gentle murmur of her own.

'And what would that be?' Lisiarna replied.

'A Kiss' Afriti answered without a moment's thought. 'For old time's sake.'

Lisiarna sighed inwardly, being careful to mask her disappointment, outwardly forcing herself to appear unmoved. She knew Afriti would do something like this. Lisiarna had a role to play after all. That role she would relish and complete, no matter what thrown at her.

Barely a moment later and Afriti was upon Lisiarna. Slight lips pursed and on her own before she could move. Of course, if Lisiarna were in any real danger, the Yunsi woman would be open to attack, but as it was Afriti had only lust and not hatred upon her mind.

Lisiarna kissed her back, best she could manage, *more white lies*. Afriti eventually pulled back and smiled, absolutely beaming with glee.

'Thank you and long may the gorgeous Yun shine down upon you.' Afriti said.

Lisiarna smiled back. Her role as Ahma completed. Soon she would Form-Shift into Beatrice once back in her adopted room.

Without another word or exchange, Afriti departed, swift as the wind, with her Yunsi outriders. The clan's folk galloped back to her campsite in the near distance just over the green clad hills to divulge to the rest of Afriti's clan of the events that had hitherto transpired.

Luciarn clamped a gentle hand on Lisiarna's shoulder.

'Well, it looks like my people have a role to play.' Luciarn said the man was smiling.

'You best be off to complete your role then, Lucairn.' Lisiarna.

The big merchant nodded.

'And Luciarn' Lisiarna called as the man made to

make his exit.

'Yes,' Luciarn inquired.

'Please do not follow us, your skills are far too invaluable to be wasted on what we are about to do.' Lisiarna begun, Luciarn made to object, with a raised hand but Lisiarna continued despite him.

'Think of your husband go to him. Don't risk your precious life in our affairs. Be careful and safe, one day we may yet meet again.' Lisiarna stated, holding back a rogue tear that inspired to escape her eye.

Luciarn's smile dropped and he nodded grimly, not speaking a word, the big man departed back into the timber journey house. With any luck, though with no small amount of bittersweet sadness that would be the last the Pact would see Luciarn.

Raijin approached Lisiarna, standing several paces from her, the Draul, after all, was not as at comfortable with physical touch as the Aurmen as a means of congress.

'It's for the best, Luciarn is no soldier.' Raijin proclaimed.

'He has far too much to live for.' Lisirana replied without taking a breath.

'The Channellors will know we are coming' Raijin replied.

'Probably' Lisiarna stated.

Raijin beckoned for Lisiarna to follow him back into the journey-house. She complied but pulled up short just at the top step in.

'You still have much to live for too Raijin.' Lisiarna stated.

'As do you' The Draul instantaneously replied.

Lisiarna nodded.

'That Afriti woman, you had a history with her?' Raijin inquired.

'Ahma did.'

'Ah, you assumed this Ahma's form on her passing?'

'She was good to me, she ….helped me once.' Lisiarna said.

'And Kail?'

'That form is more of....'Lisiarna paused considering her wording very carefully and for a moment was caught in the memory of events eight arcs ago. '…Amalgamation.'

'Ahma was different she was…'

'You need not explain things to me.' Raijin said and then under his breath, though Lisiarna made out it out nevertheless. 'There is yet a great deal we do not know of each other nor do we need to. The Pact comes first after all.'

Lisiarna sometimes felt like it all, life, this moment, emotions and the Pact itself was all just another round of High March.

Interlude
Thoughts and Threads

The Arcane Sea is not accessible to all, but it is there nevertheless.

Magik is not hard to find, the streams swirl and

eddy around us all, this is not fiction. The fact remains it is around us

it is part of us and we are part of the Sea in turn. Whether you choose

to believe our world is inseparable from the Arcane Sea or not is opinion only.

Trust is a fine thread we dance upon daily, however the 'Sea

is the truth that binds us all to our Stone.

Section of Sar Wrendal Dastin Morke's Address to the Reclaimer's Confederation Council

The Trial and Un-Knighting of Sar Wrendal Dastin Morke (Various Sources)

Nertharnlands Confederation, Aurmora, Reclaimers Isle

Confederation Council Chambers

2978 ATF

They had descended into darkness incarnate. Down
stairwells, and barely held together ramps,
through altogether slim crannies and back out
again. Eventually Judeson and the part had come
upon a dim light hallway of grimy, mould ridden
cobblestones, the sounds of a noisy steam and
flaring fires could be heard somewhere just ahead
in the gloom.

'Steady on Aurman' The squat kobold called
Prestan called out the shrill voice rising in
crescendo, excitement clearly raised, the lizard
creature's voice barely audible over the
boisterous machine ahead of them.

The murky gloom of the tunnel seemed to fold
outward beyond to the adjacent facing door. Huge
iron bars stayed the impressive portal at the
centre. Ominous decoration pieces of Kobold
artistry formed the bulk of the outward design of
the door. Cruel, twisted faces as if in pain came
out from the hard rock work.

The relentless turn of arcs had taken it's toll
on the shattered chamber, the ceiling caving
downward as if the structure itself were tired of
striving to hold itself together. Further down
the chipped and cracked stone stairwell, deeper
in the dark gloomy chamber a flare of dim
firelight was born. Several squat figures stood
ahead, waiting. More Kobold. Prestan gestured to
them and the four apparitions seemed to be able
to see her despite the darkness around them.

'Your chariot awaits aurmen' Prestan stated
gesturing to the four figures ahead.

'No offence but I can't see how those four will
make the journey any quicker on foot through
these gloomy caves' Judeson stated, a chuckle
present in his voice.

The four Kobold laughed in snorts and a curious hissing sound in unison and Prestan joined in as the yet more lights came on and a sight neither aurmen had ever set eyes upon lay just behind the other four kobold.

'Ah there it is.' Eckard said, nudging Judeson. 'Kept us in suspense.'

'And what is it exactly?' Judeson asked.

'Our chariot apparently.' Eckard answered, moving forward with the kobold and into the open door of the vessel.

The hulking monstrosity of steel, alloys, gears and hissing pipes hurled Judeson through countless leagues of midnight dark underground tunnels. That thought alone was staggering. Judeson found himself wondering about the operation of the Kobold creation he, Eckard and the aforementioned race we in. The most lingering thought in the forefront of all this was whether this machine was really as safe as its architects claimed it to be.

*

Four days passed in surprising relative comfort. Once you got past the incessant swaying of the iron box they were in. After awhile Judeson thought he could ignore the constant rhythmic humming beneath you feet, Judeson thought the journey was actually quite pleasant. Then again, anything could be perceived as pleasant to what they had departed from.

Vengeance was not his. Nor had he discovered upon his father's killer. Now Judeson however had a purpose reborn. He would fight with Eckard just as the man had done with him. The Rakoni would be fought on any front, they must be fought on any front with any means necessary.

Eckard had been distant for most of the journey.

His eyes closed at times, but Judeson was entirely sure he was sleeping. The tall man had more so seemed to be deep in concentration. When the man was not meditating or whatever it was he was doing, Eckard would be drinking out of a flask that seemed to never be emptied. Judeson had partaken in with several mouthfuls of the sickly sweet amber alcohol at times but Eckard's drinking was seemingly never-ending.

Judeson felt remorse at striking out at Eckard in his rage back at Letesah. But it seemed all was forgiven on that front. Eckard's nose seemed to be fully healed and impossibly looked as if it had never indeed be broken. Judeson felt himself going mad trying to ascertain how the Northman could recover from blunt force trauma as if it were nothing.

Judeson stirred himself awake and looked over to a sprawled out Eckard who had removed his boots and maille gloves but not his chain mail jacket.

'You are drinking quite a great deal.' Judeson stated.

Eckard grunted in response, though whether in agreement or annoyance Judeson could not discern from the man's distant gaze.

'Your Pact Eckard, if you want me to be a part of it, I need to know it well. Much more than I currently do. I cannot join something I don't void-damned understand.' Judeson stressed, wringing his hands against each other in frustration.

Eckard paused for a minute, it was difficult to read the man's expression and for a moment Judeson reckoned Eckard would never answer. He ventually placed down his drink however.

'The Pact of the Grey Mantle was formed more than three thousand arcs ago.' Eckard said, breaking the silence to Judeson's relief.

'A man known to us as Greycloak, though it would seem he possessed a whole host of other names and titles. This Greycloak was an incredibly powerful Arch-Mage.' Eckard continued.

Judeson could sense the emotion rising in Eckard's tone as he regaled this particular tale. It was Silvershard clear that this all meant a lot to the Northman.

'Greycloak formed your Order then, hence the name, very imaginative I must say' Judeson smiling back at Eckard for the last bit. Hoping humour would elevate their collectively solemn moods.

To Eckard's credit he did smile, even if it was for a hastily fleeting instant. Judeson swore he saw the strange storm of dark swirls pass over Eckard's eyes, albeit for an incredibly fleeting moment.

'Greycloak did not form the *Pact,* others with him or her did. A small collaboration of soldiers, enchanters, healers and newly freed slaves formed what we have come to know as the *Pact* of the Grey Mantle.' Eckard seemed to emphasis the word 'Pact' each time as if it was vitally important.

'Sorry' Judeson teased, pausing for dramatic effect. *'Pact'* emphasising the crucial word in question. 'Why was this Pact formed then?' Judeson said.

'It was all done in honour of Korin Greycloak. Who sacrificed himself to bring down a tyrannical Empire and send the Channellors back in their devious fucking work.' Eckard answered, for a second, the Northman looked angry, furious even, that faded quickly and his trademark smirk reappeared like it had never gone.

'So you wish for me to be apart of this Pact,

this alliance of Mages that knows so much of Magik and movements of the world, of men's thoughts and political threads.' Judeson asked.

'You are more far more clever than you believe yourself to be, Judeson' Eckard replied.

'I'm not suited to this Eckard, I have no idea nor do I see how this hoodoo shit even works. To me it is all void-damned foolish, fucking...well, nonsense. '

'Magik is all around us, it's flows and ebbs pass through all living things. We are on a world that is the closest to the Arcane Sea, we one with it all.'

'A world? You speak if you have passed to another Realm, Zadma knows only holy entities can do such wonders.' Judeson challenged the incredibly and frustratedly confounding Northman.

Just when it had seemed he had pinned a topic down and started to understand and get proper tutelage from Eckard, the man had spiralled off into more confusing territory. Judeson mused, baffled.

'There are other worlds then this one.' Eckard replied.

'You will have to tell me about that some time.' Judeson replied, Eckard nodding in reply. The Truth was finally coming.

Murmuring from the opposing side of the cast iron wall broke up the momentum of the conversation. When Eckard spoke again he had alternated the topic at hand once more.

'When we arrive in the Collective we will be briefly be unconscious.' Eckard declared.

Judeson pushing aside his earlier frustrations, he was now, absent of confounded thoughts and solely confused instead.

'What? How could you possibly know that?' Judeson questioned.

'The Kobold are saying so ahead of us' Eckard replied.

Judeson raised the man a searching look.

'Oh and how pray tell do you know this o-wise-one?' Judeson mocked.

'Magik' Eckard quipped, smirking.

Judeson narrowed his eyes in annoyance.

'Ok truths then.' Eckard motioned.

'Yes please.' Judeson answered, still cautious that the man would not say anything in turn.

'We label and title everything around us, we give notions and names to that which we long to understand. Certain things horrify certain people and in turn they reply with demeaning terms. We hate the unknown, we fear the unknown. Apprehension is a direct causation of one's ignorance.' Eckard began, seeming to slow down and draw out his normally heavily accented speech. His million-leagues an hour dialogue broken down, Judeson reasoning it was not to demean him but to inform him minus the smirking grins, bad taste jokes and up and down tone of his natural accent.

'Go on' Judeson nodded.

'Well with this in mind, Magik is magik, Judeson. We don't know everything it is as simply as that.' Eckard continued.

'Which means?' Judeson inquired, not following Eckard's confabulated road of reason.

'Which means, magik for many arcs has been a source of concern and fear for those that believe themselves in control.' Eckard replied.

'Did this Imperium you speak of not govern with magik and hold down their slaves with their powers?' Judeson noted.

'They did. But even they did not understand the magik from the Arcane Sea. They did not know how it worked. They harnessed a narrow path of control and furthered their endeavours by holding onto their control.'

'So this Arcane Sea is a place?' Judeson asked.

'In a manner of speaking yes, it is the source of our abilities to alter our own physical space. With my aspect we now call Gray I weave various threads if you will. Tones of all the other magik aspects, of which come into play and something else.'

'You are most descriptive.'

'Because I don't understand it all properly, it is so mind bendingly difficult I am only scratching the surface. Reaching out into the unknown, mate. I am fucking around with something beyond me.' Eckard said.

'And yet you believe there is no God' Judeson answered.

'No. The Arcane Sea is something else, something beyond us. But there is no voice, no commanding presence we are not slaves to it's servitude. We are free, our own misunderstandings are what is holding us back.'

'Yet there are people that can exist between life and death you say?'

'Yes, but they are people, souls or some such. I don't void-damned know really. Not gods though, my friend. They are existing differently than us but they are not our masters.' Eckard urged.

'Higher powers' Judeson finished for him, were they speaking on the same level? Judeson started to question himself.

'Fucking aye.' Eckard answered smiling.

'So what make you different from these Channellors that you speak so ill of?' Judeson motioned.

Eckard dropped the smile like a hot pan in soft exposed hands.

'The Void is not the same as the Arcane Sea, Judeson.'

'How?'

'The Arcane Sea is not a place you can dive right into it is a realm, beyond our own, but also something more. I told you I am really bad at explaining these sort of things.'

'You really are'

Both he and Eckard laughed in unison. Everything felt remarkably calmer again to Judeson.

Eckard however turned away again, fell silent and drank deep from his flask. Judeson still had one more thing say.

'When two warriors survive battle they should have lost they are intertwined. My father told me this.' Judeson said, beginning a new topic, but heavily related to their previous conversation.

Eckard nodded and kept drinking. Not facing Judeson.

'They are named Brothers of the Blade, ever locked in destined battle.' Judeson said.

Eckard shifted to face Judeson with a smile on his face.

'Your late father was very old-fashioned, wasn't he, Judeson?' Eckard asked, laughing.

Judeson saw what was happening, and he did not pass up the opportunity for good humour, though in his experience his own comedic timing was not always the best.

'My father was as an excellent tracker, an outstanding hunter and by all accounts a most courageous soldier.' Judeson replied solemnly in reflection. 'But on hindsight I can see he was terrible with women' Judeson smiled.

Both men laughed in broken unison. Not that it was particularly very funny, the humour was cliché to say the least, but the two men shared something then outside of cheaply made laughs.

Or perhaps it was actually the noxious gas the kobold utilised to render them unconscious. For in a handful of moments both men had drifted off into unconscious. A deep, relaxing slumber absorbed them.

*

Judeson was a boy once again, running along a dusty rough and tumble excuse for a road. His father was ahead of him, moving in a low , purposeful crouch.

They were on a hunt.

Judisye turned, his freshly shaved face meeting Judeson's gaze. His father smiled warmly, behind those steely eyes of his. Judisye raised a hand for quiet and drew the well used yew wood bow from his back. Judeson edged closer to his father who cautioned him to remain quiet and careful. His father adjusted a bowstring onto his hunting tool. Judeson handed him a bundle of broad-tipped arrow, huge bulky heads on the things, for bringing down gigantic walking birds known as Amits that dwelt in the Mornis Hinterlands. The Amit were well known in the Southrondor to have strong, yet flexible feathers, idle for the plumes of arrows or quarrels.

Judeson remembered this, at least partially. He had to be around 7 or maybe eight arcs. His father was going to show him how to draw a bowstring. Sure enough Judisye gifted Judeson the hunters bow and began a introduction into technique. This was one of the many unrelentingly harsh lessons to come. His father never went easy on him. Each such lesson, he returned to Letesah with scars and bruises. But each hard lesson was one his father praised him for and told him what he learnt was worthwhile. With the benefit of hindsight Judeson agreed wholehearted. But at this moment in time, he was sore all over and longing to head home.

'To win the hunt, you must know your prey son. You must respect them, only then will you succeed.' Judeson's father whispered, handing Judeson a thick plumed arrow and motioned for him to nock the arrow on the yew bow.

Judeson drew back, the action exhausting his adolescent hands against the heavy draw of the recurved bow.

'Now hold your nerve, boy.' Judisye said on baited breath.

Judeson saw the Amit seat itself on it's long slender legs down on it's roast at the peak of a small hole in the near distance. He held the bow in place and targeted the bird, making sure to take in account windfall and the arrow's trajectory just as his father had shown him in Letesah at least a dozen times by now.

The large bipedal bird stirred in its slumber, nestling its bulky wings in varying resting positions.

'Steady' Judiye said, a gentle reassuring voice behind Judeson. One of Judeson's father's calloused hands resting gently on his shoulder now.

Judeson felt pooling beads of hot sweat run down from the top of his head down his brow and resting uneasily in leather vest. He felt soaked with moisture. His arms shook with anxious vibrations, his hands felt slick with sweat and felt severally strained under the weight of the draw of the bow.

'Easy, boy, respect your hunt' The voice of Judeson's father reassured him.

The Amit sat resting deep in slumber.

Judeson had to release the arrow and trust in the flight. His aim was practised he could do this.

And yet he could not do it.

Judeson released the draw and the arrow flew high and wide of the mark. He lost his nerve he could not aim at the dozing Amit.

Judeson berated himself. How could he not do it? It was easy the bird was still.

The Amit threw itself up in a startled panic and bolted further south, swift as a strong wind.

Judeson's father cuffed him across the collar as he always did when Judeson failed. Though this time, it was much lighter, almost playful.

Judeson knew he would be getting a beating for not listening and perhaps he deserved it too. He had lost his nerve after all.

Void-dammit. Judeson thought, though he was frustrated he dared not swear out loud in front of his father.

Turning around in dread and placing the recurved bow to one side, Judeson was surprised to find an expression on his father he did anticipate. Acceptance. Judisye shook his head but smiled nevertheless.

'Don't worry yourself too much, boy. You simply lost your nerve,' Judisye said, patting Judeson on the head affectionately. 'You are still very young, still much to learn'

Judeson sighed.

He father gently petted his back. Judeson was

taken back.

One day, one day he would make his father proud, he would show him.

'Come on boy, we have amends to make' Judisye said, taking up the heavy recurved bow and the quiver of arrows and beckoning for Judeson to follow him down the hill and further into the Hinterlands.

It was the last day Judeson ever hunted with his father again.

*

As his eyes closed, the outside world faded away. Eckard awoke within a dreamscape.

Not that this place was not really a dream, but what it was exactly Eckard could not name. It was like a dream, but at the same time not so. *He was not awake, but was he really asleep?* There was still so much he did not yet understand.

The remains of a battle, yes...it was...

No

Eckard thought. Not just any battle, *it was that one it was always that one.*

Cadavers of friends and foes lay scattered haphazardly about the blood, bile and shit drenched grounds. What little remained of some of them had become a thick paint on others.
Parts,pieces and sick inducing waste of people everything. Shallow trenches housed some of the fallen, scarred fissures formed in the earth unnaturally by unstable Oyra, a lesson that unfortunately those back in Letesah had just learned.

'Why is it always here? This moment? Out of all the fragments you can weave you choose this one, every time' A voice called out, a deeply resonating voice. One Eckard knew all too well.

From the drifting and stirring shadows a mass formed into a person. A man Eckard knew, a man of dark complexion and even darker temperament - at the best of times.

The man spoke again, though Eckard knew he was not here, nor was the other man with him whenever this particular here was. It still cast doubt in his mind about why and how they were encountering each other anyway. But the edge of the Arcane Sea was never a straightforward circumstance to explain anyway.

'Ah I see now, it is not just this moment but a collection. As if every moment that come after was connected. If only life were so simple to conceptualise. But no rarely do we hold focus so well, even in your...state.' The man stated, rounding Eckard and peering about this fragment of the Arcane Sea.

Eckard followed the man's eyes. Off in the distance, away from the burning heaps of corpses, upturned wagons and blasted landscape, Eckard saw the a lone figure back turned from him, as was always the case. Dirty blonde curls flowing out behind her, her slim shape in a faded burgundy evening gown, the back splashed with dried mud and darkened congealed blood.

'I see' The old man said, laughing in his deep scratchy rhythmic tone.

'Fuck off, Wrendal.' Eckard retorted.

Eckard was slightly agitated by the arrival of his old mentor it had been a long time. Albeit only in an incorporeal form, Eckard forced a smile across his dream-form face despite himself. Not gifting Wrendal an ounce to work against him.

'As charming and courteous as ever.' Wrendal uttered back. His voice dead pan and his expression matching his tone in perfectly orchestrated concordance.

Eckard beamed harder at the man, very much over the top and purely for a show of a passive-aggressive hand. Though as he knew from arcs past Wrendal did not all appear affected by it.

'It's my reverie I'll be as polite as I fucking wish to be.' Eckard said, Wrendal too had turned his back in the same direction *she* was facing.

'It's not just her and not just this place though is it.' Wrendal stated, ignoring Eckard's vulgarity.

The old man felt and prodded at the countless number of flowing and ebbing weaves that traversed across the decimated battleground now. Thin, formless shadows swirled and eddied around Wrendal and Eckard. And further off around *her,* seconds later she became someone else. Dirty blonde tendrils becoming midnight black strands, slim taking on a more mature and heavy set appearance, the dress becoming a faded tunic, Eckard forced back and emotional overload and threw the image away from his dream, the women disappeared entirely.

Wrendal momentarily glanced back at Eckard but otherwise remained staring off into the blood red wash of the setting sun.

'It is perfectly fine to mourn those you have lost, Eckard' Wrendal said, his voice still deep but now only a whisper on the howling winds.

Eckard knew he had some control over this dreamscape, his will to influence on this edge of the *Sea* was clear enough to him. However one part of the dream he could never quite seem to control was the wind, his commands went unheeded and the howl continued. The other component that Eckard had no real control over was who he sometimes saw whether they were or not withstanding.

'What do you want, Wrendal? I'm not your student any more.' Eckard stated bluntly.

'No, you are not.' Wrendal replied, this time he turned.

Eckard was taken back by the man's appearance. Cracks and deep fissure had impacted Wrendal's dark skin as if the man was made from stone. It was not natural, it was an otherworldly appearance, and the man seeming to be fading in and out of this feature. One moment the cracks were present and the next Wrendal looked himself again, well at least what Eckard supposed he looked like presently.

This oddity was not of Eckard's intending. As Eckard knew though this irregularity would not be answered straight away. The Arcane Sea did not let it's answers flow onto the shore like an conventional wave. Eckard's dream was not to be read like an open book.

Eckard made to speak, but Wrendal continued.

'You are playing a most dangerous game - patience is needed, the Channellors are not forcing any hands just yet, theirs is a prolonged gambit. The Pact, even your version of it needs to wait.'

Eckard groaned. He had heard this lesson before.

'I told you I am not your fucking student, old man. The Pact needs to move just as the Void worshippers are. People are suffering, the world is changing and you, you fucking ain't doing anything to change that. Either we alter our strategies to move with the times or we are left behind in the void-damned dark.' Eckard said. 'Simple enough really, we are doing something. We are out there making a difference. While you still sit in your dingy fucking pub, doing nothing.'

Wrendal's unnatural fissures disappeared entirely as if they were never there and indeed they did not return again.

'In the dark, shadows operate unseen. Our best chance is in the dark, away from prying eyes and twitching hands of those easily swayed by nefarious influence.' Wrendal stabbed, his tone growing stormier with every word uttered, though his straight face never changing.

Eckard inwardly cursed the old man. *Abyss take him, it would be altogether more simple if the old man did not make so much sense.*

'It's done, Wrendal. The wheels are in motion..'Eckard replied steely.

'You're going to assault the Woldte, that is incredibly risky.' Wrendal stated.

How did he know? How did he always know?

Eckard silenced his inner thoughts and simply nodded in reply.

'It's going to happen.' Eckard said, though even to him it felt a little forced this time.

'Of course' Wrendal replied.

The elderly Berussi man began to fade once more, the fissures did not make a return but Wrendal started to metamorphose into more onyx billowing smoke than man, though his squat body-shape held for a few moments.

'You are always welcome back into the Pact, same goes for the others.' Wrendal said, his voice sounded like he was being drawn away. Though even with the odd reverberating effect on his tone, Eckard could hint the soft almost emotional (as much as Wrendal could manage) touch.

Eckard shook off his own bullheaded compulsion to tell Wrendal - *that they were the Pact and he did not void-damned need the old crust's approval.*

Instead Eckard acknowledged his old mentor's frank openness. 'Thanks, good luck Wrendal.'

The old Mage was nearing complete obscurity in the smoke now, only a partial sighting of his dark wispy bearded face still visible.

'Don't throw too much of that luck our way, young man you lot will need all the help you can get.' The shifting, wafting smoke essence that had become Wrendal replied. 'Oh and Eckard?' Wrendal continued with a question.

'Yes?' Eckard asked the shadowy mass.

'Try to listen to both of those women a little more.' Wrendal followed up and in a barely decipherable hoarse whisper. Just before the man disappeared entirely; 'May your passage on the *Sea* be in Harmony'.

Wrendal faded utterly and the billowing black smoke became caught up on the howling winds in three heartbeats.

Eckard was alone once again. As alone as he could be in reverie of shattered dreams, reoccurring nightmares and women that haunted him, both living and dead.

He found himself wondering how he could listen to the two ladies that he counted as the most important in his life. One had passed from the planes of the living entirely, though with further thought, the amount of ghost he had been able to witness of late...

...the other women was of course still very much alive and he would see again, hopefully sooner than later. That one was of course an all together different prospect than the former, though Eckard did not know which mountain was the more difficult to climb, both living and deceased, both smarter than he and both hard to read. Eckard for a few moments remained on the

edge of the Arcane Sea wondering what he was to
do, before sleep, real sleep, much needed sleep,
finally took hold.

ACT III
A World of Broken Blades and Dying Embers

The First Stanza

With a tier system in place and people ordered and reformed into a manageable and in a practical way of life we can progress. The Judicirum by extension of this way of thinking are the top echelon of the Collective and they are our decision makers as they have worked the most tenuous for our comfortable way of life. Beneath the Judicirum are the Elite, the top Industry Captains and Guild-House Officers who have strained with their hands and minds to craft new and exciting prospects. Serving the Elite are the Mercantile Trade-House attendants who provide the skills and materials necessary to strive for Modernity. Last but certainly not least by any means are the Owing, the class of folks who have not managed to "Make it" yet, who are steering toward learning and *growing so that one day they can join the ranks of those hard working individuals in the Great Classes.*

- Judicirum Rulings – The Common Charter of Peoples of the Collective

The Honourable Judges; Benton Shivar, Pieter Margan and Varies Beladan the 3rd

The morning had been one of utter undiluted chaos. The metropolis of Haltin was in the thick of a crisis. An early morning storm had swept through and caused devastation to the city centre. The Stock Exchange had turned to a figurative bloodbath, as bankers and traders clambered to bring order to diabolical sequence of fiascoes. Of course in real world terms the bloodbath was to a much lesser extent but nevertheless there had been quite a number of physical punches thrown. There was some actual blood spilled on some of the Trading House floors and some teeth on the steps in.

The national wide shortage of silver had taken a flippantly disastrous turn. Someone just before dawn had dumped a wagon load of refined silver pieces right on the doorstep of the Stock

Exchange, in the dead centre of the Central Business District of Haltin. The marked silver looked suspiciously like the six hundred and a half thousand pieces which had gone missing from the National Republic Bank in Darvis Porte almost nine arcs ago.

That particular subversive escapade in the past was proving to be far more detrimental now. Whoever had orchestrated had this had performed a master-stroke. Several Trade Houses were at each other's throats over who was responsible.

Various and hastily recruited messenger boys in the shape of down and out street urchins scurried the streets with messages and errands back and forth between the many, many Trade Houses. More well-to-do garment wearing (and officially trained) House heralds roamed on horse back the winding and bending narrow streets delivering orders of recompense, requisition and stock order controls between arguing parties. Everywhere between the 'Owing' citizens, the street urchins and those in the employ of a house were the Hari'al, the secret police of the Collective.

Order could be seen by the many in the guise of the uniformed polic, their patrols strict and to the schedule. The men involved, equally strict and unwavering. Any hapless citizens caught in the path of a scheduled patrol were nudged aside with dropped elbows and stone faces. Any guilty insurgents were dealt the full wrath of the Modernist Law. Or so the Collective liked to impose.

The uniformed police were armed with halberds and short stumpy cloth wrapped steel batons, the latter weapons serving to impose the stern Law but not to leave any permanent scars. The former weapons spoke for it's self. Against the nondescriptive brown and khaki cotton of the flak jackets were bands on the upper arms or shoulder straps (depending on rank), brassards of bright yellow were sported by city guard as their favooured colour and fluorescent orange was worn by that of the regional militia, the latter group in some cases wearing metal vambraces or half-helms. Today was a day of a much-needed Silvershard-clear show of strength.

Like so much of the Cor-Dazral Collective, the guards were image of mass-produced and picture-perfect quality. But perversely the Collective always possessed a hidden depth to this perfect symmetry. This concealed entity of uncompromising will; came in the form of the Hari'al. For in the concealed shadows of buildings or just moments behind each guard patrol was one or two of hidden officers of the Hari'al. The secret law enforcers of the Collective almost always out of sight, but were almost always lingering somewhere.

The Judicirum was the leading governing body of the Collective, they dictated the Modernist view of consumer driven culture. Th mass-produced clothing, the building and limited tenancy specifications for cities, military enforcement and of course the exchange of goods and services (and their values). All of these came under the influence of the Judicirum. But the real power swayed in the arms of the wealthy families and influential Merchants that headed those families. For in the real world the pocket books were written, ran and looked after by the Trade Houses. Thus civilisation was quite in an orderly fashion.

Everything in it's place and God is in his heaven – Fancied the Honourable Mister Ahjib Dowry, Head Chair of the Hugh-Dawsren Trade House, the largest and most powerful of the Merchant families in the city and indeed much of the Collective. Ahjib was one of the most powerful men in the Collective and he knew it.

This morning's conflicts were being down-played as was national policy. In a few short hours, Ahjib knew (as he had designed), the banks would settle themselves down, and the city guard patrols would be reduced. After all the extra staff was a strain on profits for the day and that could not be held for too long. Right now in the town centre a display of will (and a justifiable distraction) was under way, the new range of long slim barrelled oyra artillery were being wheeled out by some Trade House workman, onto the multi-coloured decorated flagstones. The newly crafted cannons would be fired with blank rounds, as a show of power and ingenuity of the Collective cannon manufacturers.

Citizens of the Owing classes, the middle workers and the wealthy Trade House Merchants would be appeased with a show. For now, Ahjib would satisfy them in turn. But there would be steps to come. For whoever had designed to upset the flow of Haltin and its profits, would be apprehended and the swift hand of Modernist Law would be swung down upon them.

As was right and just, of course. Ahjib thought to himself.

The audible thunder of the cannons nearby sounded off and brought Ahjib back to the world around him with a start. He settled his hammering heart. *Merciful Lord those blasted contraptions were loud.*

The raucous cheers of the crowd melted in with the fading booming echo of the oyra cannons. A regional militia bombardier explained the workings of the artillery pieces to the crowd, though as Ahjib noted, the loud unwashed masses did not seem to take much in, as they continued to excitingly cheer.

'The invention of the third generation Oyra directed artillery emplacement, began late last arc with the Hughes Engineering Core and the most generous financial contribution of several leading Trade Houses. As you all can the operation of this ingenious machine is commited by the suppression of a large iron ball into the firing chamber or in this demonstration it was just charcoal powder being fired out. The Oyra in a seperate chamber just below the main firing barrel... '

The shouted proclamations of the Regional Militaman were drowned out in the ensuring crescendo exited noise from the crowd. Ahjib did not bother to listen in further. Military matters were a bore to him anyway. He turned away and made to leave back to his carriage just as herald on horseback arrived.

Ahjib noted the young man, Porin was his name and at the very least he thought it was. A good lad in any case, a trusty messenger, a quiet and subtly intelligent vassal, one that knew the delicate nature of their work.

'Your Honour, all reports in the banks are settling down. The guards have secured most of the shantytowns and a lock down is in effect. Here are the details.' Porin the herald said in accented *cestral*. The lad was a Kiri of the Southrondor and most of his words rushed out in an excited garble, but Ahjib understood him well enough. After all Ahjib was part Kiri himself.

Ahjib motioned for one of his scribes, a portly fair-haired Consintali woman of his escort to take the documents Porin reached out of his hardboiled leather satchel. The woman took the printed-paper sheets and scanned them with eager eyes as she should. Ahjib would look over the finer points later of course, but his time was far too valuable at the current moment.

'Very good, Herald.' Ahjib stated, patting the messanger boy on the back as he passed him.

'Mister Dowry?' The pimpled teenage herald questioned, as Ahjib was helped into his carriage one step at a time, as was proper.

'Yes, lad?' Ahjib said not looking back.

'There was one more message, Sar.' The boy said. Ahjib breathed a sigh of relief. *Yes, right on time.*

Ahjib did not voice his happiness outwardly as it would do to fraternize like that in front of his lessers, as was most definitely not proper.

'The Hawk sees....ah, the ...the Tower is is session. Fire is..... Errr you Honourable sar I did not really remember this last part...Fire is..' The Young Herald stumbled through the encoded message, it was clear the boy had a busy morning of work and the code was lost somewhere. Fortunately Ahjib knew the meaning whereas everyone else present would not.

'Fire is Blue Ice, very good Herald. Off with you back to work.' Ahjib stated, taking a seat in the furnished door, one his men shutting the portal after him.

So she had come through for him again, as he did not doubt for a second of course. When had she let him down?

Ahjib made himself comfortable and drew out his gold-lined snuffbox from its resting place under a velvet cushion, between two splits seats. Ahjib bought up some of the pearly-white powder with a fingertip from his snuffbox. He sniffed the concoction up his nose and some of his anxiousness passed.

It was a shame about the messenger boy, he had proven himself a reliable service over the last few months. But incompetence was not to be readily accepted by Ahjib and the Hugh-Dawsren House. Still this time at least the the lad would be given a second chance. Only a minor docking would be enough. Besides all the hastily acquired errand runners need to all be paid, a bread roll or two for the urchins for running a few letters would be more than enough. After all profit still must be maintained for the greater good. Nearby the armoured wagon rolled on by the flagstone high road closer toward his Trade House compound. Ahjib turned his mind to other matters, for when he arrived he would need to deal with criminals and void-damned demonic Channellors. *All in a days work*. Ahjib took more powder from the box and inhaled deep and slowly this time. His snuffbox would have to be restocked when he returned to the Dowry Estate grounds.

*

A light coordinated sequence of taps on the rosewood doorframe, made Lisiarna aware someone was on the side of the moving wagon. The taps were set to the decipherable melody of the old Draul folk song of *Avid Folly*. Lisiarna had more than a stirring suspicion who that *someone* was before opening the compartment door. Her hunch was confirmed as the slim and tall figure of Raijin popped into the enclosed wagon compartment, taking a spot on the opposite facing twin seats from Lisiarna. Though the Draul had his face concealed behind a rather demonic-looking Coriosi iron close helm and matching brevor, Lisiarna was not surprised to see Raijin's familiar face as he flipped open the helm, his grey skin drenched in sweat.

'Bit warm?' Lisiarna asked the Draul.

'It is the first day of Sumner.' Raijin replied, breathing heavily in staggered exhalation. The sickly sweet smell of Raijin's sweat filled the carriage.

Lisiarna was rather taken back by the colour of the Draul mage's eyes, that of a rather dull grey. Paired with the azure tone of Raijin's skin, it rather made the Draul look rather like a fresh corpse.

'Well that's new.' Lisiarna stated, granting Raijin a small smile at the corner of her mouth.

'Just a precaution, the eye drops wear off in a couple of hours.' Raijin replied, moving a hand slowly toward the water skin near Lisiarna. She passed the leather sack across to Raijin who gratefully accept and took a long draw.

'You have used the drops before?' Lisiarna inquired.

Raijin withdrew the water skin from his lips and handed it back to Lisiarna who placed back down beside herself on the cushioned seat.

'No, but Lucairn assured me.' Raijin paused. 'I hope so, I rather do like my own eyes, just here it might be a bit difficult if one of the puffed up guards were to see crimson eyes. They may not take it too kindly.' Raijin finished, Lisiarna nodding.

Here in the Cor-Dazral Collective, the Draul were not very well received by the unrelentingly strict regime. Racism was somewhat of a assumed lifestyle choice held up in the face of Collective propaganda. Many of the populace either by arcs of forced suggestion or by personal experiences from; hostilities toward the Draul in the last Banner War, a conflict that seemed to be brewing afresh in the last couple of days. What ever the case, all reports of the closing off of borders from the new *Sephriot Krikza* in the Draul theilm probably added more tension. Raijin was right to remain vigilant.

The Collective did not stop with their hatred directed toward the Draul however. Lisiarna herself knew that the *form* she was in was really the only choice she had, albeit without *shifting* a entirely new form, to remain safe from the corrupt guards or the void-damned Hari'al. Eckard and Judeson was of course being smuggled into the city. Hopefully they held off showing themselves too early before the plan was properly in place. Though with Eckard any carefully laid plan could go cockeyed quite quickly.

He knew what to do. Lisiarna assured herself.

As if sensing her very thoughts, Raijin spoke up.

'They'll be fine, I got a message back from the Kobold' Raijin said.

'Finally' Lisiarna replied.

'Yes it was a bit touch and go there for bit' Raijin stated, thinking about something.

Lisiarna waited for the Draul, as he formed his next words.

'Apparently they will be in position shortly.' Raijin continued.

Lisiarna nodded her approval.

'I must confess my surprise at this Kobold leader's willingness, we knew there there were Kobold who were once part of the Pact. But they just jumped at the chance this time around.' Raijin said.

'Eckard can be persuasive, when he tries.' Lisiarna added, she drew back the faded scarlet curtains to glance out on the makeshift street.

The rain had turned much of the winding dirt track into muddy gunk, refuse left by the locals added to the obstacle course that their carriage was driven across.

The sturdy stage coach was drawn by two cross-bred Yunsi grooms a eager smiling *jarvie* (the *nerthari* title of a coach driver) named Justen who Lisiaran had hired in a small town near the Wanderer's River. The town was situated right on the border of the Collective and the Yunlands. Like most of their journey it had been no accident in acquiring the sunny, mild-mannered Justen. The young man was half Yunsi and the other half Salmian. Though his former half proved the most desired and his loyalties most definitely did not lay with the Collective.

Trust was a fine thread and all that – But for Lisiarna sometimes loyalty was ensured by not prying too much. Justen could be trusted enough to take them where they wanted to go. After that he could go on his merry way and he would be none the wiser about who Lisiarna and Raijin were and what they were doing.

Lisiaran watched Raijin glanced out his window opposite her own. He was looking out onto the shanty town they found themselves in. Quite a noticeable difference from the more orderly grid work of granite block complexes and crisp-clean cobblestone streets of the inner city of Haltin.

A little Berussi girl in a torn tunic and deep, dried grime on her face ran up and then beside the carriage in a mad bolt.

'Another one.' Raijin grinned knowingly.

'Well hop to it, Hari'al' Lisiarna stated, opening the door for Raijin who complied and hopped out of the stage coach. The Draul mage re-adjusted his disguise on the way out.

The stagecoach came to a abrupt halt, the smell metal brakes clamping down on the spoked wheels. Lisiarna tapped the front facing view port window. Justen the jarvie reigning in the grooms. The little urchin girl came close to the carriage, Raijin stood dutifully (and feigning over protectiveness) nearby.

The young street girl looked wracked with nerves. Lisiarna saw Raijin give her a blink-and-you-miss it wink. Which seemed to relax her a little bit. A crowd of onlookers stopped nearby, not too close of course. There were many city guard patrols even in the narrow twisting confines of the shantytowns. No 'Owing' citizens would dare get so close to a 'Noble' carriage. Why in the Lord's name was this girl daring to fraternise with her betters?

Lisiarna beckoned the girl into the coach before the crowd outside swelled any more. The urchin struggled on the high steps and Raijin pushed her gently up. To the outsider it would look as if the Noble lady had use of Owing worker or to the more cynical minded perhaps a sex toy to be played with and discarded. After all the Nobles had the right and the coin to do as they wished.

In reality, the urchin had a message from the Kobold and Lisiarna would do nothing as crass as some of the so-called *Nobles* did and continued to do. Lisiarna brushed aside the dark thoughts she had about the Collective and waited for the dirty little girl to deliver the message.

'You have something for us?' Lisiarna asked, smiling and speaking softly.

'Yes madam.' The young girl replied, her nerves no longer a unsteady storm. She seemed much more composed. The girl dug out a tightly bunched papyrus bundle and handed it across to Lisiarna.

Lisiarna gratefully accepted the package and began work on untying the thick string that bound the piece together. She uncovered a small folded piece of parchment paper. Rough Ballpoint etchings marked the page. Obviously the writer had worked in quite a hurry. Lisiarna had viewed the written Kobold language on a few occasions beforehand, it seemed this 'P' transferred some of their traditional running cursive writing style over into that of the more broadly utilised *cestral* writing.

Lisiarna read -

Dear Those of the G

Messages received. E and J, safe and delivered

Your plan looks successful. C overinflated and insecure

Moving forward. Attack on The W. Moving Forward.

We meet at Point ???. Please destroy note. Speak soon.

P

Lisiarna handed the note across to Raijin who came up to the edge of the stagecoach door. The Draul quickly looked over the message before tearing the parchment paper to shreds and scattering the paper fragments into the dark mud that served as the shantytown road.

'Are we going?' Raijin paused. 'Milady?' Though Lisiarna could not see the Draul's face now, she knew he was most probably grinning like a madman.

'Yes' Lisiarna said in here most authoritarian tone. She had a image to maintain as Lady Beatrice of Darvis Porte after all.

The urchin girl made to get up and vacant the carriage but Lisiarna urged the girl to retake her seat.

'You girl, stay I have need of you yet.' Lisiarna stated, keeping her tone like she had a stick up her arse, just as a Noble would be percieved in this kind of neighbourhood. 'Jarvie onward.'

The stagecoach driver knew his role and urged his equestrian workers onward. Raijin in Hari'al guise shut the coach door and rode on the side like a escort would do.

Now safe away from prying eyes; Lisiarna smiled at the young, grime covered girl. Retrieving a dainty handkerchief from near to her person Lisiarna brushed at the dirty face that was smiling back at her.

'Ma am? I don't understand' The young girl said in a quiet voice, clearly perplexed.

Lisiarna dropped her smile. She retrieved several small gold pieces within a tight purse, previously hidden in a secret compartment at her seat.

'Take this we shall drop you off on the move, just around the corner. Don't squander this. Don't spend it all at once or at the same place. Be smart, be careful, look after you and your family.' Lisiarna said, this time in her more natural tone. She felt more comfortable speaking slow and carefully, without all the show and bolster that went with pretending to be a Noble in the Collective.

'Ma'am, I couldn't I…' The young girl replied.

'You can and you will. Now what is your name, child?' Lisiarna handed the purse to the girl who gratefully accepted and tucked up the pouch onto her person.

'Saffiya, ma'am.' The girl replied, absolutely beaming now.

'Good girl' Lisiarna said.

On the outside of the carriage Lisiarna saw that they were several ramshackle blocks away from whence they had picked up Saffiya. Lisiarna tapped on the outside window, Raijin obliged and opened the coach door to allow Saffiya an exit. The Carriage slowed when Raijin called to the driver.

'Thank you so much, ma'am. No one has ever been this kind.' The young girl said, tears welling at the edges of her dark eyes.

'On your way, Saffiya.' Lisiarna stated, a little touch of authority from her assumed Noble persona to urge Saffiya on her way.

Saffiya jumped from the carriage and practically skipped down the muck encrusted roadway in ecstasy. Lisiarna observed the beautiful duality of the situation Happiness in a dirty, horrible world.

The young girl Saffiya would hopefully use the money as her second chance in life. Perhaps she and her family would better their lot. But the more cynical side of Lisiarna knew that with the way the Collective was structured against the majority of their citizens (or Mordenism as their leaders called it), it would still be a struggle to get by for the unfortunate such as Saffiya. At the very least Lisiarna had done what she could. Saffiya would see the gesture as enormously helpful, though Lisiarna herself knew the world here was very unfair.

The carriage rolled onward, the jarvie hastening their pace now. For Lady Beatrice of Darvis Porte had a place to be. A plan was in motion Those of the G (The Pact of the Grey Mantle) would all have a role to play. J and E (Judeson and Eckard) would have to live up their end of the bargain. The C (Cor-Dazral Collective) would not know what hit them until it was hopefully far too late, though their affiliation with the Rakoni and the Channellors was certainly not great in the face of everything. The Pact would reconvene at Point

III, a pre-arranged meeting location and the infiltrating attack on the W (Woldte) would finally start to become a reality.

A reality as dirty as the streets they were in, unfortunately. Lisiarna sighed to herself.

2nd Stanza

The Confederation is a odd place to the outsider that had never been.

Cold, harsh landscape with beautiful fresh water lakes when Sumner comes around, its people are both hardly, challenging and at certain points; surprisingly friendly.

The government, politics and complex mixing pot that is their culture is not a easily understandable one.

In almost the complete polarizing juxtaposition to the Nertharn Confederation is the Cor-Dazral Collective, very much the familiar sight to anyone unfortunate enough to have bore witness to uncompromising tyranny. The Judicirum – the ruling elite of the Collective, a consortium of Trade House coin counters, gate-keepers of corrupt laws and vicious sell-sword generals so staunchly swear they are battling the evils of Corruptible Monarchy. But in turn they hold all the wealth, make all the calls and throw their own people who they title as the 'Owing' class underneath the wagon if they do not abide by their absolute authority without question.

The Nerthielm is very much the struggle of duality. The harsh high seas and great storms that batter our own trading ships and shores are like kittens compared to the back-stabbing and savagery on the Nertharn Continent.

The Wild Continent – A Sailor's account of the Nertheilm.

Sarko Basden, Berussi Commerce Captain 2990 ATF

Eckard awoke to an entirely different time and place yet again. Brushing aside sleep from his blurry eyes, he made out a familiar scene. One of vermilion and violet plush cushioned walls, similarly fluffed cushions scattered throughout the floor and the bed he found himself in. Of particular note was the bed Eckard was in. The whole thing was a larger than life affair. Pillows and linen sheets everywhere, an ocean of cloth with islands of plush cases and feathered centres. Eckard once at least partially awake realised he was naked.

'At last the notorious warrior-mage of the icy fringes awakens.' A feminine voice said in a mockingly sarcastic tone.

Oh great – Eckard thought.

'Good I was getting bored with waiting, I thought mages were god-like, powers beyond recognition.'

Another voiced stated, slighter higher pitched, sarcasm present

Eckard cleared his throat in the most exaggerated manner he could muster. The spluttering cough that came subsequently was not voluntary and probably an after effect from the noxious gas used by the kobold.

'That cough did not sound very god-like.' The first voice stated.

The owner of the voice came into view. A pretty Draul woman that matched the complexion of one of Kormai Isle origins, she possessed a head of dyed platinum blonde hair, most probably by using the flower of the Owldan. The Draul looked down at Eckard with knowing grin of impossibly white teeth, the second voice that had spoken was of course held by a woman that almost always accompanied the first woman. Eckard did not need to peer over to his left hand side but when he did he beheld the inevitable sight of dark toned athletically built Berussi.

Both the Draul and aurman women were barely covered in silk bathrobes, the tops of their thighs and generous view of their cleavage showing.

Eckard inwardly sighed. *This was going to interesting*.

'Khelsi, Maria always a pleasure.' Eckard said. Offering his most sincere smile.

'Bullshit.' Maria, the Berussi retorted, seating herself on the incredibly snug bed.

'You always told the sweetest lies, magician.' Khelsi the Draul said, taking her place on the opposing side of Eckard from Maria on the bed.

Khelsi proceeded to stroke Eckard's hair gently, his hair had grown improbably fast once again. The side effects of the Arcane Sea were intricately varied on its users as Eckard understood. In his exceptional case; his facial and head hairs growth was accelerated tenfold, this was manageable, somewhat. The nose and ear bleeds were disturbing to say the very least.

Maria had obtained a wet hand linen towel, and began dabbing at one of Eckard's aforementioned-busted orifices. Maria was delicate and singularly focused. Eckard could not fault the woman, but something about being waited on always felt strange for him.

'Thanks ladies, I got it.' Eckard said, brushing aside both women gently.

'Oh come now Eck, we have not seen in oh so many arcs, and you brush aside our attentions so casually.' Kehlsi stated, mocking up a disappointed and gloomy downcast frown.

Eckard groaned, though secretly he was not remotely perturbed by their presence. But the act they had been playing was simply too good to abort. That and the bed he was in, he quickly discovered was incredibly comfortable. A few more moments lying with the fluffy confines of the fresh sheets, could not be missed.

After a few precious moments of blissful dark silence with his eyes firmly closed to the world, Eckard looking up at the two women he was confined in a small room with.

It was indeed an added bonus that they were not at all hard to look to look at, though counteracting that was the reality that they could npt be wholly trusted. *Trust was a fine thread...*

Eckard shook aside any thoughts of the Wrendal and his manipulations. It was bad enough he shared an edge of the Arcane Sea with him now. He did not have to think about the one-eared bastard in his waking moments.

Both women grinned furiously at Eckard, like creatures possessed.

'Joyous occasions will have to wait when invasion is at the forefront, I'm afraid ladies.' Eckard stated, beaming a grin back at them.

'You are a real downer sometimes, Eck' Khelsi retorted. Both she and and Maria had shuffled onto the bed closer to Eckard once more.

'Where are my cloths?' Eckard questioned.

'Come now, Eck, we have plenty of time. Your compatriots are not in position just yet.' Maria said, with a twinkle in her dark chestnut eyes.

Eckard straightened up in the bed, mourning the loss of his comfortability about to come to an end.

'Did you ladies ever imagine, the reason for my absence throughout the arcs may have been your shared tendencies to call me 'Eck'. Eckard said.

The two women shared a look and proceeded to forcibly giggle like school children, with hands of mouths in controlled syndication of each other.

'You two are intrinsically skilled at your covers here' Eckard motioned.

Both Maria and Khelsi transitioned expressions as one.

'Are you calling us whores?' Khelsi asked.

Eckard shrugged.

'We were given strict instructions to keep you here until the time was right. And to ensure no harm was visited upon you.' Maria stated.

'No matter how much we may wish to, ourselves' Khelsi smiled.

'Point taken, Ladies of the night references aside, back to my first inquiry, where are my cloths?.' Eckard countered.

Both Maria and Khelsi sighed all too loudly.

'The parts we play' Maria muttered beneath her breath.

'*She* gave us strict instructions to keep you put, Sar knight.' Khelsi said, her face a mask of seriousness now.

'And did she also instruct you to taunt me and steal my cloths from me as I dozed.' Eckard inquired with a raised eyebrow for emphasis.

Maria propelled herself off the bed and skipped over to a set of elaborately craved rosewood drawers. The dark toned woman obtained a ceramic tumbler from the top mantle of the drawers.

'Here you go; kefra. Eck..ard' Maria said, drawing out Eckard's name in good humour.

Eckard received the tumbler, which had piping hot fumes wafting from it. The mug warmed his palms as he took it from the Berussi woman.

'Would you have any whisky or better yet firewater?' Eckard questioned.

Khelsi shrugged off his query beside him. Arm over the top of the blanket where Eckard's waist was.

'These Collective folk don't hold much love for Kormai's necter unfortunately. Just another misstep on their 'collective' parts' Khelsi replied, her intention to mock the Cor-Dazral society unmasked in it's mocking.

'Your cloths if you could call them that were in horrendous condition. And it cannot be comfortable sleeping in chain maille. So we have acquired for you a new coat and pants. Will look more fashionable and far more fitting for where you are now.' Maria declared matter-of-factly. She too joined in with her partner in throwing her arm over Eckard's covered waist. Though she committed further to the act and nestled down her head onto Eckard's broad shoulder.

'We always imagined you might look quite fetching in black.' Khelsi said, taking the opposing shoulder from Maria as a headrest.

Eckard sipped from the kefra and questioned how he was to emerge unscathed from this particular ambush.

*

Judeson woke up to a clean, incredibly comfortable bed. He was in his under garments, he soon discovered. The room he was in was well-decorated, immaculate wallpaper on every side. Dim, flickering lamps of dull bluish flame adorned the walls and curiously gave off no smell. Fine hand woven blankets and cushions adorned the bed he was on and all around the floor. It was like a dream, an odyssey of comfort and and a welcome departure from the grim and grime he had so readily made visitations on of late.

He made to rise but a wave of nausea washed over him. Rubbing at sleep in his eyes, Judeson propped himself up somewhat awkwardly with the assistance of a unbelievably comfortable pillow. He recalled the folk stories of the Goddess Zadma and her palace nestled in the Far Above. Of lavish feast halls and incredibly furnished bedrooms each one for a honourable and loving aurman servant. Judeson hoped that the after life was half as good as what he was experiencing now.

From across the room sound of a brass door knob turning, lured Judeson away from his dwelling thoughts of Godly luxury. The rosewood door creaked open to reveal a young, pretty girl of greysih skin tone and short-cropped dark hair.

The girl dressed in shape fitting gown of rose pink and faded emerald green, greeted Judeson with a warm smile.

'You're up, very good. Here.' The young lady held a tin carry tray that she skirted over to Judeson with. On the tray was a tin pot, with wafting bittersweet tealeaf steam hailing from it and two empty ceramic tea bowls.

Placing the carry tray onto the bedside table near Judeson, the young lady poured greenish piping hot tea into the cups and stepped away with one. Judeson took one of the teacups from the table appreciatively.

'Who are you? Where am...' Judeson started cooling his tea with some light breaths.

The young lady replied straight away before he had time to finish his sentence.

'My name is Anya, you are in the Cor-Dazral Collective city of Haltin and you are safe' Anya stated.

Judeson tried to process all of that.

'I am Judeson.' Judeson replied.

'Nice to meet you.' Anya in turn said, taking a seat on a plush cushion chair nearby.

'It is an absolute pleasure, ma'am. Not every day a beautiful young lady brings me tea.' Judeson stated.

Anya raised one fine eyebrow at Judeson in response.

'You are too kind' Anya said with a warm smile, Judeson could tell at something in her tone was quite amused by him. Not quite the response he was going for.

Judeson took a sip of his tea, as did Anya.

'Where are we exactly? This place is very extravagant. A palace?' Judeson asked, lowering his teacup. The brew was perfect. Bittersweet and well bodied.

'A palace of sorts.' Anya replied, her smile remained, and a twinkle to her eyes now. Judeson realised what he could sense in her tone. Sarcasm. She was mocking him. Though the smile led him to believe it was in good nature.

'Maybe I am a little slow in waking, though this gorgeous tea is certainly helping…but..' Judeson positioned.

'And…I am being very vague?' Anya replied.

'A little' Judeson followed up.

Anya placed her tea bowl down and started up toward the bed where Judeson laid. Though the young woman stopped a few paces off. Her expression turned earnest.

'It's a palace of pleasure. A brothel if you wish to be crass.' Anya said.

'Ah' Judeson stated.

'Don't worry about it, I doubt too much ill feeling is spent lingering on the subtleties of life here.'

'And you are?' Judeson replied, though he wished he had not.

Anya laughed in earnest.

'I'm a maid, at least in the official capacity, more tea making than love making really, in the unofficial capacity. I listen in on the loose words that tumble out from men with large pockets and many secrets.' Anya stated, the sarcasm all but drained up and replaced with a transmutable frankness.

'I see.' Judeson said. 'And are you in league with this Pact, Eckard talks about?'

'In a manner of speaking.' Anya answered. She gathered up some freshly laundered cloths from the table top nearby and placed them right next to Judeson on the bed.

Judeson peered at the garments and then back at Anya for a moment. She urged him to take them. A thick brown woollen overcoat was matched with a pair of hard-boiled leather breeches and matching leather vest with red dyed silk sleeves. All brand new unlike whatever remained of his tattered, dirty and burnt hunting leathers. The lack of armour however was worrying as a warrior in a strange place. With Eckard at his side there was always potentially more enemies.

Come to think of it where was that mad bastard?

'I would of come to this place with an absurdly tall dark haired man. Where is he?' Judeson questioned.

'He is probably being tortured as we speak. Finish your tea.' Anya replied.

Judeson felt a wave of confusion wash over him and it must have shown Silvershard clear to Anya.

'Don't worry that was a joke, Judeson. Eckard will be along shortly. Finish your tea and get dressed.'

Judeson gifted Anya a warm hearted smile and the young lady acknowledged him with one of her own. *She was really quite pretty*. Judeson inwardly shook himself Jehasli come to mind and the raw betrayal was still sinking in. Best he occupy his mind away from women, albeit for the moment.

To his surprise Anya did not vacant the room, she took a seat and sipped at her own tea, occasionally whistling to herself quietly and looking away. Judeson threw on his new garments. The pants first followed by the vest. He found the sword of Jude and its scabbard close by, and in turn he picked up the overcoat he felt a small pouch in one of the interior chest pockets.

Pulling the pouch out, he unstrung the tight
string that held the piece closed. Inside was a
assortment of gold and silver pieces of varying
sizes and differing face piece designs. Judeson
restrung the pouch, he held it out toward Anya as
she got up and gathered up his and her tea cups
back onto her carry tray.

'Take it, you could use it more than I.' Judeson
uttered, throwing his new overcoat on himself. It
fit like a dream. *Did they measure him while he
was unconscious?*

'Thank you, you...are most kind, but the coin is
yours.' Anya said, leaving the room and Judeson
with a giggle.

The young lady curtseyed as she vacated, leaving
Judeson more confused than when she entered.

Eckard came into view in the narrow corridor
outside the now open door, the tall Northman had
a beaming grin and his arms crossed.

'What's so amusing?' Judeson inquired from his
comrade.

'Do you fall in love with every woman you ever
meet?' Eckard asked. Though Judeson knew it was
certainly not a question. The twisted bastard had
been listening in.

'I'm not sure, do you see the same woman in all
the others you meet?' Judeson retorted.

Eckard laughed and smiled a little larger. There
was no vitriol in Judeson's tone therefore Eckard
took no offence. Judeson found himself smiling
back at the man.

'Good banter that, you grim bastard' Eckard
stated enthusiastically to Judeson not entirely
sure if he in turn should take any offence at
that.

Eckard was moving to leave again. 'Now enough
with all the void-damned gloom and cheap

pleasures, we have a performance to attend.'
Eckard said. The Mage slid back from Judeson's
room and out into the dim lit hallway beyond.

Judeson sighed to himself. With one last look at
the wonderful dream of a bedroom he followed in
the wake of his frustrating companion.

'I have no fucking clue what you are on about
sometimes' Judeson called out to Eckard who was
already halfway down the long winding hallway.
The polished golden timber floorboard stretched
out before Judeson and hastened double time to
catch up with Eckard.

Eckard leaned over and winked as Judeson shadowed
his side, panting.

'You are where you want to be mate.' Eckard
rebutted.

Judeson rolled his eyes, and waved Eckard ahead
of him, down the elongated basalt stone steps
that appeared at the end of the lavish hall.

'We have to meet a gentleman the Pact has kept
close eyes on for sometime. But in order to do
that we will have to first meet a few knuckle
dragging goat takers that will inevitably be in
the road and recruit some of the former
intellectually challenged individuals.' Eckard
continued.

Judeson did not bother trying to ascertain what
Eckard meant.

Eckard cast twin doors of solid timber aside, and
the piercing rays of the light of day came into
immediate effect. Averting his vision with his
palm for a shield, Judeson winced over at Eckard.
The beanpole Northman had thrown up a hidden
black hood however and held his gaze straight as
the crow flies. Without turning Eckard spoke.

'This man does not want to come out of hiding.
However our performance will ensure their timely

return to the fold.'

With that Eckard stalked forward into the maddening rush of aurmantiy that littered the muddy and disordered streets of Haltin. Judeson shook his head and paced double time after the man, pushing aside beggars, soot coated workers and shabby dressed low-end goods merchants. This was a stark contrast to the luxurious confines of the Pleasure House they had been smuggled into.

Judeson glanced around at the various breeds of aurmantiy who littered the streets, tavern fronts and pop up tent markets. He was surprised to find such a vast array of peoples. Far more than the solitary visit he had had with his father to Dosintal. Of the breeds originally hailing from the Southrondor; he spotted a great deal of the grey skinned Kiri, fair haired Tumbaians, his own people – the Dosin with their unmistakeable brown-olive hue , the stout square heads and compact shapes of the Baelese and a fair number of dark skinned, long limbed Promtezi.

Eckard informed him as they moved through the scattering masses of men and women. That the Thul-qar people were the pale, mostly lithe of shape and blonde, light brown and dusty carmine haired. Their predominately smaller eyes and noticeably fuzzier hair made them quite distinct from the Tumbians that Judeson knew well. Jehasli was a pure representation of the traditional Tumbian people. Judeson shook the memory aside. He really did not need to dwell on her.

Dark olive skinned people with furry eye brows and hooked noses were apparently those who hailed from the the Varihale and southern Flagstern Isles off the coast, a region somewhere to the south of here in Haltin. Midnight shaded people, most of them skinny and agile looking were apparently the Berussi Eckard had talked of to Judeson earlier. Far darker than Judeson himself or any of the Promtezi he had seen before. Eckard pointed out the Yunsi; a people of dull grey, brown and even black eyes with epicanthic folds far more noticeable than any other breed. The Yunsi had a various range of hues to them. Some were fairer of tone, closer to Eckard and yet others verging on the darker brown of Judeson's own skin.

The Yunsi, Judeson noticed; occupied some of the most mundane and physically demanding positions. The Yunsi breed were either bent over shovels at the edge of roadworks or carrying loads of goods, trailing behind Thul-qar or Kiri folks, dressed in merchant overcoats or decorated nobleman vests. Eckard only grunted rather expressively, when Judeson pointed this out. Judeson had not the faintest idea whether Eckard was indiferent or irate; he did not pry any further.

They rounded a basalt corner of a two-storey stock-house adorned with a host of posters in varying written languages, only one in the *trader's tongue* Judeson noticed. The poster read:

Fair Rights for all,
Fuck the Judicurm and their Trade House cronies!

Under the chicken scratch etchings of this was a brass plague nailed into the wall, which stated:

-Subversive Behaviour will not be Tolerated-
-Onward to Modernism and Liberty-
Haltin City Authority

Eckard had pulled up short to stand right next to Judeson, reading over his shoulder.

'You will see that a great deal, in the slums. There is anger here and rightfully so' Eckard proclaimed, his tone steely and his crooked gaze strangely devoid of much in the way of any emotion.

Judeson did not fully understand but he nodded nevertheless and started forward prompting Eckard to lead the way again.

A thought struck Judeson and hopefully it took away thoughts from whatever the apparently 'subversive' signs enraptured in Eckard.

'Your own people, the Nertharlanders? I have not seen too many like you, is it rare here for your own breed to be present?' Judeson inquired.

Again Eckard stopped dead in his tracks. Though this time he did not turn to meet Judeson in the eyes.

'The Nerthar people are not exactly welcome, in the Collective, Judeson.' Eckard stated. His voice cold and distant.

'But you are here.' Judeson replied.

The beanpole Nertharnlander turned toward Judeson, with a raised brow near his solitary crooked eye.

'In disguise, yes.' Eckard said, clearly surprised about something.

Before Judeson had time to say anything in reply, Eckard followed up with:

'Clearly that fucking monster of a sword on your back, has woken up.'

Judeson felt at the hilt of Jude, a tingling sensation laced up his arm and down his side. From somewhere distant a howling squall could be heard. And then it was gone. Judeson withdrew his arm and the tempest's call and the tingling halted as if it was never there.

'I really don't understand what you are on about, most of the time.' Judeson answered, sharing a brief fleeting smile with Eckard.

'Come on, I'll show you all the joys of

Modernism.' Eckard stated, picking up at a break neck pace down the filthy alleyway once more. Judeson scrambled to catch up after the man.

*

The odour of the freshly ignited jasmine incense flooded the dim lit tent with a sweet welcoming flavour. The thin vapour mixing and twisting with the intricate kaleidoscope pattern of the tent's lone spotlight. Smoke tendrils spiralling up into the canvas roof and dissipating away into invisibility as they vacated the light. The tent walls adorned with prayer sheets of illuminated paper fitted the calming scene. Dozens of multi-coloured plush cushions and coloured silk sheets added a practical comfort factor that few in a great many leagues distance were privy to enjoy. Khrislo could almost forget she was smack-in-the middle of a bustling military camp. For in this campsite that stretched for leagues in every direction was one of the largest armies in all of the Southrondor. Outside was a messy business. Scurrying masses of Rakoni soldiers camped down for the night in tightly packed ordered tent cities. Pickets and night patrols lined the excesses of the various regiments. For although this huge sprawling expanse of Rakoni armies and their *nekta underworkers* laid out like a well oiled machine in operation. The truth could not further from the this obvious sight.

The Rakoni were not united, not in the formal sense nor in any other sense at all. Very few of her own people, Servants of the Qhasa, Listeners of the divine Word of the Void; showed any sense of joining forces and settling feuds. So it was unfortunately most Channellors were not above the petty politics and intricate power plays that inflicted their Rakoni kin.

Khrislo, Madam-Channellor of the Most Holy Drike Drik Orthodox Chapter liked to think of herself and her people as above all the pettiness. She imagined her elevated position of power was not about wrestling in the mud to ultimately win the earthly throne. No as a Channellor, she had a duty, a divine calling to God and to her people to not convet earthly possessions but to restore order and clarity to a world seemingly without them. Khrislo had far more important duties.

Unfortunate then in order to perform her duties, Khrislo had to sink into the mud. Albeit for a fleeting moment, more unfortunate, aggregatively so, was how long that particular fleeting moment choose to linger.

Khrislo's silken tent flap entrance rustled apart in a wave of fabric and in marched one of her Void-Callers. The lithe form of the servant wrapped tight in dark cloak, pulled back her hood and politely to her Madam-Channellor.

Khrislo waved off the formalities.

'So, child?' Khrislo inquired.

'It was the Void-caller known as Samwell, we apprehended him en-route to meet with the Whitemark Revisionists'

Khrislo nodded. Samwell had been the horrid little worm she distrusted at first sight from days ago. It had been prudent to keep eyes on the man. Her instincts were still very much with her.

'It gives me no pleasure, whatsoever to discover he was traitor and charlatan. Have the man executed at dawn, as the God's light shines on us.'

The Void-Caller bowed once more and exited the way she had come out into the chaos of the army encampment.

Khrislo readjusted her seated position and drew

up the map of the Nerthielm in front of her. On the parchment paper existed several marked positions and notations of Rakoni loyalist forces and strongholds. Most noticeably the old Tanpasri constructed stronghold of the Woldte. The castle where Master-Channellor Tiramene should be but he was not of course. Not at the moment. Last time she had communed with the Woldte, she had spoken with some upstart Cultist who self-indulgently labelled himself a *Chosen Hero*.

What was going on up there? - Mused Khrislo. It was bad enough down here that the Revisionist and the New Canon chapters were getting bold and making plays. But if the Cultists started gaining ground on the Northern Front. *God help them.*

Khrislo shook her concerns aside. Now she had to speak to her contact in the Heathen Collective in the North. *If the Woldte have a messenger there hopefully it was not that blasted Cultist.*

'Ruus, bring me the Holy Link' Khrislo commanded in *Rakish*, to her guard captain who would be standing just outside her tent.

Several moments later, the robust Rakoni captain strode into the tent with a slight, delicate looking young girl dressed in a pale purple gown. The Rakoni looked enormous compared to the small Draul girl. Khrislo motioned for the girl to come hither and Ruus departed back the way he had come with a respectful bow to Khrislo before he vacated.

The little Draul girl bowed to Khrislo. The child shook like a leaf.

'Be still now, child. All will be well. God is with us after all' Khrislo said to the Draul girl.

The girl nodded and feigned a smile.

Khrislo opened her heart shaped gold locket piece

at her neck and drew on the Most Holy energy of the Void. The none too subtle roaring in her ears that usually greeted her as opened a tear in the earthly plane of the Stone filled her head. After less than a second this passed, the wonderful, awe-inspiring Pure Light of the Void filled her vision. Beautiful white light and a calming whistle, with nothing else. Disconcertingly Khrislo was once again not privy to the *Voice*. No words, no images. This was not unusual. It had been so for several months now. But this was also not the first time the voice of the Qhasa had disappeared. Khrislo knew the *Voice* would be back. God did not abandon the devout for very long.

The incredibly bright light of the Holy Void subsided and Khrislo could once again see the mundane mortal plane. The Draul girl in Khrislo's tent fell into a fit and Khrislo *Channelled* herself into the child's mind. A few moments of dizzying after images flashed in Khrislo's vision and the all-too familiar pulse of spiralling flashes subsided gradually as Khrislo awoke to a elaborately lavish state-room of clashing floral and satin curtains. Velvet lined walls were adorned with hanging orchids, surrealist and traditional artworks and a great many awards proclaiming the grandeur of the estate's owner.

Khrislo was of course peering at this decadent scene through the eyes of another. This one she knew for the simple fact that she handpicked the duo; and was the male twin of the lithe girl she had back in her tent. The Holy Link was complete and she cast her gaze to the far side of the room with the child's eyes. At a varnished timber table lined with bright gold leaf trim, sat her Collective informant, Ahjib Dowry. A squat Kiri aurman with a pock marked face and a thin whisper of greying moustache. The short little man sat upright, dressed in brightly coloured satin sleepwear. Looking smugly comfortable.

Ahjib was a prideful little fool, albeit a useful little one. Khrislo thought to herself. *She would allow him his luxuries for a while yet.*

To Ahjib's left-hand side was a little boy of perhaps ten or eleven arcs. The fuzzy blonde haired boy was also in the act of being *channelled*. He was a Holy Link, as Khrislo could see from the Void energy around the boy.

On the opposing right-hand side of Ahjib stood a slender, tightly cloaked woman. The feminine figure was mostly concealed in deep shadows as she stood in noticeably dim corner, far away from the oyra lamplights of the room. Khrislo knew an assassin when she saw one. She had employed enough of them in the past.

Peering around to the edges of her Holy Link's peripherals, Khrislo noted that she (at least her Link) was inside of a round iron barred cage.

'Honourable Mister Ahjib, I take it you have your reasons for placing my Holy Link in a cage?' Khrislo projected through the Draul boy, it always felt quite peculiar hearing the words you have spoken coming from another's voice.

The young boy to Ahjib's levelled a steely glance at Khrislo's Link. But moments later it was gone and the fair-haired youth went to looking about the room like pigeon searching for crumbs.

'The vermin you inhabit, Channellor is an illegal in the Collective. We must make precautions as to the restraining of such.' Ahjib finally answered. The man as ever kept his tone reservedly steady and his eyes level at all times.

Ahjib was incredibly well trained in social circles; there was never any irritation nor be it frustration in his voice or facial expressions. Khrislo did not climb the heights of the Pure Order hierarchy without being an expert at reading people. She could sense something was up with Ahjib, the little man felt metaphorically small, he did not fully understand the complexity of the current situation. Khrislo would provide enough clues to leave the Honourable Mister Ahjib feeling safe and secure. Enough for him to know the playing field, but not enough for him to have any idea on how to control it. Not that the little heathen could, even if he wanted to.

Khrislo observed that the other Link present, the boy with the wandering eyes added a source of discomfort to the whole situation. Ahjib was somewhat bemused to be dealing with another Channellor. Khrislo had a fair idea as to why that was so; the wild card in the deck.

'Fair enough, you must do what you must do, Mister Ahjib.' Khrislo stated, holding herself up and drawing on her most authoritarian persona. Though she was not entirely sure how it looked as a Draul youth.

'I'm sure all the pieces are in place now Mister Ahjib, after our little mishaps in the past, the loss of your agent in Heatra, the disappearance of the ForeSeer brat. Regardless my people are arriving in the next few weeks and we shall do business then. My associates will give you all the Oyra you require of course' Khrislo continued.

'The path to greatness always has its obstacles.' Ahjib replied, he patted down his bed wear before continuing:'There was a disturbance this morning. The missing silver from eight arcs ago returned and I think my city is invested with your *friends'* This time on the last word Khrislo could detect a discernible venom in his tone. Very un-Ahjib like indeed.

The blonde haired boy started up from his plush armchair stood at attention like he was on a parade ground.

'It is all taken care of, Madam-Channellor. The Pact are here in this city but we will flush them out.' The boy stated.

Khrislo held her tongue.

'This Channellor has informed me you have a plan to deal with the Ungodly demonspawn. He arrived an hour before you did; completely unannounced and possessed my tea-waiter here. I mean really Channellor, this was completely over-the-top even for you' Ahjib said.

Khrislo ascertained Ahjib was attempting to scold her, perhaps make her apologise for not informing him earlier. *As if she had known*. Khrislo felt anger rise to the surface. This other Channellor currently linked into the blonde youth must have some serious guile and foresight to know how and where to locate her and her contact in Haltin. Khrislo once again inwardly questioned where Tiramene was. *She would really have to look into it when she had the chance.*

 Meanwhile this other Channellor present had to be the Cultist she had spoken to days ago. The parade ground attentive stance was a ploy of course. The Cultist was not offering his due respect to his superior but was mocking her. He knew all about the Pact and their movements somehow. A mystery Khrislo could not solve from her location, thousands of leagues away. The upstart Cultist felt it necessary to rub in the fact that he present and accountable for the Pact, on the front lines. Against the Channellor's greatest enemy and Khrislo was not.

Khrislo composed herself.

'Very good, make sure the infidels do not endanger our operations there.' Khrislo said.

'Here ma'am? Oh no, I am quite sure this Aurmen city is safe. The Unholy Pact of course will be looking to assault the Woldte, where my people and I are. We shall be well prepared for this arrival, ma'am. I assure you.' The Cultist stated through his youth Link.

Khrislo once again held back from unleashing on the Cultist. *How dare he? With so much at stake he was trying to claim superiority? How did he know what he did, what was he hiding from Khrislo?* An epiphany struck her.

'I will send reinforcements of course, Channellor, to be sure. ' Khrislo replied, not giving too much away.

The fair-haired youth smiled in such in a twisted almost demonic way Khrislo was taken back. She caught her breath and the momentary expression from the boy faded like it was never there.

'Mister Ahjib, Madam-Channellor. Good day.' The boy gave his farewells and crumpled into a heap, unconscious as the Link broke.

'We shall speak soon, Mister Ahjib.' Khrislo stated, giving her own farewell. Punctual and formal, *the way it should be*. Khrislo had a great deal to think on. With that she broke her own Link and departed back to her tent.

*

His favourite tea-waiter was dead. That uptight bitch Khrislo was giving him, the third degree of passive-aggressive goat-shit and the void-damned Pact were still in his city somewhere.

Ahjib sighed. Rubbing his palms across his face in frustration.

Sofina, the dark haired assassin stood up from where she crouched checking the tea-waiter's now departed pulse. She strode over to the edge of Ahjib's desk stood like a unwavering shadow. Ahjib levelled his gaze at her. She was pretty in a sense, not overly so. A desert flower in a sense, though as Ahjib well knew the woman was extremely deadly. A intricately skilled assassin and one that was fortunately on his side, for now at least.

'So, this other Channellor this Moffren or whatever he called himself was right the Pact is here. Khrislo is out of the loop. They will recuit with all their stolen fortune. You can find them before they depart civilisation then. That witch you are after will surely be one of them' Ahjib stated.

'I don't work for you, fat man. Careful now. That almost sounded like an order.' Sofina replied, tone cold and neutral.

'Of course, of course.' Ahjib said, holding up his hands in a peacemaking gesture. 'Before you go, please take this man with you, he will help.' Ahjib continued, he gestured out to the double oak doors at the far end of stateroom.

'Guards, send him in' Ahjib called to his men outside.

The antique doors split apart and in came the hulking form of Bratoe the Salmian killer, Ahjib had requisitioned from a state gaol.

'Sofina, Bratoe. Bratoe, Sofina. Now you know each other, I am sure your skill will complement each other's. The Pact is out there in the city somewhere; the guards will show you out' Ahjib said motioning for the guards to take his 'guests' away from him.

The giant Salmian and the lithe shadow of an

assassin did not say a word to each other but locked hard gazes at each for a fleeting moment. Both of them slipped out of Ahjib's stateroom before the guards could attend to them. Leaving Ahjib alone, finally.

Ahjib opened his top drawer at his desk and worked like like a man possessed to find his snuffbox.

3ʳᵈStanza

Striking a Nertharnlander with a closed fist is never ideal.

For their faces seem to be more often than not as hard as the dusty-hued metal

They so favour. And their blade is well known to be less than a heartbeat

Away from their over sized hands.

The Charm of the North - **A Southron's account of the Northern realms**

Shamil Dura of Kirilenko

Bright coloured cloth hung on a network of chaotic lines, cooking fires flared and loud men and women shouted at the very top of their lungs that their wares were superior to that of their neighbouring merchant's own.

Citizens rushed back and forth like headless chickens; Judeson caught bits and pieces of conversations as they passed some he understood, others he had not the faintest what they meant. Several words repeated like mantra; *Hari'al – Houses and Modernism- Whatever in the abyss that all meant.*

Judeson had seen market places once in the ruins of Dosintal before the Raks threw them out. But this place he was in now; was absolute undiluted insanity incarnate. So many, people, so many sounds, sights, smells and all of it was here in pursuit of coin and substance. As Judeson was struck by the conflicting imagery and sheer character of the markets he almost lost sight of Eckard in the vast network of tents and single story tenement blocks. The Nertharnlander was off and away again. Judeson weaved through the crowds to keep up with him. The numerous market stalls and the crowds in front of them were as a obstacle course to anyone that wished to get past.

Judeson finally caught up to Eckard who had stopped at a refuse pile of broken, scattered timber crates. The man was reaching into that impossible burlap of his.

'What are those for?' Judeson questioned fixating his gaze on Eckard's hands, which had pulled out three nondescript silver coated metal rings,

which Eckard placed onto the first three fingers
of his left hand.

'Later and they are *Embedded*' Eckard whispered in
a quiet voice, his singsong scale. 'Fixed with
little nice magiks from the Arcane Sea'.

Judeson sniffed. He was not going to bother
trying to pry details.

Pulling teeth would be easier. - Judeson thought.

'Akin to that monster of a blade of yours.'
Eckard grinned furiously.

Judeson sighed.

There he goes again.

'Why do you keep saying such goat-shit' Judeson
replied. He no longer felt comfortable resting up
against the velvet carpet wall.

'When you heard your father and....'

'Eckard' Judeson cautioned through barred teeth,
glancing over his shoulder to make sure no
interlopers had stopped to pry. The little teepee
dwelling offered very little privacy after all.

'...Then your grandmother's voice. You felt
stronger; more assured and were able to press
your advantage. Did you merely think that it was
a brief hallucination? Think about it for a
second my stoic blood-brother.' Eckard continued,
nonchalantly. All three plain steel rings were
now fixed onto his absurdly long fingers.

Judeson closed his eyes and drew out a long,
frustrated breath.

'Ok then, how is that I have had the sword of
Jude for oh so many arcs and it is only now,
weeks ago. That suddenly your mysterious magikal
sea-powers are coming from this in your words not
mine *'embedded'* item.' Judeson motioned. He still
did not wholly trust there was no one surrounding
their position. If this *Collective* was as

untrustworthy as Eckard propositioned it was, the tall Nertharnlander remained remarkably calm amidst a hornet's nest of potential enemies.

'Look, fine. You do not want to hear any more about the Sea. I understand. But Judeson, when I ask you to concentrate on your grandmother and father later, please whatever you do, please do so.' Eckard said, he did not smile and by his tone there was no hidden joke.

Judeson nodded in agreement, even if he did not fully understand.

Eckard withdrew a scarlet stained glass bottle from the burlap and strung it closed with the rope pull cord. He unstopped the bottle and handed it over to Judeson who took it. Within dwelled a bittersweet harsh tasting alcohol, similar to the *Kormai Firewater* but not nearly as smooth.

'Firewater?' Judeson said, handing back the bottle to Eckard who accepted and drank like fish in the sea.

'Of a kind, not as good as the Kormai drop...you there old woman.' Eckard replied and then proceeded to call out to a passing elderly vagrant, thick tufts of dirty hair obscured the apparition's face from full view. The old vagabond pulled up short in their respective trek.

'I'm a man, mate!' The elder shouted back with barred challenging teeth and clenched fists. The old man had a thick brushing of dirty grime all over himself and a a mere nondescript torn tunic serving as his sole piece of clothing, no shoes or indeed gloves in the morning chill.

Judeson held back letting out a chuckle the old man's challenge.

'That's fucking nice. Now you can have the rest

of this bottle if you tell me where 'The Tulisi
Sparrow' hides.' Eckard indicated to half empty
bottle of amber liquid in his hand, Eckard had
punctured some emphasise on the obscure term: *The
Tulisi Sparrow*.

The old vagrant seemed to know what Eckard was
speaking of though, as the man's glassy grey eyes
widened in unadulterated surprise.

'I wouldn...wouldn't..know sir, not sure what you
mean.' The old man said, his eyes practically
bulging, he looked like he wanted to run for his
life.

'Relax you silly old bastard, I'm not a void-
damned Hari-al.' Eckard replied.

Hari'al. Judeson had heard citizens whispered
that term in hushed, frightened murmurs just
moments ago in the bustling marketplace.

The old man considered Eckard's answer.

'How would I even know if you were or not?' The
vagrant inquired piercingly.

'3rd company, Light Horse, Consintal Reds.
Disbanded without pension. Retired? Dishonourably
discharged perhaps, no ah I see...well then. You
can help us.' Eckard stated his gaze was distant.

For a moment Judeson swore he saw the odd
swirling storm of dark grey shadows in the
Northman's eyes, the same gloomy unnatural look
that had taken over the normally sky blue eyes of
Eckard. But it was such a rapid change that
Judeson was not even sure if he had seen it or
just imagined it.

'How did you?' The old man breathed heavily,
nervous sweat lined the man's brow. 'Void-damn
you, man. The Sparrow is at the Imperial Arms,
Northcote, East Street, now leave me be, I beg
you.'

Eckard handed across the bottle to the vagrant

and backed away, bowing to the man as if he were a king.

Judeson followed Eckard away, not sure what what to make of the exchange.

'What was that all about?' Judeson asked.

Eckard ushered Judeson forward and they walked down several cobblestones and hard packed dirt streets and through at least three more cluttered alleyways, without Eckard saying a single word, until they came up to the threshold of a two-storey public house. A simple quaint affair with thatched roof of straw and kiln fired brick walls. A big double door of rough finished red glum wood stood as the entrance. Pitched up on the side of doorway was a swinging steel placard sign, which announced the venue as:

NorthCote Imperial Arms

Public House

Est. 2489 ATF

Two armoured burly looking guards stood to either side of the entrance. Donning thick meaning looking cudgels. Both guards had asked for Eckard and Judeson's weapons before entering. They had obliged, though Judeson felt quite naked without Jude. Of course he would get it back as they exited, so he was not too worried.

'I told you we travelled all this way to perform and so we shall.' Eckard answered as he swung the rustic red gum pub doors open, with a protest from the creaky iron hinges.

'You are fucking mad, Eckard' Judeson said with a smile.

Eckard surprisingly just nodded in agreement and went into the pub.

Well that is new. Judeson thought as he followed the crazy Northman in.

*

Eckard knew he was right on the edge; he may fall in and *drown* at any point. Going mad was the least of his worries. Though all things considered, insanity might be a reasonable response as to what was happening to him.

He could not close the Arcane Sea, he could not stop the ebb and flow. Lines of sorcery scattered out and tangled all around him every step he took. He felt freezing cold and a minute later like he was engulfed in fire. His head swam and he felt more and more nauseous. Eckard's gore rose for the umpteenth time but he forced it back down. The rum certainly helped. At least with the foul taste that plagued his mouth.

As Eckard and Judeson walked over to a table at the far end of the busy pub, piercing distrustful eyes followed them. A giant oaf of a man with a scraggly mop of scattered hair strode over to them confidently, several hanger-on lackeys trailed in the big man's shadow. Eckard witnessed the oafish taker had a single dull metal torc on his upper arm. Concealed by his chain mail sleeve, but with the Arcane Sea flowing all around him, Eckard saw everything, well almost everything now. It was proving difficult to stop, it ached right up to back of his skull, but people were becoming much easier to read, open books.

Eckard strove to remember what Wrendal had taught him, the one-eared bastard was right. Eckard needed help, now more than ever. He had awakened the very essence of his grey magiks; the Arcane sea was not going to stop. He would be stuck with this consuming power forever.

Eckard reached out for Lisiarna, across the Sea. In his path he felt a block halting his

oscillation. *They knew.* Damn. He let the flow
take him further and he pushed the path clear. A
moment passed and then the block was gone.
Lisiarna reached back and Eckard knew she was
close. And that, for the time being, was enough.

*

Lisiarna felt that Eckard was nearby. Unique, one
of a kind, wild and raw. Eckard's magiks of the
Grey aspect were unstable and incredibly
powerful, more powerful than before. Eckard
energies were practically everything, his reach
was extending, but there was something else in
there now, just a light touch of *Red* to be sure,
sickly sweet aromas of the Void off somewhere
too, it was getting hectic. Lisiarna shuddered
and her skin crawled. *He never did do things in
half measures.*
Raijin had climbed into the wagon with her from
the street. The Draul removed his armour disguise
and from the troubled expression on his face, he
felt Eckard's reach also.
'He better be careful, all that energy. I have
never felt anything like this before.' Raijin
stated, seating himself down, opposite Lisiarna.
'I have, many arcs ago.' Lisiarna said, a memory
flooding her vision. She shook the images aside
and returned to the present here and now.
'He's close by, I'll find him before he *drowns,*
calm him down and...' Lisiarna began, but Raijin
cut her off before she could finish.
'No, you are too close too this. Personal.
Besides my *Green* energies will cool the effects
of the *Grey*. And maybe the Southron can help with
that sword of his. And importantly I am in the
whole big-bad soldier disguise' Raijin said.
*Ah yes, Judeson. That sword, that's what is
emanating the Red. Of course; the thing was*

embedded, would have be dormant for some time, but now it was active again. Somehowm still so many questions.

Lisiarna shook aside her dwelling thoughts.

'Right yes. You are right. Find him and the Southron. I shall meet our little... contingent on the outskirts. In the Downs.' Lisiarna replied, ironing out there plan.

'Here's hoping Eckard knew what he was looking for.' Raijin answered, the lithe Draul throwing back on his Hari'al disguise.

'Don't worry about that I am sure Eckard will be making a great deal of noise to bring the Sparrow out of hiding.' Lisiarna said. Thoughts going to whatever debacle Eckard was currently undertaking.

Raijin nodded and exited the coach.

Lisiarna called out to the Jarvie to take her out into the Hasperneara Downs, trading a cesspool city for a swamp, always seemed agreeable at this point.

*

Judeson was smack bang in the middle of a mind-bogglingly disastrous situation again. Like several times before over the last couple of weeks, it was mostly because of a absurdly tall Northman.

'I will ask again for the benefit of the most deaf and dumb amoung us. Where can I find a person that goes by the alias of *The Tulisi Sparrow*?' Eckard stated louder than he had just moments before.

Judeson had thought for one brief, fleeting moment that this dingy pub may offer some respite. He and Eckard had not been greeted with the most hospitable reception as they had walked in. Narrowed, distrusting gazes held on them for far too long. But after awhile, the hooded eyes at moved off them, Eckard had got himself and Judeson two frothing pints of ale. That had had been a minute ago. Now, the whole place had gone straight to the Void, as far as Judeson was concerned.

Eckard had thrown several dozen silver hexagonal shaped coins from out of his coat. The money pieces he had scattered off dozens of patrons on dozens of tables. The patrons tussled and tangled with each other attempting to grasp the silver pieces. It was a frenzy; the huge dull bronze skinned oaf that had shadowed them on the way in, was surrounded by six hangers-on, five men and a rough looking woman all clenching their fists. Eckard had devotedly not given them any coins.

'Shut your hole, you void-damned idiot, we will have no talk of subversion in this establishment.' The big ringleader called out to Eckard.

Judeson had noticed none of the patrons, fighting over the silver pieces had bothered to answer Eckard's inquiry.

'I asked a simple question, friend.' Eckard replied, raising his glass to the big man.

'What you asked was treasonous. The penalty for you and your ugly out-lander buddy will be to buy me a pint and shut your trap. Then maybe we will let you go on your merry way, friend.' The oaf stated matter-of-factually, a evil looking grin crossed his features and his tongue dripped audibly with vitriol. From behind the hulking man, his six companions smirked like idiots.

'Judging by your torcs of command or lack thereof and the solitary one you do posses is almost completely unmarked. I quite comfortably presume that you are a low ranking member amoung whatever temple you are attached to.' Eckard grinned furiously back at the big Hari'al.

'If you keep up this horse-shit idle chitter-chatter you are going to have to buy all of us all the bloody food and ale in this pub.' The enormous Hari'al warrior proclaimed boldly.

Eckard dropped his smile for a moment, and Judeson saw those terrible dark shadows cross over Eckard's eyes briefly.

'Please friends, where is the Sparrow?' Eckard asked. A moment later the larrikin smile returned.

'Six, no damn it seven pints!' The gruff and increasingly boisterous Hari'al boomed. His square jaw grimacing and teeth barred he continued; 'For each and every bloody one of us.' Judeson's grip fell to an empty belt.

'I will spare no coin, no shard and no respect to someone who does not show it to others' Eckard rebutted back at the fuming Hari'al.

'What did you say Outlander scum?' The seething temple thug asked, moving closer. Judeson centering himself with cool, collected breaths for whatever was to come. *Another battle to come.*

'I said so everyone no matter how deaf, dumb, stupid and just plain ignorant, here - I wish to meet the fucking Sparrow.' Eckard spoke his deep voice booming throughout the dank tavern halls in a rising crescendo on each word.

Judeson swore he could see the steam rise from the bronzed oaf.

'And you Hari'al can go take a goat for a ride, if you wish.' Eckard followed up, this time in his normal quiet tone.

'You black-mane bastard!' The Hari'al roared, sweaty red-faced and voice echoing off the subterranean walls.

Judeson peered across to Eckard in alarm sensing something was about to inevitably happen. Other figures pushed aside their wooden stools and stood up from their tables. What Judeson saw in Eckard's face however was not alarm nor was it any particular of painted concern. The tall man was smirking in his lopsided manner, the wonky eye of his darting about and it appeared to be that the man would break out into laughter at any given moment. If they were not ripped apart in this grungy, dim lit pub, Judeson was considering a little murder of his own.

The Hari'al just before them made to start forward reaching across the table in a prolonged stretch. The bronze-hued man's confidence shown through in an arrogant smirk, his hand straying to rest on top of Eckard's half-emptied beer glass. Looking between the Hari'al and the Eckard; Judeson noticed the Collective man still retained an arrogant demeaning smirk. Eckard on the other hand, had dropped his trademark grin and his eyes had taken on a hint of cold iron the sky-blue orbs focusing on the Hari'al's outstretched hand. In that moment the Hari'al's arm came round in a haymaker swing.

The blow never connected. Eckard's hand moved in a blur, a shifting of his dark cloak in a mere moment and the Hari'al's palm lay impaled on the table top by a broad-tipped blade. Bleeding profusely all over the table, even as the man tried his utmost best to extract himself from his predicament. Eckard had stood up and was motioning for Judeson to do so, the Southron astounded by what had transpired.

'Fucking cunt!' The Hari'al howled as he grasped at his skewered hand with his free one.

The six burly lackeys of the Hari'al began to close in, encircling Judeson and Eckard in the darkened corner of the dingy pub.

'What the? Where did you have that knife?' Judeson gushed out in more a series of battered together words than any coherent sentence.

'It was his. He was going to attack us.' Eckard answered drawing his vision out throughout the slowly surrounding crowd of onlookers and more than likely possible aggressors, his smirk returning.

Judeson took up a fighting stance and said. 'Finally some sense can come out of your mouth.'

'Well I did have to wait' Eckard replied as he climbed on the table to scout just how many in the pub had chosen to act on their aggression.

'Ah yes the Void-Damned Rule. But he was trying to punch you, not void-damned kill you...' Judeson said.

'First off my dear Judeson, he drank from my ale, drinking from another man's cup is a most primal call to challenge, a great *nerthari* insult in fact, a dual.' Eckard swung back around on the rickety table top, drawing another blade from his black coat. He continued;

 'and secondly the 1st Edict dictates not attacking first specifically. What your opponent does to you should never be countered with the same, if they mean you harm, you should visit them with worse.'

'Your cursed rules are ever changing.' Judeson said, as he heaved up a nearby stool to utilize as a weapon.

It seemed this establishment's relinquishing of arms dictate did not blanket every persuasion of person. As the men that advanced toward them were quite clearly well armed with hatchets, blackjacks and knives.

'Riddle me this though, if that was a dual why are the rest of his buddies flanking us?' Judeson continued.

In less than a heartbeat the six lackeys of the impaled oaf and all manner of ruffians, cutthroats and less than desirableness seemed sent to descend on the confused Southron and the now smirking Mage.

'Collective Duels, they love their fucking partnerships they do.' Eckard said, laughing and then appeared to seemingly disappear, as heavy shadows blanketed the small room, obscuring almost every light.

'Zadma's mercy, for a moment then I forgot how peaceful the Northern Realms are.' Judeson hissed more to himself than anyone else.

*

'Enough!' A deep voice commanded, the sound booming through the tavern hall.

Judeson pushed aside a badly aimed punch from a rather young looking companion of the skewered oaf. Another lackey who had thought to rise again and join back in the hopelessly outmatched 'collective' duel stopped where he was on one knee. The thug's nose was broken and dripping endlessly onto his tunic. Judeson shook his head; of all six offsiders of the Hari'al, only the woman had posed much of a threat. , her small hatchet had missed one of his ears by a bees cock in the initial flurry of attacks. The five men had dropped like haysacks and their badly timed and badly aimed attacks had missed he and Eckard quite easily, albeit with a few feigns and pivots.

Most of the other pub goers who had stood up when the brawl first began to start had seemed quite

content to form a ring around them and not jump
in. Especially after Judeson and Eckard had
dropped the six thugs so easily.

Eckard sat atop of on of the still barely
conscious thugs, who screamed at him to be let
back up..*And cut his balls off!* Judeson shook his
head in disbelief when he saw Eckard was drinking
from a pint at the same time as he held down
someone trying to unsuccessfully kill him.

The two guards who sported the cudgels from
outside had come in. Several dozen-armed figure
circled around Eckard, Judeson and felled Hari'al
lackeys. The bronze oaf himself had finally freed
his hand from the tabletop but heaving out
Eckard's knife but now stood frozen, grasping at
his wounded hand and sobbing. The guards gathered
up the lackeys and the oaf, Eckard was allowed to
free the last thug. Judeson backed away from his
wounded would be attacker as the man was carted
off too .

'Absolute insanity! By The Lord's fucking mercy
what a mess.' The Inn Keep cried out, throwing
his hands over his head behind the bar.

'That's the least of our worries now, Hardigan.'
The owner of the deep booming voice announced.
The unnamed man strode forward from the pack of
armed guards. The man had a freshly shaven head,
not a hair on it and his skin was that of
midnight. Judeson guessed that he was of Berussi
origin or maybe even Promqual. Though there was
something else, something Judeson had not bore
witness to before. The new man had a criss-cross
pattern work of hard lines across his skin, like
like fissures in rock. The man almost looked like
he had a layer of scales over his skin. But
Judeson knew that was impossible.

Eckard spoke in a tongue Judeson could not

decipher. A slow, meticulous drawl of a language, each word drawn out liken to a hitherto curled up string.

The big, bald Berussi seemed to understand Eckard and nodded, though he did not look entirely pleased.

'And your friend?' The Berussi inquired, this time in Cestral, which Judeson understood.

Eckard turned to grin at Judeson albeit briefly.

'He's auditioning, new to all this, Pact and politics.' Eckard replied, returning to a language Judeson could understand.

The Berussi man considered this for a time, after a moment he gestured for the two doormen to return to their posts. The other armed contingent scurried away and ran down to the back of the bar. After a very brief exchange with the barman they all departed to the back-of-house, leaving Judeson, Eckard and the Berussi man alone the tavern hallway.

'He's certainly not new to busting heads, your friend is a skilled warrior.' The Berussi man stated, meeting Judeson in the eyes.

'You speak as if I am not here. I have a name and that is Judeson, perhaps if I knew yours we might form some sort of due respect.' Judeson said, bluntly.

Eckard chuckled to himself but did not add anything to the conversation.

'You're right, we are being most rude kind of akin having a pitched battle in a man's whole fucking pub!' The bald man sighed, his irate tone settling after a moment.

'The name's Aldrik. Though you may have guessed some call me the Tulisi Sparrow.' Aldrik answered.

'And why exactly do they call you that?' Judeson
inquired. He looked to his side momentarily at
Eckard who offered nothing again.

'That Judeson, is a very long story indeed.'
Aldrik replied, a small smile corssing his face.

'Sar. There are Hari'al, just outside!' One of
the cudgel bearing guards called from the door.
Aldrik looked livid and sprung to attention.

'This is your doing Magiker, void-damn you, you
brought them here.' Aldrik said, rage rising.

Eckard raised a calming hand in reply.

'Relax they are ours. In disguise, mind you.'
Eckard said casually, as if it were common
knowledge available for all.

Judeson was glad to see the clear confusion and
irritation painted all over Alrik's face. It
reassured Judeson he was not the only one alive
who was constantly being befuddled but Eckard and
his cryptic goat-shit.

Aldrik's eyes narrowed and he looked like he
might set all his men and women on Judeson and
Eckard. Thankfully instead of that, he called
back to the guard.

'Let them in, Linesmen.' Aldrik said.

'You are making the right, choice, together we
are going to cause some serious damage to the
Collective and the Rakoni, Aldrik.' Eckard said.

'You did not give us a void-damned choice,
Magiker.' Aldrik growled from beneath barred
teeth.

Judeson saw three full helmed figures enter the
public house with Aldrik's guards in tow. As the
group made to meet up, Judeson realised what
little choice he had ever been offered in any of
these affairs. It kind of felt like Eckard was
pulling him along the entire time. Glancing over

at the grim stormy expression of Aldrik, Judeson
felt he and this man might share quite a bit in
common.

4th Stanza

The ageless Path was left to the Bitter Cold

The banners broken upon the fold

What great minds and memories would turn to dust?

Of all the Empire's swords were wrought to rust

The Sound of horns and great War Drums

Where heard here and all Around

That Day; Imperial Walls crumbled to the ground

The End of an Era

(The Sundering of Caterium)

2034ATF -Krakios the Grounded

Bratoe spat into the grim muck. The foul taste in his mouth just would not void-damned go away. He felt uncomfortable. This whole ordeal was dragging on for longer than he hoped it would. Every time he raised the point that they could strike; the black clad assassin woman in turn refuted him. On that particular woman, he felt the most uncomfortable. She was emotionless, hollow and quite frankly unnerved him.

Bratoe had met a great deal of cruel, vicious men. Hell, the memories of the arcs he had spent in gaol where filled with the faces of downright evil bastard whoresons. But this Sofina woman was on another level entirely. She was void-damned scary.

Sofina stood close by Bratoe, unnervingly still, the woman's hard face drawn tight in concentration. Bratoe thought early on when first meeting Sofina she was a certain kind of pleasant looking. Sure her nose was a little too big, her jaw a little too wide but she was pretty in a rough and tumble sort of way.

Bratoe had thought she was the kind of woman he could become attracted to over a few pints and some friendly flirtation. But from the little details Bratoe had learned of Sofina over the last few days, his mind had drastically changed about the woman.

Down the windswept hilltop he and Sofina stood upon was the assembling camp of sell-swords and hired thugs. It had proven increasingly difficult in the day just past to actually join in as part of this ragged company. *The Honourable-fucking-Mister Dowry* had sworn they would be able to find and join a company of mercenaries being recuited by members of the *subversive Pact (whatever the hell this Pact was). Follow the trail of counterfiet coins-* Mister Dowry had said. *The villains will be easy to track; I assure you* he had said.

After being led down several false trails by informants (most of whom were street rat kids), Bratoe and Sofina had shanked a couple of mercs down in a *shantytown* alleyway. Stole a cryptic hand written note and finally found a greater company of mercenaries almost a days travel outside Haltin. They had been somewhat lucky though as the trail had gone cold around then, the idiots were lost and did not know where their 'Lady' -Bratoe assumed was the noblewoman that was in charge of the rag tag outfit. However just as Bratoe was about to start having to knock heads (or Sofina killed everyone there) a lone mercenary had found them and shown them to where this *Lady's* camp was. *Had to trudge through a void-damned mire to find the takers too* - Bratoe thought, spitting on the ground again.

Sofina turned on Bratoe with a disgusted expression. When he thought she was just about to say something the woman turned back to fixate on the mercenary camp.

Three days ago Bratoe had been in gaol. Locked up, without parole. Facing execution. Murdering his commanding officer and leaving his post was neither excusable nor forgivable, no matter how justified it was- Under Modern Law.

Bratoe reasoned and pleaded with the judges of the Court. None of the three had listened to him. About how Captain Clemmins had treated them, about how the good Captain was more than willing to sacrifice most of them to save himself from the Nerthari dogs. The whole campaign into the

Confederation had been a disaster and the captain had thought to save his own hide and leave his soldiers to die. Bratoe had been a mutineer sure. But he had done so for the greater good, for his men to return to their families. On returning into Collective lands, Bratoe and what little followers he had gathered had been promptly round up and whisked off to face trial *for desertion, for abandoning the defense of their homeland, for murdering their commanding officer.*

Three days ago Bratoe had had no hope of ever seeing his daughter again.

A certain Honourable Mister Ahjib had come into his cell three days ago, with a contingent of fancy dressed Hari'al. Bratoe had been one of those secret enforcers once. Before he slit the bastard Clemmin's throat from ear to ear. Ahjib had told Bratoe his trial would not go ahead if Bratoe killed some people for him. Ahjib told Bratoe he would be given a special poison to kill the people that he wanted gone. Bratoe had thought Ahjib could go take a donkey and that he did not owe Ahjib anything. That was before Ahjib had told Bratoe in words that kept replaying over and over in Bratoe's head now.

It would be a shame if your daughter were not given the opportunity you are being afforded now.

Three days on Bratoe had done everything the taker Ahjib wanted him to do. He had met the hard-faced bitch called Sofina. He had told her Ahjib would grant her vengeance against her sister's killer. Now Bratoe had followed the trail to the mercenary camp where apparently he and Sofina were to kill the people Ahjib named.

The Tulisi Sparrow, a black-maned mystic, a noblewoman going by Beatrice and a Southron with a giant sword.

Sofina was apparently interested in only one of them and Ahjib had no control whether she would do in the others, Bratoe was to make absolutely certain the others died. Seemed easy enough Bratoe had killed many, many people before. It had been his calling.

'That fool you hired in the swamp where is he?' Sofina inquired, her raspy voice chilling Bratoe to the bone. She was void-damned creepy.

'Stirring up trouble. Using our gold to try to sway some takers over to our side.' Bratoe replied off handily.

The fool *they* had hired in the swamp, as Sofina had so elegantly put it; was named Kamin, he had navigated them to this disordered camp. He was hulk of man, bronze skin like Bratoe's own. Both he and Kamin were of Salmian blood. But any relating factor Bratoe had with the man stopped abruptly there.

Kamin was vicious and seemed to take pleasure at the thought of bloodshed. Bratoe would do violence because it was what needed to be done. Kamin on the other hand seemed to revel to delight in the very notion of killing. Bratoe had unfortunately met quite a few men eerily similar Kamin in his brief stay in prison.

'Right then, sourced em, I did. You'll wan' to ere this' Kamin said coming up behind them, his loud and obnoxious manner seemed to be a tap that could not be forced closed.

At least with words anyway - Bratoe thought to himself about his Salmian recruit, Kamin.

'What have you found then?' Bratoe queried the man.

Kamin shook his misshapen head from side to side. 'Oh noes, big man. First come the coin.' Kamin

drew back his lips in what Bratoe propositioned
was supposed to be a smile, though it looked more
like a sneer from that of a wild dog.
Sofina sighed disapprovingly nearby.

Bratoe had bribed the boisterous Kamin with
thirty golden Crowns, the highest coin of value
in the entire Collective. Thirty was the average
annual earning of a Trade House Hari'al captain,
far too much for a common thug like Kamin.
Probably more money than the Primin had ever
seen. There was a catch though Bratoe knew Kamin
would drag his weight, as any common criminal
would do. So the bribe was in three parts, ten
for getting he and Sofina into the enemy camp,
ten for information and ten for when the whole
army was in chaos and Bratoe and Sofina could
kill the ringleaders.
'Fine. But the deal still stands, ten now, ten
later when we have the bosses.' Bratoe said
steely holding Kamin's challenging stare. The big
Salmian looked for a moment like he might jump
down Bratoe's throat. But Bratoe's countryman
backed down and nodded in acceptance, at least
for now.
Before Bratoe had time to continue, Sofina
interjected herself in the discourse.
'What did you find out, details...' Sofina said.
Her expression suitably devoid of emotion, her
voice that of bitter coldness.
Kamin looked lost for words for a moment. Taken
back by Sofina's ice queen persona, albeit an
altogether brief moment. Kamin soon found his
tongue as quick as he misplaced it.

'Most of the thugs are being led, well that is to
say being led by coin by a noble lass. Fair head

of pretty golden curlies, like the light from the Far Above she is. A body of a goddess- men and women dream of taking...'Kamin grinned furiously. Bratoe swore he could see the brutish man's face flush with excitement.

'I know who you speak of.' Sofina stated, her gloved hands resting at where Bratoe presumed her weapons belt was. Concealed underneath the leather folded layers of her black cloak.

'What else?' Bratoe questioned.
'That tasty lil' piece is followed on hand and toe by a bunch of oddlookin Hari'als' Kamin replied.
'How exactly are they odd looking?' Bratoe inquired.
'Uniforms look old, they do, like from arcs ago. Perhaps they nicked em. Probably no one took much notice in the slums. But we spotted em. Not fooled. Don't think they are Har'als that is for sure.' Kamin replied.
'I'm surprised you have the capacity to think' Sofina muttered her breath. Bratoe did not know whether it was a joke or just more acid flung by the cold woman.
Bratoe raised his hands in question surely Kamin had more.
Eventually the brute continued.

'There is also Berussi pirate, a filthy Tulisi half-blood, he's got at least a score of mean looking cut throats in his charge. Oh and a black-mane and a Southron killer, biggest sword I ever seen on that one. Surprised he can lift it.' Kamin prattled.

Bratoe drew Kamin back to the point.

'The Nerthari is there anything strange about him?' Bratoe asked.

'Apart from how fucking tall he is?' Kamin replied.

Sofina scoffed behind them.

'Yes apart from how fucking tall he is.' Bratoe groaned.

'Rumour has it, the beanpole son of a whore is a magiky-man, boils people's blood or some shit.' Kamin answered, dead serious though Bratoe thought it all sounded like childish nonsense.

'That will do.' Sofina said, stalking away down the hill into the mercenary encampment.

Bratoe handed over the ten *crowns* to the eagerly grateful hands of Kamin who stashed the gold coins in his leathers with earnest zest.

'See you down their boss.' Kamin stated, retreating back the way he had come.

Bratoe, alone, thought of his daughter. The one shining light in his life.

*

Judeson bore witness to yet another fight break out. Two men and a wild haired woman, clawed, grappled and screamed at each other. Eventually falling into a tumbled heap of limbs. Meanwhile dozens of eager onlookers gathered to get a vision of the altercation break out in the mud.

'Again.' Judeson said, pulling himself back upright, stretching out his aching limbs.

Whatever it was that was in the supply crates he and Eckard were moving was definitely a heavy load.

'Unchecked aggression, Judeson, they will soon have an outlet for that.' Eckard answered, striding over to the ass-drawn wagon where several more crates waited.

'Somehow much like Yormeth's poor brainwashed fodder, I think these fools don't know what is waiting for them.' Judeson said.

'Everyone must fight for love, Judeson. Then they will succeed, that's the secret.' Eckard propositioned, placing the pine supply crate down in the pile of stacked ones. His grin was unnerving and the fact that he winked at Judeson made it worse.

'Ok then, what love do these thick-heads fight for?' Judeson inquired, watching the procession of grimy, poorly disciplined and raucous mercenaries scuttle along the ancient ramshackle road where they had made their camp.

Several leagues away there were signs of a modern highroad. White paved stone was in use there much like the pale powdery substance Judeson and Eckard had seen in storage in Leteash. Suspiciously so this Collective shared a great deal with the vicious Rakoni and Judeson was certainly not at all at ease with it.

'The same love the Channellors manipulate so wholly in most societies.' Eckard answered, quickly as a darting arrow in a brisk wind. Back to the storage crates, Judeson grabbed the last one with him.

The fight had broken up finally.

'Which is?' Judeson questioned. A group of sell-swords had broken off the beaten track and looked to be attempting to break off a few limbs from each other respectively. *It had been like this nearly all day* -Judeson realized.

Overhead in the Far Above, the Twins could be spotted coming out. Darkness was falling. Night was on the march as day reteated.

'The love of self, being so involved with oneself is easy to miss what is happening all around you. Thus Channellors are able to manipulate pride, gluttony and hunger for power from those that sought it so recklessly.' Eckard answered, placing his burden down. Judeson followed suite. Both men finished with the pile withdrew further into the haphazard patchings of canvas tents, cooking fires and bedrolls.

One of the mercenaries had floored another with well-placed knee to the guts. The triumphant victor stood over his fallen foe, within a puddle of mud. Several others brawling group backed away, deeming the altercation over.

Aldrik swung his gigantic grey mare just ahead of Eckard and Judeson, he had had just arrived. He and several of his troops had acquired horses someway down the high road. Now that a fight broke out the man was signalling for several of his mounted subordinates to attend the scene. He must have observed some of what was said between Judeson and Eckard as he imminently quipped in.

'My men and I fight for justice for the hope of one day being free from tyranny. There is no love in that, Magiker.'

'There is' Eckard pointed out.

Aldrik narrowed his gaze and waited for Eckard to continue.

'The Love of freedom' Eckard finished.

The fight just ahead of Eckard, Judeson and Aldrik was eventually broken up and the packs of howling hangers on scurried away. Aldrik's troops who now claret and blue coloured surcoats over plate or chain mail herded the altercation's participants into separate directions.

Aldrik shook his head with earnest.

'No Greycloak, I and my warriors are here because the Collective and the Rakoni cannot be allowed to succeed.' Aldrik said, swinging his giant mare around away from Eckard and Judeson he continued. 'That and you kinda gave me no other option but to flee Haltin'

With that stated, Aldrik rode away with his men and women in check behind him over to a section of sparsely wooded high ground, noticeably far enough away from the mercenaries in the muddy valley, but perversely close enough to keep and eye on the camp.

'He called you Greycloak' Judeson stated, he and Eckard exiting the sellsword encampment and starting up a narrow ancient cobbled path.

It was their own personal campsite according to Eckard. Lisiarna, Raijin and their their score or so of guards sequestrating the spot when they had first arrived. Another raised section nestled just above the vale where the mercenaries were camped. The *Pact's* camp was inside of a weather beaten and crumbling fort of seemingly ancient origins. The mould ridden and vine tangled walls jutted out to meet Judeson as he and Eckard came closer.

'He did, it's just another name for a Mage of the Pact.' Eckard said bluntly. Some off in the near distance the wind was howling.

'What was all that shit about love? Surely a jest, these are warriors fighting for their freedom.' Judeson inquired.

'I was serious, come.' Eckard answered raising an eyebrow on his lazyeye, he did not wait for Judeson to respon. The beanpole man strode further into the ancient ruins.

'You're an odd man.' Judeson stated, following Eckard in.

Eckard looked back over his shoulder briefly as he walked on.

'So I keep being told.' Eckard said with a lopsided grin.

Judeson paused for a minute, glancing back around for a fleeting instant, Eckard following suite just ahead of him.

'We are being watched.' Judeson stated matter-of-factually.

'I believe they are shadowing us, perhaps to strike as unawares later' Eckard replied in a whisper and laugh.

Great - Judeson thought, more problems.

*

Eckard and Judeson stepped into the old dim lit ruins, as night fell. The constant spinning and roaring in his ears had eased up a bit, but he could still feel a constant tugging and pushing from the Arcane Sea. Lights and shapes danced in front of his vision, Eckard could feel the magik energies flow the others close by. A slight stench of the void lingered somewhere in the near distance. *Well the others did warn him.* Eckard reasoned. *Just like what was to come in the morrow, there was no way to back out of it now.* Most of the other outcast Pact members were present in the squalid brickwork chamber. A fold out ply wood table had been placed dead centre. Sitting on a tree stump was Raijin in full Hari-al battle armour, minus the full helm, which rested as his steel cased feet beside him. He certainly looked the part of one of those bastards with the helm on Eckard thought.

Across from Raijin, Prestan stood long elongated arms folded across her. She had a iron plate-guard across her chest and and repeater crossbow strapped to her back with quarrels strapped to her hard boiled leather belt. Some doubted the Kobold as warriors, but Eckard had saw the creatures in a pinch and he was sure Prestan would hold her own.

Several Draul, also in Hari'al armour and a half dozen Aurmen in similar garb stood behind them. The Retrievers, the company of Kobold tasked under Prestan's command spanned the outer edges of the room and some outside the far door peering in. Lisiarna was seated at the far end of the table across from Eckard and Judeson. She was in her form of the noble lady from DarvisPorte. The form was framed around a real life noble, a snotty nosed she-bitch that Eckard could remember vaguely from arcs ago. Probably around the same time he had first met Lisiarna. The form Lisiarna had assumed though rather regal looking now, was dressed in a simple silk travelling gown, nothing overtly special that was for sure. Lisiarna'a eyes remained that brilliant emerald green just as they always did. Eckard could see the energy swell and eddy around Lisiarna and for a moment swore he witnessed her true face behind the mask.

Aldrik arrived with a stern looking soldier of his retinue. The woman was a Dazral breed and she seemed on edge about something.

'So everyone is here' Aldrik striding into the room with confident poise.

'The Tulisi Sparrow, I presume.' Lisiarna said.

Aldrik nodded in acknowledgement.

'Aldrik, Raijn, Prestan and umm...' Eckard declared to Aldrik, signaling to the members of the Pact one by one until he got to Lisiarna and completely forgot what this alias was called. *Ah void-dammit what was it again?* -Eckard thought.

'Beatrice' Lisiarna finished for Eckard with a little knowing smile.

A flood of memories came back to Eckard. About the real Beatrice and about how he and Lisiarna had met. Unfortunately though right now there was no time to dwell on the past.

Judeson spoke up.

'There are people in the hired help watching us. Perhaps they mean us..ill feelings.' The big Southron said in a clearly concerned voice.

Raijin tilted his head in puzzlement at this.

'Are you certain friend Judeson?'

'They were watching us' Judeson concluded. 'I'm sure of it'

'Even if they were that is the least of our worries' Lisiarna said, unfolding a ancient looking papyrus map of the region they were in.

Eckard read the piece, much as he had down with all the maps, both old and new he had seen over the last ten arcs. The Hasperneara Downs spread out on the crinkled roll in a sequence of rough illustrated woodland and valleys. The noticeable humps of hills and blue streaks serving as creeks and estuaries.

Thick deep blue lines formed the tributaries of the massive freshwater lake of Ulrico; the Helan to branching off from Haltin and going east into the Yunlands and south Fartheilm and the larger Salmian River delta could be seen to the west, several dozen leagues from their current position. Due south from them was a ominous illustration of impressive looking foritfaction, past a woodland and over a small river. That was their target – The Woldte, an ancient Imperial era fort, now the Rakoni and their Channellor masters' forward command post in the Nertheilm.

'What worries us the most currently?' Eckard inquired. 'Apart from the fact that we are going to be raiding a near-impregnable fortress with a rag tag group of thugs and exiles.' He chuckled in good humour, though no one else joined him.

From the back of the room Prestan joined in.

'The Rakoni know we are coming. The underwheres below is a flurry of activity. Our scouts report in the Southrondor, they are sending more and more raiders underground each day. The Guilds have done nothing to stem the flux.' Prestan stated, a discernible bitterness to her scratchy voice.

'So the plan remains the same then. Aldrik, Judeson and Eckard you are to go with Prestan into the tunnels underneath here. There she will show you way into the bowels of the Woldte. Meanwhile Raijin and I will draw the attentions of the Channellor and his Void Callers and...' Lisiarna spoke as the voice of authority, quiet and assured. She proceeded to pause for some time, her brilliant emerald eyes passing over to Eckard and Judeson.

'...and whatever assassins they have sent.' Lisiarna finished.

Eckard witnessed a confused expression cross Judeson's features at this. In a way he felt sorry for the man, caught up in all the events, which were already well underway, and forever catching up. Eckard however knew that he would need quite some time indeed to explain everything to his companion Judeson:

At a later date - Eckard reasoned.

'Right then, let's get started shall we?' Eckard said, grinning from ear to ear. His excitement could not be contained. Every other member of the

room looked at him like he gone completely
insane.

In a way Eckard believed they may be right.

*

Eckard and Judeson met with Aldrik the following
morning. After a few hours sleep, the big Berussi
dismounting his horse as they approached.

'You know most of these fools, will die this
day.' Aldrik said to them in faint whisper, he
leaned closed to them as he was speaking.

Eckard merely nodded grimly, as if he were
receiving his last rites.

'It's entirely possible.' Eckard whispered back.

Judeson could not believe what he was hearing.
Was that all the mercenaries were for?

Before he had any time to reflect on this
revelation, a score or so of burly, mean looking
sell-swords appeared on the crest of a mound.
Their leader, a bronze hued man with a head like
a boulder grimaced at them. Judeson glanced
across at Aldrik and Eckard who both looked back
up at the group on the hill. No words were
exchanged. Several tense moments passed. A minute
later and the score or so mercenaries departed
back over the hill and onto their separate camp
near the river.

When they had gone from sight and vision. Eckard
snorted. Judeson turned seeing the absurdly tall
Nertharnlander grinning righteous vigour.

'Something tickle the funny-bone, Eckard?'
Judeson inquired, surprised.

'The fucking ugly one.' Eckard smirked back at
Judeson.

'Hate to break it to you but you are the
prettiest picture on the mantle piece yourself.'
Judeson joked with his Blood brother.

'Fair call.' Eckard proceeded to point one finger at his own cheek. 'No it was the criss cross body paint across his neck.' Eckard replied with a smile.

'So he had a tattoo' Judeson answered, confused.

'You only get those from deserting or worse yet barreling out completely from service. It is a great shame in the military. Pretty much a stamp for a man with nothing more to give.'

Alrdik grunted.

'I think quite a few of these individuals probably have similar markings.'

'And?' Judeson inquired further.

'They could be from anywhere for all we know.' Eckard answered. 'Explains why they are whoring themselves out into mercenary work in the Collective.'

'Or it could be a marking who choose to distinguish himself as a ruffian.' Judeson replied.

Eckard nodded in agreement.

'How very astute reasoning, either way it does give off a sense that these men are not the most upstanding of citizens.' Eckard reasoned.

Judeson shrugged. Where Eckard was going with all particular line of reasoning was completely and utterly beyond him.

'They are mere sell swords in your humble opinion.' Judeson offered, sarcastically.' And ones that will soon contribute their lives' Judeson followed up.

The idea that Eckard and the others thought so little of the men and women they hired to do their bidding still rocked Judeson.

'And in my humble opinion I do disclose that these 'mere sell swords' are simply perfect the way they are' Eckard replied.

Whatever connotations and hidden meanings lay in the stubborn Northman's words, Judeson did not care enough to pry further to discover, the foul taste in his mouth was not settling as it was.

5th Stanza

To ensure our safety with the rise and rise of the Cor-Dazral Collective we must pave the way for other Aurmen nations. Our march toward Modernity has only just begun. We must halt any advance of chaotic rhetoric, either that of the Fartheilm 'Free-towns' anarchy, the populist shortcomings of the so-called Knight-Reclaimers or the unethical debauchery of the alien Draul or disgusting barbarism of the Kobold.

Now we as a race stand at a precipice with Damnation beneath us and hope just near to us: We as a race under the watchful and graceful gaze of our Lord and Saviour -Talus must unite and the Collective must grow and endure to ensure that we continue on our prosperous and blessed path. Neither manipulative Kobold nor devious Draul shall stop us, and the barbarians in the Northern Wastes will falter and fail to stop our march into Modernity. Horse-takers, scoundrels and scum will not take our land from us. And we will unite with the rising industrious Rakoni so that we can grow and prosper even more.

- Judicirum Rulings – The Common Charter of Peoples of the Collective

The Honourable Judges; Benton Shivar, Pieter Margan and Varies Beladan the 3rd

Bratoe found the void-damned assassin woman more
and more insufferable. She ordered him about as
if he were her mule. She looked down on him like
he was filth, to *the Pit with her.*

Sofina had up and disappeared an hour ago.
Stating she was beginning the plan. Bratoe had no
the faintest idea what she was up to. But he was
quite sure it would prove fatal toward whoever
she was hunting.

Meanwhile he had a job to do. The company of
assassins was being ordered into formations and
marched up the hill where the Noble lady and her
retinue had camped last night. The ranks of mercs
marched by the ruuined ancient stonework tower
now. Bratoe spotted the beanpole blackmane and
the golden haired noble lady nearby.

Bratoe turned toward Kamin, the hulking bronze
skin Salmian with a head like a boulder and a
body odour that you anathematize a warhorse.

'I need you to upset the balance.' Bratoe stated
to the more bluntly.

'The fuck does that mean?' Kamin looked back at
him empty of emotion.

'Do what you do best, hurt them anyway you know
how.' Bratoe answered back with barred teeth.

Kamin smirked at him with all three of his
remaining teeth. Without a word the bulky hired
brute marched off into the direction of the
felled Imperial tower where the Nertharnlander
and the pretty blonde had disappeared into the
derelict tower.

*

Eckard brushed past the mould-ridden wall and
followed Lisiarna into the open expanse of the
inner tower.

'Would did you make of breakfast?' Eckard
inquired with a slight smirk.

Lisiarna rolled her eyes in response.

'Fishing for complaints?' She said.

'It's called feedback and it is instrumental in
improving art' Eckard replied.

'Oh so you are artist now.' Lisiarna teased.

'I try' Eckard shrugged.

'Just as you and your angry young companion try
to sow the seeds of chaos wherever you go.'
Lisiarna said.

Eckard rubbed at the thick uneven hairs at his
fresh beard.

'Ouch.' Eckard replied.

The creaky protest of the rotten door behind them
sounded off, dreadful and uninvited. The man that
strolled in was like a metaphor made absolute to
the uninvited.

Kamin pushed Eckard aside with one strong arm on
Lisiarna's unexpected entrance. Eckard stepped
aside with little resistance and even performing
a somewhat exaggerated mocking bow on the Kamin's
passing of him. The hulking built and bald Bratoe
smirking furiously at the sight of the new
arrival, Lisiarna appearing petite beneath the
man's unwanted gaze and her half pulled back dark
green cloak, she withdrew her hood and offered
Eckard a quizzing stare which he replied with a
shrug and refrained sneer.

'Well who might you be then?' Kamin said stepping
closer to the slight form of Lisiarna with every
word.

'Beatrice' Lisiarna uttered pulling her rosy face
tight in annoyance.

Kamin was not deterred as his mouth fell upon
looking Lisiarna up and down.

'Eckard what is this thing?' Lisiarna remarked turned to Eckard from across Kamin's shoulder, seeming to elect to ignore the huge bulking Salmian.

'A blade for the cause.' Eckard stated in reply mockingly, with a rye grin appearing.

'About to defend yours and mines homelands milady, most dangerous it will be, might not even return, how about a kiss then or a dance? One where our feet don't ave to be on the ground.' Kamin announced arrogantly, inflating out his chest as he did so.

'I wouldn't.' Eckard cautioned holding one hand up to his dark beard.

Kamin turned his head back to look at Eckard and granted the man a righteous smirk, switching back to ogle Lisiarna just as fast, the man started towards her slowly with both large hands out to clasp her until he titled into a full sprint. Lisiarna's eyes closed and she struck out two fingers in a blur towards the man level with his neck and flicked them down suddenly as if swatting an insect. A shimmering of air particles scattered towards the boisterous Salmian. Kamin's huge form crumpled like a rag doll as he held his throat in clear agony and fell against and coincidentally pummeling himself against the masonry block wall; the force of the collision by Kamin causing yet more cracks and fissures to form, the ancient stone caving in considerably to accompany the big man's impact. Lisiarna was quite forceful with her *Red* when she wanted to be.

'I did warn him.' Eckard said springing his mischievous grin and laughing profusely out his nose.

'Idiot!' Lisiarna stated shaking her head and

walking over towards Eckard.

'I do hope there are more reliable mercenaries in this company of yours then this Primin.' Lisiarna indicated.

'Not really most of them are pond scum you would not wish upon your worst enemy. Shall we?' Eckard said gesturing for Lisiarna to accompany him outside the sunken old watchtower.

Lisiarna rolled her eyes at him, but there was a small smile afterward. She went out first with Eckard following close behind in her wake.

The gates that marked the entrance into the ancient Imperial tower were broken down and rusted to near nothingness. Vines tangled around the broken cobbled pave stones leading up to the empty, ancient gates. Eckard and Lisiarna dodged and weaved the aged obstacles as they made their way down to the dirt track.

A half league down the makeshift road Prestan and her company of Kobold Retrievers waited for them. The squat reptilians, fully armoured and sporting steel-case packs across their backs. Eckard for a moment imagined they looked somewhat like mailed tortoises. He kept the jest to himself, sometimes he could could at least.

'Into the dark?' Prestan asked. Though Eckard was sure there was no question about it.

Judeson appeared a moment later, with Aldrik and the latter man's uniformed rebels.

'Here we go again.' The big Southron stated. Lisiarna sighed.

*

It had been tediously slow going from the very moment they had entered the underground. The ground was uneven and jagged; razor sharp rocks adorned the walls. When they had been close the

light of the tunnel's entrance had helped
somewhat. After ten minutes in that light was a
distant memory.

Judeson had walked alongside Alrdik's soldiers
and several of the Kobold Retrievers.
Circumstances had changed, Judeson had lost track
of many of the men and women he had started out
with. He had not seen nor heard Eckard since they
had entered. Several used lamps ignited by tinder
and fuelled by oil, though as it turned out- not
nearly enough by far. Many of the mercanies left
struggling in the darkened gloom, the scattered
lamps only reaching so far. Those sporting lamps
had attempted to cover the distances. But the
tunnel spirialled and narrow at point, forcin
this action into the realms of improbability.

 Prestan and the majority of her Kobold had taken
the vanguard and were leading them ever onward
with the their raspy voices, the vocals
travelling well in the dark confines of the
passage. Several Kobolds had taken to walking up
and down the lines of the staggering, blinded
aurmen. The Kobold seemed quite adept at seeing
in the utter darkness.

Many of the sell-swords cried out in pain, every
now and again. Knocking themselves on the
aforementioned protruding stones. Some slipped in
the dark, extremely colourful curses sounded off
in conjunction and gods were called on to answer
for what was happening. Judeson kept his feet and
and followed in the Kobold's commands as they
were heard.

The tunnel had eventually become more and more
narrow as they trekked on. Judeson was forced to
crouch after a time. Though as to what time it
was at all he could not be sure of.

Eventually the tunnel had opened back up into a

huge square shaped chamber that could accommodate almost half of their little army. Though this was an extremely tight squeeze to say the least. In the panic some men and women sought to push further ahead or fall back and were wedged between each other. At some point the steel encased cube they were in was lit up, albeit in a dim glow glow.

Prestan apparently activated some hidden switch – Eckard had said in earshot of Judeson. The Northman had disappeared again shortly thereafter somewhere in the throng of Aurmanity and Kobold.

Several moments after their expedition into the gloomy confines out of the steel walled cubic room they had been set upon. The ringing steel of weapons clashing and small whizzing projectiles echoed off the walls in a loud crescendo. Judeson smelt spilled blood and bile. At certain points he saw pivoting, scurrying forms and angry, sweating faces of fighting men, women, some of their own. Kobold Retrievers also, fleet of foot and sporting crossbow and small close quarter blade-arms. Against them; Judeson witnessed, twisted, snarling faces, some scaled, some in blackened iron, others in boiled leather, faces and arms covered in thick tufts of dirty hair and some others that unmistakable pale tone of a Rak...Judeson swept aside several attacks on him and some of his the sell-swords near him. But never did he make direct contact with any adversary. The enemy was probing for weakness but not dedicating themselves to a direct sortie.

After several barbed exchanges, screams of rage and frustration and taunts, the enigmatic enemy all but disappeared. The noncommittal *fighting* stopped before it really started. They were left alone with the dark again, this time the men and women sweated and panted in the humid

underground. Judeson feared that the true horror
was only just beginning. Eckard's voice had
reverbated off the narrow rock walls and urged
them in a direction just to Judeson's back.
Somewhere in the chaos Judeson had been turned
around, Eckard seemed to be everywhere all at
once.

Their next few hours had been spent navigating
through the gloom. The dogged enemies in the dark
had intensified their searching strikes. At
increasingly frequent rates, men or women
screamed out in pain. Every corner or crevice
held the potential of an ambush. Mercenaries were
snuffed out one by one, dragged down unseen
passages and butchered by violent and hostile
hands. Judeson held his ground, the blade of Jude
finally made contact with flesh, he hacked down
enemies that sought to take his life away. He
helped fight off an endless tirade of ambushes by
the squat, hairy adversaries that endlessly
dogged them. Eckard, Prestan and Alrdik called to
him and eventually he was trudging through grimy,
foul smelling brackish water alongside them.

The Nightmare dragged them all along.

Until the party came to a dead end, backs against
a wall of sheer and solid granite.. Prestan
pleaded for protection as she moved her fingers
up and down the molten rock. A metallic sounding
screech echoed across the rocky passages. It was
as if metric ton of steel plates were being slid
across the damp rocky ground they stood on. The
protest of forged metal scraping stone mixed with
the crunch of crushed armour and bones being
broken. Men and women howled in anguish. Snuffed
out like candles. Lamps went out nearby.
Something monstrous moved about the tunnels, a
killer of gigantic proportions. Mercenaries
announced that it was the arrival of demon from

the vast pits of the Void itself. In the stale and humid confines of the underground an impossible cold seeped in, the moss-covered walls felt cold as Judeson brushed against them. Eckard's voice called for calm.

Prestan announced they were safe, even as the whining protest of ancient gears and cogs heralded the opening of a door.

The sheer granite face parted and the Kobold and Aldrik's soldiers hurried in to the breach. Judeson and remaining sell-swords rushed in after like a flood unleashed.

Brilliant all-illuminating lights forced themselves into Judeson's peripherals. The uncompromising lights spanned out from crystalline structures high overhead. Narrow tunnels had been replaced with a vast sprawling cavern and he averted his eyes at every given chance. The sudden and unexpected lights blinded and burnt.

Judeson's attention was drawn back to the *doorway* they had come in from. The monstrous entity behind them was attempting to force its way in. A thunderous sequence of crashes announced this. The sounds of of scurrying metal feet and weapons brushing against the damp shale declared the squat Rak hunters joined the abomination.

Glancing around the company of mercenaries scattered about the broad chamber, Judeson realized just how many had been lost. *Like forgotten names in the dark now...*

Prestan and several Kobolds began chanting, a deep resonating bass-tone coming from the reptilians. Whatever the sound was that Prestan and the other Kobold had created- worked a charm in chasing off the puzzling but monstrous creature, as the battering at the door all but

ceased and the charging Raks turning distant.
Like they were retreating.

The phosphorescence given off by the crystals in
the wall became brighter still the further one
descended down into a vast opening, for the
cavern seemed to be a on a slight decline.
Further and further down it went. Machinery could
be seen scattered about haphazardly. Stonewalls
were joined by those of manufactured timber beams
and stainless steel racks.   The bright lights
became nascent as they went on. the descent
become more ominous, stairwell after stair-case,
abandoned room after empty hallway. No longer a
vast network of tunnels, but a labyrinth of
Kobold-made mines, living quarters and abandoned
manufacturing centres.

Less than a hundred- exhausted sell-swords
trailed in the wake of Judeson, who in turn
followed steadfastly behind Prestan, her Kobold
Retrievers and Eckard who strode forth all in
black. Judeson swore he could see tendrils of
smokey haze swirl about the man, but in a moment
it was gone again. Perhaps Judeson was seeing
things, either through strenuous overexertion of
his own or maybe he losing his mind.

Either thought was not a welcome one.

'Where are we going?' Judeson asked, forcing out
of dried and cracked lips, his voice matching his
tiredness.

Prestan pulled up short and with a raised a
three-fingered claw up, the Retrievers all
holding up right next to her on queue.

'These tunnels are infested with Gnolls, ancient
enemies from the arcs when we the Kobold dwelt in
the Deep Dark. The ashen-faces have ensnared them
as they have done with so many others. Despite
all this there is a weakness and only we know

where it is and how to get to it.' Prestan said in answer.

The Kobold Retrievers around her nodded their short snouts in unanimous accord.

'And that giant-fucking demon out there?' One of the sell-swords yelled in clear refutation from the back. A squeaky voiced dull hued woman with a head of messy mousy brown knots and sporting ill-fitting leathers.

'You all will be generously rewarded for your selfless deeds this day.' Prestan answered.

The mercenaries between deep exhausted breaths vented their frustrations.

'This void-damned place is a death trap!' One said.

'To the abyss with these lizard-bastards, I say we go back to the surface away from this!' Another announced.

'We should of never come here!' The squeaky voiced woman at the back declared.

Several Kobold strode forward into the dividing fold that was quickly forming between the mercenaries and the Retrievers. Judeson felt caught between the two. As he looked up Aldrik and his soldiers stood nearby. Aldrik held the ever-shaking body of one of his soldiers, a short, dark woman with a face of visible battle-scars.

'Show them!' Prestan announced, her softspoken voice curiously amplified above the shouts of the mercs.

The dozen Kobolds who had started toward what remained of the mercenary company took off burlap sacks from their backs and gently turned them out onto the dusty limestone floor.

Generous lumps of that greyish ore came out. The

mineral Judeson had heard Eckard refer to as; *oyra*. Of course he knew it more commonly as; *Kobold ore*. At least that is what his father had called it many arcs ago.

The mercenaries as one gasped in awe. After a handful of moments, the disparate group of a hundred or so of hired men and women snatched up the dull agleam *oyra* like hungry hounds.

'There is plenty more where that came from.' Prestan said joylessly over the commotion. 'Let's all get some rest and be prepared to move out. We are safe for now. But there is still a ways to go yet.' The Kobold followed up.

The sell-swords dispersed and sat down in separate little cliques, flopping themselves down like fish out of water onto the grimy limestone. Aldrik's soldiers sat down and exchanged food and water between one another. The Kobold Retrievers joined them and exchanged their own supplies.

Prestan, Alrdik and Eckard strode off a dozen or so paces away from their compatriots. Alrdik had handed off the wounded and unconscious woman he had held in his arms to a comrade. Judeson joined the triumvirate leadership group.

'You can put that chunk of iron away, if you like.' Eckard said..

Judeson still had Jude unsheathed, he hardly noticed the weapon felt lighter than usual, implausible as that seemed. He probably had had the blade in hand for sometime now. It was difficult to tell. He placed the claymore back into its resting place at the sheath on his back. As he did so, curiously a very faint echo, a voice called out to him.

It was his father.

Judeson looked around at the others, no signs of confusion.

No one else had heard it.

Some moments later; Judeson's grandmother's soft but commanding tone stated;

'Keep going, keep faith, and keep strong.'

Judeson shook himself. No. He was hearing things. He had to have been, just as he mistook seeing shadows around Eckard earlier, a trick, a sign of his fatigue showing.

'How far now?' Aldrik asked. The Berussi man's face a grim mask of determination.

'We find that a most difficult question to answer, half-kin.' Prestan said in answer.

Judeson had given up attempting to understand what these people were on about most of the time. Needless to say he did not bother to work out 'half-kin' was or how far they had to go.

'They will need to know....' Eckard interjected, he obviously was alluding to their mercenary escort. The grumbles and complaints were still ongoing behind them. 'Something at the very least.'

Prestan flared her large nostrils in a most exaggerated fashion.

The Kobold spoke amoung themselves in hushed tones. Their own language was a strange fortuity of snorts, prolonged hums and tongue clicks. Prestan turned back to Judeson, Alrdik and Eckard after a few moments.

'It will be near on one day at least.' Prestan said 'Maybe eighteen hours if we march hard. But the way may or may not be clear. It is most difficult to tell for us. Once there was a order and a clear path in these tunnels. Now the ashen-faces have had their way our people's creations are no longer easy to read. The Stone tells lies where once there was direction.'

Alrdik nodded as if the vague assortment of words Prestan had used was answer enough. The big man started back over to his soldiers. It was obvious he cared deeply for his people. A welcome sentiment for Judeson after witnessing the almost alien organized callousness of the Collective.

'We should all try and get some rest, we will march again in seven hours.' Prestan stated.

Judeson was not entirely sure how the Kobold were measuring time in this abyss nor now any of them were to get any inch of rest with enemies right at the gates.

The Kobold retired, hunkering down tin a distant corner of the factory floor leaving Eckard and Judeson alone.

'This is crazy. Even for us' Judeson said.

Eckard nodded and turned meeting Judeson in the eyes.

'It's about to get worse, there is dissent in the ranks.' Eckard offered, nodding toward the mercenaries.

Judeson saw the bronze skinned hulk staring at them, eyes of steel on that one.

As time crawled in the gloom Judeson got barely a wink of rest and dreaded whatever was to come.

6th Stanza

There will come a time, when all things shall fall apart

But by the Qhasa's Grace we shall be reborn

Madam-Channellor Makaresh

New Canon Charter

Verse 46

Aruku Shab Demul Tor -To stare into the Nothing

Extract interrupted from a Morba-Rakoni 'Holy Text'

Rakoni to Cestral Translation by the University of Tamisk for the Royal Court of Nesfhal

'It's going as well as most of our plans do'
Lisiarna stated.

She was back in the *form* of Ahma, wearing travel
leathers and feeling far more at ease. The
elaborate masquerade that was Beatrice proved
exhausting at points.

Raijin turned toward her.

'That badly, huh?' Raijin replied.

'Have we ever done any better?' Lisiarna asked a
hypothetical in answer.

Raijin nodded, choosing no more words to say.

Lisiarna starred out at the dark forested hills,
the winding jutted foothills angled up into the
steep impregnable range known as the Boundary;
the dividing mountain range that spanned most of
the Nertheilm. Somewhere out there was the
Woldte. Which was the ancient castle that was he
main forward command base of the Channellors and
the Rakoni. Somewhere far below was Eckard,
Judeson, Prestan and the Collective thugs they
had hired. The odds were against them all and the
Raks had hired help of their own.

Lisiarna had made the assassins out easy enough.
The fool she had *emoted* into a wall was possibly
just a distraction by the others. She knew there
would be more that Eckard and Judeson would have
to deal with. On closer ground was the cold-
blooded killer that had served Lisiarna's former
slaver. The woman Lisiarna was now wearing the
form of.

Beatrice - the real and original Beatrice. A
selfish, selfabsorbed narcissist had taken and
raised orphans with nothing to lose, to gain
everything for herself. The assassin that was
stalking Lisiarna and Raijin was one of those
unfortunate children, raised and brainwashed to

kill without question.

Lisiarna was not an assassin and she had not been one of Beatrice's lackeys. But she knew them well enough. She knew the woman out there in the dark, was going to hunt her without letting up.
Lisiarna knew of only one method to deal with rapid wolves.

Out in the distance near the river, many leagues away from the foothills of the Boundary a village burned.

'Your.... friend, uh… Afriti is facing challenges of her own, it would seem.' Raijin said.

'Another war, again. Void damned fools, the lot of them, full fanatical tribalism. .' Lisiarna said in answer. The billowing smoke wafted into the dense night air white on black.

The Far Above choked with the destructive vapours of what-was-once homes of innocent or perhaps not.

'We urged her.' Raijin answered.

'We asked for her help. The rest of what follows between the Yunsi, the Collective and the Confeds and all the rest that get caught up. Was not our doing.' Lisiarna said.

'You are starting to sound more and more like *him*' Raijin replied. The accented stress on the last word was clear as music to Lisiarna's eyes.
Lisiarna pushed back a fleeting moment of irritation at her companion.

'Wrendal is still helping us he never stopped. The Pact remains, it always has. ' Lisiarna spoke openly now, though it would appear cryptic to an outsider, she was certain Raijin would ascertain perfectly what she was putting out in the open.

There should have never been any secrets between them. One day she would tell Eckard everything and hopefully he would listen...

'I do believe now; Eckard suspected it was me reporting to Wrendal, despite the fact I never have met him. Eckard wrote notes in the book he gave me. Criticisms. Conflicting thoughts. The de facto leader has much to answer for in Eckard's eyes.' Raijin stated, drawing Lisiarna away from her inner musings.

'You would like Wrendal, cold, distant and suitably remote.' Lisiarna teased, gently tapping Raijin on one shoulder. ' I'll tell him the truth, there will be no more secrets after tonight.... we shall open a new chapter as they say.' Lisiarna said looking back out in the cold wilderness.

Raijin smiled back at her.

'The Pact endures.' Lisiarna said with a smirk.

'We are a melodramatic lot.' Raijin proposed.

'We are a strange breed' Lisiarna put forward. 'We are frequently our worst enemies.' She continued on.

Raijin's smile faded.

'Our other enemies out there are a little more concerning I think.' The tall-drink-of-water Draul said, changing the lightheartedness in an instant.

The grim oppressive spires of dark rock faces and low hanging black-as-night storm clouds drew Lisiarna's attention away from the petty wars of Aurman nations. The Boundary was a raw force of the Arcane, an anomaly of nature and in there, somewhere, hidden from prying eyes; the place of her former imprisonment and the present beacon of the Channellor's fanatic resolve lay.

'Eckard and this Judeson will make it. I know they will. Aldrik and Prestan will ensure they do.' Lisiarna announced. Though deep down inside a part of herself doubted her own words.

If Raijin read the emotion in her voice he did not show it.

'Well with the sensible latter two, the former two can actually accomplish something.' Raijin said.

Lisiarna granted Raijin a searching expression.

'A far more sensible team this time round.' Lisiarna urged.

'Oh somehow I am sure the sensible part will fly out the window with Eckard about.' Raijin stated with a smile.

Lisiarna knew what Raijin meant to say in his roundabout way.

'He's not going to do it is he? That was a joke surely. Arcs ago now, a terrible plan to begin with. He wouldn't, would he?' Lisiarna inquired.

'In his own little way, I think it is for you.' Raijin said in answer.

'..With veins of cold iron, the plans of war, of magik ever flowing, the Sea is here...' Lisiarna said. 'Spirits beyond. This night is going to shit.'

Raijin smirked from ear to ear across his pale azure face, the elongated almond eyes of crimson gleaming now.

'Oh stop it. You are getting as bad as Eckard. Can't I quote poetry from time to time?' Lisiarna asked.

Raijin shook himself, as if to awaken from a deep slumber.

'It's not that my many-faced friend. It's that I have never heard you swear until now. Seemed quite unlike you, in whatever *form* you are wearing.' Raijin countered.

Lisiarna smiled wholeheartedly back at Raijin.

If only Raijin knew just how alien some things in this world still seemed to Lisiarna.

Some secrets she would hold on to for a little longer.

'Well we have a siege to prepare for and quite possibly might I add, a terribly chaotic retreat to come.' Raijin said, striding off into the night.

'Sounds like more of the usual.' Lisiarna stated in reply. Raijin mock-saluted her in turn. Their in-joke was an old one and a most welcome change of pace.

Lisiarna turned her mind to her on ebb and flow. She had a *form* to remember and a trap to craft for one-who-would try to kill her this night.

*

The mercenaries had grown far more unmanageable. They were now in open rebellion. Aldrik and his soldeirs had called for calm, to no avail. When Prestan and the Kobold had called for them to move out, that was the final nail in the proverbial coffin. The alliance was in tatters. The sell-swords began turning on them.

Dividing lines as if they were about to commence a pitched battle had been drawn. On one side were the mercs on the other was Judeson, Eckard, Aldrik's soldier company and the Kobold Retrievers.

Eckard could read the anger, the thirst for blood and hatred directed toward them. His mind was open to the lingering thoughts of the mercenaries. Beneath that all, the *Void* lingered.

'We have had enough, we are not dying down here in the fucking dark' The Big bald Salmian that had identified himself as Bratoe and the makeshift leader dissenting mercenaries.

Curiously many of the cutthroats readily agreed with all his sentiments. Aurmen were fickle creatures after all.

Bratoe stared down Eckard with uncompromising rage, grinding his teeth in a snarl as he did so. Yet behind that clearly discernible anger was something else, something cold. The fire that raged on the surface appeared to be a front to Eckard who through the flow of the Arcane Sea could feel that this Bratoe was harbouring feelings quite distant from anger.

There was something else beneath the surface. This Bratoe fellow was not a common thug.

Eckard could sense a deep resonating sadness from the Salmian, a distinct flourishing of hopelessness. Eckard felt pity for the man, for he knew soon, he would have to end the man's life.

The Aurmen around them shouted and voiced their opinions; Cries ringing out for bloodshed or for it to all stop instead. Eckard looked back at Judeson who nodded with lips sewn tight at Eckard's gaze. Bratoe strode forward into the ring of Aurmanity now encased around him and Eckard: The bald Salmian holding up his broad sword in one hand and indicating toward Eckard.

'This man, this bastard-son of a whore witch, would have you die in this hole. He is not your leader and neither is his Southron pup. It's time we decided the right action to take. We fight the Raks but not in this fucking place. We fight em as they come outta the hole we push them back into the darkness from where they be coming...' Bratoe voiced boisterously to the rapidly excitable crowd around him.

'And be heavily outnumbered in the process. No I am not your leader and neither is Judeson, Aldrik

or even Bratoe himself but we are part of this.
The Raks have no idea how close we are, this is
the time and place we can stop them from entering
the Nerthielm, stop the invasion. And if we do
not succeed we deliver them the best Void-damned
mug hit we can muster, hightail it out of here
and prepare for their counter.' Eckard
interrupted, standing still and unyielding in
place, blade still safely in its hilt unlike his
aggressor standing close by.

'Is this your idea of honour big man? You think
anyone else gonna 'elp us, the Kobold ain't comin
apart that sorry fucking lot, neither are the
Draul we are in this for ourselves.' Bratoe
rebutted, gripping his bulky broad sword in both
hands now and widening his stance for attack.

'Neither will the Collective or Confederation
until the Raks are on their doorstep. We fight
now and assist any effort we will get in the
future…' Eckard said drawing his hooked sword
from his scabbard and standing tall directly
facing Bratoe.

'I've heard enough!' Bratoe shouted.

Bratoe closed in on Eckard, charging at full pelt
at the Northlander who pivoted in his stance,
tilting to the side slightly, shuffling his feet
as he did so. Bratoe's full uncompromising swing
met naught but thin air unbalancing the man and
sending him forward a step more than he intended.
Eckard did not counter and stood in place,
waiting. Bratoe repositioned himself upright and
swung his blade in a haymaker across the air,
into the direction of Eckard's neck, steel should
have met, the swipe all to fast, yet nothing.
Again Eckard shifted ever so slightly, ducking
and weaving away from Bratoe's reach. The bulky
Bratoe became infuriated swinging and hacking at

Eckard more frequently now; All of Bratoe's attacks making no real contact, landing no mortal blow, despite his unrelenting vehemence.

'Are you to dance about all day, boy or fight like a fucking man?' Bratoe mouthed off, breathing heavily and unsteady.

The bald Salmian lunged forward broadsword tip angling towards Eckard's exposed chest just mere inches distance away from stabbing true. Eckard brought himself into a crouch and slanted his weight to the left away from Bratoe's sword. Holding his scimitar in a reversed grip Eckard acquired the blade into the direction of Bratoe's pouncing form angling the curved sword across Bratoe's now completely exposed belly. The forward propelling momentum of Bratoe's attack caused the man to run full face into Eckard's countering move. Steel met flesh and a massive gaping wound appeared across the majority of Bratoe's abdomen, the Salmian stumbling still ever forward, stunned. Eckard pivoted off the back foot and gripped his scimitar in a more traditional hold, the young dark haired man slashing out at Bratoe's back, the blade biting deep into exposed flesh and driving forth gushing crimson blood.

Bratoe staggered on for several drunken steps before collapsing heavily onto the mason worked stone surface. Laying down his back, twitching unnervingly, blood and bile dripping freely from open gash marks, Bratoe's facial expression did not however read of pain to Eckard but of amazement like a small child on his first name-day. Eckard stood over the insufferable dying man and peered down into Bratoe's involuntarily fluttering eyelids, the likes of which caused Eckard to grimace away in aversion. The crowd around the fallen Salmian and Eckard standing

over him had become deathly silent like a
funeral. Eckard swung out one-handed with his
scimitar across Bratoe's pulsating neckline the
blade-slicing true through the soft flesh. Blood
spurted up meeting Eckard's face and the man
wiped some loose droplets away from his eyes and
cheeks. The jolting form of Bratoe continued for
several moments before laying out stiff.

'Is this what you desired? Fighting each other?
The Raks are coming to burn our homes and make us
slaves and you lot are transfixed on violence
among our own fucking kind!'Judeson shouted in
clear undistributed distaste. 'Well there you go.
Another idiot dies for fucking nothing.'

The previously lurid and animated throng of
mercenaries did not utter a sound all of them
casting heads down and looking worryingly about.
Eckard walked off out of the gradually disbursing
ring of Aurmantiy and into the foreboding factory
confines behind them. Judeson pierced a look to
as many men as he cared to before following
Eckard out of the spacious cavern hallway. Aldrik
and Prestan the shamed Kobold exited shortly
thereafter from the group proper and followed
also. The remaining swords for coin staggered
aimlessly about attempting to piece together what
had just occurred.

*

All Bratoe felt as he lay dying grasping onto his
last breath was pity. It was pity for his
daughter who would never see her father again.
Dear sweet Pertia. She was far too good to be
his. If there was ever a moment in his miserable
life he cherished it was *her, his daughter.*
Bratoe's heart was slowing; his blood ran cold
even as he thought such things.

He struggled to draw any air into his lungs. He

cursed all the decievers, all the manipulators; The Honourable Fucking Mister himself, Ahjib and all the other Judicirum cunts. *To the Void with em all!*

Bratoe cried, at least he felt a deep and resonating sadness, he had been used spat out and used again and again.

Once again Bratoe prayed that his sweet little Pertia could grow up and be free, be loved and find love; *unlike him.*

But before the darkness took him. Bratoe had one final parting thought that chilled him. His beloved child would never be *free.* She was a prisoner just like he had been. Just like they always were going to be.

...To the Void....

*

They were exhausted by the march. They were harassed by voices and snarls from the dark. They were near to finished with what supplies they had. And now their enemies harassed them again.

Any ounce of rest and recuperation they could have hoped for was taken by the darkness that threatened to swallow them whole.

The next wave of Gnolls and other things came not in a staggered disorganized clash like the first that had assailed them moments ago. This time the rush of attackers ran and moved like a well-oiled machine. The Primen soldiers formed rank and charged. Shields leveled and spears out.

Mercenaries fell, impaled on sharp edges now marred with blood and gore. Bile, blood and urine spilled from retreating mercenaries filled the ground. The haphazard file of aurman sell-swords crumbled.

Eckard motioned for Aldrik and Judeson to follow his lead. Prestan in the rear prepared yet another volley of Oyra-proppelled arrows, downing dozens of their foes.

Judeson followed the counterattack in with Aldrik and his soldiers. Pushing back their attackers. The battle was brief the Gnolls were completely routed. But the losses were staggering.

The mercenaries were ravaged, barely a shadow of their former numbers. Aldrik's soldiers, of who still stood, drawing in exhausted breaths were maybe half of their original total. Nearly every Kobold Retriever nursed a wound of some sort.

Judeson counted his luck and blessed Zadma under his breath that he had not been afflicted.

Glancing over at Eckard who had drying blood on one brow, the side of of his lazyeye, a deep, smeared wound just below the hairline. Judeson had not noticed before. The tall Northman was once again drenched in that impossible swirling shadow that lingered around. Even in the gloomy confines of this necropolis.

'Quickly there is no time, this way.' Prestan called as her savaged Retrievers made a calculated turn for battered down hallway.

A few grunts, *void-dammits and fuck-offs* followed but no one ignored the Kobold and followed after them. Prestan had led the survivors this far, they were not about forget that now.

*

'History is a harsh lesson.' Judeson said after awhile of prolonged silence.

He had just finished wrapping a linen binding around Eckard's head, strangely the wound had seemed to have somehow shrunk between the minutes they had been outside fighting off the Gnolls and now.

They were in a narrow cavern right at the back corner from where the others lingered in a huge

hallway; huge iron pillars barred the walls of
limestone and granite back from them. The floor
was of smashed up pave stone. A similar alabaster
shade and tone of the rocks Judeson had seen at
Letesah. Though the whiteness of the stone had
been marred by dust and mould here.

'If history has taught us anything it is to
outwit your opponent, steal his land and build a
city on top of his town, to prove a point.'
Eckard stated matter of factually. 'At least that
is the side the Channellors long to preach.'

Mercenaries, soldiers and Kobold, nursed wounds,
helped others to bunker down for much needed rest
nearby. What little food stuffs could be handed
out were. The last of the water skins were gulped
down at an alarming rate.

'What point would that be exactly? Judeson
inquired.

'A sharp one' Eckard answered flashing a grin
across at the brooding Southron. The blood above
Eckard's brow had completely disappeared.

Judeson turned and shook his head. 'You use
humour both as an ill-timed resource and also as
a insult oh so elegantly Eckard'

'And you and Aldrik are going to die of frowns
and distant contemplatives.'

Judeson narrowed his gaze at his companion. How
could the man remain so upbeat, so positive, with
their back against a wall and facing absolution?
There was no way any of this was funny, they were
slowly being *fucking bled out here.*

Eckard drew up his black cloak made to his feet.
Judeson followed in his wake despite himself and
they left the dim lit antechamber for the great,
high ceiling-ed hall where the others waited,
Prestan nursed her arm as she had previously
done. Aldrik still stayed Malio's ever-shaking

form; the woman had obviously taken another fatal blow since.

'What can we; as flesh and blood possibly do against a tide so harsh? Against lofty ideals of divine rights and the Oneness of the Shroud, of a God ever-watching and all-powerful.' Aldrik stated from the floor.

'We fight' Eckard answered, springing up from his crouch. 'We fight the tide that holds such fucking harsh and extreme ideals. We fight the hate of which tumbles and swells in a crashing wave. We fight the lofty fucking idealised and idolised tide.'

Eckard had began pacing around the dusty antechamber now, his bandage hung loose about his head and small droplets of blood dripped down his face and onto his tattered tunic and smeared down his chain-metal sleeves. Judeson nodded in the corner where he sat against the obsidian doorway, urging his comrade on but knowing the concussion could be getting worse. At least it should be. Normally concussions were enough to floor a man or eventually kill him. But as Judeson knew well by now, Eckard was very much something above and beyond normal.

Prestan looked up as did a handful of mercenaries, though a great deal more of the latter stared in shock at the uneven stone floor. As if the beckoning Void opened before them.

Eckard continued. 'For we fight my friends, not for survival. No we fight for something that is so much more.'

'Fucking right!' Judeson shouted in high spirits, his face a stone wall. Some mercenaries looked up from their self-absorbed wallowing abyss.

'Survival is giving in. Just focusing on barely surviving is precariously balancing at the tide's edge on a doomed island that is sinking in. No why would we fate ourselves against such a depressing outcome?' Eckard spoke, his tone rising in crescendo, emotion heavy in his voice now.

'Why do we fate ourselves against this dismal proverbial-fucking edge? We must rise above the depths; we must look onward to a purpose. Survival is just scrapping by as the Void comes to swallow us whole. A purpose is needed, a goal in mind to be used to fight, to fight against idealism to fight against against extremism. Fighting for and eventually with purpose is leaving that drowning fucking shore and charting a course to a new island where no Void-damned tide has come.'

A squat mercenary who wore a badly wound sling around one arm and possessed a pockmarked face of tanned hue started up at this. The acne scarring mixed with a face of rage.

'Would you fuck off with the entire mystic shit! We are going to all die here because of you and that blonde bitch that tricked us with coin into this hell!' The sell-sword blurted out.

Judeson grasped at Jude on his back posthaste. *Zadma's mercy they were going to fight each other again.*

Eckard smiled in answer.

Though as Judeson noticed it was not the *fuck-you-too;* mischievous, *come-on-then* smirk Eckard flaunted as he had done. The sky blue eyes did not gleam but just stared nonchalantly back at the angry little sell-sword. The smile did not extend further up then should be possible. There were no teeth shown. No challenge. Eckard seemed to be genuinely pleased, beside himself even. *He had gone void-damned bonkers.* Judeson thought.

The mercenary made a move for his blade and
Judeson followed up with unsheathing Jude.
Judeson was more than ready to fight even if he
imagined his bloodbrother Eckard to have left the
realms of sanity; they had been through so much
already.

Eckard did not stop smiling, but instead of
drawing a weapon. He sat down on the dusty floor
and gently turned out his burlap from his hip
onto the floor.

Out from the small bag came a flood of foods, a
feast of meats and a smorgasbord of beers and
wines.

First a tablecloth nearly the length of the hall
folded out. Then cutlery, brass cups, clay-pots
and side plates. The whole dining affair seemed
to arrange itself in turn. Slow-roasted Pork legs
followed, succulent, dripping with their own
flavoursome jus, smelling of hefty thick smoke,
drenching in rich dark honey and clove. Bowls of
steaming spicy-sweet sauce arrived, boat shaped
plates of steaming carrots, broccolini came.
Ceramic containers upon vessels whole roasted
spuds followed. Jugs of amber ale and rich red
wine sat delicately and perfectly poised nearby.
A feast that Judeson could not have imagined
arranged itself on the floor of a dusty, dead
city in front of his very eyes

The mercenaries, Retrievers and Alrdik's
soldiers, stood frozen and transfixed.

'Bless your gods or whatever you wish, apologies
about the lateness. Our ordering system is a
little askew and the delivery method takes quite
an age. But the chefs cannot be faulted, you will
see this in a moment.' Eckard announced.

7ᵗʰ Stanza

Pathing is one of the most difficult exchanges to master within the disciplines of using the Arcane Sea

Magik is all about balance, equilibrium of energies as previously touched upon in earlier chapters.

Spells or Exchanges as I prefer to call them are performed by balancing out what was

seemingly impossible prior to the Exchange. Into manifesting energy to change -to Turn for the Green, to Shift for the Blue, to Emote for the Red or to be Woven for those small few of the Grey. There is always a cost, both to the Magiker and to their surroundings.

In the case of 'Pathing (the transferal of form and energy from one area to another) this

Exchange is complete and utter. A form is broken down, torn apart and rebuilt back together piece by piece which is Absolute destruction and creation manifest.

The 'easier' option is to have a dedicated area transfixed with Arcane Energies. This takes arcs to do, constant nudging and easing of the fold between the physical Stone and the Arcane Sea. The harder method is to transfer energy (and form) from one place to another by memory and familiarity. This feat is incredibly dangerous to say the least. To the Magiker, to both areas the Magiker is departing from and arriving to and to anyone or anything else around the Magiker.

A Brief Introduction into the Workings of the Arcane Sea Vol. I

Sar Wrendal Dastin Morke

Sofina huddled in the tangled cradle of branches provided by the red gum. From where she safely nestled, hidden from prying eyes in the dark of the night she witnessed the chaos that unfolded. Off in the distance a besieged Fartheilm town descended into a war zone as two separate forces arrived to strike up old feuds. *Lord knew who those two forces were*. Sofina had more important matters on her mind.

The Rakoni reinforcements she had been promised eventually arrived. Merging into absurd lateness, the creatures were abrupt and showed disrespect. Still she passed that off as they were uncultured savages, little could be expected from them.

More disturbing for Sofina however had been the Raks sneaking up on her before. She had heard not a peep, nor sighted them or indeed sensed them at all until they were practically on top of her. She had wisely elected to not let her concern show. The parley had been brief, only one of the party of a dozen had spoke with her. As seemed the Rak's regular custom. The remaining near-men had stood silent and waited. That cold-minded dedication to a cuase Sofina could confide with.

Now Sofina, waited in her well-concealed vantage point. The dozen Raks had left her. Apparently they were meeting other *Ravagers* as they called themselves, together with *void-callers and Sofina's help they would find the heretic Pact*. Whatever that all meant.

Clutching the pouch of the poisonous liquid that Sofina had been gifted with from her Rak allies. The assassin counted her blades and throwing stars. Of which she had a great many. Some others of her trade liked to think she had too much but Sofina reckoned her arsenal was just enough for certain circumstances.

One such special case was a matter of moments away. Sofina waited several more heartbeats to follow the guard patrol into the ruins just ahead. She moved like a shadow incarnate and stalked her prey.

*

Eckard sat in the dim flickering light of a magikally induced candle flame. He realized thoughts and words of another who reached out to him.

Eckard, please hurry. They are onto us. I can feel the Void-Callers probing and their master is pushing the Void out in all directions. The element of surprise is against us.

It was never going to work, sneaking up on a Master-Channellor- Eckard auto-wrote back.

Which is all the more reason, you should rethink this whole scenario, Eckard.

It can be done, in and out. Remember, like old times- Eckard answered.

Those old times mostly consisted of our lives dangling by a thread.

More or less like today. Eckard replied bluntly.

Which would bring us full circle then. How did you intend on actually getting out once you are into that forsaken place, Eckard?

I'm sure you have worked out that already. Eckard wrote back.

That's what I was afraid of. Lisiarna gave in reply. Her words came thick and fast, Eckard jotted the sentences down with an increasingly erratic and uneven pace, his hands shook in panic or madness. Either possibility disturbed Eckard.

Eckard glanced over at the remaining mercs, soldiers and Kobold who ate and chatted as if they were old comrades. Judeson, Alrdik and Prestan stood off to the side. They ate with a steady calmness that matched their low and serious tones as they conversed with one another.

Thank Yahasa's hairy-fucking-gooch for Peaks and that dingy pub- Eckard thought to himself. He was quite sure Lisiarna did not need to hear his every thought.

The reverberating buzz that accompanied a auto-writing came through Eckard's head once more. Lisiarna was sending something.

If you go through with this Eckard, there is no turning back. You would have shown your hand, the Channellors would be like bees to honey...

I know – Eckard countered.

.... that is not not even mentioning what such a weaving could do to you..

Be careful out there Lisi, we will see each other again soon. Eckard wrote. Attempting to make some light of the heavy conversation he was in.

For a time the buzzing dissipated entirely. There was no reply in Eckard's minds. He had no words to write down.

A thousand terrible thoughts tumbled through his head. *What if Lisiarna had come under attack? Or worse...The Channellors had discovered how she and Eckard had been communicating via the Sea and even now were sending some of their Void-Caller lackeys and a host of Rak thugs down on her. What if she had given up on them and his latest scheme was one step to far for her- after all they had done to each other, Eckard partly could not blame her.*

Just before panic and hysteria overtook Eckard entirely- the buzz returned like a much-welcomed campfire song and he jotted down the thoughts of another on dirty parchment paper.

Just return to us alive, Eckard, alive and well, or as as well as a Grey Mage can be. Oh and Eckard...

Eckard read and found the dramatic pause

incredibly odd even for Lisiarna.

Yes? - He wrote back to her.

Don't ever call me Lisi again, thank you.

Eckard laughed in raptures out loud.

The present company Eckard kept; turned their collective heads toward him and through bulging eyes and furrowed brows looked at him as he were deranged.

Eckard was quite used to that kind of reception. He laughed harder still.

*

The Farthling guard fell boneless still in Sofina's hold. She retrieved her sticker from the unsuspecting man's throat and lowered him into the long grass noiselessly, *the wretched bitch was close now, and Sofina could smell her.* - Sofina, a tempest of emotions rising to the forefront as she realized she was etching closer to her target.

Sofina exhaled sharply. Excoriating the thought of seeing blinding red anger, she still had a job to do. Absolute focus was needed. There was no woman or man alive who had escaped Sofina, her sharply honed skills and arcs of experience was up to any disposal. No *mark* had escaped her attentions. Yet for nigh on eight arcs now, one single girl had had done so. *It was only a matter of time though* -Sofina realized, as she approached the abandoned sugar mill in a furtive crouch, her footsteps muffled by the soft tufts of grass underneath her flat shoes.

Sofina pushed into the back entrance of the old sugar mill, expertly stealh like, reflexes and sense properly attuned to her surroundings. But what she witnessed in the dusty room ahead...

A little frail girl stood back to her, tugged within a bulky, tattered old wool cloak.

The pale child wore a shaved plat. Visible scar marring from a rusty, blunt razor blade.

No....

The child turned toward her, a face much like her own; small and lemon shaped the face of Sofina's baby sister starred right back at her. Though she knew it was wrong, the child was arcs ago gone....and yet...and yet.

Sofina pulled up in her tracks. *What in the abyss was this?*

She charged against her better instincts, rage filled her veins. Had Sofina's even drawn her blades?

The child disappeared into a blur of rapid successive motions. The wool cloak hurled high into the air in a heart beat. Sofina stood where the child was, the sheep's coat on the grimy old floorboards now, a dozen paces away a mockery of Sofina's mistress stood facing up to her, as beautiful and as commanding as ever- in little more than a petticoat. Sofina knew this was not her mistress even if it looked like her. It was a demon that stood before Sofina who stood wearing her mistress' face.

Enough.

Sofina sprung off the balls of her feet, she hurled throwing stars in a controlled motion, faster than any could anticipate. Yet the void-damned demon did so. The throwing stars plunged into the far wall. The abomination in her underwear stood off to the side, the demon's stance unnervingly casual.

Her overconfidence will be her greatest weakness. Sofina rationalized.

Sofina threw a dozen stars at her enemy again.

The Sassanian backed up these initial attacks with several hurtled projectiles to both the left and right hand sides of where the demon stood previously.

Yet no weapon touched its mark. Sofina pivoted like a startled cat on her feet, with throwing blades drawn. The demon had somehow in a rapid blur of motion now appeared behind her.

The demon had to have some unnatural sight, seeing Sofina's moves before she made them. - Sofina had an idea. She was always one to adapt to her situation. Sofina had to utilize an unorthodox alternative to dispatch of this wretched bitch before her. Sofina squeezed her eyes shut, going against her deeply ingrained survival instincts.

If the blonde strumpet could anticipate my actions before, she will find it nigh on impossible now – Sofina thought, as she hurled two of counter-weighted throwing daggers in the direction of her crafty adversary.

As Sofina threw her knives she lunged into a battle-roll to the side. Avoiding any possible counterattack the blonde demoness may throw at her in desperation. Sofina opened her eyes in the roll and pulled herself to her feet. The scene before her was not as she anticipated, not at all. What Sofina should have been seeing was her knives - skewered in the witch. However the demon was nowhere near to that end. Sofina's throwing daggers were embedded in the soft rotting timber wall on the far side, alongside several pointed throwing stars from earlier.

Meanwhile the demon-witch had somehow impossibly arrived right next to Sofina, standing a mere pace off from her side. Sofina reacted expertly and with little thought, two more knives, this time- stickers arriving in her hands like a thousand times before, she struck out, what should have been clean and precise strikes for the blonde demon's exposed throat.

The blows never landed, Sofina's arms had come up in arc, faster than most could see, but somehow the demoness had stopped her strikes. Not with weapons, not even with fists but with to Sofina's surprises and horror, with two open palms. The demon had merely touched Sofina's cloaked arms with outstretched fingers, dainty little ones. But it proved more than enough, for Sofina's arms somehow bent back sickeningly behind, with a terrible and unnatural force and in moments both of Sofina's arms were broken, useless. Sofina saw black spots mar her vision and immense pain threatened to overwhelm her.

Sofina pushed it aside. *She would prevail. She always did.*

But with both her arms out of commission she was cut off from performing her art.

Sofina made to strike out with a boot at the witch. - Instead both her legs gave out and she crumpled into a ungraceful heap.

What in Talus' name was happening?

A swirling twisting contortion of faces and shapes appeared where the demon had been and in a manner of moments, a new face looked at Sofina, a face that was a small, angular Yunsi face, hair of midnight and tan skin tone. The petticoat hung loose on the skinny new shape of the demoness.

Sofina felt sick, searing, burning pain lanced up and down her arms, legs and back. Black spots formed at the edges of her vision.

She made to rise but flopped unceremoniously to the dusty floor.

'Are you quite finished, Sofina?' The barely

dressed demon said standing over the top of her.

*

The feast had been devoured in a dim, wet and dusty antechamber.

A much needed, albeit brief rest, though tension was still rife.

Eckard's sudden proclamation after his maddened fit of laughter that he and Judeson would go into the Rakoni stronghold alone was not at welcomed.

Dark thoughts clouded Judeson's mind. There was to be not reprieve.

Only more confusion it seemed.

'Are you touched by the fucking abyss, man?' Aldrik asked in a furious rage.

The hulk of a Berussi man was singularly concentrated on Eckard.

From what Judeson had heard he could not entirely begrudge Aldrik for his fury at the beanpole Northman.

'Firstly you conjurer up grub from seemingly nowhere then you proceed to laugh like a void-damned madman in the corner. And then to top it all off you now bloody tell us you and Judeson and going into the Woldte on your own and we lot are to what now? Go with the Kobold to a safe space for fucking pudding!' Alrdik said in a booming resentful voice.

Judeson could sense the outrage in Aldrik's voice but also something else, an adherence to a strict code maybe. It was obvious with the way the Berussi move, spoke and voiced his opinions he had a military background. Judeson should know his own father had been a soldier at one point.

It was from this standpoint, that Judeson saw the man was not simply emotional but was considering Eckard's tactics to be unhinged. *Which was more*

than reasonable with all that was happening -
Judeson rationalized.

It was not Eckard that broke the tension bubbling
over like a boiling cauldron pot.

'We have all done our part, the Woldte cannot be
besieged by a handful of troops with notched
blades and boomers' Prestan stated matter-of-
factually.

Aldrik turned on the Kobold.

'What was the point of all this death then?' The
Berussi said.

'We dealt the enemy a great blow. Dozens if not
hundreds of those wretched Gnolls and Raks would
have raided villages. More death would have
occurred had we not come here.' Prestan answered
without hesitation.

'And now two void-damned fools will wander into
the Woldte which is most probably a rigged bloody
trap now!' Aldrik said, from somewhere nearby
vermin scuttled away along dusty cobblestones.

'Then we will face the trap as we are the only
ones that can now.' Eckard stated. 'And you, the
sell swords and the Kobold will live to fight
another day. An alliance is forming and more
followers will come.'

Judeson saw that they were at a precipice, on the
edge of falling into yet another inferno. He
spoke and hoped it would be enough.

'Our appreciation for what all of you have done
here cannot be understated, thank you.' Judeson
turned in a semi-circle regarding all Alrdik's
soldiers and the mercenaries alike.

'Thank you all, one day we can fight together as
one again, I'm sure of it. May Zadma's blessing
be with you all' Judeson continued. He hoped his
earnestness would be appreciated. Or at the very
least not misconstrued as more fuel for the fire.

The mercenaries downcast their eyes, they looked a ragged lot. Probably experiencing shock at what they had been through, they were not used to fighting the Raks that was for sure.

Aldrik's soldiers looked refreshed with vigor in contrast. Though as a unit they collectively looked to their leader.

Aldrik shook his head but offered no more protests. Prestan and the Kobold Retrievers led Alrdik's soldiers and sorry rabble of mercenaries down a tunnel, Prestan had opened in the far-side wall.

Apparently Prestan had acquired a way of bringing in the Kobold *Iron Horse* toward them here. A feat that was not possible from the start for reasons Judeson could only stab at in the dark.

Eckard motioned for Judeson to follow him up a set of deteriorating and moss ridden stone steps.

The narrow, almost collapsed passage had to be half climbed and half forced through to get anywhere, it was an excruciatingly labourious routine. Judeson pushed and pulled his weight through increasing claustrophobic spaces between detritus and collapsing mouldy walls. Eckard led the way with a string of colourful curses and heavy grunts. All featuring the Nerthlander's God or Gods, Judeson still did not grasp what Yahasa was exactly.

Judeson not for the first time since meeting Eckard wondered what he was doing here.

Pushing aside what could be taken as the remains of a door, Judeson followed Eckard into a dim light promenade and was left wondering again.

Wondering why he followed the crazy, wonky eyed Northman in the first place and why he continued to do so.

A cohort of heavily armed Rakoni awaited them.

The Ravagers were fully organized entrenched into defensive positions. Shields, blades, bows and determined alien gazes cast on them.

Judeson, tensed, a cold sweat dropped down his forehead. He shook with fury. Already in a battle stance, reaching for Jude at his back...

As Judeson's hand fell upon his hilt; single Rakoni stepped forward, noticeably more slender and less armoured than its compatriots, the creature spook:

'Hands away from weapons gozka-kels' The skinny Rakoni said in a audibly high voice, though still heavily accented with that guttural speak that Raks possessed.

'Easy, Judeson' Eckard said, drawing up level with Judeson to stand side by side.

Judeson felt repulsed by Eckard's nonchalance. He was sick with anger and the Northman beside looked as if he were out for a stroll.

Eckard offered a warm smile and placed a hand on his shoulder. Judeson fought against the urge to throw his bloodbrother's hand away from him.

'Please' Eckard pleaded, almost seeming to beg.

Judeson was taken back.

In the end all he could do was nod and respect that Eckard had a plan for them.

Hopefully he had a plan....

*

Lisiarna was not at all surprised to see Sofina again.

Disappointed. But not surprised. A little irritated in fact, but Lisiarna acknowledged that was more than possibly a side effect of posing as Beatrice for such a prolonged period of time.

It was well known to Lisiarna that Beatrice had never been the most patient person in the world.

Taking on the form and indeed imitating the personality mindset of another sometimes took it's inevitable toll. Be it minuscule or some case devastatingly disastrous. A Mage who could perform Form-shifting was subject to the form they took, ironically.

Mostly Lisiarna was disappointed in herself (her real self) for allowing Sofina to get so close to her and for probably killing innocent bystanders in the process of doing so.

On a important side note however Lisiarna was quite disappointed that the personal assassin of her former tormentor had even come here or got this void-damned close, sloppy on her part. Lisiarna would not make the same mistake twice. She rarely did.

Of course Sofina probably craved revenge and as was common for the Channellors; masters of manipulating that blinding white flame that was hate. Sofina had never got over the indisposed state of her Mistress. Lisiarna using the former Lady Beatrice's form was probably not a very settling factor for Sofina.

There was very little time now to argue semantics of who wronged who. Though Lisiarna had quite a case against Sofina, as it was if the killer wanted to argue her points.

It all matters so very little...

Lisiarna shook herself awake.

'Listen assassin, I won't end your little life. Not now. I have far too much to do this night. You can go.' Lisiarna stated, trying to choke on her emotions.. the torrent of memories were on the periphery. Forcing to flood back in...

'Our mistress was never privy to this new found mercy of yours'

'*Your* Mistress still breaths unlike quite a few

of her unfortunate victims, that in itself is a small mercy.

Lisiarna backed out of the room.

'I will kill you one day, you void-damned bitch!' Sofina screamed back at Lisiarna. A world of rage and pain painted on the assassins face.

Sofina passed out in a heap.

Lisiarna starred down at the nasty little woman, studying the unconscious Sofina, taking it all in, the history, the short, sharp plain features. The short mop of messy dark curls.

...And shifted her Form to that of the vengeful killer.

Lisiarna felt the full force of the Arcane Sea move about her. Swirling and eddying - sharp goosebumps laced her skin even as it *shifted in* tone and shape. Lisiarna went from her rounded Yunsi face to the sharp and rat like features of Sofina. Her body shifted into the change. The same uncomfortable contorting turns and twists, the lacing intense pain of bones, skin, muscle and tissue pulling into place. Lisiarna cried out. A new form was always the most painful.

From nearby in a crumpled heap laid the real Sofina, now eyes closed shut but still breathing by the rise and fall of her chest. Lisiarna left her would-be killer where she lay.

Lisiarna brushed herself off and hastened out of the squat, dark ruin and out into the wild.

About a half hour or so up the old tangled over trail and in the dark confines of the forest, Lisiarna ran into a heavily armed party. Not of her own.

A score of Rakoni Ravagers and a lone ironclad figure wrapped up in a dark purple hued shawl. The unmistakably sickly sweet stench of the Void, absolutely reeked from the party.

Great. Lisiarna dreaded what came next and hoped
to heck that her form held up and that she was
able to act it out.

'Assassin ' The Void-caller in the shawl asked.
The creature, the Rakoni abomination was a
Channellor's own Mage killer. A creation of
whatever devious science the Rak and their
Channellor masters so zealously subscribed to.

'I dealt with the Mage before she knew it, the
bitch had even tried to disguise herself as me.
Left her rotting carcass back there' Lisiarna
motioned toward the ruins just barely visible in
the dark of the forest bbehind her where she had
left Sofina.

A little part of Lisiarna hoped her would-be
killer had regained consciousness by now and made
a rather hasty retreat. At least that was her
hope.

The near-man creature leered down at her. It's
disgust evident in how the scarred and dried lips
peered back in a clear grimace. The creature's
blood-shot and googly protruding eyes hung on her
for a terrifying long period until it turns it's
disproportionate head away and barked orders at
the other Raks.

Lisiarna's gambit was up. She was done for. Even
if she was able to fight off this army, which was
nowhere clearcut she could or not, it was more
than probable the creatures would lure more
enemies unto her. She would be hunted
relentlessly.

The Void-Caller looked back at her with those
haunting features and smirked between barred,
needle like teeth.

'On your way now killer.' The Void Caller said.
Lisiarna held up the act as long as they could
muster, stalking away, until she was out of the

line of sight of the Raks the Void Caller and
then broke into a full-blooded sprint.

8Th Stanza

It comes time to tell a tale

It is a tale of us all

A tale of how we rise and fall

But most of all

..it is a tale of us all

Verse 1

Speakings of the Nameless Fallen *Sculester and Pondly - 2722 arcs ATF (After The Fall)*

Nothing could have prepared Judeson for what they would see on their way through the Woldte.

Eckard offered nothing, electing to just be all sorts of stoic, brooding and did not say a word.

The ancient once High Born era fortress was host to a huge modern Rakoni flurry of industry. The white marble work was stacked with weapons and armaments some familiar to Judeson, others not so much. The methodical nature of the enterprise was immaculate. Freshly swept floors stacked to the ceiling with piles upon piles of crates in nice neat ordered pile.

Draul, Aurman and Kobold slaves were being rushed and hurried by steel clad Rakoni enforcers often violently into clean up duties, stacking the crates and carting an array of armaments around the place. The fortress was a vast, teeming well-oiled display of oppressive industry.

It stuck like an unwelcome spear into Judeson who had witnessed this all happen to his own people in Letesah, but now it was remarkably monumental scale.

The forced labour crews were not the most sickening aspect of the entire affair. Not by a long shot. For as Judeson and Eckard were taken further up and through the winding, endless hallways there was something far worse.

Rows and rows of knee high cages ordered and lined up and down a a great host of hallways and antechambers. Home to meek and malnourished, others living in blood, bile and vomit beneath them or in some cases laid out unresponsive in their own filth. Aurman, Kobold and Draul.

In the spaces between the ordered cages, Raks not adorning armour but instead pens and paper stalked like lurkers. Jotting down notes on paper and board like the suffering slaves were specimens to be studied as they passed from this life to the next. The Raks placed small ceramic bowls just within arms length of the cages. The bowls had what could only be described as masses of grey mush in them.

The Rak Mord'ha'ja that was their impromptu guide described in *cestral* how the whole affair was to be the future of them all in Nertheilm, *by the Qhasa's decree* apparently. Though Judeson really did not listen past that. He could not. Not properly. Rage boiled in his blood. It took every essence of his being to hold back jumping on their guides and pounding his fists into them. Despite the very clear fact that *knuckles against steel was never going to make a difference.*

Eckard led Judeson further down the hallway following the Mord'ha'ja and the Rakoni patrol's path. The Raks pushed aside a hulking set of double oak doors, the hinges protesting as they were forced to swing inward. The Rakoni motioned for Judeson and Eckard to go inside. The room beyond had been cleaned up nicely. A throne room to be sure. Ornate banners lined the stained glass windows to either side of a long crimson carpet. At the end of this runway was a rather grand looking dais of white stonework. A over-sized throne sat centre stage, also of whitewashed stone. Curiously the Rakoni guides dropped their weapons on the floor and strode off several dozen paces behind them to stand like statues. Judeson gathered up Jude and passed Eckard's array of sharp implements across to him. The Raks did not even attempt to stop them.

A figure bundled up in a dirty ancient looking cloak stirred on the throne. The person had been sprawled out, lounging on the regal chair as it were but a mere cushion for its seating pleasure.

'Blessed be the Qhasa, for by God's grace alone
can we see through the Darkness into the Light'
the bundle of clothe offered in a scratchy,
altogether cacophonous tonal voice.

'Is this the tyrant? A raspy old codger in a
dirty fucking smock?' Judeson said. Though
whether he was trying to incite the figure on
dais ahead of them or whether he was more
bitterly disappointed their adversary was to be
such an anti-climax.

'I am no tyrant, I am a servant of God and you
are Eckard Delmose Farth and Judeson son of
Judisye' The Masked apparition replied, taking
quite some time to speak out their names. There
was a satisfied tone to the creature's voice.

The figure seemingly threw itself up from the
throne.

Judeson felt cold shudders crawl down his back.
*How in the abyss did this bastard know their
names?*

'Riddle me this, why do you rest your arse on a
throne if you ain't a tyrant?' Eckard called, no
illusions as to what he intended to do, his tone
a transparent challenge.

'Ever so provocative, heretic, is that what that
was?' The shrouded apparition uttered in its
course gravelly voice, gesturing toward the
stonework throne it had sat on.

Judeson peered across to the Nertharnlander and
for once he saw a sight he had never seen
previously. The other man was without an answer.
Not challenging grimace nor any nauseating smirk
present on his feature. Judeson did not know how
to accept this and felt a cold chill spiral down
his spine like a icy wind had blown through
unabated.

'You are not Tiramene.' Eckard answered, no stinging tone discernible, in fact no real emotion at all in his voice.

'Morvhren is what they call me, heretic, and no Tiramene is preoccupied with...' The apparition paused.'... Other activities. As of late his skill set is determined to be useful elsewhere' the shrouded form continued.

Judeson started forward and raised the bastard claymore of Jude in his hands aiming at the impossibly shimmering figure.

'How do you know who we are?' Judeson said, calling out this Movhren.

'I have been following your little heresies for sometime, aurmen.' Movhren replied causally, too casually as he was observing the weather outside.

Judeson snorted. Partly to trump the absurdity of the whole situation he found himself in but more so to silence his growing anxious fear of how absurd was becoming more and more normalized for him. *Magik, plots within plots, Eckard....* beside him did not offer anything further. *He looked lost in thought even.* Judeson shrugged the distraction aside; Eckard was unreadable at the best of times. Instead he chose to ready into a battle stance, widening his feet. If there were to be a fight he would be ready.

'Well if Tiremene is not here than it is you who will answer for heinous crimes. Consider us; justice incarnate.' Judeson said.

A loud boisterous laugh sounded forth from the robes and Judeson found himself backing away, not frightened but appalled by the unbearable cringe inducing sound that echoed all about in the dim lit hallway of the keep. The hoarse screech seemed to have a reverberation off all the latticework.

'Justice you say aurman' the figure said as it threw back its hood revealing his features.

This was no Rakon beneath the shrouded folds of cloth, an aurman though not quite so. Movhren was young and boyish looking, handsome no doubt in some circles, in a very adolescent softness. The eyes were what threw Judeson. They were blazing orbs of light, almost pure white. Not at all Aurman, something perhaps heavenly or perversely otherworldly demonic or angelic depending on what one was willing to believe.

The young man on the dais before Judeson and Eckard had a head of dull darkish brown curls, a ring small brass ring puncturing his septum and another through his bottom lip, across one side of his face and going down his neck was tattooed markings of a language not all together unfamiliar to Judeson, he after-all had seen the Rakoni script before. The last time he had read their indecipherable words; they had been painted on the houses of Letesah in the blood of those he had once loved.

'You are altogether on the wrong side if it is justice you long for.' Movhren continued.

'Is that why you have Raks kissing your arse then? Cause you are the proverbial side of good? As for justice why don't you come down here and we can discuss terms' Judeson said.

Eckard beside him once again did not say anything.

'They are free unlike you fools, the Morba-Rakoni *choose to* serve under the Divine Rights.' Movhren answered striding down the dais toward them.

'Divinity you say? Well I must be fooled. I must have got it confused with slavery and murder.' Judeson growled between barred teeth. His voice was cold, his gaze steadfast.

Judeson strode forward but Eckard stayed him with one hand, as the Northman's other held the pommel of his weapon.

'You are fooled. Your eyes have been closed for your whole existence. The Qhasa will set you free. In life or in death if you wish.' Movhren said in answer. Coldness seeped into the Channellor's voice, a deadly seriousness that hinted at far more. Judeson was taken back… Albeit for a fleeting moment as he refocused...refocused his anger, his rage and all the frustrations.

If anything was for certain the Channellors would pay dearly.

'Oh yes please lecture us good and proper. But first where are the big *grown up* Channellors?' Eckard said mockingly, trademark grin spread from ear to ear.

'Mock all you will. For that is what you so desire to do. But let me tell you both exactly what will unfold from this day on. For it is decreed as clear as the light of day by God's Holy words.' Movhren announced, his words seemed to be rehearsed as if this was all a stage show. The Channellor had thrown his robe open and revealed an elaborately garnished plate-email chest piece. Rubies adorned the front and underneath it could attain he wore a nobleman's petty coat of fine silk. Judeson was taken back was this same vein of evil Channellors Eckard had described to him? This dandy seemed hardly capable of much in the way of war or the violent subjugation of peoples.

Movhren advanced on Judeson and Eckard.

'We are the Holy Order of the Shroud and servants of the Void. I am named a *Chosen Hero* as I have been deemed a Holy warrior to bring order to this shadow that hangs thick over the Nertheilm, our light is a blessed one and our fire will burn away the corruption this mortal Stone has taken in.'

'Blah blah blah, are we going to be fucking lectured to death?' Eckard replied, smiling furiously now. Judeson could not ascertain who was the more insane, the dainty looking zealot or the eagerly grinning Northman.

'..For hasten against the unbeliever for they shall be a pestilence onto the Holy. But defence will stand strong and the Chosen's walls shall remain steadfast if they shall believe in the Shroud.' Movhren declared, the man was reciting something now, this much was more than apparent.

'Oh how profound you're right and we are fucking wrong.' Eckard answered smirking.

Judeson glanced across at his companion raising an eyebrow in disbelief.

'If this man is dangerous Eckard, why are you antagonising him so?' Judeson inquired.

'Cause it's oh so much fun' Eckard said, without turning and without humour though he still smirked furiously somehow without mirth, eyes trained on the well-groomed boyish Channellor. Judeson could sense the anxiousness in the air.

'There is a place for everyone and the Qhasa will dictate our souls toward where we so reach. For fear not thy children you will delivered onto where you so are solely needed.' Movhren continued, smiling. A devious looking grin beyond his arcs, and his eyes seemed to stare right through Judeson, as if he were not there.

'Some are born privileged, some are born into suffering, it's unfair and unbalanced, the world is a harsh home and it's happenings are like a cold blooded teacher. But we can choose to help and aid for no god will save you if you do not save yourself' Eckard answered back to Movhren, his smile dropping.

Judeson felt the air seem to shimmer and shift around them, an odd stinging heat, followed by cold snaps passed by as if the wind was fluctuating in temperatures. The swell and crashing of far-off waves were heard, he was not certain but he could swear the throne room was getting darker and lighter on disjointed intervals. *What in Zadma's grace was happening?* Judeson wondered.

'And where do you fit into all this turmoil and unholy chaos then, heretic?' Movhren challenged now only a handful of paces from Eckard.

'I'm difficult, either through choice or substance, it matters very-fucking- little, I could blame shit on this and that, but to be perfectly honest I enjoy being a bastard but I know when compassion is needed. That is what sets us apart.'

'You feel I don't know compassion?'

'No you know it, you can describe it well enough,' Eckard paused briefly.' You; Channellor refuse to practice it.'

Movhren proceeded to clap a loud, raucous display of applause, varied in timing and structure.

'I have no compassion; I'm a cold-blooded embodiment of the destructive taint of this world? Ha ha ha, I have assembled men and women here with requisite purpose, a design of which to progress. You paint yourself in selfish poetry, as if you were a flawed hero that knows the path to salvation. There is no such road, there is order and chaos, chaos is the entrapment of base emotions and stubborn backwardness, order is the progression of society, the lessons taught to us by God. The Shroud will be the lifeblood if you will of what we are to all become. That little heretic is what sets us apart, order and chaos.' The Channellor said.

'Sure, whatever you say.' Eckard answered, his voice and expression seemed determined and laced with cold iron.

Shadows gathered still, increasing in number in each passing second. Dense and thick, seeming to block out the flickering light from that of lit gas lamps. Movhren's weapon had grown tenfold brighter, the weapons white absorbing light destroying the forming shadows around it. Judeson felt a great weight push down on him and the crash of waves was absolute now as if they were underwater.

The heavy timber doors swung open as the halberd holding the door shut; snapped in twine. Heavily armed Raks poured in like a vengeful tide. Eckard spoke but did not turn his eyes from Movhren and the flaring light.

'Go hold off the Raks. I got this.' Eckard stated, laughing as he did so.

'I will not abandon you.' Judeson answered drawing Jude from the scabbard at his back.

'Judeson, this taker before us, it is no man. Your steel though *imbued* with Magik will not help you against this …thing.' Eckard paused staring down the prissy outspoken Channellor before them. Eckard continued sternly;'What is about to happen will be very fucking violent. Just remember.. .'

Judeson managed a momentary puzzling look for Eckard who had began to breath much heavier than before.

'What?' Judeson inquired, urging his bloodbrother onward.

'Remember. Your father, remember your…family.

Remember them with cold iron rather than the fire of hatred. Hold onto that.' Eckard forced out in strained breaths.

The youthful Channellor at the foot of the steps was absolutely scouring at them now. His boyish face took on a look of undiluted rage. Judeson swore the light that bathed this Movhren's face was growing ever more vibrant. In the warm glow of that light, the Channellor's form seemed to shift, changing. Behind the youthful appearance, something else....

Judeson held onto his memories, not with bitter flame, but with a cold-blooded zeal that could only come from a accepted clarity. Clarity he himself must believe in.

Judeson nodded in answer to Eckard and pivoted to face the encroaching Raks. He did not understand exactly what Eckard meant, the dandy before them looked hardly threatening, even if the man seemed to becoming something else...something monstrous even. The light was burning Judeson's eyes now. Faces merged and blurred on the Channellor's own.

Judeson shook himself back to his senses; he had come too far with Eckard, he had done to much with him, to now to start doubting.

Though he did not fully understand himself, he would fight, he would follow and he would listen once more. Judeson dropped into a defensive stance, lowering his centre of gravity, completely and utterly prepared to face the heavily armoured Rakoni who were just mere paces from him now and were circling like predators before prey.

It was in that moment the world around them exploded in blinding luminescence.

9ᵗʰ Stanza

There is war right underneath your very noses, a secret war that is being fought for our very existence. Not the Banner War, no the Collective and you all are pawns being drawn into place. The Draul and the Kobold do not see it, they believe Aurmen and the Rakoni one of the same, that there is major issue. The Rakoni are a subservient slave army being manipulated by the Channellors. Not Mages, not users of the Arcane Sea. The Channellor are the real enemy, wielders of destructive power.

The war, the real war is against Channellors. That is the only real war that ever was right there ladies and gentlemen of the Council.

Section of Sar Wrendal's Address to the Confederation Council

The Trial and Un-Knighting of Sar Wrendal Dastin Morke (Various Sources)

Nertharnlands Confederation, Aurmora, Reclaimers Isle

Confederation Council Chambers

on the eve of 2978 arcs ATF (After the Fall)

Lisiarna felt like she had been thrown against a wall. Her senses swam in contorted spiraling dizziness. The Arcane Sea flowed like a torrent unleashed. *Something was very void-damned wrong. Eckard called to her.*

His usual sarcastic, cynical but quietly assured voice sounded strained. Desperate even. Lisiarna had heard Eckard like this before. She had seen what he was like firsthand before, before everything...

Lisiarna! I need you....

Eckard screamed out in pain.

Lisiarna panicked and reached out with all her being.

Eckard was within the Arcane Sea. He had pathed there with another presence, possibly the Southron- Judeson. Which was an incredibly dangerous prospect to say the very least. Yet there was something else, something of the void that stalked them even now.

It was closing in.....

Lisiarna reached into her aspect of the Arcane Sea at full throttle, it was a harrowing ordeal to open oneself like this.

She did not know how to *path* nor did she wish to, but Eckard could find her and bring himself back. If the creature of the Void found them first, Lisiarna dreaded what came next.

*

He felt himself tumbling, weightless in the dark. Or were his eyes closed? Judeson could not really

tell, he was not even sure if he was awake or
dreaming again. The air felt stale, cold and
somehow strangely thick, like smoke. All of it
was impossible. He could not feel his fingers, or
his toes or the rest of his body. But somehow
there was an insistent ringing in his ears and
pain laced up his brow that felt there but like
his limbs somehow not.

How could a dream hurt so?

Judeson opened his eyes to a world of impossible.

There was no land beneath his feet, no Far Above
up ahead. No clouds, no rain and no sun. There
was nothing at all.

Except...

Water, endless, flowing water, torrents, floods,
a cascade of crashing waves. But no water, as if
the water was the very air itself.... where was
he?

No animals, no insects, no trees, just flowing
watery air and a howling impossible winds that
seemed to blow both ways at once and back again.
Where was he?

Judeson's head hurt trying to work out what in
the void was going on.

Eckard appeared beside him as if he were always
there.

Though to be truthful Judeson doubted Eckard was
there.

The beanpole Northman was fading in and out, like
a shadow or sequence of shadows. Long dark
tendrils of wispy, shadowy smoke flickered out
behind the seemingly transparent shape of the
man.

Judeson's head swam.

Eckard's networked form of dark shadows spoke in
a faraway voice.

'Remember your folks, remember your grandmother. Keep thinkin about that giant piece of metal you call a sword...' Eckard said.

Before Judeson could respond - a tremendous cascade of roars and explosive crescendo of booms echoed close by. Somewhere near in the rolling, crashing waves Judeson and Eckard stood in. It was impossible and inconceivable.

A flare of unfathomably bright light came into existence right where Judeson was hearing the sound resonant. The light blinded so he averted his eyes. The light was edging closer and closer.

'We need to go.' Eckard said.

'Now!' The big Nertharnlander shouted in that eerily faraway voice of his, the shadow form of the man was already running away.

As the flaring light drew closer, Judeson felt burning, charring warmth to it. If it came closer, he reasoned it would scorch them alive.

'What is it?' Judeson asked, despite himself, he wanted to just run but he could not dismiss his own nerves so readily.

'The thing that called itself Movhren.' Eckard stated by Judeson side as the two men ran through the impossible waves and howling winds.

Judeson barily registering what the Northman said in the ensuring noise.

Judeson threw away any notions of asking how the blinding light was the same thing as the dandy they had encountered in the Woldte's throne-room. Instead he wanted to know the more pressing of issues in this vastly confusing time and place.

'Where are we going' Judeson puffed out, between the frantic sprint he and Eckard were undertaking.

Eckard suddenly changed direction and Judeson

bolted to keep up with the man.
'This way...'Eckard stated.'…I think.'

*

Lisiarna would not dare enter the Arcane Sea. Not
now least of all… It was obvious the Void-Callers
and Channellor had put up wards and traps to hold
off any Mages from accessing the Sea. She would
be assailed as soon as she attempted it. That
creepy Void-Caller had been far too close. Where
there was one there was a legion, like a disease.
She did not want to warrant undue attention.
Lisiarna steeled herself. Pushing away her fears.
Her Red magiks emoted straight through like a
battering ram. Tshe sent out a flare, deep into
the Sea. It was strong and fast and nigh on
impossible even for Eckard to miss. But no back
in the physical world she had to move. For if
Eckard found her so too would the void-damned
Channellors and their underlings.
Lisiarna ran like the wind, shifting her form as
she went.

*

Judeson and Eckard ran further into flowing,
swirling deep shadows. The running water turned
to thick noxious smoke. The blinding light
followed with the harrowing roar behind them
edged ever closer. Seeming to strike through the
shadows the light came at Eckard and himself.
Judeson did not know how that dainty Void-taker
was the same thing as this terrible, burning
light but Eckard said it was so and that was
enough.
Eckard turned and pivoted on a dime. Judeson
pulled up short not far from him.

'We are here.' Eckard said. The shadows eddied and twisted around him as he were one of them.

Judeson made to speak.

'The Sea.' Eckard said.

Deep, impossible shadows swirled the man like they had a mind of their own.

Judeson was beyond confused. No amount of questioning. This was something else entirely. This was Eckard's world.

'This next part will fucking hurt, get ready' Eckard answered before Judeson had a chance to even think of what to ask.

He did not have time to ask another question for this strange world just like the previous one they were in exploded all around them.

Coda
The Light That Blinds

We will do, what we can fathom, we will break what
can be broken

And we will scribe what is spoken.

Yet never enough do we give their' all to the Stone
that is our home.

For this is a reality that we do not yet know,

a life that as yet is still; broken and a tale that,
tragically;

Is rarely spoken.

   – Ancient Yunsi Wisdom

   – Extracted from the Recovered Yunsi
Wisdowms, Various authors, 1862 to 2473

arcs ATF

Distorting and blaring flames and images of
destruction, creation and everything in between;
Judeson saw death and rebirth; he was as if
nothing, a mere leaf upon an unfathomably
turbulent storm.

Before Judeson could place any further thought on
any of what was happening to him. He awoke.

Judeson's vision was blurry, his head pounded
like a thousand hangovers all rolled into one.
All the religious texts, all the lies; after all
the priests had said death was welcoming warm and
painless in the end.

Judeson's immediate peripherals started to clear,
he felt himself propped up against a tree.

The hairy, tired face of Eckard starred back at

him, a small smile on the face of the odd looking Northman.

So he was not dead. Or both he and Eckard had both passed on together.

'We're not dead' Eckard stated, as if he read Judeson's mind.

The beanpole Northman brushed back the unruly mop of onyx hair from his scalp. Had his hair grown even more since they had been in the Woldte's throne room? *That had been what moments ago -* Judeson's head hurt with the thought of what was happening. That and the very real pain -his body ached all over, his eyes stung and his mouth tasted like blood and sick.

'I am sorry about your sword by the way. We shall have to look into reforging that. Don't worry I know someone with some talent' Eckard said.

At Judeson's feet lay a blackened and scorched hilt. Several sizable metal fragmented shards were scattered haphazardly about close by. All that remained of his family's blade. Judeson felt pain of loss, his father's face, his grandmother's also, albeit for moment.

'Where are we?' Judeson forced out, his voice scratchy, his mouth tasted of blood and sick.

Eckard's reply came in a coarse hollow sounding stammer.

'Are you questioning your perception of reality?' Judeson felt struck by that cryptic phrasing from the haggardly weary looking Northman.

After all that had assailed them. After everything that had happened; Judeson felt his perception of the world was indeed changing and not necessarily for the better...

Eckard stirred within his burnt and charred coat, coughing up splutters.

'We are close by to where we were. In the woods near to the Woldte.' Eckard stated.

A series of footfalls sounded from behind them. The sleight frame of a thin figure came into view of Judeson.

'I think he is trying to mostly hold it together, Eckard.' A familiar feminine voice sounded from the figure.

The voice was that of of the false noble Lady Beatrice and before that the mysterious Draul – Kail they were indeed one and the same. Though this time Judeson saw neither the voluptuous figure of the tall blonde noblewoman nor did Judeson see the sleight frame of the Draul lady they had met in the woods all those weeks ago. This time the voice belonged to another form entirely. A sharp faced aurman girl with youthful slightly boyish features though a hardness also that could only of been gained from living in the wilds of the Stone. The woman was slight shade of deep brownish red. Not nearly as Judeson's own skin but similar in some way.

'He's not nearly as strong as he makes himself out to be, Judeson. Thank you, 'Lisiarna stated.

'For what?' Judeson asked.

Lisiarna smiled back at him wearing the face of another new person Judeson did not know.

'You two are so much alike.' She laughed.

Judeson felt the laughter infectious and coughed like a hack

Although the woman was looking at him and speaking to him, Judeson knew she was about Eckard who had just staggered behind a scattering of ancient red oaks.

'Thank you for looking out for him' the ever-changing woman said.

'I..'Judeson bite his tongue, what else could he say.

'Names, names have power Judeson son of Judisye. If we are to be true friends you should know mine. Just as you should know of the Pact in time' She continued.

Judeson held his tongue.

'My name is Lisiarna, Judeson, my real name. Though by now you have of course seen me in a number of forms I cannot show you my true but you have my name as I have yours. Eckard is one of my oldest....' Lisiarna paused for a moment.

'...Friends and in time I am sure we could be friends also.'

Judeson shook himself.

Her real name? Friends? Probably not like her and Eckard though, there was something or maybe had been something. They had just been launched in and out of reality, blown up half a void-damned castle and only now was he being introduced, actually introduced to this woman. His head hurt.

'Now, kefra!' Lisiarna perked up all of a sudden, as if she had awakened from a deep sleep. A beaming smile lined her new face.

The woman bolted off further down the hill, nigh on skipping like a elated child. The woman who could -form into at least half a dozen things and threw people with her mind *skipped*.

Eckard returned adjusting his belt and pants. With all the fantastical things occurring Judeson almost forgot that the primal matters still needed attending to. It was almost mildly amusingly that a Mage that could somehow transport he and Judeson across leagues with thought still had to piss.

Eckard did not look at all well, the man was all blood shot eyes and a pale almost blueish complexion, wafts of tangled black hair. Perhaps Judeson was by far and away underestimating what had happened to get them here.

'Careful' Eckard said.

'Huh?' Judeson forced out in a croak. *What was possibly going to happen now? More void-damned magik, Queen's blessing he hoped not.*

'Lisiarna's kefra is fucking awful.' Eckard laughed, rather boisterously which produced another coughing fit.

However the man quickly changed his tone and attempted to stifle his laughing and subsequent coughing by covering his mouth, thick blood came out in between fingers. Eckard threw off Judeson's concerned stare with a wave of his other hand. Lisiarna returned with two piping hot clay mugs and a blanket across her shoulders.

'Here you go' Lisiarna said handing over the mugs first to Judeson and then to Eckard and placed the thick wool blanket of the latter man.

Lisiarn'a hands strayed briefly across Eckard's impossible mop of disheveled hair as she let go of the blanket and seemed to massage him, oh so gently.

Judeson thought better than draw attention to it and looked away without saying anything further.

He sniffed at his mug, the thick dark liquid smelt incredibly burnt.

From nearby Eckard retrieved a silver hip flask from his black coat and generously tipped amber liquid into his mug of kefra. Lisiarna noticed but did not say a word about it. The slim woman sat to the sides of Eckard and Judeson.

Eckard offered up the flask to Judeson.

'A little vice for your breakfast.' Eckard said handing the flask to Judeson who accepted it.

'What? Now?' Judeson asked, adding only half of
what Eckard did to his kefra.

Lisiarna smiled.

'Now, Judeson, now have a couple of little tasks
to do, save the world being the foremost of
such.' Lisiarna stated.

'Raijin?' Eckard asked in between long pulls at
his *viced* kefra.

'He has not returned,' Lisiarna paused ' I am
sure he shall find us soon enough.'

Though Judeson felt she did not sound altogether
that convincing even to herself.

Judeson felt a sinking feeling in his stomach. He
hoped nothing had befallen the stick figure
Draul, he had hoped to see that near-man again.

'Right then we break camp.' Eckard made to stand
awkwardly and with a great deal of painful
looking effort, the tall man wincing and dry
reaching from the back of his throat. Judeson saw
Eckard almost fall to the ground before Lisiarna
swept herself up and placed her hands on the
Eckard's shoulders. The woman pointed to the
ground and frowned at Eckard as he were a
disobedient child. If Judeson had felt better,
the scene may have almost been comical.

'No, we will break camp you two get some rest.
You will need it' Lisiarna said, she sat down
though this time somewhat closer to Eckard.

Eckard winked back at Judeson. Though Judeson saw
straight through the jest and witnessed the
watery, blood-shot eyes of man in terrible pain.

*

Madam Channellor Khrislo was extremely agitated.
It had been an inexcusable amount of time between
briefings. She was not being properly informed of
the going-ons in the backward wilds of the

Nertheilm. What is the name of the Most Holy was
this 'Chosen Hero' up to?

'Madam Channellor?' The Rakoni Captain called in,
from outside Khrislo's tent.

'Come' Khrislo replied.

An underling, a short and squat Rakoni girl
scuttled in through the tent's entrance.

Finally.

The young girl fell into a fit of convulsions.

'Madam Channellor Khrislo' The young girl said,
in a voice that was not her own.

'Where in the Void have you been?' Khrislo asked.

The young girl starred thoughtlessly ahead.

'I don't answer to you, madam.' The eerie voice
said.

Khrislo held her tongue. A berating for this
arrogant little upstart from such a great
distance would serve no one. When she got in
touch with Tiramene again she would pull rank and
give this Cultist an absolute serving. After all
appearances needed up keeping, especially in the
Ranks of the Channellors.

'I am pursuing the heretics. Tiramene has a plan.
He will be away from the Woldte for a while
still, as will I. My second; Channellor Scrimsure
will be your contact.' The mouthpiece of the
little girl said in the Cultist's voice.

'What?' Khrislo said.

'That is all for now. See you soon, Madam' The
Cultist said and then left the mouthpiece.

The little girl collapsed into a fit.

Khrislo called for her personal guard to collect
the young corpse.

*Damn this self-proclaimed Chosen Hero. What had
happened up there, the Void and cursed Sea had
clashed there had been an unveiling* she had felt

it.

Khrislo was not one to be trifled with. When she and the army reached the Woldte she would take control and when the Cultist returned she would show him some manners, order would be restored in that cesspit.

*

Movhren, Chosen Hero of the New Canon Chapters, Master-Channellor of the 5th Dahn, loyal husband, decorated veteran of the subjugation of the heretic Southron Hand of kingdoms and father of two called for his left hand subordinate - Under-Channellor Scrimsure who was proverbly vacating his bowels at the prospect of attending to the Chosen Hero. Never had his Master - a living legend called for him personally. Today was a most auspicious day indeed. *His hardwork and enduring devotion was being rewarded.*

'Yes Holy One' Scrimsure said easing his tightly trimmed line of mustache down from his top lip. Master-Channellor Movhren turned around to face Scrimsure. Brilliantly bright and Holy White eyes, handsome features and something, something like exhaustion creased those good looks. This was something entirely new for Scriumsure to see present on his Master. The Master-Channeloor on closer inspection looked a little spent and more than a little sore from his encounter with that damned heretic Mage and the barbarian Southron.

The dirty and deserted alcove where Scriumsure and his Master now stood was like an unwelcome metaphor to thing used and abused.

'You will be appointed acting-Master here at the Woldte. Look to repairing the east wing immediately.' Movhren stated. The Master-Channellor pivoted and peered out the open window frame again. Scrimsure joining his Master and looking downward at the smouldering ruin of caved in turrets and decimated, melted walls that had been the wing where he was before the Grey Mage heretic had swept him up in a full unveiling of the terribly Unholy Sea. But Movhren had proved more than a match; the Holiest of Holy Void itself had lended Scriumsure's Master- powers to counter that terrible abomination.

The troop causalities had not yet been estimated from the incident. Somehow the slaves from that side of the fortress had just up and disappeared, those Scriumsure was quite sure the heretic mage's unholy powers probably had something to do with it. Though some patrols reported in seeing some former prisoners running erratically through the nearby woodland, many others had been simply been charred, burnt corpse of both troops and slaves alike.

'Track down the servants. Re-fortify this place. And pry whatever valuable information you can from the fools that we employed to subvert the Pact. As abysmal job as they have done, perhaps they learned something about the Unholy ones we do not yet know' Movhren said, assured and calm, his voice not straining nor at all sounding as tired as he looked.

Scrimsure cleared his tight nerve strained throat with a wet cough. Forcing words out.

'Where are you going your Holiness?' The under-Channellor asked.

'I am taking some of our troops and heading to the sinful nest that is called Outlook. There I will meet Master-Channellor Tiramene. He has promised us something, a weapon perhaps that may prove instrumental in bringing down the cursed Pact. What happened here was rehearsed and the Pact will think themselves victorious which is to be expected but Tiramene and I have anticipated this' Movhren said pausing for a moment, his underling Scrimsure holding onto his every word and *just as he should* 'The Heretic will believe their work done here so do not fear too much, they will probably follow me and I will be ready for them.' Movhren motioned for Scriumsure to depart 'You have a duty to attend to now Channellor. May the Qhasa watch over you. Out.' Scrimsure bowed in respect and made a hasty retreat from the alcove.

Sprinting down the empty corridor, Scriumsure fought to centre himself and reached for the voice of God.

There was a war coming and the Pact would have to be annihilated.

There was so much to do in such little time.

Lucky. *That* God, the *One True God* was on their side.

*

Tiramene stood on a forested knoll, looking over the smoke and devastation that had happened on the Woldte. The Master-Channellor tore himself away from the distant scurrying shapes in the smoldering ruins. Just in time as a Draul Oathbreaker arrived behind him.

'Raijin? Are you well? The others they have come back. Kail, Eckard and Judeson all accounted for.' The Draul Oathbreaker, a young lady named Felucia said.

Tiramene nodded.

'Yes I am well. Just took a little effort to throw off the Void Caller's attentions on us that is all.'

Felucia turned and waved Tiramene to follow her.

'Good, Raijin we have to regroup, come.' Felucia said, even as he started off into a run down the mound.

Tiramene stopped for a moment before following.

There was still so much to do.

With that last thought Tiramene followed Felucia back to where his unsuspecting enemies were.

Copyright

Copyright © 2020 Edward C. Oliver